JUST THE THING

MARIE HARTE

sourcebooks
casablanca

Published by Sourcebooks Casablanca, an imprint of Sourcebooks, Inc.
P.O. Box 4410, Naperville, Illinois 60567-4410
(630) 961-3900
Fax: (630) 961-2168
www.sourcebooks.com

Printed and bound in Canada.
MBP 10 9 8 7 6 5 4 3 2 1

Chapter 1

IT HAD BEEN ONE HELLUVA DAY ALREADY, AND IT HADN'T even reached six yet. He'd secretly called dibs on the last remaining treadmill, needing to run out some kinks.

Problem was, so had *she* Pink Yoga Pants.

Gavin Donnigan locked gazes with her before eyeing the distance to the machine, then saw her doing the same. A gentleman would let her go first… While an enthralled man would stand back and watch her work those magnificent glutes, those toned hamstrings and calves.

But Gavin was no gentleman, at least, not in the gym. His domain. His jungle. His—

"Dude, you're blocking the Nautilus."

"Oh, sorry." He moved out of the no-neck's path, now no longer able to see the treadmill. When he stepped around another idiot standing in the way, he saw her smirk at him as she stepped on the machine. She kept his gaze as she slowly warmed up, making a huge production out of stretching her arms up over her head, then grinning from ear to ear.

He frowned.

She gave him a mock salute—the sexy witch—then proceeded to ignore the holy hell out of him as she tuned out the rest of the world and ran. Not jogged, *ran*. That made half a dozen times she'd blown him off with that same smug expression. Then she'd pretend he didn't exist.

He'd like to throw her over his knee and spank the ever-loving—

"Gavin. Today, Bro. We have work to do before class."

He groaned, needing the stress relief from a good run. "But Landon, I need to work out first."

"Fine." The dick wrapped a thick arm around Gavin's neck and hauled him away in a headlock. "You want a workout? Let's see if you can get out of this. Then I'll throw you on the mat a few times and watch you flail as I beat your ass."

Gavin sputtered, trying to breathe as his behemoth brother dragged him down the hallway toward the self-defense classroom.

Not cool to headlock a gym trainer in front of his many clients. Gavin tried not to wheeze as he fought Landon's steel-hard muscles for breath. He glanced over and saw his pink-clad nemesis laughing at him. Crap. The damage had been done. He heard snickers, mockery, and encouragement for *Landon*.

Major Donnigan. What an asshole.

The former Marine choking him growled, "Now suck it up, princess, and let's see your moves. If you can't do it, you sure as shit can't teach it."

Two hours later, Gavin heard familiar chatter. "Oh my God. Did you see the size of his arms? They're huge!"

"I swear, I would pay money for him to put *me* in a wristlock, headlock, body lock…"

"Hey, he can carry me over his shoulder and take me

away to do bad things anytime he wants. Bring on the stranger danger, I say."

"I'd like to get some of that *strange*. Talk about a nice ass…"

Chuckling, then some dirty talk ensued. Gavin would have flushed with embarrassment…if their compliments hadn't been based on truth. And Landon said working at the gym had little in the way of perks.

Gavin cleared his throat from behind the group of early thirtysomethings still whispering things he knew they wouldn't want him to hear. Four guilty faces swiveled in his direction, their cheeks red, their eyes wide.

"Ladies? I just wanted to make sure none of you had any questions about tonight's instruction. We're getting a little rougher than just escaping wristlocks." And preventing douche bags from turning women into victims. Landon's self-defense class had been hugely successful.

The boldest of the four managed a shaky smile. "Uh, um, no, Gavin. No questions." She swallowed loudly, glanced at his eyes once, then lowered her gaze to his chest. "I found it really helpful."

The others nodded like bobbleheads. "Awesome class."

"I feel safer already."

"I'm so glad you're the ones teaching us."

"Will you have a third session?"

The first had gone so well two months ago that Mac, his boss, had asked Gavin and Landon to do a second set. "I'm not sure yet. You'd have to talk to Mac. I'm glad the class is helping though. Make sure you practice at home, and see you next Friday for our last class, unless I run into you in the gym first."

They scrambled to leave, but he overheard mention of his smoky-gray eyes and to-die-for abs between a few breathy sighs. He resisted the urge to power flex as he straightened up the large room, setting the mats to rights.

Another successful self-defense class at Jameson's Gym, courtesy of the Donnigan brothers.

Of course, it helped when *both* brothers did the labor instead of the lamer one panting over a hot chick.

Gavin sighed, wishing he could be more annoyed with his older brother, now laughing at something Ava—his fiancée—said. Trust Landon to find happiness and laziness at the same time. The guy who would throw a shit fit if Gavin forgot to put the toilet seat down or wipe up a water mark on the kitchen counter now saw nothing wrong with mats askew and a few plastic water bottles lying around.

He gave his brother a look, but Landon pretended to ignore him. "Dick," Gavin muttered loud enough for Landon to hear him, despite there still being a few stragglers gathering up their things before leaving.

The jackass continued to dismiss him in favor of Ava's sexy grin. Though the finger he stuck up behind his back hinted he might not be as focused as he pretended. Good to know Major OCD still understood when he was getting insulted. Gavin straightened after tossing another bottle into a bin and nearly tripped over the finest ass to grace the gym since he'd started working at the place.

Well, well. The treadmill thief hadn't darted out of the class the moment it ended. There was a God after all. He gave her a thorough once-over. Mostly because she was hot as hell, and yeah, it bugged the crap out of her.

But something had to get her to notice him as more than a rival for the gym equipment.

"Well, hel-lo, Pink Yoga Pants. Hope you enjoyed the class as much as you enjoyed your run earlier."

She stood, gave him a baleful stare, then sighed. "It's Wonder Boy, in the flesh. Or should I call you Smoky?"

He frowned, then smiled at the earlier reference to his eyes. "Did you hear the part about my rockin' biceps and bitable abs too? And don't forget these glutes." He turned around, presenting for her, and looked down at said ass. "Rumor has it, there's no sight finer in all of Seattle." He squeezed his cheeks together—looking impressive, if he did say so himself.

"This has been *such* a long day."

He'd swear the corner of her lip curled in the hint of a smile before she glanced down and fiddled with her shirt. He turned back around to fully face her. "Hey, if you'd rather, I can put you in a headlock so you can be up and close with the Guns of Steel." He flexed his biceps. "I call this one *Sexy* and this one *As hell*."

She sighed even louder. "A long, never-ending day."

But so worth it, if only because he got to see *her* again—Zoe York. The woman was as obsessive about her workouts as he was. Tall, athletic, gorgeous. Now if only she'd stop saying no to a date with the magnetic Donnigan everyone wanted but couldn't have. Well, not counting Michelle. Amy. Megan. Maybe Brenda, now that he thought about it...

Gavin poured on the charm. "You looked great tonight. Terrific form." He tried not to laugh at her scowl. "How about going out for a drin—"

She hefted her bag over her shoulder, and he had

to step back to keep from getting smacked in the face. "Have a great weekend, Romeo. I have more important things to do tonight than date your guns of tinfoil."

"Like?"

"Like wash my hair, clean lint from my dryer. Oh, and breathe. I have to do that too."

And like that, she was gone.

Behind him, he heard a whistle, then his brother's loud clapping. "Strike three. He's out, ladies and gentlemen."

Well, crap. "Gentlemen?" Gavin snorted, trying to ignore the fact that he'd failed. Again. "Please. It's just us, Landon."

"He's got a point," Ava agreed. "You're no gentleman."

Gavin turned to see her smirking at his brother.

"Shut it, Doc." Landon frowned, then winked at her. "I'm only trying to encourage my poor, battered baby brother to—"

"First of all, I'm only younger than you by two years, asswipe." Gavin hated it when Landon lorded those two frickin' years over him. "Second, Theo's the baby. Not me. And third, I was just kidding around with her." Joking, until the stubborn woman said yes.

Landon, the bastard, knew it. "Yeah, right. Nice crash and burn. But hey, if you need help finding a date tonight, Ava has a few mental patients who don't much care who they go out with."

Dr. Ava Rosenthal, clinical psychologist and the love of Landon's life, scowled. "What have I told you about not maligning my patients?"

"Maligning means talking bad about," Gavin added helpfully.

Landon shot him the finger. Again. Talk about a

one-trick pony. "Not your patients, baby. I was talking about your cousins."

Ava blinked. "Oh. Well then. That's true. They're not too particular. Gavin? Would you like me to call Sadie for you? Or Elliot, since he and Jason broke up again?"

Gavin snorted. "That makes what, fourteen times in the past two months?"

"More like five times, but yes." She shrugged. "What can you do? Elliot's got issues."

Pot, say hello to kettle, because I can outdo Elliot any day of the week. "First, Sadie scares me, so no. Second, I'm not gay. I don't want to date Elliot. Besides, he'd end up leaving me after taking advantage of my fine body."

Ava perused him. "Well, that's true. But I didn't mean you should date him. Just that you could hang out together." She continued to stare at him.

"Hey," Landon growled. "Eyes over here." Landon pointed to his own behemoth frame. He and Gavin shared the same height, but Landon had a linebacker's build whereas Gavin was more quarterback, all lean lines and sinewy strength. "Remember, Doc. You belong to me."

"*To* you? You mean *with* you, don't you?" Oh boy. She was using *the tone*.

Landon blinked. "Ah, right. With me, of course. Come on, I was just kidding."

Gavin got a kick out of seeing Ava take his domineering brother down a notch.

"Oh?" She raised a brow at the Neanderthal.

The twinkle in his brother's eyes skeeved Gavin out.

He'd seen this play out at home. Their version of kinked-up psychological foreplay, in Gavin's opinion. Ava pretended to shrink his brother. Landon got riled up, faked being pissed off, then swept her into his bedroom for a few frenzied hours.

Gavin started for the door, leaving the rest of the room for Landon to clean. "I'm out of here before you start doing it on the mats."

"Gavin." Ava sounded scandalized, but a glance at her cheery grin and blush said otherwise.

"Gavin," Landon mocked. "I would never…"

"At least lock the door," he mumbled and left to the sound of their laughter.

A happy couple. Two people in love who'd deserved to find that special someone. About time Landon got his head out of his ass and found a woman who could handle him. Not some casual fling, but a real woman who had opinions and wasn't afraid to share them.

As if thinking of opinionated women had conjured her, he saw Zoe by the water fountain near the exit.

She stared at two women chatting and laughing on treadmills, and her face lost all expression. That sadness he'd seen in her eyes on previous occasions showed itself, making her bright-blue gaze muddy with emotion. But Zoe didn't linger. She saw him watching her, scowled, then turned and left.

What would make a vibrant woman like Zoe so sad? Had she lost someone, like he'd lost so many? At the thought, it was as if she'd passed him the baton, letting him take the grief she'd worn so briefly.

The gym started to fade as memory overtook him. The slam of weights like car parts raining down after an explosion. The garble of low voices, the sound of insurgents around a rickety table, plotting, while he stared through his scope and—

No. He didn't need that. Not here. Not in his safe zone.

He refused to let the anger and pain get a toehold. Instead, calling on the exercises Lee, his new therapist, had shown him, he concentrated his energy elsewhere, on what he was good at. Gavin sought one of the unoccupied treadmills in the corner, the one facing the wall-mounted TV showing a stupid sitcom. He hopped onto the thing and ran. Faster and faster, until his lungs burned and his legs strained. The pain cleansed, allowing him to wheeze in laughter at the televised antics of some brainy scientist-types trying to hit on girls. Much better than raging at all he'd lost.

Balance, he kept telling himself. *It's all about balance*.

With that in mind, he once again donned a mantle of false cheer and willed himself to believe life was good. *Visualize, and it will come*, Lee liked to tell him. Gavin needed to have a discussion with the shrink, because he'd been visualizing Zoe York in nothing more than a smile, but that sure the hell hadn't happened. Thoughts of her turned his fake cheer into a real grin. He slowed down and let himself enjoy the TV show. But once it ended, he needed something more.

With the help of a spotter, he used a nearby weight bench and lifted until muscle exhaustion. Finally ready to go home and hit the rack. Where he could dream of a stubborn, sexy woman with long, wavy black hair… and sad blue eyes.

―∾∾―

Zoe drove home, annoyed with herself for getting overemotional. Treadmill girl's pink laces on her silly, adorable if useless fashion sneakers had been all too familiar. Just the kind of impractical crap Aubrey used to wear.

She sniffled, then blinked rapidly to still the tears. Pink laces? Really? But that pink led her to recall something else. *"Hel-lo, Pink Yoga Pants."*

Without meaning to, she felt her mood lift, and she chuckled. Had Gavin Donnigan actually flexed his ass at her?

Yes, he had.

For months, she'd been coming to the gym. For months, he'd said silly things to her to get her to smile and go out with him. No way, no how. He was *so* not her type. Ripped with muscle. Sexy. Doable, sure. He'd already proven that by hooking up with a half dozen— that she knew about—women at the gym. Dark hair, *smoky*-gray eyes, a firm yet sensual mouth. And yeah, okay, he had an amazing ass, overly amazing thighs, topped off with an amazing torso.

So annoying that he was charming too. Few people had been able to make her even want to smile since the accident. But Gavin had been obnoxious, obvious, and somehow charming all at the same time. He made her smile despite herself. Just what the doctor ordered.

Or *doctors*, she thought as she turned down her street in Fremont. The people she worked with had been supportive. Sensitive yet not intrusive, they'd tried to give her space while still treating her with a gentleness that showed a familiarity with life-and-death situations.

Hell, even one of the more aggressive clinic managers had been a treasure, keeping his dictatorial comments to a minimum while still grilling her about feature benefits of the software. No give in that man, which she appreciated.

She parked in her driveway and sat for a moment. The small bungalow she called home felt empty now that it was just her residing there. Aunt Piper had bought the place years ago, a sound investment that had more than doubled in value, thanks to her aunt's keen sense of renovation. All in all, Zoe didn't pay much to live in a great area, close to restaurants and shopping. But she'd been sharing the space with Aubrey when her vagabond sister had been home. Aubrey's last creative foray outside the States had gone well, and she'd taken some amazing photographs. Her trip had, for the most part, been uneventful. Until a vacation in the freezing mountain passes back at home, in Washington, had given her a few bumps…

God, a few.

Zoe stared at the house, now all hers.

For a second, she thought about calling her friend Cleo, needing a shoulder to cry on. But she'd put the nonstop tears to rest two months ago, determined to grow. Aubrey was dead. There was no taking that back. No way to replay the event to a different outcome. Time to look to the future and learn to live without her twin— the other half of herself.

She sighed, annoyed at sinking back into that familiar bog of despair. She'd always been levelheaded, leaving the raging artistic temperament to her twin. But lately, no matter how she tried, she couldn't stop herself from seeing her sister in everything around her. From pink shoelaces to an oddly turned phrase to a vibrant orange poppy. Everything spoke to her of Aubrey.

"Get a grip, Zoe. Buck up, lame-o. And quit being so dramatic."

Words to live by.

After locking the car behind her, she let herself into the lovely space she called home and dropped her workout bag by the entrance. She secured the door before settling down for a leftover salad, water, and mindless television. But this time, instead of dwelling on her sister, she saw Gavin Donnigan in her mind's eye.

He really flexed his ass at me. Why that continued to amuse her she couldn't say, but she had to hand it to the guy. He sure knew how to command attention.

Between him, his hunky blond brother, and Mac, the gym's drool-worthy owner, Jameson's Gym had turned into *the* hot spot for eye candy in Green Lake. Hell, make that the whole of Seattle. All the ladies at the gym, her office, the grocery store talked about it. She wasn't immune either. Zoe used the gym to work out, but seeing so much muscle didn't hurt.

She'd been on board for the first self-defense class the gym had offered, free of charge, back in late February. It had been well done, and she'd been impressed that Gavin and Landon, two ex-Marines, had never talked down to the women taking the class. They had treated everyone with respect and seemed serious about helping everyone learn to protect themselves.

The demand had been fierce for a follow-up session. Much as she hated to admit it, Mr. Guns of Steel had a gift for teaching the unteachable. He'd actually gotten through to the hardheads in the room, herself included.

Despite not wanting to give him the wrong idea— because she had no room in her life for charming men with nice glutes and sexy smiles—she'd signed up for the second round of classes.

Part of her knew she should steer clear of the roaming Romeo. But another part liked the way he made her feel—wanted, attractive, womanly.

She finished her salad and water while she watched reruns of an old show she'd seen a dozen times before. Cracking her jaw on a yawn, she forced herself to turn off the boob tube and went to bed grungy from her sweaty workout. In the morning she'd start on her weekly chores and launder the sheets.

With any luck, she wouldn't dream of Gavin tonight, as she'd been doing following her daily workouts. Lately, he figured prominently in her fantasies of shirtless men pumping iron. Go figure.

She woke the next morning refreshed, unable to remember what she'd dreamed about, and okay with that. After cleaning the house, doing the laundry, and taking care of the bills, Zoe stepped outside to do some weeding, appreciating the warming late-April temperatures.

The phone rang.

She picked it up while she did a survey of the back garden. "Hello?"

"Zoe, it's Piper. How are you?"

Zoe perked up. "Great, Aunt Piper. Just getting ready to clear out the flower beds."

"Nice. Want some company?"

"Sure."

"I'll weed for tea and sweets. Cookies, cinnamon rolls, something good. Not that crappy vegan stuff you buy. I want real sugar and butter."

"It's not vegan." Zoe rolled her eyes. "It's organic, and I—"

"Yeah, yeah. I want the good stuff."

Zoe stifled a laugh. "Your stash of processed sugar and trans fats will be here waiting on you."

"Great. See you soon."

Hard to believe Piper and Zoe's mother, Nola, were twins. Physically alike, yet different. Aubrey took after their mother, while Zoe and Piper shared many similarities.

One of those was a love of planting. Zoe had a green thumb. Aubrey seemed to kill plants just by glancing in their direction. A sad smile creased Zoe's face, but the memory didn't hurt this time. It was a wistful wish for what had been.

Piper arrived to find Zoe bent over the back row of lavender.

"Couldn't wait for me, could you?" her aunt griped.

Zoe straightened and placed a hand on her hip. "Seriously? This from the woman who once replanted all my daylilies because I'd dared sleep past six on a Saturday?"

"Try seven thirty, missy." Piper gave a mock glare. "You know I don't have time to waste."

True. The woman Zoe aspired to be ran the shoe purchasing line for several upscale retailers downtown. Talk about busy. Between flying to Italy and New York, Piper had little time to garden in her own space.

"Now, what do we have here?"

After showing her aunt the troubled area in the back, Zoe left to bring out the tray she'd prepared. She dragged a towel off the warm plate. "Ta-da. Freshly baked cinnamon rolls, courtesy of Pillsbury. Some hot Earl Grey tea, with honey and a dash of milk, and some processed fake meat sausages for protein—I think. Just in time to clog your arteries before heart health month starts at work, am I right?"

Piper beamed. Long, black hair with one fashionably thin streak of white, worn up in her traditional French braid, and a clear, rosy complexion made the woman look a decade younger.

After taking a big bite of a sweet roll, Piper shook a finger at her. "It's a wonder your mother tolerates that smart mouth for long."

"Yeah, I know." Zoe grinned, then sobered, recalling her last conversation with her mother. "She's on me big time lately. With Aubrey…gone…Mom is desperate to have me settled and partnered up. Man or woman doesn't matter so long as I'm thinking about getting married and having a family."

"That's my sister. Open to any sexuality, race, or religion…as long as you say 'I do' at the end." Piper chuckled.

Zoe groaned. "She just wants to make sure I'm 'not alone.'" She ended with air quotes, tired of her mother's constant prodding.

Piper shook her head in sympathy. "I feel for you, sweetie. Nola always has been more of a maternal figure. She would have had a whole brood of kids if she hadn't suffered complications after you two fought to come out."

"I keep telling her she should thank me," Zoe teased, focusing on the positive. "Kids are expensive."

"Exactly. Why do you think I choose to remain single and rich?"

"Because you're a woman of loose morals who'd rather bang her way through Seattle than commit to a loving man or woman?"

Piper nodded. "That's verbatim what your mother said to me last month. Good recall, Zoe. You even got her inflections down pat."

"Thanks. I aim to please." She watched Piper scarf down bad carbs like a pothead downing Doritos. "So I'm taking that self-defense class at the gym."

Totally not what she'd planned to talk about with her aunt, but God knew she couldn't mention Gavin to her mother without Nola shoving her into a wedding gown.

"Oh?" Piper perked up, her blue eyes sparkling. "So was Hunky Marine trying to show you how to 'man-handle' the enemy again? Did you take my advice and volunteer to be his victim?"

Zoe fought a grin. "Yes and no. Gavin's good at teaching. He's got quick reflexes." She couldn't help a smile, remembering how he'd ducked out of the way of her bag. "He's also funny. He named his muscles."

"His what?"

"His huge biceps or, as he likes to brag, his Guns of Steel."

Piper laughed. "I like this guy."

"So after he introduced me to his biceps, he flexed his butt at me. Some kind of primitive way of showing off, I think."

"Like a baboon, hmm?"

The image that conjured made Zoe choke on her tea.

"Now I'm seeing a red, puffy ass shaking at you."

Zoe had just managed to swallow, when tea once more went down the wrong pipe.

Piper gave her a sly grin. "Interesting you're mentioning Gavin again."

"Again?" she rasped.

"Yep. You don't remember all that bitching you did about some arrogant Marine at the gym who thinks he's God's gift to women? A few weeks ago, a few months ago. Hmm, the last time I was here? You do a lot of ranting about this guy. But you seem to have changed your tune." Piper smirked and ate a second sweet roll. "Sounds like you're going soft on me. Maybe up for a relationship after all?"

Piper was teasing, Zoe knew, but she took the words to heart. "No. Not me. I'm focused on my career. Don't worry."

Her aunt didn't smile back. "But I do worry. Just because I chose not to marry doesn't mean marriage is wrong. Holding hands with a man won't turn you into your mother. We both know you go right anytime your mother goes left. But just because marriage agreed with her doesn't mean it's wrong for you. Heck, it might yet agree with me if I ever meet the right guy."

"Really?" Zoe hadn't expected to ever hear that.

Piper sighed. "Aubrey's passing has affected us all. It made me look more closely at my life and what I want out of it. I'm at that point where my career is amazing. I travel, I have family I love, girls—a girl—I think of as my own." Crap. Piper's eyes were shiny. She cleared her throat. "Dating is nice and all, but a man to call mine sounds good about now. Something more permanent than Tom for breakfast and Nick for lunch."

"No one for dinner?" Zoe tried to make sense of her aunt's turnaround.

"Not lately. I'm on a diet." Piper gave a half laugh. "I'm kidding, obviously, but we've all taken a good, hard look at life since losing Aubrey. My life isn't perfect, kiddo, not by a long shot. But I've accepted the choices I've made. You're at the point in your life where marriage and babies make sense."

"Really? *You're* talking to me about marriage?"

"Okay, maybe nothing so conventional as marriage. But how about dating a guy for more than a few months? Maybe finding someone to spend time with on your days off? There's more to life than teaching medical software to doctors and nurses, honey."

Zoe didn't know how to take her aunt's new stance on relationships. For so long, Piper had been her hero. A woman not afraid to defy convention, to be all about career at the accepted cost of family. And she'd succeeded.

Now to hear her talking about men and connections and home and hearth? "Are you sure you don't need someone to help you with your multiple personalities?"

"Make fun. But I'm not the one panting after my self-defense teacher."

"I am not."

"Are too." Piper raised a brow.

"So he's good-looking." Zoe shrugged, needing to be at least a little bit honest. "Nothing wrong with me liking the scenery while I work out."

"And?"

"And nothing. He's a good teacher. I like the gym. It de-stresses me." She thought about Gavin and found herself smiling. "He's annoying. But he makes me laugh."

"That's magic right there." Piper nodded. "Why not see what a date might do? Aubrey used to tell me you needed to get out more."

"She nagged me about it too." Incessantly.

"Well, she knew you best. Maybe you ought to think about it."

"Fine. Okay." *Anything to stop this conversation.* Piper believed in handling grief head-on. She talked about Aubrey as if mention of the girl didn't still tear a huge hole in Zoe's heart. Treating the loss in a healthy, verbal way. So Zoe did the same, to prove she was dealing with losing her twin—her best friend, confidante, and the only person who could consistently win an argument against her.

Zoe gradually changed the topic to the English lavender, lupines, and overgrown daylilies in the far corner of her small backyard. Fortunately, Piper latched on to talk of gardening. She didn't have outdoor space in her condo by the water and was eager to dirty her manicured hands.

Doing her best to appear relaxed and not tense at thoughts of her sister *or* Gavin, Zoe laughed and joked about anything and everything, ignoring her aunt's sly suggestion that she too join Jameson's Gym. That had disaster written all over it. Especially because Zoe had decided to wear those same pink yoga pants to work out on Monday, just to poke the sleeping bear and see what he'd do and say.

Guns of Steel? More like *Buns* of Steel, she thought, remembering his finer-than-fine flexing, and chuckled despite herself.

Chapter 2

MONDAY EVENING, GAVIN DID HIS ROUNDS, WORKING WITH the gym-goers eager to get buff. He'd nicely but firmly put Michelle off. Again. The woman was a blond barracuda who thought their one night of raunchy sex months ago entitled her to having him at her beck and call. Yeah, that had been a mistake, and he'd known it the moment he'd let her talk him into going out for "dessert."

But he'd been drinking back then. He blamed the booze as much as he blamed his need to lose himself in something pleasurable. Damn, but Michelle knew how to use her tongue in the most inventive ways. Still not enough to tempt him back into her evil clutches. Especially not with Pink Yoga Pants working up a sweat on the elliptical.

He casually made his way over, aware Zoe didn't chat with the people near her. She only talked to an older woman about gardening, and then only during her cooldowns. He'd eavesdropped a time or two, puzzled at what she found so fascinating about dirt. But Loretta wasn't here, and Zoe currently moved with purpose.

Like a demon, when she jumped on a machine, she went full throttle until she'd sweated out a good gallon. She had her long black hair pulled back in a ponytail, and it swayed as she ran. He stopped next to her, answering a question for one of his clients about the new kettlebells Mac had ordered.

"Yeah, they'll be in Friday, Jim. No, none of them are pink." Gavin chuckled, then turned to Zoe, only to see her watching him, her gaze intense. "What?" She looked like she either wanted to run him over, punch him, or—dare he hope—kiss him.

"I'm just waiting for one of your incredibly fascinating comments about pink pants, small biceps, or fine form." She didn't sound too winded, yet she'd been on the machine for a good ten minutes at least. She was in phenomenal shape—those yoga pants didn't lie.

He frowned. "Hey now, your biceps are just fine. Nothing small about them." He didn't recall ever criticizing her shape.

"I meant yours," she said drily.

"You really are mean."

She scowled. "I am not."

"You are. That's why I like you."

"That's a terrible thing to say." Her lips curled into a smirk, and his heart raced.

"Yet true." Before a nearby musclehead could jump on the machine that opened up next to her, Gavin stepped in front of him, blocking the way. "Sorry, man. I'm training her." He turned around, searching for a free machine. "There you go. That one just opened up." He pointed out a machine in front of them before facing Zoe again.

The guy gave him an odd look and shrugged. "Well, I'm not gonna kiss you, but I get it. Poor bastard." He chuckled and walked away, no harm no foul.

Before Gavin could ask what the guy was talking about, Zoe cut in, "Training me? Liar." She slowed her machine, apparently done with her workout.

Gavin put on a hurt look. "But I *am* training you. To smile. Slowly but surely, I'm working on that last nerve. The same one I'm constantly rubbing the wrong way on everyone else, according to my siblings. They, like you, have no appreciation for my sense of humor." He bent over to touch his toes, luring her with his flexibility. When he straightened, he noticed the strange look she gave him.

Zoe glanced at him a moment more before *grinning*. Man, she had one sexy mouth. "Oh, I don't know. I appreciate humor as much as the next gal."

"Yeah?" He stared in awe. Her bright eyes were so… *blue*.

"How about this?" She added a husky laugh that shot sparks through his chest and radiated all over his body.

"You have a great laugh. You should do it more often."

"Oh, I will." She chuckled some more. "Thanks, Gavin. You really made my night." Then she shocked the hell out of him when after getting off her machine, she leaned close to kiss him on the cheek.

"Th-thanks." God willing, he would manage not to pop an erection in his thin athletic shorts in front of her and everyone else at the gym. "Not that I don't deserve that, but what made you kiss me? Uncontrollable lust? Finally owning up to your feelings? Realizing you're in love with my charming self?"

She looked on the verge of exploding with mirth. "You sure you want to know?"

"Well, yeah, before we set our wedding date, at least." He grinned at her. But she laughed again, and he had a feeling it was *at*—not *with*—him. He frowned. "Okay, what?"

She cleared her throat, her humor still plain to see. "Well, Smoky, there's a sign on your back that says *Kiss me if you pity men with small brains*."

He blinked. "What?"

"I feel for you. It's not your fault size really does matter." She snickered again before leaving him busy staring over his shoulder at the mirrored wall behind him.

Son of a… Gavin saw the marker inked into his T-shirt. No doubt why he hadn't caught it earlier. One of his idiot brothers or sister had written in black marker on his dark-blue shirt.

The war had most definitely resumed. A Donnigan family tradition—pranking on each other until somebody cried.

Well, it wouldn't be him. Sure, he looked like an idiot. He'd also had Zoe York's mouth on him, finally. And now he had a valid excuse to retaliate on one unlucky Donnigan. Hell yeah. He just had to figure out which one of them had pulled this stunt.

With Landon so deep into Ava, it probably wasn't him. Though technically Gavin and Landon still lived together, Big Brother spent most of his waking hours at work or with the doc. Theo was the more likely culprit. Little Brother hadn't liked the mohawk haircut he'd woken up to a few weeks ago. Gavin thought Theo had looked edgy, but maybe the hair dye had been overdoing it. But that had been Landon's prank, turning Theo's hair Oregon State orange. Gavin's assist couldn't count as the actual idea, and from what he knew, Theo still blamed Landon for the prank. Had Theo struck back, but at Gavin instead?

Or had it been Hope, his younger sister, showing off

the set of brass balls they all knew she had buried under a sweet smile? Conniving little witch. Hell, it could really be any of them. Ava too. The woman had a wicked sense of humor. After all, she loved Landon, didn't she?

Two women stopped him to give him kisses on the cheek. He flushed.

"It's okay, Gavin. So long as you're not small in other places," Megan taunted. Considering she knew exactly how not small he was, he felt vindicated.

Her laughter didn't help though. Before someone else could pity him, he swore and ripped off his shirt, assuaged by the momentary silence around him. Megan clapped, someone else wolf whistled, and Gavin hurried past half the gym while he went in search of a new shirt.

Unfortunately, the spare in his locker had also been tampered with. This saying much more visible—and insulting. *I might be small down below, but I have a big heart. Don't hate me because I'm tiny.*

"Oh my God. Theo, I *know* this is you," he growled and tossed the shirt right back in the locker. He had so many ideas of what to do to his kid brother that he missed Mac and Shane's entrance.

"So you're finally copping to the truth—that you have a small brain. The first step is admitting the problem," Shane Collins, Mac's good buddy and a fellow former Marine, shook his head. Shane smiled a lot, had a beautiful wife, and would be the perfect wingman for a night on the town. He'd help draw the ladies, then push them toward Gavin—the confirmed single man. Gavin liked him. Normally.

"Not funny, Collins." Gavin did his best not to belt the guy. "My family did this."

Mac grinned. "Seems a little immature for Landon, don't you think?"

"Who the hell knows? With my family, it could even be my father."

"Ouch." Mac shook his head. "Let me grab you a gym T-shirt. You know, the new uniform you're supposed to wear?"

Gavin forced an innocent expression. "I meant to. But I only have two, and I haven't done laundry."

"In what, a month?" Shane snorted. "Nice try." He turned to Mac. "I told you they hated the shirts."

"Shut up." Mac left and returned moments later with a bright-red shirt with bold white letters that said *Jameson's Gym*. No doubt about where Gavin worked wearing that thing. He felt like a stop sign with arms when he wore it.

With a sigh, Gavin threw it on. "Is this kid-size or what?" The shirt clung to him like rubber.

"It's an adult large. Not my fault you're so big you're growing out of our leftover stock."

Shane gave him a knowing once-over. "Still, it's good promo having a muscle-bound freak wearing your name."

"Hey." Gavin frowned.

"Sorry. Muscle-bound idiot with a small brain." Shane snickered. "Seriously, Gavin, do some laundry. That's just embarrassing."

"Good thing you can run fast," Gavin muttered, having watched Shane eat up the treadmill on more than one occasion.

Mac shook his head. "With a mouth that annoying, he's constantly outrunning daily beatings—and that's just from his wife."

"Please." Shane no longer seemed so amused. "She loves me."

"Good thing someone does."

Mac chuckled. "You know, Shane, maybe you should attend our self-defense classes. You might learn a thing or two."

"No thanks." Shane's glare turned even more unfriendly. "I've heard the class is all about watching those big, hunky Donnigans prance around."

"I'm hunky. Landon's just big," Gavin offered, trying to be helpful. "But it's a good thing Shelby's taking the class. I consider my prancing a public service."

"*My wife*," Shane emphasized, "has learned a few tricks from you two jarheads, I'll admit. But I'll be the one teaching her close combat, understand?"

Gavin held his hands up in surrender, stretching his tiny cotton shirt. With any luck, he'd rip holes in the arms and have an excuse to tear off the sleeves.

Mac winked at Gavin. "Best class we've had in a while. Well, next to Maggie's aerobics workouts. Do you know how many gym memberships we got after I put her, then you guys, to work?"

"Well, yeah." Gavin nodded. "Maggie's hot. Of course membership increased. Then you have me to balance out my brother's fat head. He's big, but I'm fast and handsome. So *bam*, your female membership goes through the roof." Not that Gavin believed most of the bullshit he spouted, but it seemed to aggravate Shane, who rolled his eyes. "Enough to give me a raise?"

Mac scoffed. "Dream on. No, but enough to give you the weekend off to go to your cousin's wedding."

"Huh?"

"Landon said to make sure you had the weekend off. Something about your mother throwing a fit if you even think of getting out of Mike's nuptials?"

Mike McCauley—one of the prodigal McCauleys, Aunt Beth's brood. Not that he didn't love his cousins, annoying as they were, but Gavin had already been to more than his share of social crap since being back home. He swore. Stupid Landon. "Thanks for nothing, Mac."

Before he left the locker room, Shane called out, "Nothing on the back of your shirt this time, *little* man. You're welcome for looking out for you." More laughter.

Gavin didn't deign to answer and left to finish his shift. Unfortunately, he got mobbed by a bunch of women he *knew* to be familiar with the equipment they asked about, as well as a few guys who wanted to know where they could purchase gym shirts.

But of Zoe, he saw no sign. And his mood went downhill from there.

———

Five days later, Gavin sat in a grand reception hall and watched as the oldest of his McCauley cousins twirled his new bride around the dance floor. Damned if he wanted to admit it, but Mike and Del made a nice-looking couple. Mike looking buff and shiny in a tux, while his new wife wore the hell out of a white wedding dress, with colorful sleeves of tattoos and her hair done up in some twisty braid. Gavin definitely approved. Nothing the McCauleys needed more than some fresh blood to dilute their straight-laced gene pool.

Yep, there went more McCauleys spinning around their significant others. In the nine months since he'd been home, Gavin had attended two weddings, a pre-wedding party, and this shindig. All of his cousins maturing and getting responsible.

He'd grown up hearing how Aunt Beth's kids could do no wrong. So it had been up to him and Landon to get good grades and kick ass at sports, setting the way for their younger sister and brother. His mother had some kind of weird need to be better than her sisters in all things, including the achievements of her kids. Or so it had seemed at the time. Gavin knew his mother to be ultra-competitive, but she cared about her family first and foremost. Her need to one-up Aunt Beth and Aunt Sophie came second. Mostly.

He saw his mother and father standing at the periphery of the dance floor holding hands. They smiled and laughed a lot, while his mother kept talking to Landon next to her. Landon had his arm around Ava, the pair of them sickeningly in tune. Ava smiled at Linda every time Landon looked like he'd eaten a lemon.

Landon caught his gaze, gave a subtle glance at their mother, and rolled his eyes.

Gavin grinned. Oh yeah, his mother's competitive streak still ran deep. Of course, Linda had managed to do the one thing her sisters hadn't. He glanced away from his mother and spotted Hope—the lone girl in a family that only made boys.

To his relief, his sister left the buff, dopey guy staring after her and joined him at the table. Fortunately, he and his family, including Aunt Sophie and her date, had been seated in a corner, away from most of the noise.

Hope flounced next to him, looking beautiful in an aqua-colored gown that came to mid-calf. It didn't show too much cleavage or thigh, though too much shoulder, in his opinion. "Oh man. My feet hurt in these heels."

"So why did you wear them?"

"Um, hello? It's a wedding? I had to look good." She narrowed her gaze at their parents. "Wouldn't want to embarrass Linda."

Gavin sighed. "Hope, forget Mom and enjoy yourself."

"I'm trying to. But she ordered me—*ordered me*, Gavin—to stay away from some of the bride's guests. Like I need to be told who to socialize with. Del's friends are perfectly nice."

"But are they housebroken? That's the question," he murmured, eyeballing the guys with myriad tattoos and arms as big as Landon's.

Hope continued to rant. "Give me a friggin' break. When will she learn I'm a grown woman? I'm twenty-nine years old."

"With a history of dating losers," he said bluntly.

"You're really going there?" A pause. "The guy who slept with Michelle and half her bitchy groupies?"

"Oh yeah. I'm a moron. I admit it. Hey, I already hit rock bottom. Drank myself silly, slept with the wrong people, and still have nightmares about crap I want to forget. My shit is hanging out there for all the world to see." He sighed, sounding pitiful.

She frowned, looking remorseful. "Gavin, I—"

"I'm not upset about it." Truth was truth, though he hated his family worrying about him. So he forced a grin. "And that big old pity card helps me get the girls like you wouldn't believe. Marine with a sob story—A-plus, baby."

Her pity cleared up, as he'd hoped it would. "You are such an ass."

"So they say, but normally, it's more like, 'Oh my God, his ass is so amazing. It's like touching gold. I want him *so bad*,'" he drew out, turning his sister pink.

"And here I thought sitting with you would be better than being drooled over by that guy."

Gavin immediately straightened. "What? That guy was bothering you? Why didn't you tell me that straight off? The one you just left, or some other schmuck?"

She blinked. "Why, Gavin, I didn't know you cared."

"Of course I do. You think I want some asshole bothering my baby sister…again?" He and Landon had taken care of the last creep to mistreat her weeks ago. "Which one was it?"

She paused, studied him, then reluctantly pointed to the biggest guy there. "Him." She sucked in a breath, then released a shaky sigh. "Okay, now I just feel stupid. I should be able to handle this kind of stuff."

"Hope?"

"But, I don't know. He scared me a little. Gavin, can you just nicely tell him I'm seeing someone else?"

"Are you?"

"No. But it might get him to leave me alone. I don't want a scene or anything. Nothing physical. Just convince him to leave me be," she said in a husky voice and blinked up at him.

Gavin automatically nodded, wishing like hell she'd pointed out one of the smaller of Del's many guests. The guy bothering her was one of the bride's employees, a mechanic at her garage. Rumor had it most of them hung out at a dive bar called Ray's. He and Landon had visited once, when they'd beaten some manners into Hope's ex. If Ray's groupies hadn't done time, it was a sure bet iron bars would figure at some point in their futures.

"Stay here." He left Hope, determined to set those assholes from Webster's Garage straight, when it dawned on him his sister hadn't tried too hard to get him to mind his own business. He glanced behind him and saw her smirk, which quickly turned into a frown. So, the gloves were now officially off in the Donnigan Prank Wars. Good to know.

He walked to the big guy she'd indicated, a hulking bruiser a few inches taller than his own six two. He had short brown hair and tattoos creeping up his neck and peeking under the sleeves of his suit jacket. Gavin knew the guy and the two giants next to him worked for Del. Since Aunt Sophie and Del's father, Liam, were dating, he knew more than he wanted to about Webster's Garage. It was almost incestuous how closely everyone at this wedding was tied together.

Big Guy paused as he drew closer, and Gavin realized he'd already met this asshole. The guy had danced with Hope a few months ago, back when Del had thrown a pre-wedding party Gavin had been forced—once again by his mother—to attend.

"What?" the dick, Sam Something-or-Other, barked at him. The others with him turned as one, now silent and staring.

Just then, a beautiful blond joined them and frowned. "Sam, be nice." She tugged his huge arm back down by his side. "Hi," she said to Gavin. "I'm Ivy."

Gavin smiled. "I'm Gavin. I need your man to do me a favor."

"No." Sam didn't blink.

Next to him, the two guys chuckled. The taller one snorted. "This is you being nice?"

"Fuck off," Sam said to Gavin or his friend. Gavin couldn't tell which. No emotion. Not even a glare.

Gavin ignored the suggestion. "So I need you to pretend to hit me."

"Don't you dare," Ivy admonished.

Sam gave a slow smile. "Pretend? I can do one better than that."

"Oh, now I really want to know where this is going," the other of Sam's friends said, his voice slightly accented, attesting to a Latino heritage.

Tall guy sighed. "Lou, don't encourage him. Cyn will have my head if he starts any shit."

"Don't swear," Sam said. "Not in front of Ivy."

"But you told me to fuck off," Gavin added, enjoying himself. He glanced over his shoulder at his sister and saw her sudden concern. Yeah, not so funny if he got pounded by three giants instead of just the one.

"I did?" Sam blinked. "Oh, sorry, baby."

"Actually, I prefer Gavin. But if you want to call me *baby*, I guess that's okay since you're doing me a solid."

Sam's scowl was enough to freeze hell over. His friends just laughed.

Ivy blushed. So adorable. How the hell had this bruiser landed such a pretty, innocent woman?

"You sure you two are together?" he asked her.

That got him an even more frigid scowl.

"Yeah, we keep asking her that. I'm Foley, by the way." Tall guy held out a hand. Gavin shook it. "He's Lou. And you're…Gavin, right? Where's Lancelot?"

Gavin laughed, then coughed to hide his amusement,

not wanting Hope to see it. "My brother, *Landon*, is over with my parents. He's being tortured as we speak. My mother is fixated on him and his fiancée having the perfect wedding."

Sam nodded. "Fiancée, huh? Good. I guess he did get his head out of his ass."

"Huh?"

"I gave him some advice a while ago."

Lou sputtered, in the process of drinking a beer. "Sorry. Thought you said you were giving out advice."

"*This* I have to hear," Ivy muttered.

Sam flushed, and the look was so incongruous with the badass vibe he projected that Gavin could only stare. "Come on, Ivy. I'm not that bad."

"No, you are," Foley said. "I mean, totally awful. Just the worst."

"The worst," Lou agreed.

"The advice?" Gavin prodded, loving this.

"Well, your brother was wandering around in the rain, feeling sorry for himself. So I told him to be more like my man Foley here and sac up. Go get his ass in front of his girl and make her see things his way."

"That's your stellar advice?" Ivy laughed. "Oh boy. It's a good thing you have the guys and me to help you, or you'd still be single."

"Well, maybe." Sam shrugged, then wrapped an arm around Ivy's shoulders. "But I have you, so it's all good."

She tugged him down so she could kiss him on the lips. The joy in her big, brown eyes didn't lie. "That's right, you do." She popped him in the arm. "But you still need to be nice." Then she shook her hand. "It's like hitting a wall. Well, I'm going to go over and talk with the girls.

Be good," she warned one final time, then headed toward a stacked redhead and a woman who looked familiar.

A sweet woman with cocoa-colored skin and bouncy blondish-brown curls. She was a stunner, for sure. How did he know her? And why, when presented with such a delightful package, did his thoughts instead veer toward blue eyes, yoga pants, and a snarky temperament?

"What are you looking at?" Lou asked, his low voice threatening despite his calm.

"I know her."

Sam moved closer. So did Foley. "Yeah? How do you know Rena?"

"Oh right. Rena, from Ray's. She's all right." Gavin nodded and realized how much space around him he'd lost as the men started to crowd him. The music turned from a slow ballad to something throbbing, techno punk, and *loud*. The bass pulsated through his bones, and sudden anxiety filled him. The remembrance of loud booms signaling danger. Shouting. Violence.

Not here. It's all good. But it's so loud.

His heart raced like a jackhammer.

He must have looked off because the guys frowned at him, and Lou took a step forward. Gavin instinctively clenched his hands into fists and jerked back. He bumped against the edge of a table, spilling someone's water. He stilled and tried to make sense of everything. Breathing in and out, focusing on what was real and in front of him helped. But not with so many faces too close.

"Hey, we were just kidding." Foley moved back a space. "Lou, step away, man."

Lou shrugged and moved back. "Still didn't say how he knows Rena, exactly."

Gavin tried to be subtle about evening his breathing, but he feared he looked like a scared rabbit. Still, better a rabbit than a man two steps away from chopping Lou in the throat, shoving the flat of his hand under Foley's nose to force shards of cartilage into his brain, and kicking Sam in the knee to take him down before *putting* him down permanently.

In seconds he'd evaluated and realized how to even the playing field. But hey, he hadn't acted on it.

He waited, forcing himself to be calm, wanting to be anywhere but surrounded by strangers in an unfamiliar place.

"Sorry." Sam surprised him with the apology, his eyes cautious. "Didn't mean anything."

Gavin felt like a fool. He shrugged, keeping it casual. "Nah, no biggie. I just… I, ah… Sometimes the music hurts my ears."

Foley grinned. "That crap? Hurts my whole fuckin' body. But at least it's not some bullshit country or folk music." He made a face. "You would not believe the noise the guys like to play in the garage."

Gavin forced a commiserating grin, felt the sweat gathering at the back of his neck, and slid into the space Lou had vacated—one with an avenue of escape.

"There's a nice quiet spot outside." Sam nodded to a tiny outdoor courtyard dimly lit by strands of white lights through tree branches. The doors to access it had been closed earlier. "I was out there before, when it got too stuffy after the McCauleys took forever making toasts."

"Yeah, thanks. That's probably what I need. Some fresh air."

Sam nodded, his gaze thoughtful. Lou and Foley had started arguing about something and stepped away.

"So Rena," Gavin said, wanting to put that to rest. "I met her a few weeks ago at Ray's. My brother and I had to take care of some jerk messing with our sister."

Sam didn't seem surprised. "So that was you, huh? The preppy twins who put a beatdown on Greg. Heard you guys did some nice work. You should stop by sometime for a beer and darts. You play?"

"Nah. But I might take you up on a drink." Of soda. God knew what he'd go home with at Ray's if he imbibed. No way he'd be lucky enough to snag Rena.

"You do that." Sam gave him a final once-over, grunted, then stepped away.

Chapter 3

GAVIN MADE A BEELINE FOR THE COURTYARD, NARROWLY avoiding his father and Flynn, another of his yappy cousins. Once outside, he sank gratefully onto a bench off in the shadows. He closed his eyes and let the brisk evening air cool him off, felt the whisper of the spring wind, and heard laughter and muted music. The leaves on the trees fluttered, and his calm returned in slow measures.

Then he heard a whine.

He blinked his eyes open and heard a *whump-whump*. Another whine, this one suspiciously canine. "Hello?"

A soft woof, and he spotted what appeared to be a big dog. Maybe a Great Dane or Rhodesian ridgeback? It moaned hopefully.

Gavin rose from his bench and moved across the courtyard to the dog, tied to another bench and tangled in his lead. It turned out to be a giant puppy. The dog had a water bowl and a bone but wanted to lick every spot on Gavin's face and hands instead.

Gavin chuckled as he untangled the leash, giving the dog space to move. "Easy, boy. Wow. You're friendly, huh?" He sucked in his breath when the large pup nearly gelded him. But the dog calmed right down when Gavin used a deep-voiced command for *sit*. He peered at the collar and, when he turned the tag just right, saw a name. "Jekyll, huh? Makes sense, because you are nearly one huge Hyde already." He sat, stroking the dog, and the big puppy soaked up the attention like a sponge. Anytime Gavin stopped, the dog nudged him with that huge head to continue.

Not sure how long he sat there petting Jekyll, Gavin felt himself easing all the way down, able to once again truly enjoy himself. He wondered how his parents were doing, if Landon had escaped with Ava, if Hope had danced with more of Del's guests. Had Theo, not yet of legal age, tried to snag himself a beer?

He also wondered what Zoe was up to. A date? Washing her hair? Breathing? He clearly recalled her snarky put-downs. To his surprise, he hadn't seen her last night at the self-defense session. And that bothered him. He'd tried to talk to her at the gym on Wednesday and Thursday, but both times she'd been too busy running to converse. She was definitely sending out *don't touch* vibes. And though he'd been called persistent, he hadn't wanted to look like that guy who didn't understand that no meant *no*.

Seemed like with Zoe, he was dead in the water with no place to go but down. He sighed.

As he petted the dog, a woman rushed outside straight in his direction. She seemed frantic, upset.

"You okay?" he asked.

She gave a small shriek, and Jekyll tensed.

"Shh, it's okay, boy," Gavin said to calm the pup. To her, he apologized, "Sorry, didn't mean to startle you. I came out here to clear my head. Too much loud music in there."

"Oh." The woman held a hand to her chest. He couldn't make out much of her face, but she seemed younger than Hope and had a petite frame. "You scared me. But now I can see you. Took my eyes a minute to get used to it being darker out here." She sighed. "Yeah, that music is loud." She paused. "What are you doing? Is that a dog?"

"This is Jekyll. We just met." He watched as she neared, the moonlight highlighting her features before she joined him under the shadow of the trees. Her enthusiasm for Jekyll had him sliding over in the seat to make room for her. "Careful. He likes to lick."

"Oh, he's adorable." The woman chuckled as she sat. "So big, though. I always wanted a dog when I was little."

"We all do," he said. "Until we have to clean up after it. I went through my dog phase pretty quickly."

She nodded, still enthralled with Jekyll. He sat like a gentleman as she stroked him.

"You okay?" Gavin asked.

"Yes. Just avoiding someone inside." She sighed.

"You want me to talk to them for you?" Gavin could barely take care of himself. But if a woman needed help, he could suck up his issues and deal. "Is this a woman thing, like someone being bitchy? Or is one of the guys inside bugging you?"

"Oh no," she protested. "Nothing like that, really." She groaned. "He hasn't done more than say hello, but I can feel him watching me. Not like a stalker or anything. But like he's going to ask me out, maybe. Not that he has or anything. I don't know." She groaned again, and though Gavin couldn't see her, he could hear the blush in her voice.

He grinned. "So that's a no to me beating him to a pulp?"

"I sound stupid. The poor man has done nothing

more than look at me and say hello once or twice, but he makes me nervous."

"Nervous can be good. As long as it's not psycho-stalker nervous."

"You're not helping."

He chuckled. "Sorry. But it's funny to hear it from a woman's perspective. I want to make a certain woman notice me, and I've said hello a bunch of times." And flexed for her, but that was beside the point. "But she won't give me the time of day."

"Maybe that's because you make her nervous. She's probably hiding, like me."

"Hmm. Maybe." Something to think about. "You going to be okay out here?"

"Yes. But if anyone asks, you never saw me."

He stood and saluted. "Right. Bye, Jekyll."

He left the pretty brunette alone with the dog and entered the great room again. When Hope found him right away, he turned his head from her, cupping his cheek.

"Gavin? Gavin, where were you?"

"My face. God. He has big hands." A peek at her showed his sister had paled.

"Oh no. I was kidding. Seriously, no one bothered me at all. I..." She trailed off as he straightened, dropping his hand, and looked down his nose at her. "Asshole." She marched off, her lack of concern for her dear brother heartbreaking.

Landon joined him. "So Mike finally got himself hitched again. Sucker."

They snickered, though they were both pleased for their cousin. Mike's first wife had died years ago in childbirth. That he'd found love again had surprised all of them. Gavin had to hand it to him. The guy had guts, opening himself to risk like that.

"Seen Theo?" he asked, not seeing his brother around.

Landon pursed his lips. "Maybe I have. Take a look. I sent Dad to find him."

Gavin followed Landon's gaze and saw their father walk up behind Theo, who was taking a sip of beer from a bottle clearly not his own. Then Gavin watched as Theo spit out what he'd been drinking and choked when their father patted him on the back.

"I take it you arranged everything?"

"What? Like getting my underage brother a beer with the promise not to tell anyone, then letting Dad know Theo was planning to take a drink? Nah. Not me. Must have been Hope who narced."

"Nice." Gavin chuckled. "So setting Theo up... You're still thinking it was him that put the blow-up doll in your bed." Back when Landon had been courting Ava, a doll looking suspiciously like her had ended up in his brother's bed. Landon's lips flattened, apparently still not amused with one hell of a prank. "Yeah, I do."

"I do too." Gavin knew Theo had done it. A work of genius. He had real hopes for his kid brother. "That or Hope." Payback for throwing him at freakish Sam, the giant. "She's shifty enough to do it, and she'd been the one upstairs alone that time. Remember how she bitched about my unclean bathroom?" *Try to sucker me. Ha. That'll teach you, Hope.*

Landon's eyes narrowed. "Good point. I'll have to give Hope some of my personal attention too. Wouldn't want her to feel left out."

"You do that."

After a pause, Landon glanced at him. "It's kind of loud in here. Ava and I are planning to take off."

"Me too." Gavin felt relieved that he could leave without looking like a wuss. "Can I get a ride?"

Landon nodded, and Gavin thought maybe Landon felt the same about the noise. His brother had seen some shit overseas. Sand and hot sun, mortars, gunfire. Maybe Landon also felt closed in here with too many people, too much noise. The guy had Ava to help him, though, so Gavin didn't overly worry about Landon's state of mind. Not as if Big Brother ever had a problem he couldn't handle anyway.

Gavin followed him back to Ava, musing on his evening. He'd spent some quality time with his cousins, who amused him for the most part. He'd found the courtyard and Jekyll. And he'd scammed his sister. So all in all, not a bad night.

Of course, going home to find Zoe York in his bed— minus her pink yoga pants—would have made the night perfect. But hey, he still had hope. *Envision it, and it will come*, he chanted to himself. And smiled.

Sunday morning at the gym, Zoe leg-pressed until her thighs shook. Missing her workout times had put her off schedule, and she felt like an addict undergoing withdrawal. But one of her training teams at work was dealing with an unexpected illness, so she'd had to take over his classes at one of the satellite clinics near Tacoma.

The hours this past week had been brutal. And ending on a Friday at six? The traffic had been hellacious, forcing her to miss the final self-defense class. She refused to think about how much she'd looked forward to it. Now she had no more excuses to watch Gavin Donnigan so carefully.

She'd done a lot of thinking the past week, and she'd grown tired of trying to maintain a careful distance between herself and the rest of the world. Zoe wasn't by nature a withdrawn or morose individual. Yes, she worked hard, but she maintained a sense of humor and liked being around others. Not all the time, but enough to know she appreciated socializing.

Grieving her sister had taken its toll, and Zoe wanted to smile again, to feel alive.

One person had made her more aware of the world around her. Even though he spouted nonsense and thought a little too highly of himself, she'd finally admitted to herself that she wanted to know him better. Guns of Steel intrigued her, and she figured she could at least give him the chance to charm her before he inevitably did something stupid and she walked away.

She finished her leg presses in a less-crowded gym than she was used to, completed her circuit, and decided to finish up with a light jog to cool down. She'd spotted Gavin talking to one of the regulars while they both worked out. Obviously, he wasn't on the clock today, yet he'd still come to the gym, as fanatical about routine and exercise as she was. As she watched him, her heart raced a lot faster than the easy jog required.

Zoe continued to run, studying Gavin in his natural environment. He smiled and laughed at something the older man with him said. Seeming at ease, Gavin looked too darn pretty to be working in a gym. With his smile and physique, he should be modeling for a protein powder or fitness magazine.

She sighed, wishing she was better than that—a woman who got her rocks off ogling the hot trainers at the gym.

As if he'd felt her stare, Gavin glanced over and blinked. He nodded, but didn't have the easy grin he normally gave her. This was friendly but aloof.

She didn't like it.

Frowning, she slowed down on the treadmill. Gavin said something to the man with him. They continued to talk while Gavin finished his set of weights. Then he put them down to help the guy do his reps. After a new set of bicep curls, Gavin handed the older man his towel, then slapped him on the shoulder and walked away.

Zoe left her machine, gave it a cursory wipe-down, then followed Gavin. Fortunately, she hadn't lost him to the men's locker room. She found him alone, doing push-ups in the room where they held their self-defense classes.

"Gavin?"

He didn't stop exercising, and she couldn't help but be entranced. Wow, was he strong. And ripped. She didn't get the sense he worked out to show off either, which actually impressed her even more. She watched his back and arms, his shoulders, as he moved up and down with ease.

"What's up?" he rasped and continued to move.

He paused, only to adjust his hands, then started doing triangle push-ups, which even she had a hard time doing.

She watched in silence while he finished twenty more push-ups.

He slowly stood and stretched, rounding his shoulders to stretch his lats. "Zoe?" he prodded.

She'd made up her mind. Time to see this through. "I missed the last session, and I was hoping you could show me what we did. With classes being over, I can't make up what I missed."

"True." He considered her. "Where were you?"

Nosy, but if he planned to help her, she could concede him an answer. "One of my trainers couldn't make it to work. Sick kid, so I had to step in and teach his class. Put me over on my time and stuck in Tacoma late on a Friday." She sighed. "Totally screwed with my gym schedule, but hey, it's my crew. My responsibility."

"What do you teach?"

"Electronic medical record software. I work at SMP Medical Group."

"Yeah?"

"You know when you go to the doctor, and he's busy tapping away at his computer, documenting the exam?"

"Yeah?"

"That's us."

Gavin smirked. "And when he's swearing at it because it's not doing what it's supposed to?"

She sighed. "That's us getting the software company to fix the bugs. Though nine times out of ten, it's actually user error. Just because the doc's wearing a white coat doesn't mean he or she is computer literate."

Gavin chuckled.

"Seems like it'd be easy, but there's constant turnover of the medical staff, and we have to do periodic updates and roll out new work-flow systems. Especially when the software is new to us," she rambled, annoyed with herself for doing so. His easy smile and laughter made her edgy. "Well? You going to show me what I missed, or what?" When Zoe grew nervous, she tended to take refuge in assertive behavior. Great when at work, not so great when trying to attract a man.

"Huh." He looked her over. "So you're pretty smart."

She frowned. Had that ever been in question? Before she could say something sarcastic that would no doubt get her banned from his presence, he waved her closer.

"You missed the fun stuff." He wiggled his brows.

She wished he was less handsome—or less captivating. It wasn't so much his looks as the total package that got to her. That sexy tough guy that sometimes seemed a little…off. Not wacky, just apart, as if he wasn't quite with the rest of the group. She'd seen him staring off into space a time or two, and it made her feel a kinship with the man. The two of them locked in a knot of emotion that no one else would understand.

Of course, he might have been dwelling on choices for dinner, for all she knew. But she didn't think so. Gavin had depth. And persistence. Or so she'd assumed. For four long months, he'd been bugging her to smile. Now that she felt ready to, he suddenly gave up?

She scowled. "You know, if you're too busy pumping up in here—all alone, watching yourself in the mirror—I can always find someone else to show me the ropes. When will Landon be in?"

"Now, now, Yoga Pants. Don't get in a snit. Let Professor Gavin show you how it's done."

She rolled her eyes, biting back a smile. Man, she'd missed his sense of humor. There was something really wrong with her. "I am more than my yoga pants, Professor."

He sighed. "*So* much more."

Not wanting to ask what that meant, she said nothing and simply followed his instructions.

They tugged each other back and forth, gripping shoulders, and Gavin showed her how to break free from his grasp. Their proximity caused the butterflies in her belly to spasm and dance, no matter how hard she tried to see him objectively. A self-defense instructor. Just her teacher. Her hot, sexy, totally built teacher.

They seemed to be touching a lot more than they normally did in class, but since he'd done nothing inappropriate and had agreed to help her, who was she to judge?

He said something else, but she couldn't think beyond the feel of all that muscle under the thin T-shirt beneath her hands. He was so hot…literally. Like a furnace as he moved, all that power bunching under supple flesh. God, he even smelled good. Not funky, but clean. A healthy sweat that did nothing but rev her engines.

I have got to stop touching him. He's frying my circuits.

"You got it?" he asked.

She nodded. Sure, sure. Maybe Piper had been right about her fixation—

He yanked her off her feet and flipped her onto her back, flat on the mat, though he'd moved with her, easing her landing.

Leaning over her while she sucked in a breath, wheezing, he stared down in concern. "Zoe? You okay?"

She glared between pants, trying to catch her breath, and rasped, "You…threw me…to the…ground."

"You said you were ready."

It took her a moment to realize that had been the

meaning behind *You got it?*—which she totally had not. Served her right for ogling the man.

When she was finally able to stop gasping for air, she took hold of her embarrassment and let him help her to her feet. "Show me that again, but slower."

Gavin nodded, unsuccessfully biting back a smirk, and took her through the steps of using his counter-weight and her own body mechanics to basically trip her opponent over her, adding her opponent's momentum to increase the pressure of his fall.

After a few dry runs, she motioned for him to grab her again. "For real this time."

"Okay."

"And don't take it easy on me."

He scoffed. "Sure. I'll punch you in the face a few times and slug you in the belly, bend you into a pretzel, maybe pull your hair too. Then I'll see if you can flip me over. You sure you're ready for this, lightweight?"

"Smart-ass." Though if he really wanted to, he could crush her. He clearly knew how to use deadly force. "Hey, you're the one teaching us this high-level stuff. If you didn't want us using it in real life, why bother?"

"You'd never use this if someone was attacking you, not unless you were really advanced in martial arts or self-defense." He shrugged. "But it's the last class. I want you to have a little fun. I mean, the class needed something punchy to liven it up." He grinned. "Get it? Punchy?"

"Oh my God. Please stop. No more talk. More action. Now come at me."

He rotated his head, cracking his neck. Then he stretched his arms over his head. Seeing her obvious impatience, he held up a finger. "Hold on. I'm preparing

for the role of a lifetime." After another annoying minute
that felt like half an hour, he gave her an irritating leer and
advanced. "Hey there, little lady. You sure are pretty."

"You going for cowboy or southern thug?"

He blew out a breath and muttered, "Bitch and moan,
bitch and moan." After clearing his throat, he tried again.
"I'm looking for a good time. How about you and me go
into a dark, dangerous alley and have hot monkey sex?"
He grabbed her shoulder. "And I mean *now*. I won't
take no for an answer. Not even if you pay me. Because
I'm mean. I'm hungry, and I'm… What are you doing?"

Instead of trying to move away, Zoe slid closer and
wrapped her arms around his neck.

He froze. "Uh, Zoe?"

Off-balance, just the way she wanted him. She tilted
her face up for a kiss. When he leaned down to meet
her, she slid back and, in the same motion, pulled him
down, then used her legs to kick him up and over her.
Not exactly what he'd shown her, but she'd tried this
move before at her friend's gym, and the modified lever-
age worked.

He landed flat on his back with a hard thump. She
rolled to her hands and knees to face him, grinning with
victory. But he lay with his eyes closed, unmoving.

"Gavin?"

Nothing, just the slightest rise and fall of his chest.

Oh hell. What if she'd hurt him? Waiting for him to
catch his breath grew worrisome. "Hey, *lightweight*,"
she teased, anxious, "wake up."

When he still didn't move, she hurried to his side and
looked for possible injury. She put a tentative hand on
his neck, and he pounced.

Gavin rolled her under him, pinning her to the floor with a triumphant smile on his stupid, handsome face. "Well, well. How the tables have turned."

"You cheated," she sputtered.

"Oh? Really? I was just taking a cue from my supposed victim." He settled against her, and he felt heavy, solid.

She squirmed under him, as much to distance herself from the arousing heat building inside her as from his actual presence.

He snorted. "Really? This is how you escape from a jerk bent on harassing you?" To his credit, he didn't lower his whole lower body to crush her, yet he held her too easily.

"We never got to floor work," she muttered, unable to look away from his eyes. Lord, they really were smoky, mysterious, alluring... "So what do you suggest, Professor?"

He glanced from her eyes to her mouth, then leisurely back up to her gaze. "I suggest you try to distract me again. Then you should definitely knee me in the balls." He grimaced. "So let's say you did, and I'll get off you now."

She clutched his shoulders when he would have moved, and he tensed. "You mean, like this?"

He immediately dropped like a rock and shoved his thighs between hers, so that her knees splayed on either side of his muscular legs. A nice move. No way to knee him this way, she thought with a moment of humor. Then she met his gaze and stopped breathing.

The look he gave her... She was afraid of going up in flames.

"Like what, exactly?" he asked, his voice husky, his face so close she could count each individual eyelash. And man, he had a forest of them, shuttering the sudden brilliance of his stare.

"Huh?"

His lips curled. "You said, 'You mean, like this?' Like what, Zoe?"

The rumble of his voice vibrated through his chest to hers. Caught like a doe in the eyes of a hungry wolf, she dared not blink.

Then she amended her analogy. *More like a hungry she-wolf staring up into the eyes of a rangy buck. You're mine this time, Smoky.* "This," Zoe whispered, as caught in his spell as she'd ever been. She tugged him closer, until she felt the warmth of his mouth against hers.

Zoe didn't do spontaneous. She didn't kiss men she didn't know that well. She didn't instigate passion until she'd thought through every possible outcome of such a union. Aubrey lived for the moment. Her twin had grabbed life by the tail and pulled with all her might. Yet Zoe couldn't stop herself…and she couldn't find it in her to care that she was acting so contrary to her nature.

Like magic, she melted under Gavin, lost in his taste, his touch. To her delighted surprise, he didn't turn aggressor. Rather, he followed her lead. She deepened the kiss, then heard him groan and yanked his shoulders closer, pressing them together as tightly as two people could be, running one leg against a muscular thigh spreading her wide.

She teased with her tongue, sliding inside his mouth, stroking, licking, and clutching the steel-hard biceps that had gone so tense beneath her hands. To her astonishment, she felt light-headed. And not just from a lack of air.

Whoa. Hel-lo, chemistry. She ended the kiss and blinked her eyes open. He leaned his head back, his eyes closed, as if savoring the moment.

Her entire body tingled, with an express heat centered squarely between her legs, where he pressed most insistently. He had grown more than happy to see her, and that shocking fact sparked a return of the old Zoe.

Did he make out with all the girls on the floor of the gym? Was this par for the course when being "courted" by Smoky Donnigan? Did rolling on the mats lead to rolling in his sheets? Big assumption for Gavin to make, despite her instigating the kiss.

He'd played possum before going on the attack, but no playing pretend now, not with that lead pipe nudging her in just the right spot. She shivered when he did it again. Jesus. She wanted him to mount her right here, right now.

So not standard procedure for Zoe York, dateless extraordinaire.

He opened his eyes, and the pale brilliance snared her. Then he cleared his throat and said in a husky voice, "Great moves, Zoe." He ran a finger over her cheek, and that unexpected tenderness threw her. "So what now?"

She could handle sexy, raunchy, carnal. But gentle? That unnerved her. So she smiled up at him, then surprised him for the second time that day. She ran her foot up and down his leg again. Unfortunately, that had the side effect of shoving him harder against her.

He sucked in a breath, and she pretended she wasn't gearing up to orgasm.

Then she rolled him under her in the next second. She sat up, straddled him, and pinned his forearms to the mat.

Leaning over him and panting, she watched him grimace and catch his breath.

"You okay?"

"No." He sounded hoarse. "Shit, don't move."

She realized his predicament at once. He remained huge and aroused, and her position wasn't helping. She sat with her legs spread, her dampened crotch directly against his erection. Talk about arousing—*embarrassing. Geez, woman. Quit thinking with your ovaries.*

"Oh," she said breathlessly.

"Yeah, oh." He chuckled, then groaned again when that rumble vibrated, shifting him against her. "So what now, Mistress?" The wicked look he shot her breasts made it hard to breathe. Her nipples clearly stood out against her shirt, even through her stupid sports bra.

"Stop it, you lech."

"Hey, I'm the innocent one here. I'm flat on my back, being taken advantage of by a stronger, fiercer competitor."

"Please."

"Please what? Whatever you want, it's yours."

She tried not to laugh, tried even harder not to realize how sexy she found his arousal. "Shut up. I'm in charge now, buddy."

"Do you own a whip? Chains? Black leather? Because I am dying for a little more of your dominance, Mistress Z."

She snorted. "I thought I was Pink Yoga Pants."

"You have many names." He sighed and stared at her chest. "None of which I can recall right now, because you've scrambled my brain. I'm so intimidated by your strength, your power, your amazingly beautiful breas—"

"What the hell is going on in here?" Landon barked from the doorway.

Zoe froze.

So did Gavin.

She started to rise when Gavin gripped her by the arms. "Don't move. *Please*," he added in a low voice.

Realizing that if she did, evidence of their play would be all too apparent, she remained where she was, totally out of sorts. Zoe didn't do public displays of affection, and she sure as hell didn't roll around on the floor with an aroused hottie who felt like he had a ten-foot pole in his pants. Where the hell had he been hiding that thing, anyway?

"Zoe?" Landon asked, now frowning.

"Ah, well, I missed the last self-defense class." The hands holding her relaxed, letting her once more control him. But the heat of his palms caused a shiver deep inside her. "Gavin was showing me that throw move you guys did."

"What throw move?" Landon seemed to be confused.

"You know, the one where you lever your opponent over…" Her voice trailed off. "So you never went over that?"

"Hell no. We did show the class a couple more advanced wristlocks and leg sweeps though. Some stomps, smashing your opponent's face with your foot, heel, whatever's handy." He coughed. "Guess you're working on more advanced techniques. Ah, well, I'll leave you guys to it. Gym's starting to get a little more crowded though." He nodded to the glass walls on either side of the doorway, then closed the door. Yet that didn't prevent him from watching them as he walked away.

Oh hell. How many people have walked by and seen us kissing?

Zoe glanced back down at Gavin, who watched her with an expression she couldn't read. How would she get herself out of this predicament when she could feel her cheeks heating to a bazillion degrees? And good Lord, he was still hard beneath her.

"What?" she asked, not sure whether to belt him for conning her or applaud him for tricking her into…what, exactly? Kissing him? Rolling around with him? Feeling up a potential lover before dying when her cheeks spontaneously burst into flame and her head exploded?

"Would this be a bad time to ask you out again?" Gavin asked, sounding casual, as if he didn't lie directly beneath her dampened crotch. "I'd planned on leaving you alone, because even I'm not so dense that I couldn't see you just wanted me to quit bugging you. But now…" He swallowed when she shifted, and she stopped breathing. She still held his arms down, and her chest was all too close to his face.

"Well, you did scam me." She tried her best not to look discomfited.

"Hey, I showed you a killer good move."

"Which I ran with," she agreed, grinding over him again, now a little annoyed he didn't seem more embarrassed about their situation. Once again she wondered if he did this with all the gym girls.

"Stop it," he rasped.

"Make me."

"Shit. Come on, Cruella. I don't have an extra pair of shorts with me."

"Oh, I like that one. Is that one of my many names?"

"Seriously. I'm about to lose it," he warned. Yet he made no move to throw her off.

She felt for the guy. At least if she had an orgasm, no one would know. But in his athletic shorts, the evidence would be tough to miss. "So you're asking me out again? What? Is that, like, the twentieth time?" She slowly inched higher on her knees, no longer pressing against him.

He let out a relieved breath. "Nah. Eighteenth, tops."

She couldn't help smiling at him. "You really are persistent. A tick that keeps burrowing until he's fat with blood."

"Such an image. I'd prefer something a little more seductive. Like a gentleman feasting on his lady in all the right places."

"Lovely." She stood on her knees over him, with only their thighs still touching. She did her best to keep her eyes on his face.

"Hey, I'm the victim here. I was just trying to be a good teacher, showing my young pupil how to master the martial arts."

"By getting your hands all over me?"

"Well, I'm also a guy." He grinned. "Besides, you really did throw me."

"True." If only he'd be less charming… Yet she was glad he hadn't given up on her. *Well, hell.* She couldn't help it. She glanced down at his package and felt dizzy.

"I did do my best to be an obnoxious tough guy with plans to defile your body, like you told me to."

"You did." She had to work to pull her gaze from his shorts. Did he stuff socks in his jock? It couldn't be that big, could it?

"See something you like?"

She shot her gaze back to his face, embarrassed all over again when *he* should have been the one wanting to hide his face.

His laughter sounded hoarse. "Look, I'm sorry. I can't help it. Stand over there, and it might go down."

She rose to her feet, not sure why he'd had to ask her to do that when a normal woman would have shot off him like a rocket. That made her think of *going off like a rocket*, as in orgasm. She blushed even harder.

He groaned. "I'm sorry I'm embarrassing you." He said again, "Worst timing ever, I know. But that date? I swear I'll be a perfect gentleman. I'll wrap myself in a girdle. And I won't use any moves on you."

"I won't let you use them," she shot back, refusing to look weak.

"No surprise there." He rolled over onto his belly and groaned into the mats.

She saw him trying to regain control and admitted she liked the fact she'd pushed his buttons. And okay, she'd really liked sitting like a queen on top of all that maleness. Her rules, her date, her sexy man to dispute the notions her aunt and twin had of her.

"Okay." She nodded. "You got yourself a date."

He looked up at her in surprise. "I do?"

"Yeah. But no more of this." She waved her hands at him. "This is a gym, for God's sake. Not a whorehouse."

He bit his lip.

"What?"

"Whorehouse? Do they even use that term anymore?"

"How the hell would I know?" She could still feel him under her skin.

"Never mind. Not important." He leaned up on his elbows, looking more in command of himself, as if he had nothing to hide, just hanging out on the floor. "How about Thursday night?"

"Okay." Should she dictate the plans for their date? She normally did. Maybe this time she'd try something different.

He watched her, looking for what, she had no idea.

To set him straight, she explained, "But I'm not going out with you for happy Zoe time."

"Huh?"

"No sex, buddy."

He flushed, *finally*. "Yeah, well. This was…an accident. Forget it."

"You mean you don't normally roll around in the gym with a poker in your shorts?"

He laid his head down and groaned. "No, I do not. Tell no one about this, and I swear I'll buy you a kick-ass dinner."

"With dessert?"

"Sure, whatever. Now go away so I can be presentable again," he said, his words muffled.

"Well, at least you're more presentable than you were the other day in that fire engine–red gym shirt."

"I know." He paused. "Tell me I didn't look like a stop sign while wearing it."

"I was thinking more like a yield sign, actually. You know, because you have nice lats, your back like a V."

"Thanks, I think." He turned his head, glanced up at

her, and turned back to the mat, swearing softly. "Now go away. You're not helping."

She walked toward the doorway, her awkwardness vanishing with the emergence of his. "I'll leave my cell number with the front desk."

"You do that," he said, sounding pathetic.

Zoe laughed. Talk about mastering the art of self-defense. Zoe, one. Gavin, zero.

Chapter 4

Wednesday evening, Gavin stared at his family seated around the table. With everyone working different schedules and attending mandatory weddings, hump day had become the only free night this month for a get-together.

As usual, his father had cooked the meal. Van Donnigan could make anything tasty, even eggplant, which Gavin usually couldn't stand. Tonight, his dad had prepared an eggplant lasagna that had melted in Gavin's mouth. Despite looking like a carbon copy of his father, Gavin hadn't inherited any culinary skills. Those he got from his mother. Like Linda, he had a hard time boiling water. So whenever anyone promised a free meal, Gavin made sure not to miss the occasion.

He'd already cleaned his plate and planned on having seconds. Except Theo, sitting next to him, had the same idea, gauging Gavin while inching his fork closer to the lasagna pan.

Their mother sighed. "Honestly, Gavin. If you're not arguing with Landon, you're fighting my baby for the last bite."

Gavin grinned. "Your baby. Aw, poor little Theo."

"Shut up." Theo flushed.

Across the table, Landon and Ava tried not to smile. Hope had no such qualms. Sitting on Gavin's other side at the end of the table, she burst out laughing, as did their father as he rose from his seat.

"Easy, you two. There's another pan in the oven. I'll get it." He took the nearly empty pan from the table and returned with the full one. Once again seated at the head of the table next to Linda, he shook his head. "Free food brings out the worst in my children."

"I don't know about free," Landon grumbled. "Ava said I have to do dishes."

"I said *we'll* do dishes," Ava corrected him, her green eyes gleaming. "You cook, Van; we clean up. It's only polite."

Hope groaned. "Can I just tell you how annoying it is to have another suck-up in the family?"

Theo snickered while shoveling food into his growing body. The boy was twenty and skinny as a reed.

"You said it," Gavin agreed. "Landon was bad enough. Major Clean, over there, can be anal like nobody's business. You sure you know what you're doing agreeing to marry him, Ava?"

Landon glowered. "Seriously? This from the human pig at the table?"

Van coughed to cover a laugh.

Gavin shrugged. "Hey, at least I don't sleep with the toilet brush and the glass cleaner by my side. Did you make him lose the duster yet, Ava? He's got a sickness." Taunting Landon made the world right every time.

"Ass," Landon muttered, to which their mother glared. He opened his mouth, saw Linda's raised brow, and shut it.

"Very good." Linda nodded. "Now, I'd like to make an announcement."

He heard Hope groan under her breath, but when their mother gave her a sharp look, she pasted an innocent smile on her face. "What's up, Mom?"

"Your father and I are moving."

Gavin stared at her, glanced at the rest of his stunned family, and asked, "What?"

"Why?" Theo frowned.

"Well, I had another argument with your father. I realized I'm too hard on my children." She sniffed, and her eyes watered. "And that I'm causing the family some real distress with my attitude."

Linda Donnigan? *Crying?* Gavin's mother didn't cry unless she lost a million-dollar listing, and then it was more an allergic reaction to losing than a true feeling of grief. Now, he could see his father rolling around in emotion. Yet the old man remained dry-eyed and tight-lipped.

"Mom?" Landon asked. "What's up?"

"That's a great question." She leveled an angry glare at Van.

Ava glanced back and forth between Linda and Van but said nothing.

Recalling how his aunt and uncle had undergone some marital difficulties not too long ago—which he knew because his mother had let it slip that Beth had needed her help—Gavin wondered if Linda's apple hadn't fallen too far from the tree of disharmony.

"Seriously, Mom. Are you and Dad having problems?"

"This is about me, isn't it?" Hope asked. "You think I won't grow up if you're constantly strangling me with advice."

Trust Hope to turn this into a mother-daughter battle. "Hope, shut up," Gavin growled. "Mom, explain."

Van quietly left the table, and Gavin's heart started pounding.

"It's just…your father and I…" She sighed, then pointed at Landon. "Ha! I got you. I am now queen of the prank wars!"

Gavin blinked, blew out a breath, and forced himself to relax. One crisis averted.

"That was low." Hope scowled.

"Yeah, Mom." Theo glared.

Landon shook his head. "And here I thought at least *you* were above it all."

Linda grinned, an older, meaner version of Hope. "Please. I reign victorious! Do you really think your father and I can't work out our issues after thirty-five years? If we even think about a hiccup, we deal with it then and there. And now we have even more assets at our disposal able to help." She looked to Ava.

Ava shook her head when Gavin raised a brow. He'd asked her for therapeutic help not long ago, and she'd referred him to a colleague. His current shrink. Something about a conflict of interest because she was doing his brother. Though she hadn't put it exactly like that.

"I know people who can help. The only person I can shrink here is Landon." Ava nodded at the bonehead. "Except I would never do that, because that conflicts with keeping my relationship stable. Right, handsome?"

Landon nodded, fat and happy with a woman who understood him and loved him anyway. "Exactly, Doc."

"Wait. I'm still confused." Gavin held up a hand. "How is it that our parents are even aware of the prank wars?" Everyone gradually looked at Theo. "You told, didn't you? Twenty years old and still running to Mom and Dad."

Theo flushed. "I did not. Dad coerced it out of me. He's some kind of freak interrogator."

"Oh? Did he rip out your fingernails?" Gavin snorted.

"No." Theo looked mutinous. "They kind of figured it out from the orange hair." Ah, the prank to end all pranks, the forced dye job.

"Theo isn't the type for Oregon State orange," Van said as he came out of the kitchen, a large grin on his face. "I knew it had to be Landon."

"Ha." Theo pointed at their big brother. "I knew it was you too."

Landon shrugged. "My idea. His execution." He nodded at Gavin. Figured he'd dime out his coconspirator. The traitor.

Theo turned a hurt gaze Gavin's way. "Seriously? You're ganging up on me with *him*?"

"Oh please. It was either gonna be me or Hope. Sac up, boy."

"Gavin." His mother didn't like rude or crude language. Even at thirty-two, he wasn't immune from the wrath of Linda.

"Sorry." He grinned. "But Theo, you really rocked the mohawk. And hey, it's all grown back. Mostly."

Theo had shaved his head, leaving it longer on top, going for more of a flattop look. Unsurprisingly, he wore it well.

"You look regulation," Landon added. "USMC all the way." He smiled.

Theo flushed. "I'm still kicking that around."

Baby Brother wanted to join the Marine Corps, to

follow in Landon and Gavin's footsteps. But he hesitated because Landon had been medically discharged due to injuries sustained during battle. And Gavin... Gavin was all messed up. A bullet in the ribs had healed well enough. As had that punctured lung and torn quad. But the bombs that had killed his friends had brought on some god-awful nightmares and shakes he hadn't been able to subdue on his own. Made his job as a sniper difficult.

So like his brother, he'd been medically discharged, but without the primo retirement pay *Major* Donnigan had earned. Instead Gavin, now a medically retired master sergeant, had a tiny-ass pension, medical benefits, some spiffy medals, and a GI Bill he had yet to put to use.

"Well, I for one think you'd look good in green," Hope said.

Linda frowned. "Theo, take your time. The military isn't for everyone."

"Mom." Theo sighed.

She changed the subject. "How is work going?"

Everyone homed in on the kid, and Gavin felt bad. Theo went through jobs like Linda went through assistants. Nothing satisfied the guy. But then, working at a place for more than a few weeks might prove the key to finding the perfect fit. Theo grew bored at the drop of a hat. The Marine Corps would chew that shit right up.

"Where are you working now?" Gavin asked. "You said you were going to leave the coffee shop a week ago. Did you? Are you back to unplugging toilets with Flynn and Brody?" His cousins, the plumbers.

Theo glared at him.

"Yes, son. Where?" Van asked.

With everyone focused on Theo, Gavin felt safe to sneak to the kitchen, away from the limelight, with his dirty plate.

Hope soon joined him. "Man, Mom really had me going."

"Me too. Guess this means we have to include them in the war. I'll TP Dad's car; you short-sheet Mom's bed. It'll drive her nuts," he suggested, only half teasing.

"Hmm. Not a bad idea."

"I was kidding."

"Yeah." Yet Hope looked too speculative for her own good. "So what's this I hear about you and some woman at the gym?"

He swallowed a groan. "Where'd you hear that?"

"Where else?" She smiled. "Before you got here, Landon was telling everyone how Zoe York keeps shooting you down. I like her already."

"Yeah? Well, she and I have a date tomorrow night. Guess you don't know everything, do you?"

"Seriously? The woman who's been rejecting you for months said yes? What did you do? Spike her Gatorade?"

"You know, sometimes you're sassy and smart and pretty," he said with enthusiasm. "Just like Mom."

"That's just mean."

"Yes, it is." He laughed.

"So back to you and Zoe."

He groaned. "Persistent, just like Mom." He gave himself a point for annoying her into a scowl. Then, before she could pull his hair, knee him in the balls, or pinch him, he said, "What do you want to know?"

Hope was nearly thirty and still clueless about crap

Gavin would have thought she'd know by now. She had a decent job working with their cousin, Cameron, in finance, and she rented a nice apartment away from home. Had friends, a family who cared, obviously. But her personal life had been worse than his for too long. She dated losers, and their mother never let her forget how much growing up she still had to do.

"You like her." Hope blinked. "For real."

For all her needed maturation, his sister had an uncanny way of seeing through bullshit to the heart of a thing. She'd always been able to read him, and that chafed because Gavin was older, the one supposed to protect and guide *her*.

"So what? She's pretty. I like her. Yeah."

"No, you *like*-like her."

He sighed. "We're past the third grade, honey."

"Well, *honey*, do you want a second date or not? I have some advice I'm willing to share for free. Just because you've been so pathetic lately."

"And because you owe me from the wedding? You remember, when you tried to get my ass handed to me by Goliath and his friends, the Titans?"

"Maybe," she muttered. "Look, do you want my advice or not?"

"Might as well. You're a chick. You probably know how they think."

She sighed. He could almost hear her counting to ten in her head for patience. "Look, you horndog. From what I hear, you've pretty much rolled every available woman in the gym."

"Hey now."

"Shut it. You like this woman, you leave off the sex."

"Hope." Great, now he felt icked out by his sister saying the s-word. He'd teased Theo about not being a virgin anymore. Was Hope? In this day and age, probably not. And now he wanted to scour out his brain.

"Listen to me. I know how women think. And I know you. If this Zoe has rejected you for months, it's because she's not interested in being a notch on the old Gavin bedpost. Say what you want," she said hurriedly before he could interrupt, "but we all know you had a rough time adjusting when you came back. You did a lot of stupid things — and stupid women — before you realized sex and happiness do not go hand in hand."

"What? You're taking shrink lessons from Ava now?"

"Maybe I am. She's smart, and I can admit I've been as bad as you, steering myself in the wrong direction for a long time. Heck, Gavin, you've admitted the same thing. You confessed it at the wedding, remember?"

"So?"

"So you can't have sex with Zoe on the first date. You have to show her you want to be with her for more than that. So no slick moves. No trying to shove your tongue down her throat before she's out of her car. Do something unexpected. Take her somewhere different. Somewhere fun."

"Saying my bedroom is both fun and different would be immature at this point."

She sneered. "Very."

"Well, where the hell should we go? Dinner and a movie? That's boring."

"What does she like to do? Please tell me that you know something about her besides she has a great ass."

"How did you know?"

"Ew. I was kidding."

He shrugged. "She teaches software to doctors. She likes to work out, and she looks amazing in pink."

"Keep trying. I'm sure something will come to you."

He recalled other things. "She has a big brain. She's into fitness, but I don't think a run together will be much fun. She's the competitive type. Instead of talking, we'll end up racing to the finish line. Then she'll get all pissed off 'cause I beat her." Gavin had his faults, but being slow wasn't one of them.

"What else?" Hope asked as she placed her dish and his in the dishwasher.

"Hmm. I've overheard her talking about plants a lot. She's way into gardening."

"There you go."

"What? We should plant something together?" How lame.

"I know that look. It's not lame." Sometimes his sister scared him. "I happen to have access to an amazing garden that needs some tender care."

"What?"

"I'm house-sitting for a friend." She shrugged. "One of Cam's clients. She's loaded, and she's into gardening. I'm keeping an eye on her place while she's in the Caymans, and she told me I can do whatever I want. Part of watching the house means tending her garden. You want to come over and dig in the dirt with your wannabe girlfriend, go for it. Just don't kill anything."

"So you're trying to use my need to impress a date to get me to weed the gardens you're supposed to be tending."

"That's one way of looking at it." Hope narrowed her

gaze, looking uncomfortably like his mother. "Another is I'm doing you a favor by setting you up as a guy with game. Not just a player out to shag the next woman on his Do Me list."

"Where the hell do you come up with this stuff?"

"Do you want the garden or not?"

"Yes, okay. Jesus, ease up."

She smiled. "Awesome. Follow me home, and I'll get you the keys and show you around. And remember, you owe me."

He felt a little as if he'd sold his soul to the devil, but worst case, he could finagle his way around his baby sister. He hoped. "Gardening on a date? You think that will work?"

"What do you have to lose? Think of it this way. She'll never see it coming, and then she'll think you actually have a brain in that head. One that's thinking about more than getting into her pants."

"Would you stop talking like that?" He scowled.

"What? Is it the innuendo?" She batted her eyelashes. "Hearing me talk about *s-e-x*?"

He darted out of the kitchen.

"Gavin?" his father asked. "You okay?"

"Hope's picking on me," he whined, grinning when his mother reprimanded her only daughter while his father sat back and shook his head.

"Narc." Landon looked disappointed, as did Theo, but Ava laughed.

"Have I told you how much I love this family?" she asked Landon. "It's all the dysfunction I need to study in one place."

Van lifted a brow, and Theo groaned.

Linda continued to snipe at Hope, who of course sniped back.

Landon didn't look too pleased. "Hey, I thought you used your cousins for that. What's the rule? No shrinking me."

"I'd never do that," Ava protested a little too emphatically. Gavin bet she'd found a gold mine in his brother. Mr. Self-Assured had to have issues out the ass. "I do like to study my cousins. But when we do dinner with your family, I learn so much more about family dynamics."

"Glad to be of service," Landon muttered.

Ava beamed. "So tell me, Linda, how do you really feel about Landon wanting to elope with me to Hawaii?"

"Elope?" Linda's eyes bugged. "*What?*"

Van sighed.

The earful that followed would put Ava on top of her game for months to come.

Gavin shook his head and followed Hope out the door, the only safe option he could see.

—∽∽—

Thursday evening, Zoe gaped at the address Gavin had sent her to. She'd been lucky enough to dodge her mother's phone calls, had missed Cleo stopping by earlier this evening, and had ignored Piper's texts. Otherwise, she would have shared news of a date she wanted to keep to herself.

Now she had to get through said date without jumping the poor man. Every time she thought about how long she'd sat on him in the gym—knowing exactly what he felt like in those thin shorts, every inch of him excited to be with her—her world turned upside down.

Not a prude by any means, she'd still never ground over an aroused man in a public place when she barely knew more than his name.

Well, she'd wanted to do a one-eighty from her normal routine. Cleo and Piper would be pleased. Or at least, they might be if Zoe decided to confide details about this date. Then again, depending on how tonight went, she might never speak to Gavin again. She sure the hell wouldn't be sleeping with him on their first night out together.

So sad she had to keep reminding herself of that. No one-night stands.

Ever?

Ignoring temptation, she shut her fantasies down tight. *No, never.*

After parking in the stone driveway of a huge old Victorian house on a nice piece of property in Magnolia—a pricey area of Seattle that boasted quiet streets, lots of greenery, and amazing views of Puget Sound—she cautiously left the car. She stared at the house with suspicion, wondering just what Gavin had in store.

He opened the door to greet her. Wearing a pair of well-worn jeans and a faded blue sweatshirt, he looked at home and way too handsome for her peace of mind.

She'd dressed down in jeans and a sweater over a thin T-shirt. With the cool spring evenings, she normally dressed heavier for comfort. A smart idea, considering she had no idea if they'd be indoors or outdoors tonight.

"This is your place?" she asked, not believing for a second he lived in such a grand, landscaped home. It just seemed all wrong for him.

He chuckled. "Nah. It belongs to a friend of my sister's. Hope's house-sitting, but she's letting me borrow it tonight."

Zoe followed him into the huge house. It had rich mahogany furnishings, a few sculptures that looked like they cost in the thousands, and the feel of a professional interior designer. No dust, no mess, and everything had its place.

Following him through the entrance and down the hallway, past the stairs to the kitchen, she stopped and gawked. The kitchen had to be as large as her living room, dining room, and pantry combined. It had an island, marble countertops, two sinks, stainless-steel appliances, and a Viking stove—the same high-end one Piper had in her kitchen. A large vase of flowers sat on the island, while the glossy oak table off to the back looked over an expansive patio, which in turn overlooked the ocean.

"Holy crap. This is amazing."

"I know, right?" Gavin nodded. "Go on, check it out. But keep your sweater on. The fun's outside."

"Not sure what that means, but give me a minute. I need some time to take this in." She walked around the kitchen some more, while he went out to the patio and down some steps to the backyard.

After sadly affirming that she'd never have a kitchen this grand, she made mental notes to share with Cleo, a fellow HGTV addict who would go gaga over this house.

A few moments later, Zoe stepped outside on the patio, looking for Gavin. She still had no idea why he'd brought her to someone else's home, but it had been worth the drive just to see that kitchen.

"Gavin?" The stone deck ran the entire length of the back of the house and had plenty of room for a table and chair, potted flowers and plants, and a snazzy fire pit embedded in the ground. It was surrounded by rock that had been built up, no doubt to provide a measure of safety.

A glance beyond the deck showed the Sound in all its glory. The sun was setting, and an indigo sky surrounded a blanket of clouds trying to block out the rising moon—and failing. The wind picked up, bringing a chill to the air. But the crisp scent of salt water cleaned everything around her.

Zoe breathed in and out, knowing a sense of serenity she'd been missing of late.

"Over here," Gavin called.

She gave up her view of the water and found him on the side of house, in a corner of the lot with trees on one side and the patio on the other. Talk about a nice amount of privacy. The clearing had several boxes filled with green and growing things. And there, in the distance, a small greenhouse.

She blinked, feeling as if she'd stepped into her version of heaven.

"Well? Don't just stand there." Gavin nodded at a small assortment of gardening tools on the ground beside him. A trowel, a weeder, a spade, and a shovel. "The gloves are for you."

They looked brand new. She picked up the pink set, tugged off the tags, and put them on. "Pink?"

He smiled. "You like 'em? Maybe you can wear them with your yoga pants at the gym sometime."

"You're obsessed with those pants, aren't you?"

He chuckled. "Come on. We need to weed." He crouched down and reached a hand out to some overflowing green. "But I'm not sure if that's a plant or—"

"*Stop*. That's not a weed." She gently nudged him out of the way before he could kill the coreopsis and garden phlox around some limp tulips. He handed her the snips, and she clipped the spent tulip blooms, then did a bit more pruning and pulled a few real weeds. She showed him the difference, then answered his questions about what to plant when and how to separate a few daylily bulbs that really should have been split before now. So lost in the gardening, it took Zoe a good half an hour before she realized this was to be the extent of her date.

Peering over her shoulder, she frowned at Gavin and turned to face him, standing so that they could look eye to eye. Or rather, eye to throat. She had to glance up to see his gaze. "This is our date?" *Gardening?*

The pleasure seemed to leach out of him as he looked down at her. "Uh, yeah. Why? You don't like it? We don't have to play around all night in the dirt or anything."

"You thought I'd like weeding someone else's garden for hours?"

He sighed. "Stupid idea, right?"

"No, not at all." She stared at him. "How did you know I'm into plants?" Fascinating. He'd chosen one of her favorite things to do, and he seemed to be interested in her explanations about planting and zones and soil type.

"I overheard you at the gym. You and Loretta talk about gardens as if they're the second coming. I wanted to do something different with you, and I thought you

might like this." He smiled. "You did say sex was off
the table."

She nodded absently, disconcerted that he'd read her
so well. "I like this. Do you?"

He flexed his dirty fingers, because he apparently
hadn't bought himself any gloves. "Surprisingly, yeah.
It feels…good." He looked bewildered. "It's just dirt and
flowers. But I like putting it all together, maybe seeing it
grow." He stared at her as if she had the answers.

"That's what I like about it too. I have a small garden
in my backyard. I spend a lot of time caring for my
flowers and veggies. It's fun for me, and I like knowing
my hard work will pay off in tomatoes or green beans,
maybe even cucumbers."

"Fresh is best," he agreed.

She smiled with him. The moon darted behind clouds,
then broke out over them both once more. She shivered
when the wind made another pass.

"Wait here," Gavin ordered. "I mean, don't stop digging and stuff. I'll be back."

He left, and she assumed a new spot by another bed,
where lilies and clusters of out-of-control lavender con-
gregated. He returned with a tray of cocoa and marshmallows, all served on some fancy-looking crockery.
"Wasn't sure if you liked coffee or tea, but thought I
couldn't go wrong with cocoa."

"Yes." Chocolate, one of her major weaknesses. She
tried to eat healthy, but the heaven known as liquid
milk chocolate constantly called to her. As did those
mini marshmallows.

He handed her a mug and watched her with intense
eyes.

After a few decadent sips, she frowned. "Do I have marshmallow on my lip or something?" Then she licked her lips just to be sure they were clean.

"Did you have to do that? I've been so good, behaving myself." He took the mug from her and set it on the wooden border of the flowerbed, then moved into her personal space.

She refused to back up, so they stood so close that she nearly bumped his chin when she tilted her face up to see him better.

"You're so pretty. Even when you're not wearing pink," he teased, his voice soft on the cool wind.

The moment seemed like a freeze frame from the most romantic scene ever. She still tasted chocolate. The moon overhead lit everything with a preternatural glow. The scents of earth and lavender and Gavin filled her head, until she could focus on nothing but him.

"Gavin?" She didn't know what she was asking him for, but the promise of safety in his eyes drew her closer.

"I'm gonna kiss you now," he said, his voice low, warm.

She nodded.

He leaned closer at the same time she did.

Their coming together felt amazing. Perfect. *Right*. The kiss shook her. Deep, sensual, yet not as close as she wanted. His tongue swept her mouth, caressing while he took charge of the embrace. But not once did he overwhelm her. Instead, she followed him, sip for sip, and let the rush of her heartbeat pull her into a tide of longing she couldn't suppress. Not now, surrounded by all her favorite things.

"Gavin," she murmured when he kissed his way from her mouth down her cheek to her throat.

He pulled her to him, but their clothes kept them too far apart. Gentle bites down her throat ended in a soft kiss that caused a full-body shiver.

"Cold?" he whispered as he straightened.

She shook her head, unable to speak, and blinked into his shuttered gaze. Then he made everything worse. He tucked her head under his chin and hugged her with affection. No way she could chalk this up as a gambit to get her to bed, not when he had the gall to make her *feel*.

With a sigh, he ended the embrace and pulled back. "Now show me which ones I can pull and which ones I can't." He nodded at the third flower bed they hadn't gotten to yet, not winded or affected by their kiss, apparently. *Hell*. Zoe couldn't feel his heartbeat through their clothes, but hers raced like a thoroughbred intent on taking the Triple Crown.

The bastard had the nerve to wipe a clean thumb over her lower lip, causing that thoroughbred to run past the finish line with no signs of stopping.

"I have the urge to flip you again, right here," she rasped. For starting something he wouldn't finish. And for making her want to finish it, regardless of their newness.

He smirked, as if reading her mind. "I know. I can't stop thinking about us in the gym either."

"That's not what I meant."

He wiggled his brows. "I think it is. Next time I'm flat on my back, I'll be thinking only of you, Mistress."

"You're such a pain."

"I know. It's a gift."

She wanted to smack him, so she did. When his laughter ended, she pulled him close and planted a kiss on him that had him panting and grabbing for her—but this time she had the presence of mind to disentangle herself. "Now," she said, her voice hoarse, "grab that trowel and let's get back to work."

He kept staring at her mouth. "Trowel?"

She groaned, because she wanted to get back to that kiss as well. "Why me?"

Chapter 5

THE NEXT MORNING AT THE OFFICE, ZOE COULDN'T STOP thinking about her night with Gavin or the fact that she'd agreed to a second date with His Annoyingness. Why had she agreed when she'd finally satisfied her curiosity about what a night out with him would be like? Oh right. Because he made her laugh, made her burn, and replaced her sad memories with bright, happy ones.

Who knew that the man who could bench press two-fifty, flex his ass to impress, and thought himself hilarious could also be sensitive enough to care about what *she* liked, going so far as to arrange a gardening date?

She hadn't enjoyed herself with a man so much in ages. Maybe years. They hadn't done more than talk about flowering plants and vegetables, and kiss and hug, with no hands in any inappropriate places. She'd learned little about him though, other than that he was one of four siblings and that his parents had a small garden tended by his father at their house in Fremont. That and the fact he lived with Landon in a suburban home that didn't lend itself to much greenery. And that was just fine with him.

Though he'd protested he had no idea what to do with plants, he'd been careful about not killing them. His large hands had been gentle when patting the few transplanted bulbs she'd overseen.

The magic of the night had gotten to her. A little too

much maybe, because she'd made plans for a second date, enjoyed kisses that had ended way too quickly, and wanted another shot at the gorgeous and addicting Gavin Donnigan.

Her friend Cleo stuck her head in the office door. "Hey, woman. FYI, Swanson has a bug up his ass about the latest version of BymaHealth. Ginny made the mistake of picking up line 2. He wants you." Ginny, another of Zoe's trainers, loved dealing with Swanson, but he wasn't interested in a date with the young woman, to her dismay.

Now that Zoe was firmly grounded, thanks to Cleo and the tenacious Mark Swanson, Gavin fled her mind. "Right."

"Oh, and another thing. Ginny said Bill stopped by. He had to head out to resolve an issue at one of the clinics, so he'll need to make up his evaluation. In other words, he won't be here for your meeting in"—Cleo checked her phone for the time—"ten minutes. Also, I suggested to Tina that she see you Monday, after our new director's committee meeting. Because you're busy now."

"Wait. What Monday meeting?"

"All the department heads need to start standardizing work flows. You'll be there too…seven a.m. sharp." As operations coordinator for SMP Medical Group, Cleo handled the logistics for everything. When it came to scheduling, her word was final.

"Seriously? Tina at any time is frightening. But on a Monday morning?"

Cleo grinned. "Drink lots of coffee and deal."

"Right. So why am I busy now, exactly?"

"Because you have a meeting with *me*. I want to know why you're daydreaming when you should be creating the training plan for our new immediate care clinic, which opens in… That's right! Three months!"

Zoe groaned. "Don't remind me."

Cleo smirked. "Yet I see you in here daydreaming about something far more important than work. Hmm. What could it be? I know. It's that studly self-defense coach at your gym, right? I want details about your date. Stat! Well, after Swanson's done lighting your tail on fire."

"Thanks so much."

"Anytime. I'll be right back." Cleo left the office bubbly and no doubt thrilled not to have to deal with Mr. Scary.

Where was Bill's sick kid now, when Zoe needed to cover for the guy far away from the office?

Dreading the call blinking at her on hold, she picked it up and forced herself to think positive thoughts. "Hello, this is Zoe speaking."

A deep voice answered. "Jesus H…. *Lana, not now*." A woman's voice rose in the background.

Zoe blinked. "Jesus H. Lana? Is this some new religion I'm not aware of? I thought that usually ended in Christ."

She heard him snap at someone and considered herself lucky not to be on the receiving end. Despite his brusqueness, she liked Swanson. He was their top clinic manager. Wickedly smart, shockingly handsome, autocratic, and a total hard-ass who didn't mess around when it came to his job.

He growled, "Look, Ms. York. Today is *not* the day to screw with me. I'm covering for one of our other managers because his head is so far up his nineteen-year-old girlfriend's ass he can't see for the rainbows and unicorns she still watches on Nickelodeon." Zoe totally knew who he was talking about. Unfortunately, the manager, Dan Garrison, had friends in high places, retaining his job at the expense of others. "Then there are our medical assistants who"—he raised his voice—"apparently think it's okay to go on strike because I forgot to bring the replacement for the damn hazelnut coffee creamer!" He muttered a few more choice words under his breath while Zoe winced, feeling for him. The MAs working with Swanson didn't mess around. Especially not when it came to their caffeine habit.

"So, uh, Mr. Swanson, what can I do for you?" She pulled out her trusty *problems* notebook. Sometimes old school worked best when she'd have to be on the move later. She had a feeling she'd need to do a face-to-face with IT to get this handled. Ugh squared.

Lana's diatribe in the background faded, so Swanson must have moved away from her before he said, "I need some remedial training for our two newest hires, because they've been fucking up the intakes."

Swanson must have been seriously stressed for him to be swearing so much.

"Okay. I'll talk to Lana to book their training time." Zoe mentally selected her best trainer for the assignment. Lana was a top-notch MA who coordinated for all the medical assistants in Swanson's clinic. She knew her stuff…and her coffee creamer, apparently. Zoe had to fight not to laugh.

"Good. *You* talk to Her Highness about scheduling." He sighed. "We've also had complaints of laptops crashing when our people try to put in notes under the new patient template. Can you fix that ASAP? Oh, and the medication refills are slow. We're getting a lot of pissed-off patient complaints from the pharmacy. And the patient demographics button sometimes has to be tapped three times before the data screen comes up. What's that about?"

Zoe wrote it all down, asked him a few more questions, and was about to hang up when Swanson jarred her with a question she'd been hoping not to hear.

She cleared her throat. "I'm sorry. What?"

"I asked if you'd meet me for lunch on Monday. I have a few more tweaks for our consult template, and I'd rather not harass you over the phone about them. You're much easier to get a commitment out of when we're face-to-face."

Swanson could outstare Satan himself when he wanted something. And he had a habit of getting her to agree to fix his problems before everyone else's, even when they were minor. Zoe still had no idea how he pulled off his Jedi mind tricks. But she'd smartened up. Lately, she'd dealt with him via phone calls and emails. Or sent Ginny. Apparently that wasn't working for him anymore.

She sighed. "Fine."

"Hey, it could be worse. I could ask our no-show manager to handle it. He'd spend the time pretending he wasn't trying to see down your blouse, no doubt wondering how he could somehow justify having sex with a woman no longer in her teens. I just want to talk to you about work."

"Funny, Mr. Swanson." Though he had a point. She couldn't stand Dan Garrison either.

He snorted. "I thought so. You owe me."

"For what? Making your job easier? More like *you* owe *me*."

"Please. I'm keeping Garrison contained and making myself look like the bad guy with Lana. So when you schedule that training, she'll still be madder with me than with you for taking her people away."

"Um, didn't you piss off Lana all on your own? You know, by forgetting the creamer?"

"It was all part of a larger plan."

Zoe laughed. "Someone needs therapy to take care of those delusions…and it's not me. Okay, I'll get on the software issues and meet you on Monday for lunch."

"At eleven."

"Better make that noon. I have a feeling the new directors' meeting Cleo scheduled Monday morning is going to add a whole new pile of work for me."

"Monday morning? What time?"

"Seven."

"Seven? That's when we have our providers' meetings—at seven. *I* schedule our clinic's meetings." He sounded strangled. "You said Cleo Brewer scheduled it?"

"Yes," she said, cautious. Swanson sounded ready to explode again.

"Damn it," he barked, added, "Don't be late," and hung up without a good-bye.

Not too bad, considering she hadn't been frozen by Swanson's icy displeasure. He burned with a cold tongue. But he reserved his cutting remarks for those who deserved them. Fortunately, Zoe's diligence had served her well. Her coworkers took her seriously, and she loved her job. She and Swanson rarely had run-ins, though she'd heard more than her fair share about him from Cleo.

And speak of the devil… Bright-green eyes peered at her from behind the doorframe.

"Might as well pop your head back in and have a seat."

Cleo joined Zoe in the office once more. Handing over a cup of steaming coffee, she sat back and slurped her own. "So how's Mark McDreary?"

Zoe took a sip of her coffee and grinned. "Don't you mean Mark McDreamy?"

Cleo snorted. "Please. That man has no heart, no dreams, and nothing more than a handsome shell going for him. If it weren't for his dark good looks, he'd be the epitome of a troll. Like the kind that lives under the Fremont Bridge. Hmm. Now I think about it, there's a resemblance in that stony glare."

Zoe chuckled. "He's not so bad. He had some valid complaints. And Lana's giving it to him for not replacing the coffee creamer."

Cleo shared her mirth. "Oh man. I'd never get between Lana and her coffee. Not if I wanted to live. That's like telling you that you'll have to miss your exercise classes because Bill's son got sick." She gave Zoe a pointed glance.

Zoe flushed. Obviously Ginny had been telling tales. "I already apologized to Ginny for being bitchy. But you know how it is when your routine gets interrupted. I was cranky because I—"

"Had to miss gym time with Sergeant Studly. I know."

"Smooth, the way you worked that in."

"That's why they pay me the big bucks." Cleo placed her coffee down and rubbed her hands together with relish. "So what's the deal? How did the date go?"

"Date?"

"Please. I know everything that goes on around here. Our own microcosm of reality, and I'm the reigning deity who sees everything."

When Cleo got that all-knowing look in her sparkling green eyes, she spooked Zoe a little. "What? Are you reading my future again?"

Cleo had hinted once that the women in her family were highly intuitive. But the way she ran the administrative section of the medical group so smoothly was more than unnerving. No one should be that organized.

"Yes. I read your tea leaves…and your day calendar. You penciled in Gavin's name yesterday." She gave a wide grin. "Besides, I'm your best friend. It's my job to know these things."

Zoe sighed. "I tried to keep this quiet. Piper and my parents don't know."

"I get you not telling your mom and dad. But come on. Piper? She's cool."

"She's on this relationship kick right now. It's weird. For so long she was against marriage, and now she's talking about joining at the hip with some guy because time is short." She felt a familiar pang. "With my sister gone, everyone's all shaken up."

Cleo nodded in understanding. "I miss Aubrey too." She gave a dramatic sigh. "Yeah. And I'm still not falling for the whole woe-is-me change of subject, woman. Tell me about Gavin. What happened last night? Did you two have sex?"

"Cleo." Zoe's cheeks heated as her gaze shot to the open door.

Cleo grinned, and honest to God, she totally resembled a feline in human form. Jet-black hair, green eyes, and if she'd had whiskers, they'd have been twitching.

"Well?"

In a low voice, Zoe stated, "We did not have sex." *Unfortunately*. She cleared that thought right out of her head. "He took me to a place in Magnolia."

"He lives out there? Nice."

"No. His sister's friends with the owner. So we're at this house with the most amazing kitchen ever." Zoe described it, familiar with the envious expression on Cleo's face. She'd felt the same. "Yeah, marble countertops as far as the eye could see. And even better, they had amazing plant beds."

"Really?"

"Yes." Zoe still couldn't believe how fun the night had been. "Gavin bought me pink work gloves, and we played in the garden beds all night. He made me cocoa too." *And kissed the breath out of me*.

"Wait. By played in the garden beds, you mean—"

"We weeded and replanted things. It was amazing."

Cleo shook her head. "I feel so sad for you. You're pathetic, and you don't even realize how pathetic you are."

Zoe flipped her off.

Cleo pretend-caught the gesture, kissed her fingers, and flipped it back to Zoe. "Now if you'd literally gotten down and dirty rolling in rose petals—"

"With all the thorns, roses would be a bad idea. But candytuft or geraniums would work if I didn't care about crushing flowers. Which I do."

"Hey, nerd girl. I'm trying to make a point. You had him all to yourself last night, and you pulled weeds. How is that romantic?"

"You had to be there." Zoe frowned. "Come to think of it, he promised to take me to dinner." Since she'd promised to keep quiet about his state of arousal at the gym. "Good thing I made that second date then. He owes me." She grinned, pleased with herself that now she could rationalize her need to see him again. Because she missed him already. And that was too damn weird. Gah. She could feel his lips on hers as if he were still there, closing her in the warmth of his embrace.

Cleo stared at her, wide-eyed.

"What?"

"You look kind of weird. Smiley. Dopey."

"Hey." That took care of the smiley.

"Tell me *exactly* what happened last night. Leave nothing out." Before Zoe could protest, Cleo moved to close the door behind them, then sat back down on the edge of her seat. "I told Ginny you needed her to cover the phone for a solid hour. I'm taking an early lunch break for this. You're mine until eleven. So come on and share. My love life is nonexistent until Scott gets back."

With her boyfriend deployed overseas, Cleo was at loose ends romantically.

Zoe groaned. "It was bad."

"Bad how?"

"Bad in that I had to keep telling myself I don't do one-night stands."

"Yes." Cleo fist-pumped in the air. "I *knew* you liked him."

"So what? He's likeable. Good-looking." An understatement. "And he kisses like… Well, it's like devouring a s'more in one bite."

"That good, huh?" Cleo's smile was way too wide for her face.

"Yes." Zoe remembered the kiss and felt warm all over. "He kissed me under the moonlight. He took me on a gardening date, because he knew I liked plants. It's like he's thinking about more than just doing me. And it's a little scary."

"Because…?"

"Because I want to do him too." How painful, yet freeing to admit. "Piper thinks I'm obsessed with him."

"Um, you are. You've been talking about the cute jerk from the gym for months."

"I have?"

"Yeah." Cleo snorted. "Even I could tell you have a crush, and according to my brothers, I'm clueless about stuff like that."

"*Obsessed* is a strong word." At Cleo's raised brow, Zoe amended, "I mean, well, I wasn't exactly *obsessed*…until last night. The date was too good to be true, Cleo. So I'm giving him tonight to show his true colors."

"If he's smart, it'll take him way many more dates than just two to expose himself." She paused, then chuckled. "See what I did there? *Expose himself*?"

Zoe intentionally ignored her. "If he tries to get into my pants on date two, I won't have to go any further." And maybe she'd save herself some drama early on, because Gavin had trouble written all over him. She liked him. A lot. "Although I did tell Piper I'd try to be more like Aubrey." She took a deep breath and let it out. "No, *I* want to be more like my sister. I want to have fun with life."

Without warning, her eyes welled as grief intruded.

"Damn it."

Cleo's smile gentled and seemed to shift to shared understanding. She took a tissue from Zoe's desk and handed it to her. "When my mom died, I was a basket case. Then my dad and uncle passed the next year. I'd be fine, then just break down for no reason. But that's part of the healing process." She pointed to her face. "Look at me. Just talked about my family. No tears."

Zoe blew her nose. "How long did that take?"

"Ten years. But hey, no more crying about it. I'm still sad inside, but it's a healthy, buried pain. I think. That's what Matt and Josh tell me. Then again, they're assholes."

Zoe sputtered a surprised laugh. "Your brothers are not assholes. I like them." And if she hadn't been so busy with work before the mess with Aubrey, she might have asked one of them out. Cleo's brothers were hot.

"Just because they wear badges does not make them good guys. Well, technically they are the good guys, but…you know what I mean. Now stop stalling and tell me about Gavin and his kisses."

So Zoe told her everything. About Gavin's charm at the gym, trying to get her to smile. About rolling around on the mats with him and getting tricked into "wrestling" before his brother looked in. And about the most romantic date she'd ever gone on that had ended in hot chocolate with real whipped cream, mini marshmallows, and a sweet kiss good-bye. Not one gropey instance where he pushed for sex.

Cleo kept nodding. "He's into you. Really into you, not just for the wham-bam. I'm shocked."

"That the man doesn't want sex?"

"No, that you haven't thrown him over yet. I like this new you, Zoe. Time to give a relationship a try. Look at me. Took me a while, but now Scott and I are tighter than ever. I think we might even get engaged when he gets back from his temporary duty in Germany."

"Really? I didn't know it was that serious." Scott's temporary duty had already been extended months longer than the six he'd initially been gone.

Cleo beamed. "I know. The last time he was back on leave, we had the best time. He was so sweet and attentive, more than he usually is. I don't think he wanted to go back. And we're talking about Stuttgart, Germany. The land of beer and blond chicks."

Zoe laughed. "Beer and blond chicks, huh? Funny, I thought Germany was about more than that."

"Not for Scott." Cleo teased. "So what are you doing tonight?"

"I invited Gavin to my place for dinner and a movie. I thought we could watch something on Netflix together and hang out."

"Seriously? I didn't know Netflix and chill was your kind of deal."

Zoe frowned. "What?"

Cleo sighed. "Like I said. Pathetic. So what are you cooking?"

"That's not the point. Gavin passed the first test.

Let's see what he does on the second." She frowned. "Now what's this Netflix and chill business about?"

⁓

Gavin had no idea what to do about the upcoming evening. According to his sister, sex on the first date would have been bad. But the second should work, right? Except he didn't think he could do it. And that freaked him out.

He could fuck a woman, no problem. Detachment—check. He was the king of meaningless sex. Of course, it meant something during the doing, but after, he and his partner would part ways without a problem. Also, the reason he'd been with those particular women at the gym was because they'd wanted nothing more than a few orgasms and clean sex.

But Zoe meant more than a mindless screw. The pleasure with her was in being with her. Not just *being with her*.

He groaned and covered his eyes with his forearm as he lay back on the couch in his living room.

"Seriously, Gavin. The whole patient lying back on the couch while confiding his problems is a stereotype. I don't really use the couch in my practice except as a seat," Ava said, her wry smile a testament to a terrific sense of humor in a shrink. "When you asked me for some advice about Zoe, I thought we'd talk. Sitting up. Like normal friends."

"Is that what we are? Friends? You're going to be my sister-in-law someday, if Landon doesn't screw up your relationship. You're a future sister. That means I can hang all out with you. Pick my nose, walk around in my boxers, include you in the prank wars…" He peeked from under his forearm and saw her grimace. "Too immature for you?"

"Yes, as a matter of fact."

"Yeah, right. I know you encouraged my brother yesterday to switch out Mom's toothpaste for that numbing agent you got from your dentist."

She buffed her nails on her shirt and glanced away from him. "I have no idea what you're talking about."

He snorted. "Right. Hey, it was damn good. And Mom is still blaming Dad, which means we're all safe from the wrath of Linda for a while. Now help a brother out."

She sighed. "Fine. Continue to lie on the couch. Tell me about your problems, Gavin."

He frowned. "Shouldn't you have a notepad to write this down?"

"Gavin." She tapped her fingernails in a rhythm that only someone with an interminable amount of patience could have. Of course, she was dating his brother. With Landon, patience was not just a virtue; it was a requirement.

"I'm kidding." He sat up. "Tell me how to handle Zoe. I mean, we'll eventually get to the good stuff. I hope. But I'm oddly reluctant to rush it, and I'm not sure why."

"Because you care for her more than your other casual partners."

"I was waiting for you to call them my conquests. Good on you for being a feminist and refraining."

Ah. There. That tic in her forehead. And his job was done.

"Kidding, Ava. I respected those other *casual partners*. I think a woman wanting to have sex should go for it whenever she wants. I'm a forward-thinking guy."

She blinked. "I'll say. You have a much rangier vocabulary when we talk one-on-one. Interesting."

"Yeah, I try to underwhelm at every opportunity. Gives me an edge."

"But not with Zoe."

"Nope." He shrugged. "She rejected me for months. Last night we hung out at Hope's rich friend's place and dug in the dirt. And Zoe was into it." He didn't understand why he'd been having so much fun too. "I liked it."

"And?"

"And it was kind of…I don't know…close. When she and I kissed, I felt it here." He tapped his chest. "Not just there." He glanced down between his legs, saw her flush, and grimaced. "Sorry, that wasn't me trying to embarrass you. I was being honest."

"I know." She sighed. "Forgive me. I need to readjust my mind-set. It's different when I talk to an actual client than when talking to my *brother*." She gifted him with a warm smile. "I think you like this woman, Gavin. So treat her with respect and go slow. There's no timetable to keep, is there?"

"Ah, no." Which he kept telling his cock. The damn thing refused to stay down in Zoe's presence. And squatting to dig while erect? Not comfortable. Nope.

"Listen to your instincts. That's my advice."

"You're not helping. I find myself wanting to… Never mind." All of the sudden, confiding his sexual desires to Landon's fiancée felt too much like talking to Hope. Gross. He rose from the couch and glanced around the pristine room in disgust. "You and Landon were made for each other. Did I see you dusting earlier?"

"Yes, and you should take note. Most women like a clean house. It shows you care about your environment."

"Guess I'll see if she cares about her environment tonight." When he met Zoe at her place. She didn't seem like the type to put out on even the second date. But she'd invited him to her place for dinner—and Netflix. He felt nervous again, not sure what to do or how to behave around her. Should he try for more gentle kisses that sent his heart racing? Or should he be all caveman and bend her over the couch and...

"Gavin?"

"Hell," he muttered and hurried down the hallway toward his bedroom, trying to hide his newly sprouted wood. Frickin' Zoe. "Yeah, Ava?"

"Landon said he'd told you about this weekend, but I don't trust that he did." He hadn't. "Your brother and I are going away and won't be back until Monday morning. So you have the house to yourself. And I heard Theo talking with an old friend of his, and they're heading to Port Angeles for the weekend."

"I know," he called out, doing his best to focus on not being aroused around Landon's fiancée. Once he could control himself, he stepped into his room, pretending he'd meant to really go in there, then returned after picking up his cell phone. A good enough excuse. He met Ava again in the living room. "Oh my God. Are you straightening up *again*?"

She groaned. "The magazines weren't aligned. Oh, Gavin. It's a sickness. Your brother is turning me into an obsessive personality type."

He chuckled. "I managed to resist it for years until

the Marine Corps got ahold of me. But now I'm back to being slovenly."

The front door banged open, and Gavin hurried to lie on the couch and cross his arms over his chest. "So there I was, dreaming about you and me. Is that normal, Doc?" he asked her. "Because we weren't wearing anything more than Oregon State orange stripes. Oddly enough, Landon was playing referee. He even had a whistle while we—Oh hi, Bro. What's up?"

"You're so not funny." He glared at Gavin before planting a kiss on Ava that made her unsteady on her feet. She was gasping by the time Landon pulled away.

"Need…air…" She drew in large breaths.

"Wow. How romantic." Gavin nodded. "Getting your woman all hot and bothered. And breathless. Nearly dying."

Landon laughed. "She was swooning, weren't you, babe?"

She glared. "I couldn't breathe, you animal."

"We're so in love," Landon gushed, then lifted her in his arms and twirled her until she laughed. "Now what's for dinner? I'm starved."

"Whatever you're buying," Ava responded a bit tartly. "The only thing saving you from an argument about the merits of men versus women in the kitchen is that you look amazing in that suit."

Sadly, Landon did. The big guy worked for some business logistics firm managing people. Just what Landon needed. To be in charge. Gavin eyed his brother, those huge arms not in the least camouflaged by some expensive slate-gray jacket. Then he glanced down at his own jeans and T-shirt.

"So should I dress up, Ava?"

"I think you look fine. Be yourself, Gavin."

"What? Another date for you? Who with this time?" Landon asked. "Not Michelle."

Gavin made a face. "No, dumbass. It's with Zoe."

"Oh, the chick who secretly hates you. Go for it, man. She can't possibly cut you off…again." Landon snickered. "Kidding. Ava's right. Be yourself. If she can stand you two nights in a row, she's probably on her way to falling in love."

"That's what I was thinking," Gavin agreed. "Chicks. So easy."

Ava shook her head and walked away, muttering under her breath.

He and Landon shared a grin.

Gavin stood and gestured down at himself. "So seriously. Would you dress this up?"

Landon considered him, glanced over his shoulder at Ava now puttering in the kitchen, and said in a low voice, "Wear my dark-blue sweater. It's a little tight on me and will make you look even more buff than you are. Chicks dig that. And put on a little cologne. Look good. If you like this one, play it safe. Take nothing for granted. The women you really want take effort. Hell, look at my doc in there. She's a handful…" He paused.

"Please don't say it."

"…in all the right places. Trite, but true. And she's mine," Landon reminded him.

"Whatever. I don't have time for your macho head games. I have a woman to win over." He blew out a breath. "She wants to watch Netflix and just relax over dinner. Does that mean what I hope it means?"

Landon blinked. "Zoe York? Nah. No way."

"That's what I thought." He glanced at the clock on the mantel. "Well, gotta motor. Wish me luck." He dashed to the fridge in the kitchen, took the flowers he'd been saving, and saw Ava's startled gaze. "I'm not totally lame when it comes to wining and dining women, Ava. Geez. Hurt my feelings, why don't you?"

"But I—"

He passed Landon. "Ava's making me feel bad about myself, Bro. Give her a talking-to, would you?" he asked loudly enough for Ava to hear.

"Gavin, that's not true." She tried to exit the kitchen, but Landon's wide shoulders blocked her.

"Doc, that's just not right. You know Gavin's got self-esteem issues."

"But I wasn't…"

Gavin laughed to himself as he raced to Landon's room to borrow his blue sweater, then left. Yep. Landon owed him one. Now Ava and Landon could do their version of verbal foreplay. And he, bless him, would be far away while they got their shrink on.

He shuddered at the thought of his brother getting frisky. Now if it were Gavin and Zoe, that would be more than okay. The entire way to her house, he continued to tell himself she couldn't possibly mean they'd be having sex tonight, all casual and hot. But what if she did? Should he do the gentlemanly thing and say no, or give the lady what she wanted? What *he* desperately wanted, despite wanting to go slowly with her.

Decisions, decisions…

Chapter 6

Zoe couldn't stop blushing after she took the flowers from Gavin. Once she'd Googled just what *Netflix and chill* meant—because Cleo had laughed her ass off but refused to tell her—she'd been flabbergasted. Did Gavin think he'd been invited over for sex? She had ground all over him at the gym. Maybe he now thought her promiscuous and flirty.

Aubrey would have been all over that. Her twin had liked to go with the moment. But right now, all Zoe felt was embarrassed. She cleared her throat as she accepted the flowers and ushered Gavin into her home. "Thanks. They're lovely."

He nodded. "Nice place. It's so bright and happy in here." He looked around, then back at her. "Not what I would have expected from you."

"Thanks." She huffed, now annoyed. "You were expecting black walls dripping with the blood of sacrificed goats instead? Should I show you my broom in the center of the pentagram in my kitchen?"

He grinned. "Now that you mention it, that would be really cool. Is it similar to me showing you my etchings?"

She tried not to smile. "Oh stop." She hurried into the kitchen and put the cheery bunch of flowers into a vase. Turning to exit she found him right behind her.

"My bad. Sorry." He put his hands out to stop her, and they both froze at the contact. His palms rested against her shoulders. So innocent, yet heat blazed inside her. Everywhere.

He slowly pulled back and stepped aside. "So I think I owe you dinner, but here I am at your place. This is gonna cost me, right?"

She blew out a silent breath and forced herself to calm down. Why should her pulse race so fast from just a casual touch? After putting the vase on her dining table, she faced him once more. In control of herself. And the situation.

"Gavin, there's something you should understand."

"Yeah?"

She opened her mouth to let him know there would be no *chilling* tonight when she froze, her brain unable to process more than the sight of him waiting for her answer. So handsome. Dark hair cut short, those gray eyes so brilliant, so smart. And his square jaw, the shoulders begging her to reach out and touch. Then farther down, those long legs and that impressive part of himself she'd felt so intimately against her just days ago. *Yum*.

"Zoe?"

"Gavin?"

He looked serious. "My eyes are up here." He pointed to his face.

She blinked, totally mortified to have been caught leering, for God's sake.

He burst out laughing. "Man, if you could see your face."

That he hadn't taken offense soothed her some-what. "Well, it's no more than what you do to me at the gym."

He calmed down, still grinning like a maniac. "So you caught those subtle once-overs, hmm?"

"Yep." And they'd flattered her regardless. "You need to know something important."

"Oh?"

"There might have been some confusion about tonight's date. But to clear that up, you're here for dinner and a movie only. No sex. No foreplay or fooling around. Understand?"

He regarded her as if she were an alien species.

"What?"

"You really say what's on your mind, don't you? Honest to a fault."

"Is that a problem for you?"

"Not at all. I love it."

"Well then. Spell it out. What do you want from me, exactly?" She crossed her arms, waiting.

"Nope." He crossed his arms, mimicking her. "You started this. What do *you* want from *me*? I've been asking you out for months, then you say yes. Out of the blue. Was it because you finally felt what you'd been missing?" He glanced down his front at himself.

"No," she snapped. "It was a pity date."

"Bullshit." He shook his head. "Did I say *honest*? Let me take that back."

"Stop. Wait." She decided to lay it out for him. "Fine. You want the truth? I need some changes in my life. And you're different than what I'm used to."

"What are you used to? All work and no play?"

"Yes."

He looked as if he wanted to make fun of her but didn't. "Okay."

She didn't want to go there, but she wanted honesty from him, so she'd give it first. "I've recently had something bad happen. Something terrible." She swallowed, saw his concern, and did her best to ignore it. "A family member passed away unexpectedly. It's made me reevaluate things. Since I'm the buttoned-up twin who can't seem to relax, I'm doing my best to be the opposite of me and enjoy life. I mean, I enjoyed it before, but apparently not enough."

"Twin, huh?" He glanced back at the photo on the bookshelf, the one where she and Aubrey had stood with their arms around each other in Vancouver. What a fabulous trip that had been.

Her eyes pricked, so she cleared her throat and focused on him, not her sister.

Surprised to see the compassion and understanding there, she continued, "So my point is I decided to try you out. Not sexually, I mean." God, could she take her foot out of her mouth for two seconds? But Gavin didn't laugh.

"I get it." He watched her, waiting, then added, "I lost friends not long ago too. It's tough. Really hard sometimes when the memories catch up with you."

She hadn't been wrong about him after all. That emptiness she'd sensed sometimes. He understood. "Yeah. I don't mean to be a downer. I'm just explaining why I said yes. To *a date*," she emphasized.

He smiled.

"Your turn."

"Hold on now. You didn't say what you wanted from me, exactly."

"I want excitement. Fun. Laughter and great times,"

she added with a bit of sarcasm. "Do I need to spell it out? I'd like to date you. And if we connect, maybe sex. After we know each other better. Okay now?"

He blinked. "Yeah. Great."

"And you?"

"And me what? Oh right. I want you. I mean, I'm attracted to you," he admitted, not glancing away from her eyes. "You're sexy as hell. But I like you. You're funny."

"*I'm* funny?" Was he on drugs? No one had ever accused her of having a decent sense of humor, though she thought of herself as a laugh riot.

"Well, more like biting and sarcastic. But hell, I grew up with that. I'm comfortable with mean chicks."

She sighed. "Back to me being mean again? I'm assertive."

"Try aggressive."

"I'm blunt and honest, remember?"

"Yeah. And blunt can be brutal. But I like brutal." He winked. "Mistress."

"You just had to bring that up." She refused to look at his crotch again.

"Speaking of up…"

"You did *not* just say that." She kept trying not to look back at his groin.

"Oh, sorry. I don't mean my dick. It just does that when you're around. Kind of like an affectionate salute. I was in the Marine Corps, you know."

She slapped a hand over her eyes. *Do not look. Do not look.*

"I meant you bringing up us not having sex tonight. See, I wasn't planning on it, as much as I'd like to."

She lowered her hand. "Really?"

"Yeah. You confuse the shit out of me, and that's the truth. At first I wanted to make you laugh. 'Cause you're this hot chick all the guys want to bang, but you look like you tame lions when you're working out. All intense and pissed off at the world. Except you're like that when you're done too, and I think you scare people."

"You are not helping my self-esteem any."

"Nah, see, you're confident. And that's a turn-on in my book. So I wanted to see that beautiful smile. Then bang the hell out of you."

"Gavin."

"You smiled. And then I wanted… Hell, Zoe. I don't know what I want. And that really confuses me. I was in a bad place for a long time when I got back to the States. I drank more than I should. Slept with people I regret. And I'm not totally together now. But I'm good enough for some laughter and great times." He shrugged. "I can't tell you what I'm after until I know. But I'd never do anything you didn't want me to.

"And, well, hell, this will sound stupid. I actually had a lot of fun last night digging in the dirt with you. And kissing. Yeah, that was amazing." He blew out a breath. "So that's my take. Oh, and though I was hoping like hell you wanted to fuck while listening to a movie in the background, I also kind of didn't want to. I'd like us to be something more. But I don't know what that *more* is. It's weird as hell for me."

She stared at him, not sure what to think. This Gavin Donnigan was layers—worlds—deeper than she'd assumed.

"If what I said isn't what you wanted to hear, I can

go. You can keep the flowers." He didn't blink, and she wasn't sure if he was teasing or not.

"I plan to." She nodded to the kitchen. "You still owe me a dinner."

His slow smile melted those icy corners of her heart. "I do."

"So when the pizza guy comes, you're paying."

He laughed. "Sounds like a plan. So what movie are we going to watch and not have sex to?"

She couldn't help laughing with him. "You are such a pain. What would you like to watch? And for the record, porn, soft porn, and topless collegiates are off-limits."

"Well, hell. That blew my wad." He sighed. "How about *Guardians of the Galaxy* then?"

"I've only seen it five times." She pointed to the cabinet that held her movie collection in the living room. "How about we make it six?"

"Did you say sex?" His eyes grew wide.

"Gavin, I—"

"Kidding, Zoe. Just…*chill*."

She groaned.

The front bell chimed, and he laughed as he went to answer it. "I got the pizza guy."

"I'll leave the tip," she offered.

"Nah. Dinner's on me, remember?" He opened the door. "Well, hello there. You don't strike me as the pizza delivery type."

"You got that right."

Zoe froze. Disaster loomed.

"Well, well. You must be the Marine," her aunt said with way too much enthusiasm.

"I am he." Gavin stood back from the door and bowed. "And who are you?"

"That one's favorite aunt," she said with a nod at Zoe. "I'm Piper Andrews."

"Favorite?" Zoe said. "Try only."

"So you're Guns of Steel." Piper entered and greeted Zoe with a kiss to the cheek.

"That would be me." He glanced at Zoe to see her red in the face. Hmm. What had she been telling her aunt?

"Come sit by me on the couch, Gavin. Let's chat." Piper sat and patted the spot next to her.

Zoe sighed. "To what do I owe the honor of your untimely and unwelcome visit?"

"Is that any way to talk to your beloved aunt? I worry for you, being so alone on a Friday night. I was going to invite you out with me and a few friends. But you're not alone, are you?"

Gavin grinned and sat by her. "So Zoe never dates, huh?"

"I wouldn't say never, but it's been a while. The men she works with are in love with her, but she's too professional to ever make a move in that direction. And they're doctors. Can you imagine?"

Gavin didn't much like hearing that. "Doctors. Well, that's some tough competition."

"Oh, I don't know. Let's see those Guns of Steel."

Zoe blew out a breath. "Piper, don't—"

"It's okay, Zoe." Gavin flexed for them, mentally thanking Landon for the tight sweater. He did look more buff than usual. He offered his biceps for a squeeze, and Piper did it, delighting him while Zoe stood away from the sofa, looking like she'd rather be anywhere else.

"It's part and parcel of being a trainer. People want to know if you can back up what you're selling. I sell fitness, so I should be fit. What do you think?"

Piper nodded, still squeezing. This woman was who Zoe would grow to be some day. Beautiful, confident, sexually powerful. Granted, Zoe seemed like that now. But add in not embarrassed about anything, and you had a real winner. Gavin liked Piper on sight.

Piper Andrews had dark hair with a cool streak of white, a youthful glow, and a killer skirt and designer top that emphasized her lithe frame, accented with heels no one should be able to walk in without dying. She had to be in her late forties or early fifties, but she seemed more like an older sister than Zoe's aunt.

"I have to know. How old are you?" he asked.

Zoe gaped. "Oh my God. You're as bad as she is."

Piper, who had finally quit squeezing his arms, patted him on the thigh, then leaned back. "I'm forty-eight."

"No kidding. You look amazing."

"For forty-eight?" She raised a brow—one of Zoe's mastered mannerisms.

"Aunt Piper." Zoe gritted her teeth.

"For anyone," Gavin said, and meant it. "You resemble Zoe enough to be her mom, but you don't look old enough."

"Oh, now I really like you."

"See, Zoe? Your aunt likes me. Now we have to get married and have babies. But not in that order."

Piper blinked, and Zoe's lips curled into that smirk of a smile he'd grown addicted to seeing.

"Oh, I don't know, Gavin. Netflix and chill seems off the table now that my aunt is here."

"What?" Piper stared back and forth between them. "Did you really invite him over here for that?"

Zoe snorted. "No. Seriously? Do you think I'd be talking this to death if we meant to get crazy all over the house? And how do you know what that means, anyway?"

"How do you not?" Piper huffed. "Well, I can see you two are busy. Not babies-and-marriage busy," she said to Gavin with a nod and a smile. "Good one. But you're busy all the same. I'll get out of your hair. Call me for Sunday brunch, sweetie. I'm heading to New York on Monday and won't be back for a while."

Zoe walked her aunt to the door.

"Bye, Piper." Gavin waved. "When you get back, come to the gym. We can always use the eye candy."

She blew him a kiss. "I really like him, Zoe." She said something else he couldn't make out, laughed, then left.

Zoe had just closed the door and leaned back against it when the bell chimed again. She turned to open it, only to have the pizza guy standing there.

"Ah, now this one I can handle." Gavin hurried to the door to pay. "Milo?"

He made small talk with one of Theo's friends before taking the pie and handing Milo his payment with a big tip. Gavin closed the door on the younger man's thumbs-up in regards to Zoe.

"You know everyone in town, don't you?" She took the box from him and headed into the kitchen.

"Just about, because at one time or another, they've all worked with my younger brother."

"Landon's the oldest, right?"

"Right." Gavin stood with her at the counter while she divvied up slices and served a decent beer, still chilled and bottled. "Um, could I get some water or something else to drink?"

She nodded, not making a big deal of it. "How about a home-style root beer?"

"Outstanding. Thanks."

"So, Landon?" she prodded. "And before you ask, I'm not interested in your brother except as how he pertains to molding you into that charming personality you have."

"Okay then." *Good*. "You know Landon. Bossy, big, and blond. Takes after Mom."

She took a few bites and nodded, so he continued.

"Then there's me. I'm like my dad—dark-haired, laid-back. But I have my mom's focus. Linda Donnigan is sharp, let me tell you. Hope is my sister. Not sure if you met her or not, but we used her to demo some of the self-defense moves in class. Sometimes she comes by the gym. She's three years younger. Then Theo. He's the spitting image of Dad, a late addition to the family. Not sure, but maybe a mistake."

"I'm sure you delighted in telling him that while growing up."

"Well, yeah."

She shook her head.

"I was twelve when he was born."

"So he's how old now?"

"Twenty. I'm thirty-two. You didn't have to do the math. You only had to ask."

"Whatever," she said around a mouthful of cheese.

He liked that about her. She wasn't trying too hard to impress him. Just being herself.

"Tell me more about the Donnigans. You were pretty close-mouthed yesterday."

"Only because you wouldn't stop talking about dirt."
He ate some pizza, disturbed to find his appetite off.
Being so close to Zoe, all he could taste was the memory
of her lips. Man, what a crock. Had he told Ava he didn't
want sex with Zoe? Right now he had a difficult time
concentrating on anything but her fine, fine body. Her
scent, the sound of her strong voice. The mouthwatering
breasts pressed against the thin T-shirt she wore.

Zoe put the pizza back down on her plate. "Is that
right? As I recall, you wouldn't stop asking me stupid
questions about what to do with that dirt. I mean, who
doesn't know what a trowel is?"

"It's a mini shovel. Why make things complicated?"

"Because they just come that way."

"Huh?"

"Complicated." She shrugged and ate, so he continued talking before she blasted him for being ignorant
about zone types.

"What about your family?"

"We're not done with yours yet."

"What else do you want to know?"

She crossed her eyes, and even purposefully looking
goofy, she was beautiful. "Okay, it's like this. Example:
Well, Gavin, my family is pretty tight. My mom and dad
live in Portland, and I see them once a month at least.
Mom is an artist. Dad owns a natural foods shop. My
mom and aunt are twins, which explains how Aubrey
and I are twins. I mean, *were* twins."

She swallowed but forced herself to look him straight
in the eye. He could see so much pain in hers. "Aubrey
was in a car accident back in January, and she didn't
make it."

Hell. When she'd told him there had been a death in the family, he hadn't made the connection to her twin. That seriously sucked.

"I'm sorry."

She nodded, seemed to shake it off, and continued. "I work for a major medical group, where I train users on the software the medical staff uses. It's fun. I'm good at it, and life is great."

"Well. That was concise."

She grinned, showing a lot of teeth. "Yes, it was." She took a large swallow of beer, which physically hurt Gavin to see—her lips wrapped around a phallic-looking object.

He glanced down at his pizza and forced himself to take another bite.

"Now it's your turn."

He swallowed and chased the pizza with half his bottle of root beer. "Nice brew. Tastes great."

"Thank you."

"Now that I've been properly schooled in how to respond to your question—and see, I can totally tell you're an educator—my family is filled with driven people. My mom is a real estate agent who hates to lose. She's damn good at her job too. My dad works at a pharmaceutical company. Did twenty years in the Navy, retired, then went to work in the civilian sector and is a bigwig at his firm. I give it another five years until he retires, then spends all his time cooking or playing golf."

"Cooking?"

"He's an amazing cook. Always makes our dinners, or did when we were kids. He still dotes on my mom, which is nice. God knows Linda can be a handful."

She stared, all that feminine energy focused on him, and it made him warm inside. Like, freakin' hot. He reconsidered his option about bending her over the couch…

"Go on."

Head out of the gutter, Gavin! "Landon you know. He works out to stay in shape. Medically retired from the Marine Corps after a bullet hit him in the knee and messed him up. Now he's a manager at some logistics firm bossing people around."

"That would suit him."

He shared a grin with her. The kitchen felt intimate, just the two of them standing at the counter and eating. "Hope works for my cousin at his private finance company. Cam is smart and obnoxious, but he takes care of my baby sister. Plus he's the easiest of my cousins to tolerate."

"Your cousins?"

"Yeah, my mom's sister and her husband live in town. She's got four boys. I spent my childhood with Landon competing to be better than Aunt Beth's crew. Well, technically only three are Aunt Beth's, but they took Brody in when he was little. He's just as annoying as the others. A real McCauley."

"Wow. Big family."

He nodded. "So where was I? Oh right. Theo. My poor baby brother isn't sure what he wants to do now that he's out of high school. I think he wants to join the Corps, but with Landon and me coming back kind of screwed up, he's not sure."

She studied him. "You're screwed up?"

She had no idea. And he wanted to keep it that way. "I was shot and medically retired from the Marine Corps too. Saw some shit overseas. Not good. Anyhow, it's done. So I'm back here, trying to figure out what to do. I work at the gym because it de-stresses me and I'm good at it. Being physical, I mean."

Before he could fall into the memories, Zoe distracted him. "Oh, I bet you're good at being physical. Or so I've heard from Michelle and Megan. And a few others."

He flushed. "Yeah, well, I made some dumb choices when I first got back. I drank a little too much, so I don't like to drink anymore."

"Are you an alcoholic?"

"Didn't you just minutes ago yell at me for asking your aunt blunt questions?"

"I didn't yell."

"It felt like it."

"Yeah, but I'm mean and aggressive, remember?"

"There is that." He took another swig of root beer, grinning. "No, I'm not an alcoholic. But the fact I was starting to drink too much scared the crap out of me. Now I stay away from it. I don't want my thinking impaired. So yeah, no drugs either. And no cigarettes. I have no vices."

"Except your poor taste in women." She paused. "Present company excluded."

"Oh, that was a nice add-on."

"I thought so." She smirked.

He couldn't help it. He put down his root beer, took her beer from her hand, and caged her against the counter.

"Gavin, what are you doing?" she sounded breathy. Aroused.

Lord knew he was.

"I just need one kiss. Then we can go watch the movie. Okay?"

"O-one. I guess." She licked her lips.

He leaned down, feathered his breath over her mouth, and kissed her. The taste of warm beer and woman went right to his head, making him drunk on her in a way he'd only ever felt with Zoe. The kiss last night hadn't done them justice. This one just...

He slanted his mouth over hers, deepening the kiss when she put her hands on his waist and tugged him closer. She had to be feeling him hard and thick against her, but she only gripped his belt loops and refused to let go.

Zoe participated in everything. She followed his lead, stroked his tongue with hers, and shoved those amazing breasts against his chest. Nothing with her was tentative or half done. She gave him a full-body kiss that threatened to undo him the longer it lasted.

Gavin yanked his head back and leaned his forehead against hers, trying to regain his control. Right now, his body screamed at him to satisfy his needs by sinking inside her. She'd be hot, tight, wet.

But his brain warned him to slow down. To not rush or scare her, because they had so much more to share.

And his heart...the damn thing did nothing but race in his chest and ache for a woman he still barely knew. Except he felt like he knew everything about her. Which made no sense.

He pulled back and met her gaze. She seemed as bewildered and turned on as he was.

He had to do something, or he feared listening all too well to his baser instincts.

"So no sex tonight, right?" His thick voice attested to his desire. "Bending you over the couch is a no-no?"

She blinked, blushed, and scowled. Instead of berating him for being crude, she yanked him back for a kiss that about blew his mind—and his balls clean off. "Nope. Not even close."

She was breathing hard, her eyes straying to his mouth time and again, her hands still clutching his sweater. She stroked his chest, brushing her hands over his tight nipples.

"Not even close," he agreed. "Not thinking about it at all."

"Not at all."

And they both knew they were lying.

Chapter 7

"I'M SO CONFUSED." GAVIN STARED AT THE SMALL BOY AT AN ungodly hour Saturday morning. Colin McCauley, his cousin Mike's son, had to be seven or eight now. The kid—his first cousin once removed, and yeah, he knew that because he'd gone through a genealogy phase as a teen—was cute and a handful. He'd even brought his monster of a dog, Jekyll, who turned out to be the same dog Gavin had met at the wedding. But why Colin stood at the base of Gavin's bed, Gavin had no idea.

"This is our cousin," Theo said slowly, having entered the room they shared. "His name is Colin. Colin McCauley. Remember him?"

The boy nodded. "Yep. I'm Colin. Dad said you were the smart one, Cousin Gavin. I'm not seeing it."

Gavin glared, especially when he saw the seven thirty on the clock. "Theo, what the hell?"

Theo shrugged. "I told Flynn we'd watch him because the guys and their wives are out on some bonding camping trip or something."

"Yeah, but Mike is his dad." Gavin couldn't quite wake up. A glance next to him showed the lavender cutting Zoe had given him last night, protected and cared for in a clay pot. Seeing the small plant made him happy.

A gift from Zoe. An amazing date. No sex but great root beer and a killer sci-fi movie next to a woman who fascinated him. His night had been magical.

And now…this.

Turning to Colin, he asked, "Isn't Mike your dad? Why is that idiot Flynn involved?"

"I love Uncle Flynn." Colin glared, and it was like looking at a pint-size version of Mike. "Jekyll and I need to be watched. It's a grown-ups-only trip."

"Oh. Sorry, buddy." And the McCauleys had no one better to watch the kid than Theo…wearing work clothes? "Theo, why are you dressed like that?"

Theo had been working at the coffee shop, or so Gavin thought. But his brother now wore a moving company's collared shirt. "Not my fault, Gavin. I start today." Theo sounded nervous. Gavin didn't trust him. "I was supposed to start tomorrow, but well, schedules change. So you have Colin."

"I *what?*" Gavin sat up, shocked awake, and the sheets bunched at his waist.

"Wow. You're big, Cousin Gavin. A lot of big muscles, like Dad."

"Dude, no one's that big." Except Del's prison employees at the garage. "But thanks. I work out a lot at the gym. It's my job."

Colin nodded. "I know. Dad told me you train people to not brain themselves with weights."

"That's one way of describing it. But it's not a permanent gig."

Theo perked up. "You work temporary jobs. Like me."

"No, not like you. I don't get how you can go from job to job the way you do. Make a decision and stick with it, boy. You'd do fine in the Corps."

"You didn't" came out of Theo's mouth with more

rancor that he'd expected. His expression of surprise said as much.

Colin nodded. "Yeah. You got all squirrelly, which is funny because Jekyll loves squirrels." The dog came to sit by Colin, appearing obedient and passive while vibrating with energy. "You probably don't know what you want in life because the Marine Corps messed with your head. That's what Dad said. Jacked you up. Cracked you up. So now all you can do is lift heavy weights while you get better. Del thinks you're cute. Dad didn't like that. Hey, are those bullet holes?" Colin pointed to Gavin's chest.

Theo stared, not moving, no doubt waiting for Gavin to lose it over the mention of his time in the service. Granted, Gavin had been a little squirrelly when he'd first come back. But he was getting better. As long as he didn't think too hard about the past.

Gavin sighed. "Your dad talks a lot."

"I know," Colin grumbled as he neared Gavin and traced the wound on Gavin's chest, where an enemy round had torn into his left lung. "That's so cool."

"Yeah, cool." And while he'd been healing up from it, his friends had gotten blown to bits without him. John, Mick, Luke. His friends, and half of his fucking squad. They'd all left loved ones behind. Fucking Mickey had left a pregnant wife all alone. She'd given birth months ago and had even invited Gavin to a get together with some of the other family members left behind. Gavin felt that tug of despair and swallowed it down, burying it deep, where it ate at him in the silence of his nightmares.

"Dad's getting worse, Cousin Gavin."

Focus on the kid and pretend Theo isn't studying you, looking for signs of weakness. "Just call me Gavin, Colin."

Colin talked over him. "Because Dad is always talking or saying stuff about babies or kissing Mom. Not my dead one. She's buried in the cemetery. But I still talk to her in my head. I mean Del. She's my new mom."

"I know that."

"Yeah, well, she's gonna give me a baby brother soon."

Gavin smiled, trying not to flinch at the ticklish feel of tiny fingers over his scar. So strange to see a little kid in his room. "Del's pregnant?"

"I don't think so. But Dad said he's doing his best to get the job done."

"I'll bet," Theo murmured.

Gavin shot him a grin. With a woman as fine as Del, Gavin didn't think Mike was suffering too much hardship. "Well, he's trying, I'm sure. But you know, sometimes guys like your dad get too old and weak. Maybe he needs help getting the baby. He might not know what to do, since it's been so long since you were born. Tell him I'd be happy to help Del out with the problem." And Mike would suffer a fit of apoplexy. Serve him right.

"Wow, Gavin. That would be awesome. I'll tell Dad. I want a baby brother, like Theo. But smaller."

"Theo used to be really small." Gavin scooted over and patted his bed. Colin joined him. Then Jekyll did too.

"Jekyll, don't—" Gavin *oomphed* as the dog knocked him back, slobbering a huge tongue over his face while Colin and Theo laughed.

"Can we go for a walk? Or go in the park? Bryan is

doing air guns today. Can we do that?" Colin revved himself so that he talked faster, if that were possible. "Can we? Can we, Gavin? And is there more Lucky Charms for me? Theo only gave me one bowl, but I can eat the whole box. Wanna see?"

"Gotta go, Gav. You're the best. Bye." Theo darted away.

"Coward," Gavin called out. He heard the front door slam. Then just a panting, overgrown puppy dog and a hopeful little boy with Mike's dark-blue eyes stared up at him. "So this means I'm taking care of you today."

"Yeah. But I don't know why Gramma isn't. She and Grandpa are home. But Theo asked if he could watch me for money. And they paid him." Colin leaned in and whispered, "I don't think he's working at a job. He and his friend are going to get beer and girls. I heard them talking about it when Theo drove me here." He screwed up his face. "Girls? Blech."

Gavin remembered Ava telling him that Theo would be out of town this weekend. Port Angeles to party. Right.

"What a punk." Gavin had apparently been sacrificed for beer money and Theo's good time. "Well, there's nothing saying we can't get him back for the trick he pulled. Let me get a shower, and we'll pull some nasty pranks on my family. You game?"

Colin beamed. "I sure am. I'm really good at tricks. I can even cry whenever I want. Watch." To Gavin's astonishment, the kid sobbed as if he'd lost his favorite toy.

"Nice one." Gavin grinned. "Now give me a 'Yes, sir!' with a salute. Like this." He showed the boy, who caught on fast. Jekyll wagged his tail and barked. "Jekyll, off the bed."

The dog immediately leaped down.

"Wow. That's pretty good." Colin seemed impressed. "So how are we going to trick your family? Aunt Linda and Uncle Van too? Can we do my uncles and aunts when we're done with them?" So bloodthirsty. Gavin liked him.

"Oh, all of them, kid. They deserve no mercy." He snorted. "And your dad thinks I'm messed up. I'm clear-headed enough to win the prank wars."

Colin's eyes grew wide. "What are those?"

Gavin smiled. "Tell you what. Go watch some cartoons, eat the rest of Theo's Lucky Charms if you want, and relax. When I finish my shower, I'll tell you all about the prank wars. Then we'll make plans to sabotage the whole family. One sibling and one cousin at a time." He rubbed his hands together with glee. "Won't that be fun?"

"You are awesome, Gavin! Better than Theo even." Colin raced away and shrieked like a demon while the dog barked and knocked things over. Uh-oh. That sounded like a lamp crashing to the floor. Ah well.

"I really am awesome," Gavin said to the now-empty room, thoughts of revenge brightening his day.

With no plans to see Zoe until later tonight, he had time to kill. And a reputation to uphold.

No time like the present.

———

Standing in her driveway, Zoe held the phone away from her ear as Cleo yelled her excitement. She brought the phone back close. "Yes, a third date, the third night in a row. What? Oh, Gavin suggested this one. More gardening at that friend of his sister's. But he wants to learn some ways to—" She paused. "Wait. Piper called you? My aunt?"

Piper and Cleo knew and liked each other. But Zoe hadn't realized they were on regular speaking terms.

"So Piper said he has an amazing body, huh? She would know. She all but felt him up in my house." On the couch. *Zoe's* couch, touching *Zoe's* man. It disturbed Zoe to feel so possessive, and especially about her aunt. But Piper still had her looks, and Gavin had not been immune.

I am not *jealous of my aunt. What is wrong with me?*

She made an excuse to hang up the phone, then shoved it in her purse. Once in her car, she headed for the house in Magnolia. Apparently Gavin wanted to see her in action again with a trowel. That lavender plant she'd potted for him on a whim had meant something. She'd seen his awe and surprise, then that sweetness, his true joy in the gift.

She'd thought he'd kiss her again at the end of their date last night. Instead he'd taken the plant and mentioned tonight's time and place for their third date.

And stupid Zoe had accepted.

"Oh, who am I kidding? I like him. Time to be honest with myself. He's fun and sexy. What's not to like?" Piper and Cleo would be so proud.

And so would Aubrey.

Zoe blinked away useless tears and drove to the stately home, once again parking in the driveway. After coaching herself to relax and not lock lips with the man the moment she saw him, she drew in a deep breath and let it out, then met him at the door.

He opened it right away, as if he'd been waiting for her.

"Hello there, Zoe." He smiled. The devastating expression of warmth heated her up, combating the windy May evening. The clouds overhead continued to gather, an ominous foreshadowing of the rain sure to come.

"We might need to hurry this up. Looks like it's going to pour."

"Hmm. Good point. Come on." He yanked her inside and through the house to the backyard again.

"Whoa. Slow down."

"No, hurry up. I need you to show me how to transplant my lavender before we're drenched in a Seattle monsoon."

She blinked. "Really?"

"I'm kidding about the monsoon. Though I agree. Looks like rain."

"I mean about your plant. You like it. Good."

He flushed. "I brought a bigger pot for it, because you told me that little one was going to be too small eventually. I don't want the little guy to die or anything."

"Um, okay." She saw the gardening supplies on the porch and smiled. "You're ready this time. Good." She also saw a few other plants to go with the lavender. He had brought a large pot.

"I thought I could put all the color together. To give my guy some friends, at least. Then it can go outside the front door. I'm told my house needs some charm. Especially because Theo's living there," he added in low growl.

"What's that?"

"Nothing." He sighed. "Do you know what it's like dealing with a little brother?"

"Can't say I do."

"It's a nightmare. Theo stuck me with babysitting duty today. All day. And the kid—my cousin's kid, actually—turns out to be a ticking time bomb when you fill him full of sugary cereal." Gavin brooded.

Zoe tried not to laugh. "Oh?"

He explained what Theo had done by sticking him with babysitting duty.

"So who's winning your war?"

"Oh, me for sure. But it's the principle of the thing. I was supposed to have my weekend to myself, the house all mine for once. Instead I was stuck with a seven-year-old going on forty. That kid is scary smart. And cunning."

"Really?"

"Yeah. Good thing he's not a Donnigan. Or my mother would have molded him into the next president. That or a genius dictator who'll end up bringing down big government. I think Colin could go either way."

"Ah." She watched him babying his plant, oddly touched by his fussing. "You don't like kids?"

"Never thought about it, really. But Colin's cool. I was older when Theo was born. I wasn't a fan of the diapers, but he was a really cute baby. Don't tell him I said that."

She twisted an invisible key over her lips.

"Now show me how to protect my lavender plant so it thrives. I've already named him Leon."

"It's a he, huh?"

"Yeah. My plant might smell girlie, and he's a little purple, but he's a very masculine flower. You know. 'Cause he's mine, and I'm very manly."

"Yes, aren't you," she said drily.

She helped him repot the plant, adding some color—Leon's "ladies"—to it in the form of a few pink geraniums, with a mix of green mint and grasses. By the end, they had a well-planted container that would fill out.

"It's kind of sparse." He frowned. "You sure it'll get fuller?"

"You have to give plants room to grow."

"I guess." He gave it a critical eye, then nodded. "The veggies need some love too." He nodded to one of the container beds they hadn't gotten to the last time.

"Is this the price I pay for being able to hang out at this house?"

"Yeah. And gardening is my price for dealing with my sister."

She grinned. "Lead on."

They worked well together for close to an hour, under the cool wind and dappled moonlight making fairy patterns on the grass.

"Fairy patterns?" Gavin asked when she commented on it. He hunkered next to her as he patted at the soil around a freshly weeded cucumber plant. "Someone's a little too fond of *The Lord of the Rings*."

"Why is that the only movie series people associate with fairies? And they were elves and dwarves, technically." She paused. "And hobbits."

He rolled his eyes. "Fine. Name another fairy movie."

She opened her mouth and closed it. Suddenly blank. Before she could come up with a better argument, she felt a raindrop hit her cheek. Then another.

Gavin glanced up. "Hell. At least it held off for a while."

She would have agreed, but then the sky opened up, and a torrent of rain fell from out of nowhere.

In seconds, she was drenched. "I'm getting soaked!"

"Shit. Let's go." He hauled her with him to the back porch, then left her to ease Leon and his new pals under the eaves, so that the water wasn't pummeling directly on top of the transplants. Instead, the wind sprayed the drops like mist over the fragile blooms.

Once inside again, they stood dripping onto the kitchen floor.

Gavin swore. "That rain is not gentle or warm. I think a few more minutes out there and we'd be missing skin. Damn storm."

"No kidding." She started to shiver.

"Wait here." He hustled away and came back with towels and a robe. "I raided the downstairs guest room, where Hope's staying. This place is better than the Ritz. Leave your muddy shoes here. You can change in the guest room around the corner." He pointed past the kitchen toward the main hall.

She left and returned, clad only in the fluffy blue robe. She refused to feel self-conscious, because the wet cold of undergarments had been like torture. Especially in contrast to the soft warmth of the robe.

She found Gavin in the kitchen in nothing but jeans, towel-drying his hair. Droplets graced his muscular shoulders and biceps. A dusting of hair covered his firm chest and ran down his corded abs.

Holy mother of… She pretended to yawn to cover her gaping mouth.

He froze when he saw her. "Blue's your color."

"Tan is yours," she quipped, earning a grin.

But there was no mistaking the hunger in his gaze.

"So, ah, what now?"

The loaded silence about killed her, until Gavin nodded to the hallway. He skirted her, careful not to make contact, she noted. Then he walked past the living room, leading her back down another hallway toward a smaller living space. It was cozy, filled with a large-screen television, a soft, thick sectional, and a fireplace. With the flick of a switch, he had a fire going.

"Gotta love natural gas."

She nodded.

"Yep. No chopping wood for these folks." He smiled. "And no smelly smoke from the flue being blocked. Had that happen a time or two growing up, back when my mother thought it would build character to take us all camping."

"What happened?"

He placed the towel down over a faux bearskin rug in front of the fire and sat, his back to the fireplace. "My mother and father realized we are not a 'roughing it' kind of family. Landon and I basically tormented Hope, Mom, and Theo with spiders. Dad refused to cook in such a primitive setting, without his designer pots. And it rained on our borrowed tent…that had holes. Unfortunately, Mom hadn't listened to Aunt Beth about trying it out and checking for tears before we camped."

She chuckled. "I consider myself a hotel kind of camper."

"Yeah."

"But you were in the Marines, right? You must have done plenty of camping in the woods."

To her surprise, his face closed up, and she realized his time in the service had come with a hefty price. He said he'd seen horrible things. It appeared the memory of them wasn't far away.

Then Gavin seemed to shake off the memories, because he smiled. "I'm a better camper than Landon, that's for sure. I was enlisted. I worked for a living. My prissy older brother was an officer. Major Pain in the Ass, for sure." He snickered.

"What rank were you, if you don't mind me asking?"

"Master sergeant. I wanted to stay a gunny, but they forced the promotion. Most of my time was spent away from a desk, thank God. I'm not an admin, peacetime kind of Marine. I do better out in the field."

He seemed calm talking about his time in. Then she noticed his fist by his side, clenched in the rug. He saw her watching him and relaxed it, brushing through the fur. "Great place, isn't it? Want to watch a movie or something while our clothes dry?" He blinked. "Ah, speaking of which, let me find the dryer. I'll be right back."

He darted from the room, returning minutes later. "I threw the stuff in the dryer. Hope that was okay."

Great. He'd seen her polka-dot panties and plain cotton bra. *Way to go, May West. Wow 'em with your sexy lingerie.*

She nodded and moved closer to the flames, hoping he'd attribute the heat in her cheeks to the warmth of the fire. Keeping her back to him, she held out her hands, enraptured by the flickering oranges and reds.

She started when his breath swept her ear. "Love those panties, by the way."

She went from nervous to hot and wanting in seconds. Even though she knew it wouldn't be smart, she turned and saw bare, muscular flesh inches away. Lifting a hand, she stroked his shoulder and saw him shudder. Then she followed the trail of muscle, and one thick vein, down his biceps to his dense forearm.

"Yeah? Well, I love your shirt too." She stroked his fingers, then traced a pattern over his chest. Deliberately grazing his nipples, she stared up into his eyes, now dark with need.

"Do you?" he growled. "'Cause I'm not wearing one."

"Uh-huh." She bit her lip, aware she was aroused all over. Wet between her legs, her nipples taut, her belly doing somersaults as she breathed in Gavin Donnigan. "I don't do casual sex," she reminded him—and her.

"Right. No one-night stands," he agreed, his voice impossibly low.

"Exactly," she whispered.

And then, somehow, his mouth was on hers, and the passion building between them exploded.

Gavin couldn't take it. Two seconds from coming in his pants, just from looking at her. Knowing she wore nothing but skin and that sensual, fluffy robe killed him.

But the nail in the coffin—her fingernails scraping his chest.

Lost in her taste, her touch, he felt her hands everywhere. Gliding across his pecs, his stomach, grazing the button of his jeans.

He swore against her mouth as he unfastened his

pants, then unzipped to give himself some room. Fuck, but he was thick and hard. Ready to come without much more prodding. So when her fingers grazed his cock-head, sliding through the moisture there, he could do nothing but give the lady what she wanted.

Gavin had been doing his best to keep his hands away from the robe opening, controlling the kiss and being as much of a gentleman as he could. But shit. No longer.

He pulled away and yanked off the rest of his clothes while she stared, her eyes wide, her lips parted, quiet. Her hands moved to her robe, and he covered them so that they removed her robe together to pool on the floor. He spared her a glance, wanting to *feel* more than see the feminine shape that so tantalized. This first time.

They met, naked, body to body, and he groaned at the silky feel of her against him. So soft, pliant, yet firm as she yanked him closer and kissed him until he couldn't breathe. Not sure who made the first move, they ended up on the rug. He kissed her, palmed her breasts, and nudged a leg between hers, needing to be inside her in the worst way.

His desire skyrocketed when she moaned and grabbed him back, her soft panting and mewling cries like pin-pricks of arousal stabbing him everywhere.

Sanity tried to rear its head—to slow down, make sense of it all, be smart. But there was no reasoning once she wrapped her ankles around his waist and nudged his cock between her folds.

He kissed his way to her ear, biting her lobe with insistence. "So hot. You feel so fucking good."

She gasped and rocked against him, causing the head of his shaft to slide inside her.

"Zoe?" he managed, pulling back to stare into her eyes.

"On the pill," she confessed and dragged him back for a kiss, digging her heels into his ass in encouragement.

Gavin thrust the rest of the way inside her. "Oh fuck." He pulled out only to surge back in, faster, harder. No patience left.

"Yeah," she whispered and clasped him tighter, tugging at his shoulders as he rammed in and out, no finesse, just raw need.

It didn't take long before she cried out and seized around him, her body so hot and slick she sucked him into an orgasm without thinking.

He shuddered as he came, emptying inside her until he could no longer maintain the carnal frenzy. She squeezed him again with her body, and he swore and jerked, finding something left inside him after all.

They lay in each other's arms, breathing hard, sweaty and joined. All the way, body to body.

Without a condom.

Gavin paused, not used to feeling like an imbecile while sober. Hell, even drunk he'd always known to wear a rubber. But two seconds inside Zoe and he'd come, and come hard.

"I guess it's kind of late to ask about the safe-sex question," Zoe said, drowsy, content, as she stroked his arms.

He raised himself on his hands, still locked inside her, making no attempt to pull from her heat. Staring at her, he lost himself in her beauty. "You're gorgeous, you know that?" He loved that she blushed. "And yeah, too late for the safe-sex quiz. Though it's your fault. Once you said you were on the pill, my brain totally shut off."

He groaned and started moving in her once more, now taking the time to appreciate her full breasts and tight abs. Those silky thighs and that rockin' ass.

His cock had softened, but not totally. The more he studied her, the more he wanted another round. He'd been waiting for this moment too long for it to be over so soon.

Gavin leaned down and took a nipple in his mouth, sucking gently, then teething the taut nub. "I've been with a few women since I came back," he admitted. "But I've always used protection. I'm clean. That's one thing you don't have to worry about."

She uttered a sexy groan. "Oh, me too. Safe, I mean. I haven't had sex in a while."

"Yeah? How long's a while?"

"Not counting you or that dry humping in the gym…"

"*Zoe*." Did she have to bring that up?

She chuckled. "Sadly, it's been seven or eight months, I think."

"Whoa." He swallowed the *No wonder you were so hot for me*. Especially because he'd been even hotter for her, and he'd been with Megan a month ago, a fact he now very much regretted. "So you're discerning."

"Good word for it." She pulled him down for another kiss, surprising him. Zoe reveled in her sensuality. He'd have assumed she'd jump up from the floor, race away with a horrified look on her face, and deem tonight an utter disaster and mistake. Instead, she seemed to be encouraging him for round two.

He leaned down into her again, but this time playing with her breasts, enthralled with her contrasts of softness and muscle. "I love your body."

"Yeah? Well, I love yours too. Would help if you moved a little faster though. No one-night stands for us."

"Oh?"

"Keep going past midnight, and that'll definitely make it a two-nighter."

"Or we both come again, take a short nap, then go at it again tomorrow. Maybe Monday, and again into next week," he offered, praying she'd take him up on it. No way in hell he'd be done with her after one night.

She stopped stroking his shoulders, and he tensed, thickening inside her.

This, right now, was a turning point.

"So you want to keep hanging out and having sex?"

"Or, as your people call it, dating?"

"My people?"

"Yeah, womankind. Because my people are crude." He shifted a bit, wondering if she'd notice, but he had to. God, she was so tight around him. "Dudes would be calling it all sorts of insulting things."

"Like?"

He slid slowly out, then pushed back in. She bit her lip. He moaned and said hoarsely, "Like banging and balling. Riding the sweet shoot. Dining and dashing."

"Wait. I know that one." She gasped when he angled deeper inside her. "That's about eating and taking off."

He smiled.

She blushed. "Oh. We haven't gotten to that yet."

"The night's still young."

She stared up at him, searching. Then she pulled his head close and whispered in his ear, "Then what are you waiting for?" She stuck her tongue in his ear. An erogenous zone she'd homed in on with ease.

He slammed back home. This time he didn't stop until after she'd cried out his name. In five long, howling syllables. Then, and only then, did he leave a little bit of himself behind.

Unfortunately, he had a bad feeling he'd left more than a physical piece of himself. He'd left an emotional one as well.

Chapter 8

LATE SUNDAY AFTERNOON, ZOE FELT ODD ABOUT HAVING Gavin over. Sure, they'd had a lot of sex Saturday night into the wee hours of the morning. And again after waking up—which had worried her. She'd done her best to think sexy thoughts, hoping her morning breath didn't scare him away for good. So caught up in what he'd done to her, she hadn't worried about it a moment more until after they'd finished. And by then she hadn't cared.

Life had been one exhausting bag of loveliness. Until Piper had seen her walk of shame from the driveway to the house. And man, had her aunt made her pay. Lots of *I told you so's* and laughter at her expense. Still too sated to care, Zoe had only laughed with her.

After waiting on Zoe's quick shower and then sharing brunch downtown, Piper had left. Zoe had turned to her weekly chores with little enthusiasm, haphazardly cleaning her already clean house while she thought about Gavin.

Who would be joining her later this evening for more sex.

Should she insist on conversation as well? Zoe didn't know. She hadn't been so well pleasured in, well, forever. Okay, so they'd gone Mach 10 to orgasm that first time. But then they'd slowed way down. And this morning, he'd had her begging him to take her, going so far as to use the f-word and a few other four-letter ones too, insane to have him inside her.

"Go, me." She grinned as she straightened up. Talk about the right person to break her dry spell. Gavin not only looked like Prince Charming, but he acted like a perfect gentleman. He took charge in bed, just the way she liked.

She got goose bumps remembering how he'd held her hands over her head while he slid in and out of her with way too much patience...

She shivered and finished throwing the laundry in the dryer. Then she gave a full-body sigh. Time to stop thinking about sex and focus on the day-to-day. Monday crept all too near.

More gardening, a quick salad for dinner. Which she might as well not have made, for all that her appetite had deserted her.

That damn Gavin Donnigan. What a dreamboat and pain in the ass all in one. He was her own personal Two-Face, but much more handsome than the Gotham archvillain.

Aubrey totally would have loved him. Gavin had a lot of her qualities. He was fun-loving, humorous, laidback. But that distance when he'd mentioned his time in the Marine Corps. Zoe found that part of him fascinating. Like her, he tried to control his grief. Whatever he'd been through, it had seriously bothered him. So as much as she'd wanted to pry, she hadn't. Oddly though, she felt like they shared grief in common.

What a wacky thing to be glad about—a similarity in experiencing sorrow.

A glance at the picture of her and Aubrey, arm in arm and smiling, brought forth memories.

Teasing, the *He's your boyfriend* game, spiking each other's eggnog at Christmas while teens and trying not to get caught. So many wonderful things they were going to experience. But Aubrey would never walk down an aisle in a funky, fashionable, nontraditional gown. She'd never hold the baby she'd planned to name Zoey "with a *y*." And she'd never grow old with Zoe, sharing the rest of their lives together, the high and lows, the firsts and lasts.

God, that hurt so much. To lose that zest and joy in life Aubrey had possessed in abundance.

The guilt that she remained alive while Aubrey lay dead returned. If one of them should have had to go, it should have been Zoe. The too-serious twin. The hard-ass who didn't know how to laugh at life, too busy making plans to cover even her eventual death.

Hell, she'd been the one to make her family plan for the future. She'd been the one who'd invested in a plot where the family could lie in rest together. And here she stood, staring at a picture of the funnier, more-adventurous twin while Aubrey entertained the world no longer.

Tears trickled down her cheeks.

"God, Aubrey. I miss you. You should be here with Gavin. Not me."

Even as she said it, she knew she was being overly dramatic and ridiculous. Aubrey would kick her ass for thinking like that. *Life was for living, not planning for an early grave*, she'd liked to say.

"Guess I showed you," Zoe said through a watery laugh.

Determined to stop being such a wuss, she turned

to more pragmatic thoughts, the kind that might help her adjust to the here and now. So she put away her grief and numbed her mind with next week's schedule. After running through her work calendar and figuring in a girls' night with Cleo, where they could talk about everything over wine—yet another thing she could no longer do with Aubrey—Zoe's thoughts once again turned to Gavin.

When she saw him at the gym later in the week— because no way in hell would she stop going just because they'd played the old slap-and-tickle—should she pretend not to know him? Or would they be adults about the relationship and acknowledge each other? Should she high-five Megan, Michelle, and the others because she'd joined their not-so-elite club?

The petty thought both ashamed and amused her.

"Gavin's casual one-night stands on the left and two-nighters on the right." She wondered about his prior relationships. From what she'd overheard a time or two in the steam room, his lady friends had enjoyed a casual time, but not much else. Michelle and Megan had crassly compared notes. Neither had been thrilled that he hadn't come back for a second "date." But they'd been hot to point out how well-endowed and talented he was in the sack, even if he hadn't stuck around to talk afterward.

They had that part right, at least. But no way had she been treated to any kind of dine and dash. She smirked at the thought.

She had a right to know about his sexual past and planned to ask him about it. He liked her honesty. Well, she'd see how much.

Two hours later, when he rang her bell at eight on the

dot, she let him in. And just stared. "Er, you dressed up for me?"

He grinned. "You like? It's a Mac special."

The red Jameson's Gym T-shirt threatened to burn her retinas. "Could that shirt be any tighter?" Or the dark shorts, which hugged him in all the right places?

"I don't know. But I can't feel my left arm anymore."

She sighed. "You actually do look like a stop sign in that."

"I know." He shrugged. "What can I do?" He jerked his arm, hard, and she heard a rip. "Oh no. It ripped! Witness." He pointed to her. "I did nothing to cause this, just tried to hug my new girlfriend."

Her heart raced. Girlfriend? They had labels now? Best to keep it casual and not act like she cared what they called each other. Though she did. But how did she feel about that? She'd figure it out later, after he'd gone.

"Is that so? Looked to me like you moved really fast and in a jerky motion. Damaging work property, not to mention flouting his authority by not wearing the uniform when everyone else is. Are you at all worried Mac could fire you?"

He snorted. "Yeah, right."

"Good point." Hell, even she knew that the recent gym crowd came for the Donnigans and their self-defense class.

"I work for peanuts. He's lucky to have me."

"Then why stay?"

He pulled off his shirt, leaving him in thigh-hugging nylon shorts that left little to the imagination. "Because I love the gym. And if I can work and have fun, right now, that's good enough for me." He nodded. "I mean, at some point I'll want to do something else with my life. But I'm taking it slowly. One day at a time."

She nodded absently, unable to look away from all those muscles. It was like a biological map. Zoe could see the lines of his ab muscles begging to be traced with a marker. Or her tongue. "Not that I'm complaining, but what's with the tight gym clothes? Are we going to work out or something?"

He chuckled. "You, sexy, give new meaning to the term *workout*." He moved closer, drawing her against his incredible body for a kiss. "I should be too worn out to even wonder about sex with you tonight. But it's all I've been thinking about since you left this morning."

She flushed. "I hope your sister was okay with us staying over."

"She doesn't need to know. Besides. You've made that garden shine."

"Speaking of which, how's Leon?"

"Just fine, surrounded by all the ladies." He smiled and kissed her again, this time slipping her more tongue. "Hmm. You taste delicious."

"Like a big old apple, I'll bet." Since she'd just polished off a Honeycrisp in an effort to have some sustenance before she worked it off in bed.

"Nah. Like an appetizer before I get to the main course. I'm going to go slow tonight. Not like yesterday."

Her heart raced. "You mean this morning, and you were pretty damn slow then."

"Did I tire you out?" He smirked. "Hard to keep up with me, huh, baby?"

"Oh right. The pet names." She loved him calling her *baby*. And it was so macho and sexist. She hated herself a little for enjoying it. "Now that we're going steady and all"—she looked down her nose at him—"is this where I call you *sugar lumps*? You know, in case I forget your name in the middle of sex?"

He looked at her in awe.

"What?" she snapped, still turned on despite herself.

"See? That meanness? Gets me so fuckin' hard." He took her hand and drew it between his legs. "You do this for me…baby."

She gripped him, not surprised to feel him so large. But she hadn't taken a good look the other night, having been too keen on riding him to orgasm, or letting him ride her. "Strip. I want to see what I'm getting." So much for that conversation they might have.

"Yeah? Feeling me deep in you when I came wasn't enough?"

She wanted to be a little more worldly, but she blushed.

He grinned. "You're so cute when you turn red."

"Shut up and get naked, would you?"

"Guess we're skipping right over the foreplay tonight, hmm? I'm game." He had no problem stripping down. And why would he? With a body like that, he had nothing to be ashamed of. But in this light, she saw many of the scars she'd felt last night.

He followed her gaze. "Ah. Those are nothing. A few bullet wounds. A knife fight over there. And the one higher on my collarbone? That's my brother shoving me on a bike with no brakes down a major hill. I crashed well though."

He glossed over the military scars easily enough, so she took his lead. "Which brother?"

"Really? It's the job of the bigger brother to lead the

younger one down the wrong path. This scar is all Landon. Bullied by my big brother and disfigured for life."

"So sad." She wiped an imaginary tear, saw him grinning, and noticed his cock had yet to go down.

"Yes, Mistress," he said, his voice growing deeper. "Now how about I let you in on some more deepseated trauma?"

"Do tell."

"I've got these hidden fantasies, and they keep me up at night."

She eyed his pride and joy. "I can tell."

"It's this woman. I can't see her face, exactly, but I can see her pink yoga pants."

"Oh really? Wait. Don't tell me. I'm having a vision." She put a hand to her forehead, then glanced at him. "Is this the fantasy where you bend me over the couch?"

He licked his lips and eyed her up and down. "Ah, no, not this one."

"I know. This is the one where we roll around in the gym, where there are glass windows where anyone can see inside. Then you have me straddling you, and you pull down your shorts just enough so your cock pops out."

"Damn, girl." He gripped himself.

"And we move my shorts to the side—I'm not wearing any panties—so I can slide over you. Is that the one?"

He stared at her crotch.

"Or is this fantasy the one where we pretend we're at the gym, and you take me in the hall closet? We go at it like dogs in heat, and everyone in the gym can hear us, but they don't know it's us."

"You have one hell of a vivid imagination. But no."

"How about—"

"How about you let me show you?"

"Wow. Already?" she teased, loving how his breathing sounded uneven. Why should Zoe be the only one desperately in lust? "And we didn't even get to my proper hostessing skills. I have more root beer. I even bought cream soda just for you."

He nodded, his gaze intense. She couldn't forget he stood nude before her, while she wore a casual jersey skirt and an off-the-shoulder sweatshirt. Not too fancy, but in honor of the seductive evening, she'd worn lacy underclothes.

"What?"

"You talk too much."

She frowned. "Hey."

"Ms. York, zip it. Get up against the wall."

Sensing he wanted to play, she gave a sniff, playing her part, and did as ordered.

Gavin stalked her. There was no other word for it.

Yet again, without even touching her, he'd made her wet and aroused just watching him.

He leaned into her, pinning her to the wall. "Hello. I'm Gavin. Your sexy new trainer."

"Oh, I see. Hello, Gavin. My, what big muscles you have." She stroked his chest, and he blew out a breath.

"Ms. York, how can I help you? What are your goals for tonight?" He brushed against her belly, his erection prodding.

God, he was sexy. "Hmm. My goals for tonight?" She wrapped her arms around his neck, plastering her body to his. "A few orgasms. Maybe lifting a ten-pounder. Doing some reps to get buff."

"Hmm. You like 'em big, yeah?"

She raised a brow. "The bigger the better. I told you before, size matters."

He chuckled. "So you did."

"It's just…I always wanted a *boyfriend* with a big cock. And now I apparently have one." She hadn't meant to bring that up so soon, but heck, why not?

"Knew that *girlfriend* mention would get in your loop," he said with satisfaction. "You're not sure you want to belong to me yet, are you?"

"Belong to you? Like a pet, you mean?" How wrong was it that when he put his hand around her throat, she grew very, very wet between her legs?

"Now hold on a minute, Ms. York." He ran his other hand up her thigh, dragging up the mid-thigh skirt. "Let's see if you're wearing your equipment properly." He found her bikinis and shook his head. "Sorry, Mistress. This is a no-panty zone."

He tugged them off, leaving her bottom covered only by the skirt. "And what's the deal with your top? It's ugly."

"Hey."

"Women don't work out in sweatshirts. You'll get all sweaty. You need to go au naturel." He smiled, a mean grin that had her groaning his name. "Put your arms up."

"So I guess we really are going right into the sex," she said, her voice muffled while he drew the sweatshirt over her head. With that gone, her bra soon followed. "Did you like the lace?"

"The what?" He leaned close and sucked a nipple into his mouth before she could argue with him.

"Oh." Threading her fingers in his hair, she held

him close while he played with her breasts. He cupped her, pinching her with excruciating gentleness, which only exacerbated the tiny sting of the tug he gave at the end. She went from hot to cold, not sure how to feel except aroused.

Last night had been about satiating themselves on each other. Tonight, apparently, would be about savoring the experience.

"That's it. Keep your hands there. Hold me close, Mistress."

Oddly enough, instead of laughing off the silly pet name, she felt turned on by it. An intimacy he'd given her. And the way he said it made her want to show him just how much of a "mistress" she wanted to be. But she was helpless against her body's needs. Gavin played her like he owned her. And after so brief a time being sexual with each other, she found that astonishing.

He continued to suck her breasts, drawing forth carnal sparks that ramped her arousal. But those naughty hands of his drove her insane.

"Gavin," she gasped. "What are you doing?" He kept running his hands up her legs, between her thighs, making her widen her stance. He'd get so close to her sex, then he'd slide his hands back down her legs. Each time he came closer to grazing her clit, sliding the edges of his hands through her wet arousal.

She unconsciously leaned toward him, thrusting her pelvis forward. And he heard her unspoken plea, let her guide his head lower. He dragged her skirt down until she stepped out of it. Then his mouth was there, between her legs, and his tongue found her.

She cried out, engulfed in desire. Those thick fingers

of his continued to move up and down her legs, coming close but not close enough.

Until he drew her clit between his lips and teethed her with enough bite to cause painful pleasure to blanch everything white. Just as she reached the pinnacle of her release, he shoved a thick finger inside her.

Zoe clamped down on him as she came, the pleasure so intense she felt ripples of it up and down her spine. And the ecstasy continued, shocking her that it hadn't ended. Gavin, bless him, continued to lick her up, moaning as he did. He whispered something against her, and she shook, now overwhelmed with sensation.

"Zoe," he growled. "Turn around."

"What?" Dazed and just flat-out impressed he had the skill to make her lose herself completely, she let him turn her and braced herself against the wall. He pulled her hips toward him, bending her, and then she felt him there, at the entrance to her slick flesh.

He slid forward, triggering more shocks in her sensitive channel. She moaned, wishing he'd been inside her before when she'd come, so she hadn't felt so empty. His finger had been good, but not as good as the rest of him.

"Fuck me. You feel so wet. I'm not gonna last." His breathing grew choppy, his thrusts frenzied as he moved faster, harder. He dug his fingers into her hips, sawing with a brutal pace until he seized and moaned her name, pumping inside her.

Zoe didn't know why, but having him release in her was a huge turn-on. She had this part of him. Joined even when he'd no longer be there. It was a closeness she'd rarely had with the men in her life. By rights, she shouldn't be having it with Gavin.

But she wanted it. Wanted this, with him.

He groaned and started to withdraw. "Zoe, baby, you destroy me."

"I only gave back what you gave me." She felt every inch where they were joined. Gavin had strength beyond the muscle, a fortitude that had gotten him through some hard times. And it was that concentrated power that sucked her in, made her feel that in his arms, she would be safe enough to really let go.

"Hey, you got me all hot and bothered first," he complained, still breathing hard. "Demanding I strip. Being all bossy and mean. It was damn hot. And those fantasies of yours. We need to take care of those, stat."

"Well, let's at least give me time to clean up. I think you made another mess in me."

He chuckled. All hot, male satisfaction. "Do you have any idea how much I love coming in you?"

"Do you have any idea how stupid I was to let you do it that first time?"

"Yep. Pretty dumb," he agreed and slowly withdrew from her. Before she could dash for the bathroom, he lifted her in his arms, startling a gasp out of her. "Easy. I got you. You weigh surprisingly less than you look."

"What the hell does that mean?" she snarled.

"So hot." He sighed again and walked her back to her bedroom, going into the attached bath. Once there, he wouldn't let her clean herself. So she stood embarrassed through it all as he wiped her clean with a washcloth, then patted her dry, following the towel with kisses.

When he started revving her engines again, insatiable with that oral fixation, she forced him to stop.

He immediately ceased and scowled up at her. "Why?"

"Why?" *Because I don't want to come again so easily. I have no control around you.* "I thought we could talk too. Or did you just come over to drain the weasel?"

He grimaced. "Bad euphemism. That's more like taking a piss, and not something I want involved in my lovemaking." He stood and made a face. "Go lay down in bed, and we'll cuddle."

She blinked. "Did you just say we'll cuddle?"

"And talk. I know you chicks dig that." He gave her a knowing smile, just waiting for her to blow up.

"Oh yes. All of us chicks on your fuck list. Let's talk about that, shall we?"

He shrugged, seeming not at all bothered by the bite in her voice. "If you want to. You can tell me all about the men in your life too, if you want. I'm game."

"Fine."

"Fine."

She left him to clean up and stalked to the bed. Refusing to dress, she waited, naked, and ignored the slight chill in the room.

Gavin joined her shortly, looking fresh, buff, and determined—which surprised her.

"I'll start," he said, still naked and lying down next to her. He leaned on his elbow so he could face her, on his side. She did the same, needing to see his expressions. Then he confused her—again—by tracing her facial features with a callused fingertip. When he stopped, he was smiling.

"Wh-what was that?" And why had it made her feel as if he was touching so much deeper than her skin?

"Just memorizing your features."

"Through touch?"

"Yep." His gentle smile annoyed her.

"Don't try seducing me again. We're going to talk like regular people."

"Okay."

"So start." She flicked her fingers at him. "Your mistress demands it."

He chuckled. "I was teasing with that *you chicks* comment. I won't lie and say I'm all virginal. Truth is—Zoe, you want the truth, right?"

"Yes, I do."

"The truth is…"

Gavin stared at the woman he couldn't stop thinking about. They'd only been sexual for the past two days, but he wanted more. He'd never been so into a woman before. If it had just been sex, he thought he'd be able to walk away.

Each time he slid inside Zoe and looked into her eyes, he connected with her. He loved her snarky attitude. Her take-charge vibe that refused to let him get away with shit. And when she grieved for her sister, that realness, that honest love, hurt him. But in a good way. Zoe's grief was as it should be. Untainted with guilt and revulsion.

He wanted that. To feel love without all the bad stuff that came with it. With Zoe, it felt right. The sex, the emotion, the laughter always bubbling inside at her peevishness. "Still waiting, Sir Sex-A-Lot."

"The truth is…'I like big butts and I cannot lie.'" He laughed at her gradual comprehension. "Sorry, sorry. But you said Sex-A-Lot. I heard Mix-A-Lot. And please, you have the finest ass in Seattle. Baby, you ain't got much back, but what you have is tight."

"Thanks. I think."

He snorted. "Yeah. Anyway. The truth. That's what you want." And what he had to tell her. Gavin didn't want to play around with Zoe. No lies, no kidding to cover shit up. If not all of his issues, he wanted at least the big ones out of the way, so he and Zoe could get past them and never discuss them again.

He cleared his throat. "So I was in the Marine Corps. Joined up at eighteen and got out last June. Fourteen years. They weren't all pretty, but they mattered. I mattered."

She put her hand on his and squeezed.

"So I joined up with a bunch of my friends. We moved apart, then came back together, so that some or all of us seemed to be in the same unit a lot. Until I had different duties. But that's not important. What is important is that while I was injured, recuperating, the guys went out on a routine patrol and died in an explosion. It was bad. I lost a lot of friends." *Just say it fast and never mention it again.* "Then I ended up coming home. I was fucked up. Not handling being back well. So I started drinking. I had a lot of sex. Things that felt good to make me not feel like such shit."

"I get it."

"I know you do." Her wounds from losing her twin had yet to heal. "To make a long story short, my family intervened. Saw I was being a dumbass and helped me get some clarity. I'm no saint. But I never asked those women at the gym for anything they didn't want to give. And before you ask, I used protection. Probably the only smart thing I did back then.

"I look back on it now and wish I hadn't slept with some of them. Yeah, I admit it. I made some mistakes. But at the time, I needed what they had to offer. And so did they." He paused, putting it out there. "I like you a lot, Zoe. I want to hang out more. You and me. Gardening or hiking, taking in a movie. You know, Netflix and chill," he teased, seeing her flush. "I'm not out to use you. I'm not out to call you my girlfriend or get you to commit to something you don't want. Yeah, I was yanking your chain before. We're finally getting to know each other. Well, more than how to get you to orgasm, that is."

"You know, I was with you right up until—"

"So I want to spend time with you. I like being with you. You make me laugh. And I'm damn sure attracted to you." Zoe was different from the others. "But I'm not sure what you want from me. And I'm not sure I could give it to you if I did know. I'm not totally together yet. I'm a work in progress, you could say."

She studied him, and he saw so much more than a naked woman who could have had her own spread as a centerfold. The caring in her bright-blue eyes, that zing he felt when looking at her smile. With her, he felt at peace, despite the fact his entire body flamed with desire.

"Okay. I get you."

"Do you?"

"I think so. So here's my truth." She drew in a deep breath and let it out slowly. "I'm the boring twin, the responsible one. The twin who has a burial plot, a 401(k), and my future planned out to the nth degree. But when Aubrey died, it made me think hard about what I was doing with my life. She was fun and carefree. Everyone loved her. I miss her so much sometimes," Zoe admitted in a soft voice.

He saw her eyes well up, and his heart dropped. "Aw, baby, come here."

He pulled her into his arms and felt her tremble. She cleared her throat and sniffed.

"Sorry. I hate when that happens. I'll be fine, and then...*bam*. Waterworks."

"Better tears than booze and Michelle," he muttered, not thinking.

She stiffened in his arms, and he felt like a heel.

Until she laughed. She laughed so hard she cried.

"Those are good tears, right?"

"Yeah. Booze and Michelle. What a combination." She huffed. "And maybe next time, consider it might be better not to mention specific names of the women you've had sex with while being naked in bed with me. I'd rather they were faceless. Because...Michelle? Ugh."

"I have been known to talk without thinking." He groaned and hugged her tighter, until she squeaked. "I'm sorry. I really do understand what you're saying. That came out wrong."

"I know." She pulled back so she could look at him. "I know you don't like to talk about your military time. We all have to deal with our stuff our own way. But I'm glad we're finally *hanging out*."

He frowned. "Ah, do you mean hanging out, as in having sex? Or as in us talking?"

"Both." She rolled him onto his back and lay over him like a blanket. "I like being with you, Gavin. I don't know what that means, but this is nice."

He scowled. "Wait. Hold on. Nice? The mittens your aunt gave you for Christmas are nice. A halfway decent haircut is nice. My brother doing the dishes for my mom is nice. I'm not nice."

"No, no. Not nice."

He glared. "Why are you smiling?"

"Gavin, that was a compliment. You're a real bastard and a prick, but your cock is huge and manly, and I'm totally impressed. Did I say nice? I meant exciting. Passionate. Being with you makes me horny all the time."

He nodded and huffed. "Better."

"And I have more fantasies that we need to get to. Maybe later this week though. Because if we keep going at it this hard, I'll be bowlegged at work and people will be asking questions."

"Good. Let them ask." And that brought up a great point. "While we're *hanging out*, it's just you for me and me for you. No other dudes or chicks to get in the way. Right?"

She stared into his eyes, hers warm and smiling, the bright-blue gleam entrancing. "Right." She leaned down to kiss him. "You're cute when you're possessive."

Now he felt like an idiot. "Nah, just making sure we can still be condom-free with sex. I'm not planning on screwing that up." Gruffly he added, "You either."

"Sure thing, Smoky."

"I prefer Guns of Steel." He pumped his arm, showing off his biceps.

"Oh, nice. Want to see mine?"

He nodded, feeling warm because she kept moving with slow, sensual gyrations against his body. For someone who wanted to cuddle and talk, she was getting him fired up instead.

"Yeah." He cleared his throat, trying not to fixate on her breasts as she sat up.

She straddled him, then took his now-hard cock in hand and eased over him.

"Zoe? *Fuck.* What are you doing?"

"See me flexing?" She made a muscle with her biceps while sliding down his shaft, seating him all the way inside.

He felt his eyes roll back into his head and moaned.

"Now, now, Smoky. Pay attention. When I say cuddle, I mean cuddle with every bone in that body."

"Every boner in my body?" he rasped.

"Sad you had to go there." She started riding him, up and down.

"Yes, Mistress, you insatiable thing." He stared up at her, wanting to pinch himself to make sure he wasn't dreaming. Hot chick, tender heart, riding him so he could jet inside her? Really? This was his life?

His heart sped when she moved faster over him. He panted, getting closer on the climb to orgasm. "Let me tell you my fantasy about a certain pair of pink yoga pants tied around my wrists while my wicked mistress has her way with me."

"You mean those yoga pants?" Zoe moaned and pointed to a pair folded neatly on a chair. "Next time."

She kept grinding over him, and then she leaned to kiss him, and it was like she had read his mind.

Chapter 9

"…THE NEXT ITEM ON THE AGENDA IS ADDING A NEW DEXA scanner order," Cleo said, reading from a PowerPoint slide projected on the far wall. "So Dr. Fenton, did you…"

It was the Wednesday morning managers' meeting, and Zoe was zoning out. Six thirty on a Wednesday morning normally wasn't too early by her standards, but Gavin was wearing her out.

In the best way, physically. Mentally, he baffled her. She still wasn't sure how she felt about her new relationship. Because yeah, she and Gavin were more than just friends with benefits. They had sexcapades that thus far had ended with her having many—and at one point, multiple—orgasms. He remained charming, sexual, and unstoppable.

He continued to surprise her. By mutual agreement, they'd decided to take a break on Monday. And Tuesday, seeing each other at the gym and greeting with a nod. Low key but certainly not dismissive. He'd smiled wide. She'd grinned back. But they'd left each other mostly alone.

Until last night. Gavin had knocked, entered, and left her exhausted twenty minutes later. Another session of wham-bam, come screaming again.

So why did she feel sated and not used? They both got enjoyment out of the deal. But they'd talked and been deep with each other on Sunday. That meant something, and not just to her.

Gavin had invited her to lunch today. Hmm, something about lunch struck a chord…

Oh hell. Swanson had been responsible for the change in Cleo's precious Monday morning meeting. He'd also mentioned he planned to rescheduled their lunch, for which Zoe had been more than grateful. She'd hoped to dodge that bullet, but he'd rescheduled it for today. Meaning the lunch she'd gotten out of on Monday with Mr. Crabby was happening in another four hours. Joy.

"Approved. Who's on point for rolling this out?"

Cleo and the rest of the room stared at Zoe, waiting.

"Huh? Oh, right. I need to check over our calendar, but I'm shooting for Friday."

No one had any issues, so they moved on to the next item on the agenda.

By the time the meeting ended, Zoe had managed to wake up, ignore the tempting box of doughnuts sitting way too close, and scoot out the door before Swanson could catch up with her. Somehow, she had to get out of lunch with him. She had a feeling if she spent too much time under that piercing gaze, she'd end up promising him her firstborn child and signing over the deed to her soul.

The morning passed swiftly. Her meeting with IT went about as well as expected. The poor bastards in that department worked hard, but they worked for an idiot. Jim liked to make meetings to have meetings. They'd talk for an hour and get nothing done. Not this time.

Zoe left after forcing Jim to accept her terms, committing to actual times of delivery instead of vague references to the future. She'd also suggested, rather strongly, that if he didn't want to deal with hundreds of unhappy users, including Mr. Swanson himself, he'd better figure out why the wireless was so slow. Jim hadn't looked too panicked until she mentioned Mr. Crabby.

Score another one for the dictatorial manager.

And speaking of which, she shot Swanson an email with a request to reschedule today's lunch. Fingers crossed he'd buy it. Zoe was no coward, but she had enough on her plate without trying to manage Swanson's many dictates. After all, he was a client, and her job made customer service a number one priority, which the guy took clear advantage of.

After working with Ginny and a few of the trainers on the implementation schedule, a *huge* project, Zoe filtered her emails from most important to not so much, set up a few more meetings, and informed Bill she'd be sitting in on his training session this afternoon at the cardiology clinic. For being the new guy, Bill had gotten up to speed quickly. Zoe loved her people. They worked hard with few hiccups and did a spectacular job of communicating to the customer—the doctors, medical assistants, and office staff who used the software.

Eleven o'clock rolled around all too soon, and she moved with leaden feet to the lunch shop next door. It was a favorite hangout for the admin staff and the general surgery and cardiology clinics close by.

She entered and ordered a chicken Caesar salad and iced tea, her food of choice to get through the rest of the day. The protein would do her good, because she was dragging. She didn't wait for Gavin to show before she dug into her plate.

"Hey there, girlfriend." Cleo joined her with a burger and fries in the seat across from her by the window.

"Uh, hi. I didn't realize we were having lunch today."

That's what she got for grabbing a table with four chairs.

"We aren't. I decided to be spontaneous."

Time to bite the bullet. "Actually, I'm expecting someone else—"

"Ms. York. There you are." Swanson plunked down next to Cleo after giving her a small frown. "Cleo."

"Mark."

"So that's what the M stands for," Zoe teased, wondering how to extricate herself from the opponents across from her. "I thought it was—"

"Macho? Murderous? Malignant?" Cleo filled in, her voice soft, innocent.

Swanson huffed. "Yes, because those are common male names beginning with M. You're so clever, Cleo." Clearly, he didn't mean a word he said. "Why am I not surprised?" He bit into a wrap, dismissing Cleo with ease.

Before Cleo could get a verbal bite in, Zoe said, "You know, this is great, you two being here. Because I have a prior—"

"Zoe. Hey there." Gavin swooped down and planted a kiss on her cheek. "You're looking good, as usual."

She blushed, not used to having her personal life mix with business. Though she shouldn't be embarrassed. It wasn't as if working for SMP mandated she live a monk-like existence.

Cleo gaped at Gavin as if unsure he was real. Not that Zoe could blame her. Gavin wore jeans and a dark-gray T-shirt that clung lovingly to his torso, exposing every inch of muscle. The gray color made his eyes pop, and she'd bet ten bucks he knew the fact and exploited it.

Swanson gave Gavin a thorough once-over she couldn't read.

"Who is *this*?" Cleo asked, though she knew darned well who it was.

Zoe frowned at her to behave. "Cleo, Mr. Swanson, meet Gavin Donnigan, a good friend of mine. Gavin, they work with me at the medical group."

"I'm also her best friend," Cleo announced and took Gavin's proffered hand with enthusiasm, holding longer than could be considered polite.

Gavin just grinned.

Zoe sighed. "Cleo."

Cleo winked at him. "Oh, sorry. Forgot I was holding him, blinded by all his muscles."

Gavin chuckled, and even Zoe grinned. Cleo could say things Zoe could never get away with, sounding cute and flirty but not over the top, probably because she looked so mischievous and innocent at the same time. Not like Zoe, who was often compared to a steamroller or an Amazon. And that had been complimentary.

Swanson offered his hand, and he and Gavin shook and let go. Propriety upheld, though she didn't see any friendships blossoming there.

Gavin glanced at her and the group. "Should I come back another time? If you're busy, I can—"

Cleo interrupted. "No, no. We're butting in on your date, apparently. Aren't we, Mr. M. Swanson?"

"No, we're not. This is a working lunch." He

grudgingly conceded, "Though you're more than welcome to join us, Gavin. And call me Mark."

"Thanks." Gavin smiled, squeezed Zoe's shoulder, and said, "I'll be right back." He left to place his order.

"If you'd said you had a prior engagement, I'd have understood," Swanson said.

"I sent you an email," Zoe told him.

"Oh, that." He took a sip of his drink. "I thought that was you trying to weasel your way out of a meeting. I didn't know you really had plans."

"Nice," Cleo muttered. "So you're not a total dick all the time."

"Cleo!" Zoe wondered if she'd have to pry the pair apart once the gloves really came off. Swanson had never been one to let bygones be bygones without a reckoning first.

"Not all the time, no," Swanson said with a half smile. Amused?

Cleo snorted. "Well, at least you're honest."

"More than some." He glanced at her.

Zoe watched the back-and-forth, entertained despite herself.

Cleo raised a brow. "What does that mean?"

"Weren't you the one bragging to everyone the other day about your Army boyfriend soon becoming a fiancé? Yet today you're flirting with Zoe's good *friend*."

So no one had missed the fact she and Gavin were more than friendly.

"First of all, yes, that's true, Scott and I are going to get engaged soon." Cleo sounded proud and happy. "And second, I was only teasing. Gavin is built. Anyone can see that. He's also Zoe's *friend*, and I would never move in on a friend's *friend*."

"Okay, you two, stop with all the *friend* emphasis. And while we're here, if you can stop going at each other's throats, that would be super helpful too. Now, what is it you wanted to meet with me about, Mr. Swanson?"

He'd been chewing and had to swallow first to talk. Gavin returned and sat next to her, across from Swanson. Everyone watched Gavin and his tiny tray of food.

"What?"

"Eat much?" Cleo eyed his plate. "That's a salad. Shouldn't you eat something with meat or protein?"

"I have a tuna melt coming up," he said. "Go on. Don't let me interrupt you. I'm starving anyway." While Gavin tucked into his salad, Zoe waited for Swanson to speak.

He sighed. "First, you might as well call me Mark. It's been four years. I think we're past the point of being distant professional colleagues."

"So now you're what?" Cleo asked, a dimple in her cheek. "Closer professional colleagues? Or, gasp, friends, even?"

"Colleagues is fine, Cleo." Mark shook his head. "I still have no idea who you bribed to get to such an important position in the group. It's not as if you're a people person."

"I'm a little more people-oriented than you are," Cleo snapped.

Gavin chuckled. "Who would have thought medical talk could be so entertaining?"

"I know, right?" Zoe accepted the hand he put on her

thigh, feeling melty inside. She squeezed his hand, then put hers back on the table.

"I'm sorry," Mark apologized, not to Cleo, but to Gavin. "Cleo's a little too autocratic for my taste. Now Zoe, on the other hand, is *much* easier to work with." He shot her a blinding smile. "So about that training for the new staff. I was wondering if we could make that happen as early as this Friday…"

Minutes later, still baffled at how she'd agreed to make something happen with only one trainer available, Zoe realized Cleo had segued the conversation.

Cleo was asking Gavin, "So you work at Jameson's Gym, huh? The one in Green Lake?"

"Yep." He had returned moments ago with his tuna melt and ate in small bites. Odd, because she'd have thought him the type to chomp down his food. Lord knew he burned his calories honestly.

"I've been thinking about switching from my place."

"You should come check us out. We have free trial memberships. And if you tell the front desk I sent you, they'll give you a few extra days as well." Gavin turned to Swanson—Mark. "You too, Mark. The facilities are top-notch, and the owner's a hell of a guy."

Mark nodded. "Thanks. So how long have you been a trainer?"

"Since he got out of the Marine Corps, right?" Cleo nodded. "A few of our staff go to the gym, and they mentioned the terrific self-defense instructors." She gave a smile. "That's you, right?"

"Yep. Me and my brother."

"So you were in the Marines?" Mark's gaze sharpened. Zoe noticed the stillness that seemed to come over

Gavin before he shrugged and smiled. "Guilty as charged. Infantry all the way."

"Did you like it?" Cleo asked, and Zoe wanted to tell her to stop prying. Though Gavin looked fine, she could sense his disquiet.

"It's a terrific institution. A brotherhood, excuse the expression," he said to Zoe and Cleo, "that you're hard-pressed to find anywhere else. The civilian sector is way different."

"I'll bet," Mark said. "How long were you in?"

"Fourteen years. Got out thanks to a bullet. But it's all good," Gavin added with a grin at Zoe. "You meet some of the most interesting people in Seattle."

Cleo laughed. "Yeah, you do. That's where I met Scott. He's a sergeant in the Army."

"I'm sorry," Gavin said.

Mark snickered.

Cleo frowned. "What?"

"I'm kidding, Cleo. Anyone who serves is okay in my book…even if he's Army."

"Funny stuff coming from a jarhead," Cleo teased back.

Zoe thought that maybe she'd imagined Gavin's earlier tension, because he appeared light-hearted throughout the lunch banter. And he asked enough questions about her, to be sure.

"So what's Zoe like at work?" he asked Mark.

"Focused. Driven." Mark gave her another of those weird, penetrating looks. "I'd say she's a ballbuster with a smile, but that wouldn't be politically correct. Like calling someone a dick to his face."

Cleo squirmed in her seat.

Zoe took pity on her. "Good thing you're more about getting the job done than being PC."

"True." Mark grinned at blushing Cleo. "So yes, Gavin. Your girlfriend—sorry, *friend*—is a ballbuster. But then, with our IT department, someone has to be."

They all lamented Jim's inability to manage or make decisions, though Zoe tried to stick up for the poor guy a few times. In the end, she gave in because she knew Mark and Cleo wouldn't spread tales.

Mark glanced at his watch, one of the few people who still wore one. "Heck. I need to get back. Nice meeting you, Gavin." He turned to Cleo. "Ms. Brewer."

"Mr. Macho Swanson."

He sighed and left.

Cleo made a face at his back, then saw Gavin watching her. "Sorry. That was immature, but that guy gets under my skin."

"I thought he was okay." Gavin pushed his plate aside, having all but scraped it clean. Not a bit to waste.

"He's firm but fair," Zoe said just to needle Cleo.

"He's an asshole, but he's one of the best managers we have. I hate to admit it, but if everyone ran their clinics like he does, we'd have way less problems getting things done."

"Don't sound so depressed, Cleo. I'm sure he'll annoy someone, and you'll be able to direct HR to breathe down his neck."

Cleo brightened. "There's that. Well, I'd better go too. Bye, Gavin. I've heard so much about you," she gushed, "that it's nice to put a face to the name."

"Oh?" Gavin looked interested. "What have you heard?"

"She's got to go. Bye, Cleo." Zoe nodded to the exit.

Cleo laughed and departed, leaving Gavin and Zoe alone.

"Finally." He wasted no time in moving across from her. "Ah, now I can see you."

"Sorry about that. Cleo dropped by unannounced, but Swanson cornered me into lunch."

"Cleo's right. He's a dick. I don't like him."

"Really?" Shocker, because Gavin had been nothing but polite to the guy.

"He was eating you up, staring at your eyes and mouth like he wanted to plant one on you while I watched."

"Mark Swanson," she said for clarification.

"Mark," he gushed in a high-pitched voice. "An ass-hole. And not your type."

"Oh?" She didn't know how to feel about Gavin being jealous. Her insides fluttered with happiness, while the rational being that was Zoe told her jealousy was a use-less, negative emotion. "What's my type, Gavin?"

He stretched his legs into the aisle and laced his hands behind his head. To her chagrin, she noted a few women glancing their way. "Your type. Hmm. You love a guy who works with his hands."

"Mark is a high-ranking executive. He types a lot."

Gavin's expression darkened. "He should be charm-ing, have a sense of humor."

"Mark can be snarky. That's kind of funny."

"He's not charming," Gavin muttered. "And his ego is huge. You can just tell. I guarantee you he's got a tiny dick."

"Gavin." She shushed him, especially when a few raised eyebrows swung their way.

"Sorry. But that's a fact."

"Fact?"

"When a guy has to prove how great he is, he's compensating. And since all guys, no matter what they tell you, are dick-centric, it's always about sexual expertise. I'm telling you. If he's not so small you need a microscope to see it, he sucks in bed. Totally not your type. You need a man who can satisfy you, baby."

"If she doesn't, I do. Here's my card." A woman snuck it by him as she sauntered out of the sandwich shop.

"You're married, Betty," Zoe yelled after one of the cardiology MAs and tugged the card from Gavin. "You don't need this."

"Jealous?" His wicked grin startled her into laughing.

Then she forced a scowl. "I thought we said no one else while we're being all friendly."

His amusement left him. "About that. You know, it's okay if you want to define me as your boyfriend to other people. I won't take it the wrong way, and it might tell other guys to back off."

"Oh? Is that what you're calling me behind my back to other men at the gym?" she asked, expecting him to say no.

"Hell yeah. And it's awesome, really. I'm a real stud now."

"What?"

He nodded. "Everyone knows how focused and kind of snarly you are. Even Michelle has backed off on the flirting. Way to go, baby."

She just stared. "So everyone thinks we have a thing going?"

"We do." He toyed with his napkin. "Ah, did I do

something wrong? I didn't tell that many people, actually. Just the ones leering at your ass. It wouldn't kill you to wear longer shorts, you know."

It wasn't as if Zoe was interested in anyone else. And Gavin's declaration had put the gym bunnies off his tail. But now he seemed defensive. She loved it. "I don't know. What if there's a guy there I'm thinking about asking out? Now he'll never go out with me because of you."

Gavin leaned forward, no more teasing grin. "Is there?"

"Not right now." When he relaxed, she added, "But there could be."

"Sure, sure. When you find your next Mr. Right, let me know. Until then, you're off-limits."

"Okay, Tarzan" came out with more sarcasm than she'd intended.

"Ah, my woman knows her place. My Jane," he said lovingly, his eyes limpid pools of longing.

"Ew. Sac up, Gavin."

His guffaw turned several heads. "Man, I love that mouth. Sac up. Righto, sugar pants." His phone rang, and he glanced at it, then quieted the phone.

"Do you need to get that?" Another woman, perhaps? His family? No one of importance, apparently.

"Nah. I'll deal with it later. Now before I get to work, how about you show me your place? I mean, can I get a tour of the amazingly focused Zoe York's office?"

She blinked. "You want to see where I work?" She stood to dispose of her plate, but Gavin beat her to it.

He stuffed his hands in his pockets. "Is that a problem?"

"No, not at all." A pleasant surprise. A man only interested in sex wouldn't care about her workplace, her friends, or her feelings about her sister. Just what were she and Gavin, anyway? And why did the notion of them being close enough to be in a relationship make her so damn happy?

They crossed to her building, and she showed him around. As expected, her female coworkers gobbled him up with their eyes. Sweet smiles and lengthy handshakes abounded.

"Everyone is so nice here," he said.

"Really? You're buying all the insincerity?"

"Huh?"

"Gavin," she said in a lower voice after pushing him past a gaping, blushing Ginny into her office, "they all want a peek at your tight abs and tighter ass. You're man candy, and every woman out there knows it."

He stared at her, and she wondered if she'd insulted him. She hadn't meant to.

Then he walked toward her, took her chin in his hand, and kissed her. "You say the nicest things." The kiss deepened, and she found herself clutching his waist, hoping not to fall into the river of lust she hadn't realized she'd waded into.

A cleared throat showed Cleo at the door, not bothering to hide a smile. "I had one more question for you— about work, I mean—that I forgot to ask earlier."

Gavin pulled away, caressed Zoe's cheek, then groaned. "Guess I'd better go. See you later, Zoe."

"Bye." She dropped weakly into her chair and watched him leave.

Cleo watched as well, and when she turned back to Zoe, she gave a thumbs-up. "Oh my God, is that man fine! And that kiss." She fanned herself. "I felt like it was the beginning of a very X-rated documentary. All we need is a massage table and essential oils, maybe a toy or two."

"Shut up, Cleo." Zoe worked to still her racing heart.

"Yes, Ms. York." Cleo laughed. "Something I thought about after the meeting. Hey, I know this new implementation has you guys swamped. So do you need any help booking rooms for training?"

Brought back to earth, Zoe focused on her answers. An hour later, she found herself wondering what Gavin had planned for them later in the week. Then she decided to stop letting him make the decisions and devised an outing she hoped he'd enjoy. And one she knew she needed to take if she ever wanted to get over Aubrey being gone.

Chapter 10

GAVIN LEANED BACK ON THE COUCH, SITTING UP THIS TIME, while his therapist droned on about inner peace and finding one's zen. Lee had helped him a lot. They'd worked out a payment plan, because weekly sessions with a shrink cost a pretty penny. It helped that Lee had been approved by the VA, but not enough to take away all the cost of an out-of-network doctor.

"Gavin? You've been pretty quiet today."

Tall, thin, and prematurely gray, Lee had to be in his mid-forties. The guy had a quiet bearing and inner strength that would appeal to the mentally ill, as Gavin laughingly thought of himself. On a serious note, Lee was easy to talk to, nonjudgmental, and he'd helped Gavin learn to deal with stress, tailoring the sessions to Gavin as an individual. Because in psychology, as Lee liked to say, one size did not fit all. The office sat in the same building Ava worked in. That might have made Gavin uncomfortable if he hadn't trusted one hundred percent in Ava and Lee as professionals.

"I met someone," Gavin admitted, though he hadn't intended to bring Zoe up.

"Oh?"

"She's this woman I've been trying to talk to at the gym for months. Really nice, beautiful... Well, wait. Not too nice. She's kind of smart-alecky."

"And you like her."

"Yeah, I do." As a person, not just a woman he wanted to sex up.

"Right. Interesting, and something we'll definitely discuss in just a moment. Just as soon as you answer my favorite question." Lee paused, and Gavin knew what came next. "So how are you holding up?"

"With?" he asked, just to be contrary.

"The nightmares. Triggers in everyday life. Talking about your time in the service. Not the harsh wartime activity, but the good times with your fellow Marines. Remember, right now we're all about stabilizing you. Getting you to a place where your coping mechanisms allow you to function without stress."

Gavin squirmed. He hadn't mentioned his cousin's wedding at their last meeting. And he felt like he needed to. "I kind of had an issue at Mike's wedding."

Lee sat quietly. "Go on."

"Mike's my cousin. I told you about him a while ago. It was the Saturday before last. The wedding was really nice but crowded, mostly with family and people I know. I was dealing. Then I was talking to a few guys I didn't know too well. They're big, tough dudes with attitude."

"There was a problem?"

"Well, not with feeling threatened by them. Not that I wanted the fight, but I pretty much already knew how I'd take them out if they came at me." And he'd been confident he could incapacitate them before grabbing something heavy, maybe a knife—something to *really* take them out. "They got a little aggressive, thought I'd messed with a friend of theirs. Which I hadn't. I'd just talked to the woman. Pretty, nice. Not my type."

Lee nodded at him to continue. He didn't take notes,

but he listened. Super intense, that gaze. Like Gavin was the only one who mattered right now.

"So anyway, I was still okay. Then the music got loud, thumping. Some techno crap that tapped into memories." He hated when that happened, when bad scenes overwhelmed him. Gavin loved the USMC to this day. But he wasn't a robot who could turn on and off that killing switch in his brain. He'd done his duty, but there'd been a cost.

"What did you do?" Lee asked.

"I breathed in and out, deeply. Calmed myself, reminded myself I was safe, that it was just music, and I was at another mandatory family wedding in Seattle. Not under a desert sun. Helped that the guys kind of backed away, so I had a place to move to if I needed it. But I pulled myself out of the moment. I was good."

Lee smiled. "That's great. So the breathing and focus are helping."

"Yeah. It's a lot better now. Plus I'm clearheaded. Not drinking or anything." He paused. "And, well, it was weird, but when I was with Zoe, the girl I mentioned, we were gardening, and I felt that same kind of ease. I feel that way a lot when I'm with her."

"Gardening is wonderful therapy for dealing with issues of posttraumatic stress, you know."

"It is?"

"Yes. You're getting your hands dirty, out in nature, under the sun."

"In my case, the stars."

Lee blinked. "Or the stars. You tap into Mother Nature, and something instinctual responds to that caring and nurturing. You were building, helping to create life."

"Yeah." He felt damn good about that. "I have a plant. His name is Leon." Gavin grinned at Lee's surprise. "He's a lavender cutting Zoe gave me. I hooked him up with a bunch of lady flowers, and they look pretty damn good outside my front door."

"Lady flowers? So your plant has a harem, eh?"

"Well, yeah. Though there might be a guy flower in there too. I'm game for my boy being an equal opportunity lover. Everybody wants Leon."

Lee snorted.

"But in all seriousness, the gardening made me feel good. And Zoe…she, ah, she makes me feel that too. Not just because the sex is out-of-this-world fantastic either." He was still trying to make sense of that incredible connection.

"So she's different from those others before."

Gavin had told Lee all about his flings and his growing dependence on booze. "Yeah. She's special. We're new to being together, but she's fun. I feel good around her, clean. And as much as she makes me want to burst out of my skin when she's around, 'cause she's all kinds of sexy hot, she calms me too. I can't explain it."

"Because she's more than a physical anchor. She's become an emotional one."

"I guess. Her sister died not long ago. And I know Zoe gets it. That she knows real loss. Zoe really loved her."

"I see." Lee leaned forward. "You're still going to the gym?"

Change in subject, but okay. "Yeah."

"And the nightmares? You didn't say. Are they still with you?"

"Now that I think about it, not so much. I mean, I still have one occasionally, but not like all the time."

"That's good. You need to be prepared to deal with the resurgence when, not if, you get them. Anything can trigger you, even subconsciously. But the key is to not let it drag you back down, but to cope. Gardening is a wonderful tool I'd planned to mention in this session anyway. Another method of easing your worries is a pet."

"A pet. Hell, I have Leon."

Lee's lips curled. "I meant something with fur or feathers. Dogs are wonderful, actually. Pets can be very therapeutic. The furry texture, that stroking, can be calming. And bonding with a living creature who loves you unconditionally, who accepts you for you are, is ideal." He gave Gavin a hard look. "It's so interesting how we can accept that kind of love from someone else, yet often we can't give ourselves what we really need, out of some notion we aren't deserving of that kind of devotion and affection."

Gavin sighed. "Not this again."

"We both know you won't really begin to heal until you can accept that you're allowed to be happy, to live a full life without any regret."

"Aren't regrets a part of living?"

"Sure. Like, I should have chosen the chocolate instead of the vanilla. Not, I wish it were me and not my friend in that grave." Lee shook his head. "But we'll talk about when you're ready. Later. Now, something about this Zoe."

"Yeah?"

"Are you sure you're not replacing the relief you get

from exercise with the joy of a new romance, with the physical side of sex?"

"A good question. I've thought about that a lot." Gavin leaned back, staring at the ceiling with his head resting on the back of the sofa. "At first, it was about trying to get her to smile. I'd flirt, she'd ignore me. Tell me off. Then she became a challenge. It was when I backed off, figuring she wanted nothing to do with me, that we finally connected. But it wasn't just sex at first, much as I wanted her. Now that we're going out, kind of, I know it could end." And that scared the piss out of him, but he wasn't ready to tell Lee that yet. Because he wasn't ready to admit it out loud to himself either.

"And that's okay with you?"

"It would upset me, sure. She's fine as hell, and she makes me laugh. But we're not serious or anything. She's the first woman who makes me feel good about myself, I guess. So yeah, if it ended, it might hurt." Like having his heart ripped out through his chest with bare fingers.

"That's what concerns me. You're still learning to ground yourself. I think a relationship is healthy, Gavin. Don't get me wrong. But I don't want you to rely on her to make you feel good. You have to do that for yourself."

"I get it. I really do."

Lee seemed to relax. "Good. Is there anything else you wanted to talk about?"

Gavin still wasn't ready to discuss seeing his dead buddy's sister at the grocery store a few weeks ago. Nor did he relish talking about his anxiety over Nicole, Mick's widow, leaving him phone messages. Messages he still hadn't listened to, because he couldn't. Not yet.

"I'm good."

"Okay then. Now sit up and show me how you meditate. Without all the bitching and moaning this time, I mean."

Gavin groaned. "You still need to get laid. I just know when that happens, you'll be much more fun to be around."

As usual, Lee ignored his remarks. "Let's see it, show-off."

So Gavin got into the zone, but instead of keeping the world out and himself centered inside a warm golden cocoon of safety, he imagined Zoe's smile building a wall around the pair of them.

Gavin saw Zoe's text and smiled. He'd wondered when she'd push for a no-sex date. No doubt the stubborn woman thought she'd have to force him into spending time with her that didn't end with some part of his anatomy buried in hers.

But the truth was, he wanted to spend time with her any way he could. After his session with Lee yesterday, he'd thought long and hard about Zoe's impact on his life and his psyche. No way could he see her having a negative impact on him. Even if she were to dump him and break his heart into a million pieces tomorrow, he wouldn't regret a second with her, and he wouldn't turn violent, become a meth head, or start shooting at people from a rooftop.

She'd done nothing but enhance his life. If he'd learned anything from dealing with loss and from Lee, it was to appreciate what he had in the now. Not look for possible problems tomorrow.

While working at the gym, he ignored Mac's insistence that he wear the double-XL gym shirt that had come in. He put in a solid eight hours, including a harrowing training session with Max Grenly, an eighty-nine-year-old athlete who wheezed through his exercises. Gavin kept waiting for the guy to have a heart attack, prepared to give CPR. But the old man only cracked jokes about the women in his assisted living center and did his bicep curls like a pro.

Now cleaned up and ready to impress, Gavin waited for Zoe outside the Chihuly Garden and Glass exhibit in Seattle Center. Ava and Hope had mentioned it once or twice, but he'd rather have his teeth pulled than walk around a place decorated with glass. Personally, he didn't care for museums. Unless someone mentioned the Pro Football Hall of Fame. And he still wanted to head to Lambeau Field in Green Bay to check out the statue of legendary coach Vince Lombardi in all his glory. But yeah, Zoe had chosen glass, which was basically melted-down sand. Whoop-dee-do.

He saw her coming and pasted a smile on his face. "Hey, baby."

"Sweetums. How are you, Smoky?"

"Just dandy. I can't wait to look at all this pretty glass."

She snickered. "Come on. This is real art. Let's go look around." They bought their tickets and continued inside.

Sure, he could readily admit that whoever had made the amazing, colorful glass fixed to the ceilings and hanging in spikes had mastered his or her craft. But for seventeen bucks a ticket, he could have had two beers and fries while watching a Mariners game. And all while seated on his ass in a cozy little bar.

Zoe oohed and aahed over everything, and he slowly found himself oohing with her. Enjoying her pleasure in the sights. She reached for his hand, and he gave it gladly, walking with her like they were a real couple.

Maybe this art place wasn't such a bad deal after all. The sun had begun to set, but even shadowed, the sculptures outside glowed with alien, fluidlike life. Blue spikes, tentacle-like spires, and round, meditation balls dotted the greenery like an alien landscape. Gavin and Zoe moved back inside, where the primary colors of glass molds and forms in the ceiling were cast down at them, providing a muted glow.

"This is just amazing," Zoe said, her voice hushed.

"You can talk louder. It's not church, you know," he teased.

"Shh. Come on." She tugged his hand, and they moved through the museum, stopping, staring, and commenting. Her childlike joy made him see it all through her eyes. And he loved every second of it.

By the time they finished two hours later, he couldn't believe how much time had passed. They'd meandered through one and a half acres of exhibits.

"All right. This was fun," he admitted. "I can't believe you've never been here before."

"It was Aubrey's favorite place to go," Zoe said quietly. "I used to tell her we'd go later. When I could get the time. I preferred hiking or going to the mountains." She shrugged, but he could see Zoe wished she'd taken the time to go with her sister.

"Didn't you tell me your sister was an artist?"

"A photographer." She nodded. "She had some

amazing pictures of this place. What was your favorite part?" she asked, her voice deliberately cheery.

He had to hand it to her. Zoe didn't try to avoid her pain. Not like he did. She met it head on. He squeezed her hand, amazed they had only separated from each other a few times in all the time they'd been there. "This place is amazing. I liked *Mille Fiori*. It means a thousand flowers, right? I mean, come on. The glasshouse was like forty feet tall."

She nodded. "I read that it's 4,500 square feet in size. And that centerpiece sculpture is one hundred feet long."

"That's a lot of glass."

"Yes. Oh, and one other thing."

"Yeah?"

She gave him a quick peck on the lips, and the tingle shot all the way to his feet. "I told you so. Ha."

"You had to rub that in."

"Yes. When I told you where we'd be going tonight, I knew you'd think it would be boring."

"Really? Now who's stereotyping? Just because I'm a guy doesn't mean I can't appreciate art."

She took her hand away—*damn it*—and crossed her arms over her chest. "Really? Because I distinctly overheard you talking to Shane about it at the gym, about what a—your words, not mine—*pussy* he was for hitting up all those 'stupid museums' just to keep his wife happy."

"You should never eavesdrop, Zoe. It's very unbecoming," Gavin said in a deliberately prissy tone.

She tried not to laugh. And failed.

As she collected herself, he nudged her toward the

sidewalk, and they walked back to the parking garage on Mercer. "So it was okay going there, even though you miss your sister?"

"Yes. I'm glad you went with me."

Touched that she'd asked him to go even though she'd known it would be difficult, he nodded. "This was about more than your sister though."

"Oh?"

"This was about trying to torture me. Confess."

"Well, the trip did have that going for it."

They continued to tease, passing a few other couples out for a stroll. But the encroaching darkness, and the unknown, kept Gavin on edge, especially when he spotted two unsavory men walking their way. They seemed a little too aggressive for casual strollers. And they were focused too intently on the lady and her kid coming toward Gavin for him to ignore them.

His adrenaline buzzed. "Hey, Zoe. Wait here for a minute, okay?"

She blinked. "Ah, sure." She paused on the sidewalk, watching with understanding when the skeevier of the two guys, the one wearing a beanie and an olive-green jacket, reached for the lady's purse strap.

"Hey," Gavin yelled and moved closer.

The young boy with the woman looked frightened, so Gavin smiled.

"Hey, Mike, is that you?" he said to Beanie, who was still reaching for the purse. *Almost there…*

Beanie froze. Next to him, his friend sneered. "His name isn't Mike, dickhead. Get lost."

The lady and her boy moved quickly away, now behind Gavin. Content innocents wouldn't be caught in the melee to come, Gavin kept his smile and stepped closer to the thugs. Both men smelled as if they hadn't bathed in weeks. Up close, their pupils didn't look right, and their jittery mannerisms hinted at drug abuse. Beanie was the taller of the two but didn't have the mean look his tweaker friend did.

"Not Mike?" Gavin frowned. "Hmm. Must be his doppelgänger."

The tough guy said, "What?" Then he looked Gavin over, glanced at Beanie, and shrugged. "You'll do. Give me twenty bucks."

"Or what?"

"What do you mean, or what?"

"I mean, if I don't give you twenty bucks, what then?"

Beanie raised his shirt and showed off a gun tucked into his pants.

It looked dirty, and Gavin marveled that the guy hadn't accidentally shot his dick off, if the thing was actually loaded.

"Is that a 9mm? Do you mind?" He tugged the pistol free, ejected the magazine, and cleared the round from the chamber in seconds. Then he tossed the gun into the dirt beside him, along with the magazine and round. "What do you have?" he asked the mean one.

But Mean Guy was already pulling a knife. He looked stringy but strong, and no match for a Marine with a grudge against bullies. Gavin heard loud chatter near them as they gained an audience. Then a siren in the distance. But this being the city, there was no guarantee the wailing sound signaled police coming for these two idiots.

So he handled things. He grabbed Mean Guy's hand,

twisted his wrist to make him drop the knife, and used his free hand to punch Beanie in the nose when Beanie took a step toward him.

Beanie dropped, holding his face, and moaned. Mean Guy shrieked in pain and held his wrist. But Gavin hadn't snapped it, as much as he'd wanted to.

"Gavin, the police are on the way," Zoe said from a few steps behind him. Calm, collected, she eased him as well. A good thing, because for a second, he'd wondered how much trouble he'd be in if he bent down to let Mean Guy get closer, then tossed him to the ground and stomped the fucker's neck. Nothing like an internal decapitation to cut down on a crime streak.

Instead, Gavin eased away, kicked the gun and ammo farther from the criminals, and waited with Zoe for a pair of uniforms. He gave a quick statement, echoed by the woman with her son, Zoe, and a few others who'd gathered to witness.

"Fastest takedown, man," a twentysomething guy was telling the cops. "Like a ninja. Dude did some kind of kung fu."

The cop looked to Gavin and raised a brow.

"Simple hand-to-hand. Marine Corps."

The cop nodded. "Thanks. We'll contact you if we need anything else."

They had his number. Gavin nodded, still trying to come down off the adrenaline high. Would this give him bad dreams tonight? He didn't know.

Zoe tugged him away, and to his mortification, he heard clapping behind him.

"Semper Fi, man," one of the onlookers yelled out.

He put up a hand to wave and walked faster.

"Slow down, Mr. Marathon. My legs don't go that fast unless I'm running."

"Sorry." He let out a breath, subtly trying to calm himself.

She didn't touch him, but Zoe helped all the same. "You know, that was pretty damn heroic."

"Yeah, well, I didn't like the way they were looking at that woman and her kid. Christ. It's nearly broad daylight."

"Well, it's almost nine, but you're right. That was pretty gutsy of them. That or desperate."

"Should have broken his hand. Thou shalt not steal."

She chuckled, and Gavin relaxed even more. "Exactly. But I'm serious, Gavin. What you did was heroic, and you should be rewarded."

His body thrummed. "Oh?"

"But not with sex. It wasn't that impressive."

Gavin barked a laugh at Zoe's outright lie. Not impressive? *Good God*. He'd disarmed two dangerous men with his bare hands! One had a gun, the other a knife, and he'd handled them as if back in the class at Jameson's demonstrating a simple self-defense technique.

"You never showed us that clearing-the-gun move at the gym. I'd like to learn that one."

"Hmm. It's a little more advanced."

They entered the parking garage, and she saw him become alert for trouble. The way he'd been while they walked back, but more so. She wondered if this episode with the purse-snatchers would bother him. Coming back from the service and having issues would surely lead to other problems with conflict. She'd seen TV specials on war trauma and PTSD, which might be what he suffered from.

Nightmares, the inability to handle crowds, body hyperarousal, sleepless nights. Just some of the symptoms of posttraumatic stress. He'd seemed okay with the crowd tonight, though to be fair, the museum hadn't been packed, just moderately filled with art lovers who respected personal space.

Gavin unlocked her car door, then moved around to his. The expression on his face was painful to see, an emptiness in his gaze, a kind of internal hurt. But he hadn't asked for her comfort, and a man like Gavin would have his pride.

Once inside his car, they sat in silence.

"Well? What now, Mistress?"

She forced a smirk. "Now we go to my place. Not for sex."

"Quit reminding me," he growled and drove her home. They chatted about the exhibit some more, and about which other cultural events he had no interest in. He agreed on *never, ever* seeing an opera or a ballet. But he liked quiet, intimate jazz bars, which surprised her. Jazz was fairly sophisticated music for someone not into art.

Back at her place, she took him outside to the patio. "Sit. I'm going to get you your reward." She ignored the hungry look he shot at her body. "Vanilla hot-fudge sundae work for you?"

His slow smile struck her right in the heart. So innocent, and so at odds with that glimpse of pain she'd seen before he got into the car. "With nuts too?"

"You really think you're that special?"

"Peanuts. Not some froufrou sugar-coated walnuts or almond knockoffs."

"Purist."

"You're damn right."

She left him smiling and returned with two bowls full of lots of vanilla ice cream, hot fudge, whipped cream, and nuts. With a cherry on top. Only to find him kneeling by her garden, shuffling dirt around.

"Hey."

He shot up with a guilty look on his face. "Oh ah, that was fast."

"What were you doing to my cucumbers?"

"Such accusation in that tone." He tried to joke it off, but she saw his fists clench.

"Oh. Weeding. I see." She totally didn't, but she felt bad for teasing. "Look, the sundae will keep. But since you do owe me for taking you to an awesome museum—"

"Which I paid for," he mumbled.

"Then you should take care of Violet. See? If you can name your plant, I can name mine."

"Which one is Violet?" He started to relax.

"The big geranium in that pot. I have to move her to replace the dead thing my aunt swears will come back to life. It won't, and she's going to blame me for killing it, though she gave it to me already dead. The potting stuff is over there. Hop to. Chop-chop."

He blinked. "Seriously?"

"Well, yeah. I'm eating ice cream over here." She took a big scoop and sighed, ignoring the brain freeze. *Oy. What I do for my* boyfriend.

His eyes crinkled, and he laughed. Then he kissed her. "Hmm. Vanilla. Not my favorite, but the fudge makes up for it. Tell you what. I'll do the hard labor while you feed me and tell me how brave and awesome and sexy I am."

"Seriously?" He really made her want to laugh.

"I have self-esteem issues. Plus I'm doing your work."

"Kind of like I was doing yours *and* your sister's in Magnolia, hmm?"

"Not the same thing at all. That was a date to impress you. Now feed me, woman."

He ate the ice cream like he was making love to it. By the time he finished, Zoe was hot and bothered. And not having any scx, because their relationship had to be more than casual.

It had to be for both of them, because Zoe feared she'd started falling for the muscular Marine with buried wounds, who owned a plant that had girlfriends and wore a smile that turned her world upside down.

And that's how Zoe found herself wishing to trade places with a spoon on a Friday night with a man made for loving.

Chapter 11

GAVIN HAD ONE HELL OF A NIGHTMARE, AS HE'D SUSPECTED he might. Zoe, the ice cream, and her lush garden had helped. He'd meditated at home before going to bed. He'd been nearly asleep, calmed down, and had just closed his eyes. Everything faded to a gentle black.

Theo must have made a noise coming home, because his bang and curse had turned into shots fired, Dan losing a leg, and Gavin shooting through a sniper's eye just as the guy got a bead on him. He shot up in bed, his heart threatening to burst from his chest, breathing hard, and yelled for cover fire.

"Shit. Gavin, it's me. It's Theo." Theo tripped over a pair of Gavin's shoes and fell hard on his stomach. "Fuck. That hurt!"

"What *the hell* is going on?" Landon roared as he stomped down the stairs. The hallway light flickered on. He soon appeared in the doorway and flipped on the bedroom light, then stared at Theo on the floor. "Theo?" He leaned down. "You smell like a cheap six-pack. Or is that Boone's I smell?"

Gavin was still trembling, his heart still racing, so he lay back and took even breaths. "Shit. I can smell it from over here. What the hell were you drinking? And hey, aren't you underage?" he taunted, calming down. *It's okay. You're home. Think about family. About Leon. Violet.*

Zoe.

This time his heart did a strange leap of delight, imagining the sexy witch with the smart mouth and ice-blue eyes. *No sex, my ass.* She totally owed him more than a hot fudge sundae. Focusing on the mundane, on his breathing, on Zoe and his family, he slowly but surely came back to himself while Landon ragged on their brother.

Unfortunately now awake, Gavin had to move. He wouldn't fall back to sleep easily, he knew from experience. He rose to a sitting position and stared down at his baby brother, ignoring Landon's less-than-subtle look of concern directed *his* way. "Theo, you don't look so good."

Theo glared, or tried to. Because in the next breath, he turned and puked all over the floor.

Landon grimaced. "Oh man. It's pink. Whatever he drank is gonna stain."

"Hey, Major Clean, go grab the carpet cleaner while I haul Little Boozer into the bathroom."

"Up…yours," Theo managed before vomiting again.

"Hell, Bro." Gavin tried not to gag. "It stinks like sugared vomit and cheap alcohol. Just tell me you didn't sleep with anyone too. Trust me. Bad booze makes for worse bed companions."

Theo tried to flip him off and groaned instead.

"Let's go." Gavin hauled him off the floor and into the bathroom, sticking Theo's head in the toilet just in time while the kid upchucked even more. Gavin hurried back to the doorway to get away from that awful smell.

More retching ensued, but at least he was standing upwind from it. "That's just gross."

"So are you." More moaning.

"Do you even have anything else in your stomach to get rid of? How much did you drink, anyway?"

"I only had three shots. Maybe a cocktail or two. It was the clams beforehand, I think." Theo spat into the toilet.

"Wait. Cheap drinks *and* bad seafood? You're a moron." Gavin yelled the facts to Landon, who laughed. No sympathy from that corner. Gavin turned back to Theo. "Stain must have come out, because Major Clean is amused. You're lucky."

Another finger. It was like his brothers lost all creativity when insulting him. No challenge there. He left Theo after figuring the boy could handle himself and his porcelain savior.

Joining Landon in the kitchen, he watched his older brother boil water for hot cocoa. They'd never done tea, and left to Gavin, they never would. It was too…unmanly.

"Where's the hot chick?" Gavin asked. "And I don't mean blow-up Ava. I mean the real one."

Landon shot him a scowl. "Asshole."

Apparently still not over the blow-up doll incident. A stroke of genius on Theo's part, that. "She's hanging with Sadie and Elliot this weekend. Cousins only. I'm not invited."

"Ouch."

"But neither is Joe, Rose's husband." Rose—Ava's younger, married cousin. "So I'm fairly okay with the exclusion."

"Hurray. More Landon time for the family."

Landon smiled through his teeth. "Lucky, lucky you." He leaned back against the counter, clad in only a pair of shorts. "So what happened? Another nightmare?"

Gavin nodded.

"You haven't been having too many of them lately."

"Keeping tabs, Big Brother?" Because no way Landon knew that firsthand, since he rarely spent the night at home anymore, nearly always at Ava's.

"Yep. Deal with it." Landon shrugged. "What happened to set you off? Do you know?"

Since Landon had seen his own mess while in the Marine Corps, Gavin felt comfortable—to a point—talking to him about things. Though Landon would never admit it, he'd had his own sleepless nights. His own stressors to deal with since becoming a civilian, from shit that stemmed from his own time in the desert.

"I know exactly what happened. I was expecting the nightmare, if you want the truth. After Zoe and I went out tonight, we were walking back to get the car when two druggies attacked a lady. Or tried to attack her. I took care of them. The violence of it shook me is all."

Landon's gaze sharpened as he looked Gavin over from top to bottom. "You okay?"

"Fine. It was fun, in a way." Not as fun as breaking their bones might have been. A surprising anger resurged. "Fuck, Landon. It was barely dark. Some lady and her kid, who couldn't be that much older than Colin, were walking down the public sidewalk. Near Seattle Center. And these assholes tried to take her purse." He snorted. "Like that shitty gun and rusty knife would do much damage against"—he struck a ninja pose—"Guns of Steel."

Landon covered his mouth, but Gavin saw the grin there. "You need mental help."

"I'm getting it once a week, dumbass."

"I mean for your ego." Landon laughed. "Okay, Guns of Steel. Nicely done. But it cost you."

Gavin shrugged. A woman and little boy's safety versus a nightmare? No contest.

"So you were out with Zoe again. Hmm."

"The water's boiling."

Landon took the kettle off the stove and poured two mugs full, then added the powdered mix.

Gavin stirred his, took a sip, and sighed. "Why do you insist on buying the cheap crap?"

"Why don't you shut your piehole and buy your own?"

"Touché." Gavin chuckled, blew on his hot chocolate, and sipped as he heard Theo's pathetic moan.

They ignored him.

"So Zoe. What's up with her?"

"Um, she's a woman. About five ten, great ass. Beautiful blue eyes, long, sexy black hair. It's witchy black, not bland. If I had to guess, and don't tell her this, I'd say she's maybe one-forty? One-fifty? But all muscle. Sweet. And—"

"You know what I mean, dipshit. I don't need her vitals, but what she is *to you*." Landon sipped his cocoa and frowned. "This is awful."

"Told you."

"Save the rest for Theo."

They nodded and pushed the cups aside in favor of sucking down whipped cream straight from the can.

"Zoe and I are friends who also have sex. We like each other. I guess we're kind of dating."

"Kind of?"

"It's new, okay? I don't want to jinx it."

"Ha! I knew it." Landon looked like their mother nailing a real estate sale. Victorious and kind of rabid scary. "You like this chick." He squirted more whipped cream into his mouth.

"Duh. I've been asking her out for months."

"But you've had her."

"Crude, Bro." Gavin's turn. He wrestled the can away and gave himself a shot of sugar.

"You know what I mean. She's not just a challenge to get into bed."

"The others weren't challenges." *Or challenging, to be honest*.

"The point, idiot, is that Zoe is smart, attractive, way too good for you, and she likes you back." Landon beamed. "Nice. You have a girlfriend."

"Well, not really. I mean, *I'd* be okay with that. But we're keeping it low-key." Gavin paused. "Though I did see her office and everything. I know where she lives and met some of her work friends." He smiled, pleased others she came in contact with on a daily basis knew she had a "friend" named Gavin. "I know her best friend, actually, and I met her aunt."

"See that? It's like you're practically married."

Gavin blanched, and Landon laughed so hard he cried.

"Dick."

"I'm dying. Water," Theo moaned from the bathroom, still conscious, apparently.

"So I was thinking," Landon said, completely ignoring Theo's entreaties for help. "How about you bring her over here Sunday night? Ava and I want to entertain." He smiled. "I was all for grilling some dogs and burgers, but Ava wants to cook you and your lady something special."

"Wait. I just told you we're dating. How do you already have a dinner planned?"

"Please." Landon huffed. The dude looked huge. Despite the fact Gavin had been working out for months like a madman to get rid of his issues, he still didn't have his brother's mass. "I keep tabs on all you pathetic slobs needing my help."

"Is that so?"

"Yes. That's so. I know you and Zoe have been seeing each other, and that you make eyes at each other at the gym."

"Mac blabbed."

"I'm not saying who it was. Let's call him, or her, my gym connection."

Gavin rolled his eyes. "What else?"

"I know Hope has sworn off men, thinking that she's dating the wrong type."

"She is."

"But she's been arguing with Mom more, and it's putting her off ever procreating. Just to spite Linda."

Gavin had to laugh at that.

"And Theo," Landon paused as the toilet flushed, "has been partying up a storm. He turns twenty-one next month."

"I know."

"Well, do you also know he's planning to make a life-changing announcement on his birthday?"

Gavin smiled. "Yeah? He's finally going to join the Corps?"

"Yep. I think. Unless he changes his mind between now and then. So keep it together. Remember, we're supposed to be good examples of what it is to be a Marine."

"Two assholes shot in the line of duty and sent home with medical retirements?"

"Exactly."

They bumped knuckles, finished off the whipped cream, then watched Theo dramatically low-crawl, dragging himself into the living room.

"That'll come in handy in boot camp," Gavin said.

Landon frowned. "Shut it." In a louder voice, he said, "So, Theo. How's the gut? Want some leftover chicken? It's just a little greasy. Let's see… We also have some baked beans, some thick, mayonnaise-y potato salad. Oh wait. Look, Gavin, in the fridge. Don't we have liverwurst in there too? And onions?"

Theo glared at him, then turned green and shot off the floor and out of the living room. After a pause, they heard him retch again.

Gavin stared at the hallway. "Sure hope he made it to the bathroom for that."

"He can clean it up if he didn't. Oh, and by the way, he puked in your shoes earlier."

"Damn it." Gavin hadn't even had the pair a month. "Hey, do we really have liverwurst? I hate that stuff."

"No way. It stinks. And with onions? Gross. The thought of it is enough to make a guy sick though." Landon smirked.

Gavin chuckled. "So Sunday. I'll invite Zoe. What should I do for the meal? Want me to bring something?"

"Yourself. Maybe dessert. How's that?"

"I can do dessert." To irritate his brother, and just

because, he added, "No wine or beer? I picked up a six-pack earlier today." He nodded to the fridge.

Landon darted to look, then glared at Gavin upon seeing nothing alcohol-related in the refrigerator.

"What? I drank it all. Right before I shot up, took some pills, then slept with all of Seattle's desperate singles. But I still had time for a museum trip with Zoe. Am I the shit or what?"

Landon advanced, took Gavin in a headlock, and then proceeded to show him that spending more time at the gym did not make him stronger than his older, obnoxious brother.

"I'm not saying uncle," Gavin said, strangled and not giving in.

"Uncle, uncle," Theo said, moaning loudly from the bathroom to be heard. "I think I need a mop," he shouted, still sounding weak.

Landon chuckled, then removed his Hulk-like forearm from Gavin's throat. "Good fight, little guy."

"Fuck you."

"Landon!" Theo yelled.

"*I'm coming.* Keep your shorts on." He added in a lower voice, "Unless you puked on them too. I'm not doing laundry at two in the morning."

"Yeah right." Gavin snorted. Landon had been known to do laundry at all hours if he felt the need. The guy hated dirt, which was ironic considering all the field training he'd done in the Marine Corps.

Rubbing his neck, Gavin wondered why his brother's mauling didn't stress him out more. Maybe because the wrestling made him think of happier times with the family growing up. Landon was family, love, safety.

"You puked on your shorts *and* missed the toilet?" Landon shouted.

Neurotic, bossy, loud.

Fortunately, the addiction to cleanliness was one condition Gavin hadn't inherited from his older brother. Still, the smell of vomit was off-putting. He grabbed a blanket and his pillow and settled on the couch with an old movie on for company.

He didn't realize he'd fallen asleep until he was rudely awakened the following morning by Major Dickhead.

"Rise and shine, ladies. It's time to clean."

Theo shrieked from the front door, "Hey! Who put all my clothes outside on the lawn?"

"Why, I don't know, Theo." Landon sounded way too pleasant. "Probably the same person who dyed all of my white underwear and white undershirts pink."

Colin one. Landon, and now Theo, zero.

A shadow appeared over Gavin on the couch. "You too, Good Samaritan. Your heroics made the news, by the way." Landon yanked the blanket off him and shoved him to the floor.

"*Shit.*"

"Get your ass up, hero. We have a house to clean."

Gavin groaned, his nose to the carpet, right near crumbs that smelled like Doritos. And there, a few of Theo's favorite cheese puffs. Maybe Landon had a point about cleaning house. Without Landon home, they'd been ignoring his directives to vacuum and pick up. And the toilet? Gross. No question.

"Now," Landon barked.

Theo whined about a headache and the clothes he had to gather.

Gavin was awake now, needing coffee. "So much for sleeping in on my one weekend off."

"That's the spirit!" Landon grinned at him. "Now who wants to dust?"

—◆◆◆—

Zoe felt nervous. Hanging out with Gavin was one thing. Spending time at a dinner with his brother and his brother's fiancée was something else. She knew Landon from the gym. He seemed nice enough, if a little overwhelming. Geez, the Donnigans sure did make them good looking. She wondered what Gavin's parents looked like.

She parked in the driveway of a nice enough house, even if it did look like it had been stamped with the same bland, suburban print the others on the street possessed. This house was blue and had a colorful pot of flowers outside it, pretty much the only thing differentiating it from the neighbors.

"Hi, Leon." She smiled at the perky bit of lavender amidst a chaotic assortment of clumsily placed flowers. The effect was charming and sweet, a lot like the man who'd planted it, though he'd likely be horrified to be told so.

She knocked. Gavin answered, wearing a half apron over his jeans. Another T-shirt, this one olive green. She was dying to see his wardrobe, to know if he owned anything other than colored cotton. This shirt sported a bold USMC across his broad chest.

Then again, Gavin didn't need to wear much—if anything at all—to dress up his perfect frame.

"Hey, baby. I mean, Zoe, *my good friend*," he said in a louder voice.

She sighed.

"Come on in."

She knew tonight would be a challenge, especially because she kept vacillating between just getting it over with and accepting they were really dating, and keeping a bit of distance between them to protect herself. But Aubrey would have gone whole hog, so Zoe spontaneously bit the bullet.

She waited until they stood before Landon and a gorgeous brunette, the same woman she'd seen a time or two in class at the gym. She tapped Gavin on the shoulder.

He turned, and she yanked him to her for a kiss that left them both breathless. "There. We're dating. You have boyfriend status. Now go make my dinner."

His shock soon turned to a heartwarming smile. "Sure, Lady Hot Pants. My studly muffinette. Dream of my loins. Ye who turns my mind aflutter, my body—"

"For God's sake, Gavin. Go get her something to drink," the brunette cut in with a laugh. "Hi, I'm Ava."

"My fiancée," Landon added. "Hi, Zoe."

Ava had a sincere smile and kind eyes. Zoe liked her immediately. "Hi, Landon. Ava, nice to meet you. I'm Zoe."

They shook hands. "Another woman sucked into the Donnigans because of that self-defense class." Ava shook her head. "I wonder if Mac knows he's running an athletic dating service."

"Yeah, right." Landon laughed. "Mac is about as tactful as I am. I can just see him trying to play Cupid."

Zoe agreed. "Nope. Never happen." Standing in the dining area, she could still see Gavin, who'd gone into the kitchen via the large, spacious pass-through. "So what's he making?"

"A mess." Landon frowned. "Don't let him fool you. He is not, in any way, shape, or form, able to prepare food. He can barely slap together a PB&J. Ava's cooking us noodles out of squash with some Asian stir-fry. But don't let the squash throw you. It's good." Landon moved to nudge Gavin from the kitchen, where she could see he'd been chopping vegetables for a dip.

They argued about how to cut the carrots and how long to make them, big brother trying to boss the younger one.

"For the record, I like squash," Zoe felt the need to say. "Thanks for having me over."

The argument grew a little heated until Landon shoved Gavin out of the kitchen.

Gavin threw the apron at his brother's back, smacking him in the head. Then he put on a big smile. "Ladies? Can I get you guys something to drink?"

"I'll have some of that wine on the counter." Ava turned to Zoe. "It's a nice pinot grigio. Would you like some?"

She didn't know if she should, since Gavin didn't seem to drink alcohol.

"Go ahead," Gavin said. "It's probably more sophisticated and a nicer pairing with dinner. Or you could have iced tea, water, milk, or some gross seltzer-pomegranate combination. I wouldn't recommend that."

"It's a healthy alternative to soda." Ava sounded defensive. "Anyway, it's your call, Zoe."

"I'll have the wine."

Gavin returned moments later with wine for her and

a glass of iced tea for himself. "Man, slaving over the stove all day has made me tired."

"I thought you didn't cook."

"I don't." He scowled back at the kitchen. "I was forced to clean the oven."

"Oh." Zoe bit back a grin.

"My fiancé has a thing about cleanliness." Ava leaned closer. "It's bordering on a slight neurosis, but it doesn't hurt him, so it's okay."

"I heard that," Landon called out.

"Major OCD, we like to call him," Gavin added. "And in case you haven't figured it out yet, Ava's a psychologist."

"Really? That's got to be interesting."

"Oh, it is." Ava drank more wine. "So what do you do?"

"I'm a—"

"She works at SMP Medical as their training manager. And she's really good at her job," Gavin said for her.

"Oh?" Ava smiled. "So what exactly does that entail, Zoe?"

"I..." She paused, waiting for Gavin to cut her off again.

"No, you field this one. You got it, babe."

"Thanks so much for your confidence." She ignored his thumbs-up, trying not to encourage him by smiling. "I basically manage the trainers who teach the medical software to the medical group. It can get pretty involved, especially dealing with tech support, software issues, and clinic managers who don't like to have to wait. But it's fun and challenging. I love being a teacher as much as I love being a manager."

"It's always a good thing when you love your job."

"Yeah," Gavin said. "I mean, if Ava didn't love dealing with the mentally impaired, she and Landon never would have gotten together."

Ava frowned. "Gavin."

"Hey, isn't that the pot calling the kettle black?" Zoe teased, but Gavin's smile left him.

"What are you trying to say? That I'm mentally deficient? That I can't deal with the pressure society puts on me to be a man?"

"Um, no. I was just teasing."

Gavin's big grin relieved and annoyed her. "Kidding. I'm probably the biggest mental patient Ava knows."

Zoe glared. "You're such an ass." For a moment she'd feared she'd hurt him, and that hadn't felt good at all.

"He really is," Landon said with cheer as he rejoined them, carrying a veggie tray. "Ava, you're up."

She handed Landon her glass and kissed him on the cheek, then left them for the kitchen. He set the snacks on the coffee table and drank his fiancée's wine. "Sit down. Take a load off."

Zoe sat on the comfortable brown sofa, not surprised when Gavin sat next to her and put an arm around her shoulders.

Landon sat kitty-corner from them in a side chair big enough to fit his frame. "Zoe, I need to ask you something."

She drank more wine. She had a feeling she'd need it to deal with the Donnigans en masse. "Shoot."

"You sure he hasn't coerced you in any way to be here? Blackmail, threats? What's he got on you? I can help."

"Shut up, Landon." Gavin glared.

Zoe laughed. "See, now that's funny. Well, to be honest, he wore me down. So many months of constant whining and begging. I took pity on him."

"Ha. Thought so." Landon grinned.

Gavin wasn't bothered in the slightest. "See? Tenacity pays off in the end. And now, look. Hottest woman at the gym is into me. I am *so* The Man."

"Well, you're definitely *a* man. I can agree with that." Zoe held up her wineglass and clinked it with Gavin's glass. He was such a goof.

They ate veggies with dip, argued over who had the better technique in the self-defense class—which Zoe had to admit belonged to Gavin—and discussed the latest knucklehead in Landon's office, which amused Zoe to no end.

"These people, they're morons, right?" Landon growled. "People who demand privileges and special favors because they asked for them, not because they worked to earn those favors." Landon sneered. "Fu—frickin' Ed Werner. I had to counsel the douche three times before I could fire him. First he came to work smelling like booze. Then he missed an important meeting. Right there, I would have canned his ass, but corporate policy mandated a strike three. When he showed late—no calls, no texts, nothing—*two days* later, I fired his ass."

"Wow. Did he say why he'd been gone?"

Landon shook his head. "Apparently things at home, and with the mistress, weren't going well. His midlife crisis is now someone else's problem."

"Nice." Gavin laughed. "I bet you tore him up."

"Well, yeah."

Zoe wouldn't have wanted to be that guy, facing down a fire-breathing Landon. For all that they were clearly brothers, having similar facial features and mannerisms, Landon seemed the more aggressive of the two. Gavin was more laid-back. Then too, Zoe was partial to dark hair and gray eyes. And that smile on Gavin's handsome face when he looked at her, like he was now.

"I bet Zoe can be just as tough in the office." He nodded. "She's a hard-ass."

"Not really." She preened at what she considered a compliment. "Well, there was that one admin assistant at one of the clinics who kept screwing up our training sessions by scheduling her people at all the wrong times. I don't know if she just didn't like me or was bad at her job, but she had a real attitude when we'd deal with each other. I tried to be nice. Then I just took her aside and had a conversation, if you know what I mean."

"Oh? Catfight?"

"Relax, Gavin." She huffed. "I chewed her out is all."

Landon leaned back, grinning. "Bet that set her straight."

"Well, I was professional until she called me a bitch and poked me in the chest."

"Seriously?" Gavin blinked.

Zoe flushed. "She had some deluded notion that one of the doctors she had a crush on was lusting after me. Not the case at all, but she was too immature, and plain crazy, to see that. Soon as she touched me, I kind of went off on her." Zoe smiled, feeling the mean. "No *kind of* about it. I told her to stop thinking with her head up her ass, that she had no shot with Dr. Hottie because he only liked eighteen-year-olds, and that she needed to grow

up or get fired, because she clearly sucked at her job. I
also might have told her to fix her appearance, because
we're a professional organization, and she dressed like
a groupie at a rock concert. I don't care who you are.
No one needs to see that much cleavage." Before they
could say anything, she added, "Holly was maybe an A
cup and trying way too hard."

"Oh. Well then." Gavin glanced at her. "You know,
you could wear V-necks a lot more than you do."

"Gavin."

Landon laughed. "That's what I'm always telling
Ava, and she's professional this, doctoral that."

"I heard my name," Ava called out. "Dinner."

They chatted more about work nightmares, with Ava
adding some of her own. Nothing client-related, because
Landon was right. She took her job very seriously. But
she told some funny stories about what she observed
when out in town, putting a clinical spin on the incidents
that Zoe found hilarious.

The time passed as Zoe truly enjoyed herself, feeling
like she belonged at the table with her new friends. She
and Ava made plans to do coffee the following week.
She felt Gavin's hand on hers on the table. He squeezed
it, leaned in to give her a kiss, then asked if she wanted
coffee while he cleared their plates.

"I can get that," she tried, but he forestalled her.

"No, no. I can't cook, but I can clean." He talked over
Landon's *harrumph*. "Coffee with cream, right?"

"Yes, please. And two—"

"Packets of that sugar substitute crap. Right."

Zoe watched him walk off, then turned to see Landon
and Ava grinning at her. "What?"

"She domesticated him. I wouldn't believe it if I hadn't seen it with my own eyes." Landon shook his head and held up a glass. "To Zoe, tamer of wild beasts."

Ava chuckled and toasted her as well. "To Zoe, who can tolerate the brothers Donnigan. You deserve three sugars, in my opinion."

Zoe blushed and laughed with them. Gavin returned with a tray of coffee cups and a carafe. "At your service." He set down the tray with flourish and a bow. "And yes, Landon. My mistress has thoroughly domesticated her humble servant."

Though the others thought him funny, she hadn't missed that emphasis on *mistress* or the way his gaze deepened with sexual intimacy when he smiled at her.

And then it was time to go, and she had her wild beast all to herself in the privacy of her own home. What to do, what to do…

Chapter 12

NAKED AND BOUND, GAVIN WAITED, BREATHLESS WITH anticipation, while Zoe puttered around in the other room. She'd made good on her promise to give him a mistress worthy of the title tonight.

Man, it had made him so damn happy to have her by his side with his brother and Ava. He'd never, ever considered bringing his other bed partners home to meet his family. Not that there had been that many over the years.

He'd had one girlfriend for a few months in San Diego. And then sexy and funny Ariel during his temporary active duty assignment to Hawaii a few years back. But when the operational tempo had increased, his energies had been spent on honing his skills with a weapon, on being with his team during those times he wasn't flagged for special ops.

He'd only taken that last promotion because he had to, but inside, he'd always be Gunnery Sergeant Donnigan, platoon sergeant and all-around ball-breaker to a bunch of mouthy Marines. Melancholy darkened what should be a fantasy come true—Zoe-time with him naked and tied up.

He seriously had to stop dwelling on the past.

Except he couldn't do that when he kept getting calls from those who'd lost the same loved ones he had. People who probably wanted what he didn't have to give—happy stories of his pals and a glazed-over version of the truth. That the sad coincidence of being shot while deployed at the same time and in the same location as Mick and the guys had prevented him from being in that unlucky convoy.

He clenched his fingers around the taut material binding his wrists to the posts on Zoe's bed and forced himself to relax. God, talk about the wrong time to lose it. Seconds away from being Zoe's sexual plaything, and he had almost ruined it by getting all self-pitying and sad.

He closed his eyes and concentrated, ignoring the subtle breeze through an open window that made him shiver. Lying naked on the bed, tied up and waiting, should have been more fun than this.

"Well, well, falling asleep so soon, boy?"

Her voice sparked him to awareness. He blinked and, across the candlelit room, saw Zoe in some sexy-as-hell bustier. It had black lines crisscrossing under her breasts, emphasizing her round globes, skimming down her tight abs in red silk and flaring out over her belly, giving tantalizing hints of panties he was dying to see. Over her thighs, a matching pair of black garters with little red bows. *Garters*.

His cock rose in salute. All thought fled, his blood rushing to that other, more important part of him. He could cry later, he told himself, having a difficult time thinking about anything but burying himself inside her.

"I'm so disappointed, Gavin."

"No, no. Call me *boy*. Or *bad boy*." He chuckled at her frown. "I mean, whatever you want, Mistress."

"Thanks so much for letting me be in charge of your fantasy," she said drily. "Now shut up and listen."

"Oh yes, Mistress." He bit his lip to keep from laughing when she planted her hands on her hips and glared at him.

"You've been a very bad boy. But I think it's probably because you're so stressed. I think a massage would calm you right down."

He said nothing, not wanting to ruin the moment. Fuck all, Zoe was a queen. She wore her black hair down, the wavy mass flowing over her toned shoulders, kissing the tops of her breasts. The bustier left little to the imagination, and he could see her nipples poking past the thin red material cupping her breasts.

She'd put on some kind of shiny gloss, making her lips look bloodred and slick. He was dying to see them wrapped around his cock. But he feared that if she put them there, he'd come way too fast.

He spread his thighs wider, instinctively readying himself to thrust up so when she settled her hot pussy over him, they'd have the perfect fit.

Zoe smiled and trailed a finger from his ankle up his leg to his hip. And damn, but that light touch made him even harder. Anticipation and her naughty smile would give him wet dreams for weeks, months, *years*.

She stroked back the way she'd come, moving to the other side of the bed, where she did the same to his right side. When she got to his hip, she again stopped. But this time she turned and flaunted her ass at him, so that he could see—

"*Oh fuck*. No panties?"

She turned back around and spread her legs, and he saw her wet and slick, mostly shaved. A mouthwatering treat. She *had* to sit over his face. And soon.

"Did I tell you to speak?" She smacked his thigh, very close to his cock.

He jerked and felt a spurt of moisture leave him.

"Oh, so big, baby." She feathered a breath over his cockhead, and he moaned. But she didn't kiss him or touch him there. Instead, his sadist of a girlfriend caressed his legs, paying special attention to the insides of his thighs, always coming close but not close enough to his groin.

She turned and slid her hands up his belly to his chest, running her short fingernails over his body, tugging his chest hair, then raking over his nipples until he was panting.

"Zoe, please."

"That's *mistress* to you." She wore a cruel smile, getting off on their play, yet a special joy remained in her eyes. A care that went deeper than just a need for sex.

He could see it and knew it because he felt the same. This should have just been a hot fuck between two consenting adults. Instead, it was an intimate interlude between a woman who cared enough to give her lover his fantasy and a man falling deeper under her magical spell. They shared an emotional connection that continued to grow.

Zoe leaned down, finally following her hands with her mouth.

He groaned and swore when she trailed kisses across his body, licking his nipples, then biting them.

"Come on," he urged. "More."

She moaned and continued to kiss him, dragging her breasts over his body as she leaned across him. It seemed to take forever before she kissed his mouth, while continuing to stroke his arms, from his shoulders to his wrists tied up in spandex.

He felt like a man possessed, kissing her with desperation. Sliding his tongue in and out, needing to do the same with his cock. He arched his head off the bed until she cupped his head, easing the strain on his neck.

When she pulled away to kiss toward his ear, he begged her to come back. "Come on, baby. Kiss me again," he growled. "Mouth fuck me with that tongue."

She gave a low laugh, one that vibrated to his core. Then she nipped his earlobe and whispered, "How about if I take a seat on the bed. Would you like that?"

He bowed off the bed, humping the air. "Fuck, yes. Right over me. Put yourself on me. I'm so hard."

She laughed again, then tongued his ear, playing along his erogenous zones until he feared spontaneously combusting. "You're so easy."

"Yeah. Really easy," he agreed. "Super easy. Come on. I'm hurting."

"Not enough." She moved back, and he watched without blinking as she slowly crept onto the bed, first one knee, then the next. She was on her knees, straddling his waist, too far away for him to penetrate. The silky feel of her thigh-high stockings aroused him anew. "How about a treat?"

He nodded, and she blew his mind.

She peeled away the fabric covering her breasts, then tossed the material to the floor. Black webs of elastic still framed her, but now only accenting how naked her breasts were.

"Oh, Jesus." He was living a nightmare, dying of

sexual starvation while his fantasy made flesh wore an outfit meant for torture of the best kind.

She moved to his side, giving him no way to shove up into her. But she did lean over his mouth. "Who wants a treat?"

This sexual dynamo who'd taken over Zoe's body had him so aroused he threatened to burst. Gavin latched onto her breast, sucking and licking, needing to get her as stimulated as he was. She moved away, but before he could complain, she gave him her other breast, and he laved it with the same attention.

Soon Zoe moaned, and he couldn't stop gyrating his hips, needing to thrust inside her something fierce. Zoe eased up, and he swore she'd finally sink over him.

But she did him one better.

"Zoe, please," he begged, not too proud to do whatever he had to for a hard fuck. He'd gone past the point of desperation what felt like forever ago.

"You've been such a good boy; you deserve a reward," she said in a husky voice, her eyes pinpricks of lust. Then she crawled up his body and settled over his face, slowly lowering until he latched onto her clit and sucked.

Gavin had always loved oral. Getting or receiving, though he preferred giving it. He loved the taste of a woman in passion. But Zoe was like an eternity of dessert. All his favorite things in one glorious woman. She was so wet, as aroused as he'd been by their play. And knowing she was getting off on it made it that much more difficult to resist coming. He'd never thought he could without someone touching his cock, but he might be able to right now.

He moaned and licked, shoving his tongue inside her, stroking and taking. Giving back the pleasure magnified by her sexuality. Living out his own private fantasy, better than anything he'd ever been through or could imagine.

"Oh Gavin. I'm coming, oh God," she whispered as she rode his mouth.

He'd have given anything to be inside her at that moment, but when she cried out and came over his lips, he lapped her up like the sweetest cream.

She didn't sink over him at all. Instead, she immediately straightened while she quivered, not giving him that last bit of her pleasure.

"Come back," he managed, his voice thick.

"Oh, wow. That was amazing." She left the bed, damn her, and smiled down at him.

"You have got to be kidding me." He could feel himself seconds from losing it.

"Now, now. Be a good boy, Gavin, or you won't get your next treat."

"I'm so getting you back after this."

"Well then. Maybe I won't untie you after all." She tried to look mean, but her lips quirked. That Zoe half smile he'd gotten used to seeing at the gym.

"I'm sorry, I'm sorry," he lied.

"Yes, you are." She moved back on the bed, so slowly it was like time moved backward. She kept a close eye on him. "Well, you do look repentant, I guess."

"Mistress, now," he growled, arching up, seeking her heat as she straddled him once more.

"Mistress, hmm? You remembered my name." She positioned him at her entrance and waited, the tip of his cock surrounded by wet warmth. Heaven and hell in the same breath.

Staring up at her unbound breasts tipped with berry-red nipples, at her parted lips, those slumberous blue eyes gazing down at him with more than lust, he closed his eyes and committed the experience to memory. God, he never wanted to forget tonight. Ever.

She shocked the hell out of him by slamming down, taking him all the way in.

"*Fuck!*"

She rose and bore down just once more, and he came like a geyser.

"Yes, yes," he yelled as she remained over him, taking every fucking cell of desperation, frustration, and longing while he released into bliss. He came forever, letting it all go, and felt groggy when she finally leaned down to kiss him.

He tasted her on his lips and wondered if she liked it. He sure the hell did.

"Oh, baby. You're so big inside me," she murmured. "I like it."

"Zoe. Zoe," he whispered while she kissed him all over his face. Soft, tender presses of her lips while she cared for him.

He didn't want her to leave, but she moved off him anyway. She hurried away but returned moments later with a washcloth. She gently wiped his cock, his thighs, then tossed the cloth to the floor. Then she snuggled up to him in the bed.

"Wow. That was *amazing*." He opened his eyes to check out her outfit again. "And what you're wearing? Never, ever get rid of it. I'm thinking of framing it, minus those nipple covers of course. It'll go on my wall. Right above my bed."

"Gavin." She laughed. "You liked it."

"Liked it? Seriously? I loved it. I almost came just from looking at you. You are one seriously sexy woman."

"Thanks." She ran a hand over his chest, up his still-bound arms. She'd given him plenty of slack. "So it wasn't too much?"

"Ask me that again, and I'll spank you."

She grinned, and his heart dropped to her feet.

"So, I have to know. Is this standard for you? I mean, should I feel special or what? Because kink makes the world go round, and I'm all for it. But did you just do this for me, or is it something you're into?" He moved his hands. "And while you're answering that, could you untie me?"

She leaned on her elbow to regard him. "I bought this last week, thinking maybe you and I might put it to use. I like to think of myself as a sensual person, but I've never been much into fantasy play or sex, to be honest. It can feel good, but then I'm busy with my life at work, at home, my flowers. I haven't dwelled on it too much, at least not lately." She shrugged and turned pink, yet she didn't look away. "But with you, I wanted to try something else. All that mistress talk. And you turn me on."

"Have I told you how much I love your bluntness?"

She caressed his arm, lingering over his biceps with a touch that started turning him on again, though he didn't think that was her intention. "I'm fascinated with your body. I love touching you."

"No complaints here." Though she could release him from her bed. He had a quirky notion of her keeping him tied up for weeks as her willing sex slave. Totally worth getting fired from the gym for that.

"You make me want to play," she admitted. "To do wicked things to you. To see how far I can push you. Sexually, I mean. Because you get me so hot and bothered. It was good to see I make you the same."

"Never doubt that. It's been all I could do not to sport wood around the gym for months while you flaunted yourself at me."

"Flaunted? Really?" She frowned.

"Yep. Even in your professional clothes, looking all starched and neat. I could see that ass begging me for a slap. Or those breasts pleading with me to suck some plump nipplage." He grinned at her deepening flush. "I want you to make all your shirts with breast flaps like that. You have no idea how much work you could get done if you wore that. No one, at least, no guy, would ever turn down anything you wanted if you wore that."

She snickered. "Gavin. I can just imagine the group directors' faces if I wore this to our next meeting." She dissolved into more laughter. "Sorry. That was too funny."

He had a sour thought. "Yeah, well, just don't wear it around Swanson. He'd take the invite and run with it. I still don't like that guy."

"Oh, stop." She looked so pretty, smiling at him. "Can we talk about your groupies at the gym?"

He groaned. "No, don't ruin this."

"Well, you already mentioned Swanson. I don't normally think of him when my breasts are hanging out and my boyfriend is all tied up. So I think I'm entitled."

She'd used the b-word. He felt another thrill. "Go for it."

"Why them? I mean, I get wanting sex. But why those women at the gym? You work there."

He groaned. "It was stupid. But the thing is, I didn't think I'd still be working there, not this long. When I first left the military and returned to the States, I told you. I was messed up. I tried working for my dad's company. That sucked, and I left after a month. I'm not a corporate suit-and-tie type of guy. Then I tried another job at a staging company through my mom. Not a good fit either. Mostly because I was doing all the work while those lazy humps sat back and drank coffee for four of their eight-hour days. I thought about work at a construction company. But the, ah, the loud noises kind of bothered me."

She narrowed her eyes and nodded. And she continued petting him, which was just perfect. He'd tell her anything she wanted to know if she kept that up. She had a hell of an insidious interrogation technique.

"So I'd started going to the gym. At first, because I needed to release some stress. Landon was already a member, and I really like Mac. He's a great guy."

"Yeah, so I've heard."

"I started working there, and I was in a bad place mentally. So when these women came on to me, wanting to get laid, I thought, why not? None of them wanted any entanglements. I sure as hell didn't. And I didn't think I'd spend more than a month or two at the gym. It was doubtful I'd see them again."

"So you had random hookups with gym members."

He scowled. "Hey. My story. No, they weren't random. They were planned," he said primly and saw her roll her eyes. "You know, Zoe, I'm worried about you. Do you think you might have a condition? Your eyes tend to roll a lot while we talk. Might want to see a doctor about that."

She snorted. "Continue, Romeo."

"This is awkward. You really want to know about my past sexual history while we're naked?"

She nodded. "I'm not a fan of your groupies. I've heard the stories about how good in bed you are, and that you're hung like a moose."

"Better that than a ferret."

She laughed at that.

"Look. I was no saint. Not even trying to say I was. But I'm not normally such a horndog. I was just… I needed something, and they gave it. But it didn't last. And sadly, I'm embarrassed to say, it didn't mean anything."

Her hands found his chest and she started massaging him, easing the tension he hadn't been aware was building. Gavin sighed. "This, us…this means something. I'm not trying to freak you out. Hell, I don't know what it means. But it's more than coming into a warm woman. It's sex with *you*, Zoe.

"I can't promise much these days, but I can promise I won't fuck around on you. Having fun, being with you like this, I want it. And as long as you want it too, life is good."

Life would be better if he'd stop saying this shit out loud and giving her the opportunity to tie it off, ending it because he kept being so fucking honest about not being able to commit. *Stop telling her you're messed up. She knows it already. Don't remind her.* He might have to rethink this honesty policy. *Time to talk to Lee again.*

Zoe shrugged. "Makes sense to me. It works until it doesn't work. Why screw with a good thing?"

He melted under a wave of relief and her hot hands. "Exactly."

"Now, how about you stop sharing while I massage your poor muscles. Then, when I'm good and ready, I'll untie you."

Lulled by the promise of more pleasure, he relented. No more talking, only a few groans of satisfaction when she hit several sore spots from his workout yesterday.

They lay together, touching, close, and he wanted to hold the moment and never let it go.

"Falling asleep on me, hmm?" she teased, lying between his thighs as she kneaded his quads.

"Not really." Great. He sounded sleepy. Except his body was turning stiffer as she worked some of his adductor muscles, the ones leading up and under his balls. His dick spiked when she started kissing her way up the insides of his thighs. "Ah, Zoe?"

She kissed his inner thigh, her cheek brushing him so intimately, and he moaned. Then her mouth was there, taking him, gently sucking one ball while cupping and rubbing the other.

"Zoe, shit. Baby, so good."

Her mouth worked miracles, turning him fully erect, and then some, in the span of seconds. She slid her lips over his balls to his shaft, licking him from base to tip while she played with him, her hands in all the right places. She held him, stared into his shocked gaze, then slid those red lips over his cockhead and down.

Another memory he committed to never forgetting. Before she robbed him of the ability to think altogether. Because Zoe was a good girl, *such* a good girl.

Chapter 13

Zoe sat with Ava at one of her favorite local coffee bars in Queen Anne. To her surprise, Gavin's younger brother worked there. Ava pointed him out.

"Wow. All the Donnigans do look alike. Good thing I'd never met Gavin when I was in my late teens. I'd have been heartbroken that much sooner." Zoe sipped from her latte and watched the youngest Donnigan working behind the bar, singing to himself while he fixed another macchiato.

"Yeah, they're all like that," Ava said. "Wait until you meet Van, their dad. He's sixty-three, runs four or five miles a day, and looks like Landon's older brother. He's so handsome." Ava winked. "Drives Landon nuts when I tell him he owes his father for being so good-looking."

They both laughed.

"And Linda's pretty too. You've met Hope?"

"I've seen her at the gym. The pretty blond who likes to argue with Landon?" A knockout, but with a more feminine version of the Donnigan good looks.

"Yep. That would be her. She's the only blond who argues with him. The others usually flirt." Yet Ava didn't seem bothered by the fact.

"And you're okay with them flirting with your fiancé?"

"Heck no." Ava took another sip of her coffee, as if in thought. "The thing is, with a Donnigan, you know they're going to attract attention. They all do, without even trying."

Gavin sure did.

"So you either accept that your guy is going to be popular, and you trust that he cares for you and won't stray, or you cut him off. Period. End of story." Ava sipped more caffeine. "I work with people of all kinds who have a variety of problems in their relationships. Cheating can be a big one to overcome. Frankly, I don't think I could tolerate it. But who knows?" she sighed. "My profession, hearing what I do, makes it more difficult for me to trust in my personal life. But I know Landon. He's loyal to the bone. They all are. Even the young rooster over there."

Zoe followed her glance to Theo, now smiling politely over the counter at a girl who'd picked up her drink. The girl acted a lot friendlier than a customer just grabbing her order. After she left, he turned to the girl with frosted-blue hair working next to him and winked, then kissed her.

"That's Maya, Theo's girlfriend. He's been with her for a little over a month. They're so cute."

"Huh." Zoe sipped her coffee and watched them.

"So you think it's only a matter of time before Gavin breaks your heart?"

Theo was handsome. Like a slenderer version of Gavin, and maybe a little taller, wearing a crew cut that was a bit longer on top. So young. She had a feeling he'd fill out as he grew older.

"What's that?" She turned back to Ava. "Did I say Gavin will break my heart?"

"You implied it."

Zoe shrugged. She'd been happy to go out with Ava. Finding a new gal pal was always a challenge. But knowing Ava had *Dr.* in front of her name put Zoe on edge.

Ava sighed. "This is why I don't have many friends. I swear, I'm not psychoanalyzing you. We're just out talking, woman to woman, joined by our common bond to the overpowering Donnigans."

"Well, when you put it like that…" Zoe held up her cup in a toast. "To us, for being brave."

"Hear, hear."

Zoe drained her coffee. "Honestly, I don't know what I'm doing with Gavin. I met him at a low point in my life." She found it easy to talk to Ava, who watched with a kind, calm expression. "My twin sister, Aubrey, died four months ago. Freak car accident. It was tough, and I pretty much shut down." She gave a sad smile. "But Gavin just kept annoying me at the gym. Always bugging me to smile. So annoying."

Ava grinned. "Yes, they are like that, aren't they? Tenacious and clingy, like a virus that infects you no matter how much vitamin C you take."

Zoe laughed, feeling good despite her lingering sorrow. Aubrey would have liked Ava, for sure. "Yeah, a virus. Can I use that?"

"Be my guest."

"Anyway, I've been really focused the past few years. I'm a driven career woman. Aubrey was the artist, the dreamer. The sexual dynamo, to hear her tell it." Yeah, her sister had loved to brag, hadn't she?

"She sounds like fun."

"She was great." And just like that, the waterworks started. "Shit."

Ava didn't freak out at all. The woman chuckled. "You know, I'd be disconcerted if I didn't have this effect on so many people." She shoved a packet of tissues at Zoe. "I keep extras in my purse."

"Go, Ava."

Theo chose that moment to join them, saw Zoe wiping her eyes, and goggled. "Oh my God. Please tell me the coffee's okay. It wasn't the coffee, was it?"

"Relax, Theo. Zoe had something in her eye is all," Ava explained.

"Yeah, tears," Zoe muttered, impressed with Ava's ability to fabricate and relieved she hadn't made a scene. "So you're Theo."

Theo sat and gave her a wide, charming smile. Another heartthrob in the making. "Hel-lo."

Ava huffed. "Theo, this is Zoe. Gavin's girlfriend."

Theo gaped. "This is Zoe? But you're so pretty."

Zoe put the tissue down. "I'm sorry?"

He flushed. "I just don't understand how someone as obnoxious as my brother can get such a hot girlfriend. I mean, he's got muscles, sure. But doesn't that attitude rub you the wrong way?"

More like the right way, she thought but would never say, not to Gavin's brother. Her time with the sexual dynamo last Sunday had been magical. But the guy never stopped. He'd officially worn her out yesterday, giving new meaning to *hump day*. Still, she'd met him thrust for thrust. Then they'd mutually agreed to give each other a break.

Dinners together, home movie dates, board games; they'd been spending every available waking moment together. Even she knew that couldn't be healthy.

Theo seemed to be waiting for her answer, so she gave a casual shrug. "I find him tolerable."

He laughed, a deep boom that didn't seem to go with his slighter frame. "Well, thanks for getting him out of the house at least."

Gavin had spent time with her, way into the late hours, but he always went home after. That separation also made it easier to rationalize her time with him. But lately Zoe wanted to wake up in his arms. That she didn't mind him crowding her precious space alarmed her.

"Can I ask you something?" she said to Theo.

"Sure."

"Why were you so worried the coffee made me cry? Are you new here? You seem to know people, and you're doing a great job."

His smile looked strained. "Thanks. I've actually been working here for a while. I kind of left for a little but came back. Maya missed me." He glanced back at his girlfriend, then sighed. "A few days ago, I got a text message telling me to be careful about what I served at work. A direct threat from *your boyfriend*."

"What?"

"It's escalating."

"The prank wars." Ava let out a breath. "I told Landon to put a stop to it. But does he listen to me? No. See, the four of them—"

"No," Theo shook his head. "Mom and Dad too. You remember Mom's announcement at dinner."

"Right. The six of them take turns pulling pranks on each other. At our last family dinner, Linda tricked us into thinking she and Van were having marital problems."

"Really?" Zoe looked from Ava to Theo.

Both nodded.

"Yes." Ava chuckled. "Of course it all started back up when I was dating Landon. One of them, though they won't say who, put a blow-up sex doll in his bed. She looked just like me. It shocked the heck out of him." She laughed.

So did Theo.

Zoe grinned. "Wish I could have seen that."

Ava snickered. "He was so embarrassed. And not much gets to him."

"Don't tell," Theo said. "But I did it."

Ava pointed. "Ha. I knew it was you! I had thought perhaps Hope, but you're more devious."

Theo flushed. "Aw, thanks."

"Don't worry. I won't tell. Keeps him on his toes not to have guessed the culprit yet." She turned to Zoe. "Landon even blamed me for a while. As if I would stoop so low…and get caught," she tacked on with a wink.

"So the prank wars are still going on? How long do they last?" Zoe asked, not sure she wanted to be drawn into such a thing, even by distant association.

"Well…" Theo scratched his jaw. "After they gave me a mohawk and dyed my hair orange a couple months ago, I got back at them. Each of them. I saved Gavin for last weekend, when I sicced our cousin on him. Colin is seven. Great kid, but he's a kid. And I made it so Gavin had to take care of him."

"Ah. I heard about that." Zoe smiled. "Apparently Colin is not good with sugary cereals."

Theo's evil laugh stirred hers again, Ava's too. "Yeah. It was classic. Anyway, I think Landon messed with Gavin and the toilet—don't ask—and for a while

Hope had pink hair. Oh, and I think someone messed with Mom's toothpaste, but she won't confirm that.

"Now Gavin is getting back at everyone. I'm freaked he's going to mess with me at work. And then yesterday I woke up by smacking myself in the face with a handful of shaving cream. It's lame, but it's still annoying. Plus he took pictures," he added glumly.

"Well, I haven't seen them yet. Don't worry." Ava patted his shoulder.

"Yeah, well, it's the ones who wait to get even who are the worst. At least Gavin's getting me back right away." He noted the girl behind the cashier waving at him. "Oh, gotta go. Great meeting you, Zoe. Hope you come over and hang before wising up and dumping my brother." He left before she could respond.

"Scary, huh?" Ava teased. "It's all immature, yes, but the guys seem to enjoy it. Linda sure did. And I'm sorry to say I might have pulled a prank of my own." Ava chuckled. "You haven't met their parents yet, have you?"

"Um, no." Zoe swallowed. "But Gavin mentioned having dinner with them this weekend."

"Ah. Best of luck."

"Wait. That's it? No tips or tricks to surviving the dinner?"

"No. They're actually wonderful people. Your problem isn't Van and Linda. It's dealing with Gavin."

"Nice segue."

Ava grinned. "Thanks. Yes, I always circle back to a point until it's been covered. And you still never quite answered about your fears of Gavin breaking your heart. But considering your state of mind when you met, that seems normal. Plus anyone entering a new relationship

will wonder how to recover when and if it breaks up."
She shrugged. "I still wonder about that with Landon,
and we're engaged."

"Really? You two seem so in love."

"We are." Ava played with her ring, a stunning
square-cut emerald set between two sparkling diamonds.
"But there's never a guarantee of a happily ever after
in your future. And considering I deal with marriage
counseling a lot in my practice, I can't help but think
about it."

"I'll bet." Zoe toyed with her cup. "So can I ask you
something, in your professional opinion as a therapist?"

"And as a friend," Ava added.

"And as a friend." Zoe liked this woman.

"Please do."

"Do you think it's normal to still cry when I think
of my sister? I do feel good now. It's not all doom and
gloom for me the way it was when it first happened.
Mostly I think I'm over the grief tugging me down.
Then I'll see something that reminds me of her, and it
makes me sad. Or I'll hear a song she hated and want to
make fun of it with her. But she's not there."

"Totally normal." Ava leaned forward. "Processing
through grief takes time. I'd be more worried if you
weren't dealing with it. In my opinion, tears are therapy.
Talking is therapy. Pretending the bad never interferes
with the good? That's not healthy."

Zoe nodded. "Thanks. I kind of thought that too." She
paused. "Gavin doesn't talk about his time in the service
much. I don't push him or anything. But that's part of
what drew us together, I think. We both know what it's
like to grieve."

"He has some issues he's dealing with," Ava said carefully.

"I know. He told me about the booze and the women. Of course, anyone hanging out at the gym knows the women part already."

Ava bit her lip. "Ah, yeah. Gossip does tend to circulate there. But word on the street is he's got himself a girlfriend." She winked. "Michelle doesn't seem to like you very much."

"Good."

Ava laughed. "Seriously though, the women in his past wouldn't worry me. Gavin is a lot of things, but he doesn't strike me as the unfaithful type. That doesn't mean you're not in for some work if you take him on. But you know that."

"I do. He's not perfect. Thank God. Because with that body, that face, and all that charm, if he didn't have issues, he'd be impossible to live with." Live with. Wasn't that close to what they were already doing? No, he still slept at home.

But I don't want him to. I want him to stay with me.

"Oh my gosh. He makes my head hurt sometimes."

Ava nodded. "Welcome to my world. More coffee?"

"Yes, please. I have to get back to work, and between thinking about him and dealing with a few of our clinic managers, I think a double shot of espresso is in order."

Ava stood. "Coming right up."

―⁂―

Gavin sat in therapy, tapping his knuckles on his thigh while Lee droned on about healthy man-woman relationships. Apparently Gavin's newfound joy with Zoe had freaked Lee out. Then again, maybe Gavin shouldn't have mentioned the thought about having kids with her.

Of course, most of his thoughts had revolved around efforts *to make* said kids. And if a few years down the road, they still happened to be going out, still fucking like rabbits, and she wanted a kid, he'd happily join her in… in wedded matrimony? Being her baby daddy? What?

His phone buzzed. He wasn't supposed to take calls during a session, but he rarely got them unless it was an emergency. Especially from his family, because they knew and Zoe knew he saw his therapist from three to four on Thursdays.

"Go ahead. Get it." Lee waved him to answer.

He saw the number, muted the ringer, and put it away. "Nah, I'm good."

"Are you really? Then what's that look on your face?"

"What look?"

"You look upset, Gavin. Scared. But there's nothing here to be scared about. This is a safe zone," Lee reminded him, then patiently waited.

Gavin rubbed the back of his neck, knowing he needed to share his growing anxiety. Every time the phone rang lately, he worried. He would have put a special ringtone to the number, but then he'd know for sure when she called.

"Gavin. I can't help you if you won't let me."

"It's Nicole," he blurted. "Mick's wife."

"Mickey? Your friend who died in that blast?"

"Yeah, him." Gavin rose and paced, his anxiety building. "She's called a few times. I think she wants to talk."

"You think? You don't know?"

He shrugged. "I haven't listened to the messages."

"You should."

Gavin swallowed. "Ah, would you?"

Lee studied him, then sighed and nodded. After listening to all three messages in silence, he handed the phone back to Gavin. "Can you sit down, please?"

"What? What's she want?" His knee bobbed, and he tried to stop it, but his heart raced like a jackhammer. He swallowed. "Is she okay?" He couldn't ask about the baby, couldn't know if Mick had lost more than just his life.

Gavin sat back, feeling like a pussy when his hands started shaking. It was a phone call, for God's sake.

Lee nodded. "Yes, she's fine, Gavin. And so is her son."

A relieved breath gushed out of him, and Gavin leaned forward, his head between his knees. "Thank God."

"Your friend's widow, and Luke's sister, Amanda, want to talk with you."

Gavin tuned out everything, choosing to focus on them being healthy and hearty.

"For the record, I don't think it's a good idea. Not yet," Lee said.

Gavin blinked up at his therapist's unexpected advice. "No?"

"Gavin, it's a stressor you don't need right now."

"But I thought you were all about getting closure."

"I am when the situation calls for it. But we're still in the stages of getting you to cope with everything. You have plenty of time to heal. There's no need to rush this."

"Yeah, but I don't want to gaff them off."

"So send a text stating you'll contact them when you can. I'm sure they'll understand. And if that's too difficult, which it could rightly be, just ignore the calls. They'll stop. You have the numbers. When you're ready to face them, you will."

His palms sweated. "But then aren't I denying them some closure?"

"How? They know the status of their deceased loved ones. It's you I'm worried about. You need to be healthy before you see them. Physically, you're in amazing shape. But mentally, it's going to take time. And that's okay. That's normal, Gavin," Lee emphasized. As if Gavin worried about being a looney tune. What he worried about was doing more damage to Nicole and Amanda, and he said so.

"The thing is, Gavin, if you go to see them before you're comfortable, you might inadvertently hurt them. You might turn erratic. Or you might say things out of guilt that will put them back in a dark place. From those few phone calls, it sounds like they're moving on. It's your decision, of course. But I suggest you tuck away that number and let it go. At least for now."

Gavin thought about it. Thought about how Zoe had lost her twin, how it still hurt her months later, and how she took on the pain and dealt with it. She didn't need to see a therapist, didn't avoid problems. How could he be less?

"Um, I'm going to call right now. Just to let her know it's not a good time for me." His knee shot up and down. His heart pounded, and sweat poured down his back. "Would you, would you just sit with me through it?" Fuck, but he felt like crying.

This was not supposed to be his life right now. Thirty-two and afraid to call an old friend because he might crack up. What a pathetic waste he'd become. Jesus, how lame could he be?

Lee got up and sat next to him. Then he put a hand on Gavin's shoulder, which surprisingly steadied him. "Go ahead, Gavin. I'm right here with you."

Gavin's eyes watered. This wasn't who he was. But who he'd become. Because he wasn't still supposed to be here? His penance for surviving?

Lee said quietly, "It's okay if you don't want—"

"*No*. I got this." Gavin wiped his stupid face and dialed, then cleared his throat, hoping he didn't sound like the pitiful shit he was.

After a few rings, he started to think she wouldn't answer, that he could leave a message. But that wasn't the case. "Hello?"

Bright-brown eyes and a laughing smile. Always up for a good time, that was Mick's Nicole. Man, they'd had some great parties when they'd been stateside. Even better ones when back on leave through the years.

"Hello?" she said again.

"Uh, hi, Nicole." He had to clear this throat again. "It's Gavin Donnigan."

"Gavin." She sounded thrilled to hear from him. "I'm so glad you called. I've been wanting to talk to you. A couple of us have, actually."

His stomach knotted. He envisioned Mick grinning, flipping him off. Luke mouthing something, and John making fun of him. The guys, friends since high school. Now gone forever. "Yeah, about that." He coughed. Wiped his eyes. Prayed he sounded cheerful. "I'm kind of busy lately. Got some stuff to take care of." *Like my fucked-up brain*. "I want to talk to you… It's just… It might be a while."

"Oh." She paused, and her voice gentled. "Gavin, that's perfectly fine. Whenever you get done with what you're working on, we'll be here. You have my number."

"Yeah, okay. Sure. Bye."

He hung up, not able to wait on her answer. Then he stood, thanked Lee, and said, "Need the restroom for a minute." He calmly walked from the room and found the bathroom unoccupied. After locking the door behind him, he braced himself on the sink and stared at his ugly face in the mirror, heard Nicole's voice, so happy to hear from him.

He turned, got to his knees, and threw up into the toilet. The rush eased him, so that now he felt sick instead of anxious. Oddly enough, he felt better, as if he'd rid himself of all the shitty emotion that never quite left him anymore. An image of Zoe's concerned face filled his mind's eye, and he threw up all over again, dry heaves because he had nothing left.

God. What had he been thinking? She deserved so much better than him.

When he walked back into Lee's office, ready to grab the phone he'd left behind and leave, he found Lee waiting for him on the couch. "Come on, Gavin. Let's talk."

"My time is up, I think."

Lee smiled. So much understanding in that gaze that Gavin looked away, ashamed. "Nah. My four thirty canceled. It's just you and me for a bit longer. Just us talking, off the books. No charge. Okay?"

Gavin shrugged. "I guess."

When he left an hour later, he felt drained but cleansed, ready to get back to pretending to have a life, at least. Lee had talked some sense into him. And now that he'd actually talked to Nicole, she wouldn't call him again. So one good thing had happened today at least.

He went home, changed into exercise clothes, then went on a ten-mile run. Because he had to. He called in sick for work, in no condition to socialize. He texted Zoe the same excuse as a reason not to talk to her until Saturday, then used the crappy weight bench in the garage because going to the gym was out.

He pumped iron until his arms felt limp. Exhausted and past the point of any hint of anxiety, he took a quick shower, then went upstairs to Landon's bed. Landon would be sleeping over at Ava's. And tonight, Gavin didn't want to deal with Theo. He just wanted to be left alone.

Tucking into Landon's freshly laundered sheets, he lay there, ignoring the still-bright evening and remembered the last time he'd laughed with Mick and the guys…and felt unwelcome tears pour down his cheeks.

Hope snuck into her brother's home with a furtiveness she'd developed in her adolescent years and perfected in her late teens. She stopped still, heard nothing, and continued to look around, making sure the coast was clear. With Landon firmly ensconced at Ava's and Theo taken care of by Maya—great girl—that left only Gavin.

Rumor had it he was staying over at Zoe's most nights, though Hope hadn't been able to get through to the woman she had yet to meet. But Gavin should have been working at the gym 'til closing anyway, so she should be good to trick out the house. She tiptoed around the downstairs, heard nothing, and made magic.

Some horseradish in the mayonnaise. Hot peppers in the ketchup. Replacing Theo's underwear with Colin-size drawers. Okay, that one she could credit Mike's boy with.

Man, talk about devious. He'd even planned Theo's downfall using Liam's—his new grandpa's—phone, so as not to be traced. As if anyone would trace a seven-year-old. She grinned. Apparently the McCauleys had been suffering from the prank wars as well, with no idea who to blame. *Someone* had been messing with her cousin Cameron's things. Since she worked for Cam, she had eyes and ears on all her cousins.

Gosh, the things little Colin had been doing made her so proud. Where did that kid get his ideas?

She laughed to herself as she did nothing to Gavin's side of the room, because the anticipation would be its own form of punishment. She'd think of something worse to do to him later. Then she started up the stairs to Landon's room.

She heard something and froze. Then nothing. Moving all the way up and turning to his door, she found it closed. *Oh God. Please don't tell me he's sexing up Ava.* Wouldn't he do that in the privacy of her place though, and not at home where his brothers could hear?

A soft moan. Not one of pleasure, but of pain.

She quietly twisted the nob and peeked her head in. The sun had finally set, and only faint moonlight came through the open blinds of the window. On the bed, Gavin lay on his side, his back to her, covered to his waist.

"Gavin?" she whispered, concerned. Sleeping in Landon's room? That was weird.

Then she goose-stepped around the bed to see more

than his broad back. The sight of his tear-stained face in sleep made her own eyes water. Poor Gavin. He teased and joked, but her brother had some serious hurt buried inside.

He moaned again, tears tracking down his face, and curled into himself.

She wanted to help him, to make the bad go away, but she knew better than to touch him right now. Landon had warned her and Theo to leave Gavin alone when he was resting. They never knew if touching him when he was out would startle him to waking violently or not. Not that he'd ever intend to hurt them or that he'd been aggressive at all with family.

"It's okay, Gavin," she whispered instead. "We love you. It's okay," she repeated, several times.

Sometime later, he blinked his eyes open, though he didn't seem fully awake, and looked at her. "Hope?"

"Shh. Go back to sleep. This is a dream. I'm not messing with Landon's stuff."

He gave a tired smile and closed his eyes. She wiped her tears away. But this time she felt safe to move in close and sit on the bed with him, stroking his hair. "I love you, Gavin. And I always will."

Chapter 14

Zoe hoped Gavin was okay. She hadn't seen him since Wednesday night. He hadn't been at the gym since then either, apparently taken with that flu going around. She did some work on the circuit, then took a long drink of water, trying to stop harping on Gavin.

Mac walked up to her. "Hey, Zoe. How's it going?"

"Good, thanks." She didn't trust his smile. "What's up?"

"Could you do me a favor?"

"Ah, sure."

"Tell Gavin we're doing another self-defense session in another month. Same thing as the first one, unless he wants to change it up. But it should still be for beginners."

"Why tell me?" Zoe asked.

At Mac's knowing look, she threw up her hands. "Seriously? You too? Who *doesn't* listen to gossip?"

"I don't!" A perky, handsome guy popped out from behind her with a wide grin. She recognized him because he always seemed to be at the gym surrounded by people. Mr. Popular, apparently. "Listen to gossip? Please. I start it! Hi, I'm Elliot, and I want the 411 on you and Gavin."

"Oh hell. You're on your own," Mac warned her, then nodded at her new pal. "Elliot."

"Adonis. You have my number," he mock whispered and winked. "Use it."

"Jackass." Mac flushed and walked away, trying to ignore Elliot's whistle.

"Don't worry. His wife asks that I harass him when I can. It's good for him."

Charmed into laughter and a fun time at the gym, Zoe ended up making friends with Elliot. Who just happened to be Ava's cousin.

Small world.

They swapped some Gavin stories. Hers revolved around Gavin and his siblings. Nothing Gavin wouldn't have minded her sharing, she was sure. While Elliot told her all about the bitchy women still wanting a piece of "that fine tail." He sure did know everything about everything.

But he didn't know if Gavin was feeling up to dinner tonight.

She'd texted him just once since receiving his *I'm sick and can't talk* note, not wanting to bug him but wishing him well. It had *killed* her not to have heard from him for a few days. But who wanted a clingy lover? Not her. So she'd left him alone, content he'd call to cancel or confirm their Saturday night dinner at his parents'—but he hadn't.

She said good-bye to Elliot with a promise to text him for lunch or drinks some time. Another friend to add to Ava, Cleo, and Piper. She was on a roll. Zoe grinned and left the gym. After arriving home, she forced herself to clean and do her normal Saturday chores before sending Gavin a text. **Hope you're feeling better. Tonight? Yes or no?**

He immediately returned it. **Still on 4 tonite. Pick you up at 7:30. Wear something with cleavage. G.**

She laughed. Typical Gavin. Elliot hadn't told her

anything she hadn't already known about her sexy man, except that now she liked him even more. According to Elliot, Gavin had tolerance for everyone—gay, straight, and in between. He treated the old and young with respect. Man or woman, it didn't matter. Everyone at Jameson's loved him. Even Michelle, his "spurned" one-nighter, would say nothing bad about Gavin. About Zoe, on the other hand…

Michelle didn't care for Zoe much. But since they had nothing to say to each other, Zoe could give a rat's ass. Dwelling on Gavin's exes didn't do much but annoy her, so she spent her remaining hour figuring out what the heck to wear to meet Gavin's parents.

After a shower, she dressed in a nice pair of cotton capris and a long, flowy, floral top.

A dark-blue Charger pulled up in her driveway. Showtime.

Gavin got out and walked to her door.

She watched him, thinking he looked thinner. The poor guy.

She opened the door, not prepared for the huge hug he gave her. "*Oomph.*"

"I missed you." He tucked his head into the crook of her neck and breathed her in. "Ah. Eau de Zoe." He pulled back and looked at her with smiling gray eyes. "So, after my parents, we on for another round of Mistress Z Schools Her Naughty Schoolboy, Volume 2?"

She studied him. Something was off. "You named our sessions?"

"Ooh. Sessions. As in, plural." He wiggled his brows, and she saw the old Gavin, all smiles and laughter.

"You okay? I missed you at the gym."

"I won't lie. I felt like shit for two days. But I'm better now." He looked into her eyes again. "Seriously. I'm good."

"Well, that's too bad."

He raised a brow.

"Because I have nothing to do with *good* boys," she said, all innuendo.

"Oh. Right. No, I'm bad. So bad." He put her hand between his legs, where she found him growing larger, filling out her palm and then some. "My balls are so blue, baby. You have no idea." He nipped her throat. "While recuperating, I had a lot of fantasies about tying you up."

"Me?" came out in a squeak.

He laughed. "Oh yeah. But you have to earn it. Let's see you dance at my parents."

"Huh?"

"On my puppet strings." He held out a small padded shirt.

"What's this?"

"This is called payback. And a chance for utter annihilation against the enemy."

"I thought we were going to dinner with your parents."

"Oh, we are. All of us are. You, me, and Zoe Jr."

She stared at the padded shirt, realizing it was actually a shirt with a fake pregnant belly. "Huh? Oh no. No way. I can't meet your parents pretending to be pregnant!"

"Sure you can. Look. I have to win this thing. It's a point of honor. Besides, they can take a joke. Trust me."

"No."

"Honey, you do this, I'll give you so many orgasms tonight, your legs will fall off."

She laughed. "Um, I need those legs." Then she realized she'd have an excuse to spend more time with him without seeming desperate. "Hmm. Well, there's one thing. If you promise to go with me tomorrow and help, I'm in."

She'd expected the guarded expression on this face. "Go where? Help with what?"

"A blind yes or no, Smoky. What's it going to be?"

He narrowed his eyes, but she refused to budge. "Fine. I'm in."

"Great." She gave him a wide smile. "We can't be up too late tonight. We have to be there early tomorrow morning. And I'll need you for most of the day. Until at least four."

"Fine. Sure. Put this on. We get one over on my mother, and you will have achieved legendary status. Oh, Theo and Hope will be there tonight too. They're in on it."

"Great. How is it I'm the last to know?"

"Come on. Let's do this."

After putting on the padded shirt and covering it with her own, now showing off her—*oh dear Jesus*—baby bump when she shifted just right, they walked to his parents', taking their time while Gavin told her what to say. Goodness, but the elder Donnigans lived maybe minutes away from her house. She'd had no idea. A large tan-and-black Craftsman with a wide, cozy, wraparound porch, a double garage, and a nicely manicured lawn greeted them.

"They live here?" The house had to be worth more than a solid mil.

"Yep. We grew up here, but my mother's been updating it for years. The place looks a lot different than it used to. I think I told you Mom sells real estate. She's friends with a lot of bigwig designer types." He sighed. "Frankly I liked it more when the floor was covered in Legos, but you'll probably like it."

"Why?"

His hand went to the small of her back. "Because you're a chick, and chicks dig designer places. Now try to be subtle about that bump, okay? That shirt is perfect, because it kind of masks the bulge until you drag the fabric back. Then it's baby time." He chuckled.

"I cannot believe you talked me into this." She had a sudden case of déjà vu, remembering how she'd get swept up into her sister's antics.

"Hey, I have no idea what I'm walking into tomorrow with you. Consider it worth it. Now, like we practiced on the way over. Try to be a little creative."

Stung, because Aubrey had always said the exact same thing to her when it came to lying, and especially to their parents, she growled, "I can act."

"Sure, baby. Sure you can." *Patronizing SOB.* "Pretend you're trying to hide it." He kissed the side of her neck and put a hand over her now-distended abdomen.

She felt a strange sense of excitement, the thought of having a real baby someday jump-starting something in her biological clock, now *tick, tick, ticking* away. *Oh hell.*

Gavin must have felt her tense, because he turned her to face him. "What's wrong?"

"Not much." She smiled between her teeth. "Just pretending to be pregnant for my boyfriend's parents, whom I've never met."

"Oh, that." He shrugged. "You'll do fine." He rang

the doorbell. "Remember, act natural. Scared and pregnant, but infatuated with me."

"That's a lot of acting." She paused. "The infatuated part, I mean."

He scowled and rang the bell again. "Smile, damn it."

Hope answered it. She looked them over, then grinned. "Hi, Zoe. I'm Hope. Nice to finally meet you." Then Hope winked at Gavin. "Hey, Big Brother. Welcome. *All* of you."

He nodded, and Zoe prayed the evening wouldn't blow up in her face. What the hell had she been thinking? This would never work. She started to get cold feet.

"No backing out now," Gavin said, taking hold of her arm, leaving her no way to slip into the bathroom and out of that stupid belly shirt. "Remember, I'll pay up both tonight and tomorrow. Swear."

She blew out a breath. "Fine. But if they hate me, it's your fault."

Hope heard her. "Nah. You're good. Trust me, my mother deserves this."

Into her ear, Gavin whispered, "Have I mentioned Hope has mother issues?"

Family drama and lies. The perfect combination for a lovely dinner with strangers. "Awesome."

Once inside the expansive hallway, they turned into an even bigger living room and open kitchen. The house had a mountain-modern look, a combination of Craftsman and old-fashioned, unique decorations in muted blues and browns, accented with reds and oranges. Whoever had done the decorating deserved his or her own design show. Wow. Piper would love this place.

An older man who had to be Gavin's dad smiled at her.

"Hello there." He walked over, same black hair and gray eyes as Gavin. But this man wore khaki trousers and a button-down shirt, comfortable in his casual chic. He also looked excited to be alive, as if happy with himself and his lot in life. For all that Gavin liked to laugh, he sometimes seemed a little jittery, off keel.

"Dad, this is my girlfriend, Zoe. Zoe, Van, my dad."

"Lovely to meet you." Van smiled and accepted the hand she stuck out to him before he could hug her. At least, she assumed he'd hug. He seemed the type. "Linda, Gavin and Zoe are here."

From out of the kitchen bustled an older version of Hope. Still beautiful, but more mature. Theo joined her. It was like someone had copied Van and Linda and stamped their faces onto their children.

"Man, you guys really do all look alike." She blinked.

Theo and Hope shrugged. "What can you do?"

Linda beamed. "Hello, Zoe. Lovely to meet you. Gavin hadn't mentioned a girlfriend."

She watched in awe as he flushed and looked down. If she hadn't known better, she'd swear he felt real embarrassment. "Sorry, Mom. Zoe and I are new. We're keeping things under wraps for a while. Or we were. We felt it was time to meet each other's families."

"Oh?" Linda gave Zoe a kiss on the cheek and a hug before Zoe could stop it. His mother pulled back, alarmed, and glanced at Zoe's stomach, carefully hidden by the swath of shirt she wore. "Is your family here then?"

"My aunt," Zoe said with a straight face, trying to ignore Hope, who remained unnoticed behind her parents with unbridled amusement on her face. "She works in fashion so she's always traveling though. My parents are in Portland. It's just them and me."

Gavin wrapped an arm around Zoe's shoulders and squeezed, supportive. Their gazes connected, and the compassion she saw there, for the loss of her sister, meant more than she could say.

He kissed her temple. "Yeah, Zoe was ripe for the plucking when I found her."

She snorted. "More like stalked. He bugged me incessantly at the gym."

"Ha." Theo laughed. "Figures. He nagged you into a date, am I right?"

"Pretty much."

Van's laugh sounded a lot like Theo's. "That's how I got Linda. Took me a while, but eventually she gave up and said yes."

"Yep." Linda smiled, gave Van a kiss on the cheek, then asked if anyone wanted drinks.

"Just water for us, Mom. Eating and drinking healthy, you know." Gavin squeezed Zoe. "Nothing's more important that clean living."

Van looked surprised. "I'm so glad to hear you say that. I've been on him to try some terrific herbal tea to help with sleeping, Zoe. It's infused with chamomile."

"My aunt loves the stuff. Personally, I'm more a fan of green tea."

"Oh?"

While she and Van engaged in conversation about teas, she noticed Linda watching her and frowning every so often.

Hope gave Zoe a subtle thumbs-up, while Theo and Gavin moved to distract their mother.

When it came time to sit down, Linda gently guided her to a spot. Van sat at the head of the table with Linda to his right. Zoe sat next to her, with Gavin at the other end of the table, just on her left. Across from her sat Theo and Hope.

"I hope pepper steak is okay," Van said. "Gavin didn't mention you being a vegetarian or anything."

"Actually he didn't mention much of anything about you." Linda smiled to take away the sting. "But then, our boy likes to keep things close to his chest, hmm?" Linda glanced down at the more noticeable bulge in Zoe's shirt and stared. "What the…?"

Zoe shifted and tried to hunch over to cover the bump, thinking she just might be able to get away with sneaking off to remove the fake pregnancy. That's if the Donnigan siblings would keep their mouths shut. She could sacrifice a day of Gavin's company and take care of tomorrow by herself. Who did he think he was he fooling? He'd give her orgasms without incentive. Just because. No reason to carry on this charade any longer. And no need to upset his parents.

"Oh, uh, Gavin being quiet is my fault," Zoe ad libbed.

Linda's attention once more fixed on Zoe's face. At this point, Van was frowning at his wife's odd behavior. "You?" he asked.

Zoe nodded and drank more water while Linda passed around the first of the plates. Zoe piled on a small amount of rice and meat. Then a salad and some sautéed vegetable medley. "Yep, me. Oh wow. This looks terrific."

Van smiled. "Thank you."

"I heard you're quite the cook. Gavin can't—"

"He's not very good, no," Linda interrupted. "So what's this about you keeping him quiet?"

Hope coughed. "Sorry. A little spicy, Dad."

"Really?" He glanced at his steak.

Hope coughed again, no doubt trying to cover laughter.

Theo continued to stare at his plate, shooting small glances at his parents.

Gavin nodded, encouraging her. "Don't worry, honey. Nothing you say will upset my parents."

"If you say so. Fine. Well, Linda, it's just, I was embarrassed about my family. And I wanted Gavin to like me and not be scared off by my family. So we decided to keep our new relationship just to ourselves at first."

A glance at Gavin showed him frowning. Oh yeah, Zoe was going off script. She patted his hand, clenched around his fork. "It's okay, Gavin, we should tell them."

"Right. What we talked about." He glanced at her belly.

"No, it's okay." She turned to his parents. Hope and Theo watched, waiting. "You see, my brother is our family's black sheep. We don't talk about him much. He's in jail right now. Not his first time," she said sadly.

"Oh, well." Linda paused in the act of putting veggies on her plate. "Every family has a black sheep, Zoe. That's nothing to be embarrassed about."

"Yeah, Mom? Who's ours?" Hope asked, her tone all innocence.

Linda glanced at her daughter. "That's a good question."

"It's me." Theo sounded bummed. "Because I can't hold down a job."

"No, it's me," Hope argued. "Because I keep dating losers, and my mother thinks I'm an idiot."

Gavin groaned. "Not now, guys."

"Oh, Hope. Of course it's not you," Van tried to soothe her.

"Sure thing. Take Hope's side. Baby girl can do no wrong," Theo complained. "It's me, Zoe. I'm the screwup. I'm on my fifth job this year, though being back at the coffee shop shouldn't count as something new, should it?"

"Ah, I'm not sure…" Zoe trailed off. The family dynamics had started off harmonious and gone sideways fast. Were Theo and Hope acting? She couldn't tell.

"If Landon were here," Linda began, forcing a smile, "he'd—"

"Take charge and tell everyone to shut up and cool off," Gavin said, sounding bitter. "Jesus, Mom. He's with Ava tonight. Let's pretend we can get along without the prodigal son for once."

Shocked at how angry he seemed, Zoe turned to note the surprise on his face, as well as that on the rest of the family's.

"Gavin, it's okay," she said, trying to calm him down. They had her all confused. Should she continue this farce or get him to leave with her right now?

"It's not. My head is all wrong. Theo can't figure out what he wants to do in life, and Hope dates dickheads."

"Gavin…" Van started.

"My father thinks tea and meditation will make it all better. And my mother just wants her kids to be better than Aunt Beth's so she can win Mother of the Year again."

"Amen to that," Hope said.

"That's enough, young man," Linda snapped—clearly where Landon got his authoritative tendencies.

"Really, Gavin." Van looked disapproving.

"And then I had to go and get you pregnant," Gavin continued in a loud voice.

Everyone stopped talking. Stopped moving.

At the sudden silence, he sat back and covered his face. Man, was he good. For a minute there she'd totally believed he wasn't acting. "Shit."

"That *is* a baby bump I felt earlier," Linda exclaimed.

"What?" Van looked baffled. "What is everyone talking about?"

"You're kidding." Theo gaped. "So there really is a baby? Sorry, Gav. I overheard the truth a few nights ago, when you were talking to her on the phone." Another skilled liar in the clan.

Hope sighed. "Well, at least now I'm not the biggest moron in the family."

Zoe wanted in on the game. "No, I think I am. Because, well, Gavin…" She paused, every eye on her. "It's not yours. It's Mark's."

He froze. She knew mention of Mark—who he saw as a potential rival—would startle him. She'd made his reaction more authentic. Nice.

"What the hell are you talking about?"

"Who's Mark?" Theo asked, staring from Gavin's cooling expression to Zoe's fearful one.

Casting her eyes down for a second, she said softly, "A man I shouldn't have anything to do with."

"Are you fucking with me?" Gavin said, his voice rising. "'Cause that shit isn't funny."

"Oh, Gavin. It's not my fault. I didn't want to tell

you this. And not here. But…I tried not to, but I-I love him."

"Mark Swanson?" he asked in a voice a pitch higher than normal.

Hope and Theo resembled onlookers at a Ping-Pong match.

"No, you idiot," Zoe shouted, totally in tune with Gavin's shenanigans. "My brother, Mark!"

Everyone sat in stupefied silence before Gavin put his head on the table. Theo burst into hysterical laughter. Hope didn't seem to know what to think and stared at them.

Van and Linda didn't know where to look or how to act.

"Did you know about this?" Linda sounded half strangled.

"Hell no," Van said, absurdly calm. "Let's all take a minute and just—"

"I'm not keeping it. My brother's baby? I can't!" Zoe yelled and raced off into the bathroom, slamming the door in her wake. *Holy shit, I channeled Aubrey.* She could almost feel her twin laughing like a loon, so at home at anything having to do with theatrics. The strange connection made Zoe smile, then laugh. Her goofiness soothing the nerves once again racing up and down her spine.

Zoe lost the belly shirt, now dressed once again in the shirt over her flat tummy. Such a terribly dramatic exit. She took a well-deserved bow.

And if the Donnigans didn't hate her after her masterful audition, she'd ask for seconds on the pepper steak, because the one bite she'd taken had been delicious.

Gavin slowly raised his head, admiring the chaos Zoe had left in her wake. Out-fucking-standing. His parents were talking over each other in their haste to understand. Theo wouldn't stop laughing, and Hope didn't seem to realize it had all been a huge fabrication. The golden moment had been the introduction of Zoe's incestuous, jail-ridden brother, of course.

She'd hit him in the ego with that reference to Mark though. Nicely played.

Gavin stood to go get her when she entered the room. He could tell right off she'd removed the fake belly. He tapped his glass with his fork. "Everyone, quiet please."

His mother and father glared at him. Not amused, apparently.

Zoe came to stand next to him. "I'm sorry, Gavin. But I can't keep my brother's baby and raise it as our own. Not even for you, the man I love."

He got a weird tickle at the confession, fake though it was.

Theo went into another gale of laughter. This time, Hope joined him.

"Classic!" Hope erupted into giggles. "Oh man, Mom. If you could see your face!"

Van sighed. "I thought so."

"Oh, you did not," Linda snapped. "You bought into this stupidity like I did." She turned to point a finger at Zoe. "And you...you lied to us. With him."

"Yes, yes I did." Zoe reached for his hand and gripped it tight.

So, not as sure of the outcome as he'd told her to be. That was all right. Her payback for freaking him out about Mark.

"But sugar pants," he said to her, "with all that Federal Reserve money Mark stole, we'll be set for life if we raise his quadruplets."

"That's true," Zoe said, rubbing her flat stomach.

Van guffawed. "Jesus, that was good. You totally had us going. Not exactly the incestuous part, but the pregnancy."

His mother still hadn't cracked a smile. Then he realized. "Oh, I know what this is. You now have to acknowledge I'm the new master. Say it, Mom. Come on. I, Linda Donnigan, do announce a new winner…"

"Yeah, Mom," Hope said.

Theo added, "Say it."

Linda grumbled, then begrudgingly stated, "Gavin Donnigan, I hand over my crown. I now proclaim you king and Zoe queen of this year's prank wars. Now that's it, you three…four." She included Zoe. "No more screwing with each other. And Zoe, come here. I won't bite."

Gavin gave his lying, two-timing, brother-sexing girl a full-on mouth kiss, one with a little heat, before letting her go.

Flushed, she glared at him before joining Linda. "I—"

His mother had the nerve to pat Zoe's stomach before she nodded. "Sorry. Had to make sure."

At which point everyone burst into laughter once more, Zoe too. Once they calmed down, Zoe introduced herself properly and answered his mother's hundred-and-one questions about her life—how they'd met, her hobbies, and maybe even her shoe size. Gavin wasn't sure; he'd zoned out by then.

But all in all, the night had been a huge success.

After downing large amounts of pepper steak, the family centered around the kitchen island for dessert and coffee. The dessert was a sumptuous crème brûlée. Gavin's father had painstakingly poured it into individual ramekins and encrusted the sugared tops with his mini-torch. One of Gavin's favorite desserts since he'd been a kid. He'd even helped his father make the dessert a time or two. Well, more like he handed over the ramekins, but that counted.

"Thanks for dessert, Dad."

"But of course. Anything for my son, his girlfriend, and our pretend grandbaby. Was it a boy or a girl?"

"A girl. We called her Zoe Jr."

"Oh please. What's this 'we'? Are you suddenly French?" Zoe asked, standing next to Linda by the sink as she dug into her serving. "Van, this is amazing. Oh my gosh, goodness, topped with crunchy sugar." She swallowed and moaned, then pointed her spoon at Gavin. "But in regards to tonight's performance, I was blackmailed into helping. Totally against my will."

"Well, I'd say you more than held your own." High praise from Linda. "Nicely done, honey."

"Thanks." Zoe looked proud.

And right then and there, Gavin wanted to yank her away from everyone, haul her over his shoulder, and take her home. Then not leave the bedroom for weeks. She fit him, his family, hell, his lifestyle, perfectly. She didn't ask for more than he wanted to give. And she made him want to do anything just to see her smile.

The past few days he'd meditated—his father was right about the healing power of meditation, but Gavin refused to admit it to the old man—talked to Lee some more, and in general took time for himself. Some long hikes along the ocean, on wilderness trails, away from people.

He had to stop flying off the handle and freaking out about surviving. He knew that. It was too late to jump on a bomb and sacrifice his life for the greater good, to join his friends in service to their country. Suicide had never been an answer he'd consider anyway, not since arriving back home.

No. Gavin had survived. Now he had to deal with it.

The past few months, he'd been doing much better. Healing, until Nicole forced him to confront losing his friends. He couldn't run from it forever. Especially not after tonight. Seeing Zoe with that pretend baby gave him all sorts of crazy ideas. Glimpses into a future he still didn't know if he deserved, but one he'd like to work toward.

They finally said their good-byes after Gavin had pledged, on payment of his life if he reneged, to bring Zoe to their next family dinner. His parents and Hope had hugged her. Theo gave her a shy smile and offered a free coffee next time she came into his shop.

"Your family is awesome," she said with a laugh. The cool night had warmed enough that she only needed a light jacket. June in Seattle promised a return to sunny days and, with any luck, heartier plants to garden.

"Yeah, well, they're something." Gavin held her hand as they walked.

After a moment, Zoe snorted. "Had you going for a minute, eh?"

He groaned. "Go ahead. Get it all out."

"Oh my God. You thought I was in love with Mark Swanson? Seriously?" She laughed at him.

"You just brought that up out of nowhere. It was as stroke of genius, really, because you threw me. Made it more believable."

"I know."

"You're even gorgeous when you're smug. There's no end to your terror, is there, you monster?"

She laughed and swung their clasped hands. "That was so much fun, Gavin. It felt like what Aubrey and I used to get up to with our parents. She always had some scheme or another, and I was always the straight man. Until tonight. Yes." She pumped her fist high. Then she stopped him, her eyes shiny. "Right now, I'm kind of sad. Because I miss her. But I'm happy too. Because that was a good memory." She drew him into her arms, and he went willingly. Then she kissed him. Not a sexual touch, but a loving one that sent his system haywire all the same. "And now when I think of her, I'll also think of you." She smiled. "You made a new memory come alive. Thanks."

"Anytime." He kissed her back, rubbing her stomach. "Is it just me, or was it a little weird with the baby bump?" He stared into her eyes, so blue, so bright.

"It was weird. I mean, I'm not there yet, ready for kids. But when I touched it, I wondered what it would be like."

"With me, or in general?"

They both tensed. Such a stupid question to ask.

Then she smiled. "Both. And is that freaky or what?"

He smiled with her, feeling so much for her he had no

idea what to do with all that balled-up emotion. Gavin cleared his throat. "Speaking of freaky…I believe I owe you something." He moved his hand from her stomach and around her back to her ass. And squeezed.

"Well then, Smoky," she said, her voice husky, "let's go home so you can pay your debts."

Chapter 15

Zoe moaned.

Having already experienced one major orgasm courtesy of her fake baby daddy, she was gearing up for number two. Going without, for just a few days, had left both of them raging to have each other. Once sated, they'd succumbed to what should have been a short nap. Zoe had woken before he did, in the middle of the night, feeling warm and loved in the shelter of his arms.

But was that love coming from her or him? Or both of them?

Gavin hadn't let her dwell on the answer. Instead, he'd tied her up using her pink tights—fetish much?—and set out to destroy her sanity. Her arms spread wide, her legs as well since he'd settled between them, all their important parts aligned, she could only lay supplicant while he teased with a mouth that never quit. He stroked her belly while he sucked her nipples into tight peaks.

"Gavin, come on." She squirmed, ready for him right now.

"I love your tits. They're the perfect handful." He of course measured, squeezing and petting. And torturing her with pleasure. "Not too big or too small. Jussttt right."

She nearly laughed. But he teethed her nipple again. "Okay, baby bear. You had your fun time. Now fuck me."

He kissed his way down her belly, and she felt his grin against her skin. "What a mouth on you. It's no wonder your brother couldn't keep his inmate hands off you."

"Stop," she moaned. "That's just"—her breath hitched—"gross."

"And to think, you don't even have a brother." He chuckled, then shifted to devote his full attention between her thighs. He sucked her clit and licked her, sliding hands up her thighs.

"Gavin, please."

He continued to go down on her, adding his fingers. First one, then two, into her slick, hot sex. He pumped in time with his mouth, until she writhed, on the cusp of orgasm.

"I'm so close. Oh please, Gavin, in me," she rasped, not sure she could wait.

He moved in a blur, one moment licking her, the next pushing that thick, long cock inside her. All the way, so very deep. She stared into his eyes as her body clamped down on him.

"Yeah, come, baby. Come hard," he growled and thrust faster, harder.

Her climax took her breath away, as did the intensity of his expression as he rode into an explosion of ecstasy and affection.

"Coming in you. Oh fuck." He shoved one final time and swore again, giving her everything as they lay joined, face-to-face, heart-to-heart, their bodies completely in tune.

He moaned and gave a few more short thrusts before stilling completely, wrung dry.

She could only lie there, trying to breathe while her brain reset.

After a moment, he untied her hands but remained joined with her.

"That was…" He sighed, then kissed her. "Incredible."

"Yes." She wrapped her arms around him, stroking the base of his neck and sending him into shivers. Smiling, Zoe confessed, "It's always better when you're inside me when I come."

He nodded. "I know. Me too."

They stared at each other.

"I don't want to go," he said softly. "Is that bad?"

"Is it bad I don't want you to go?"

His relieved smile made her fall that much harder. Zoe had a bad feeling she seriously loved Gavin Donnigan.

But then his smile faded. "Zoe, I want to stay over tonight. But, well, I have issues."

"Issues?" Probably a discussion they should have when he wasn't buried inside her. "Maybe we should clean up."

His eyes brightened. "Great idea. Let's take a shower."

He withdrew, yanked her to her feet, and hustled them into the shower. He got the water nice and hot, then held the curtain for her to precede him.

She did and found her back pressed against the tile wall while Gavin made love to her mouth. When he pulled away, she felt unsteady on her feet.

"Man, coming in you is like nothing else. It's seriously nirvana."

She took a deep breath in, filled her lungs again, then let it out. "I like it too." She hugged him, feeling the water sluice down her body, cool in contrast to his heat. "I like you wet."

His wide smile turned into a laugh. "Isn't that my line?"

"Ha."

"Yeah, well, it's true. Shower wet, or sex wet." He kissed her again, cupped her breasts, and groaned. "You were so great tonight. And I'm not talking about you coming over my cock either."

"Gavin."

"And still, she blushes. You're so beautiful." He quieted. "But those issues we need to talk about. I want to sleep with you. As in sleep in bed, at rest. I mean, I have from the first. But I didn't want to be pushy, make you feel like I was moving too fast. This is your place. I respect that."

She smiled and stroked his hair. "I know, baby."

He swallowed, closed his eyes, then opened them. "Shit. You are making this really hard to say."

"What's wrong?"

"What's wrong is that I want to make love to you all over again, but we need to talk."

"So talk."

He looked uncomfortable, and she stopped teasing. "Gavin, you can tell me."

"I, ah, well, sometimes I have nightmares. I wake up yelling, sometimes screaming. And I didn't want to freak you out."

"Oh." And how that must have hurt to admit. "That's okay."

"Well, the thing is, I don't want to hurt you."

She froze. "Huh?"

"If I wake you up, and I'm moving around or something, just let me thrash. Don't try to wake me. One time I woke up swinging and nearly hit Landon. But that was when I first got back. Since seeing this counselor guy, I actually don't have a lot of nightmares anymore. When I do, I normally wake up on my own. Nothing violent or anything, but it freaks Theo out." He made a face. "We share a room since he can't handle living with Mom and Dad anymore."

"Oh." She thought about it. "I'm game. Let's try it."

"You sure? It's okay if you want me to go. I won't be upset or anything."

"No." She kissed his warm mouth. "I like being in your arms. Or is that bad to admit?"

He eased against her. "Hell no. That's exactly what I wanted to hear. So let's finish getting clean, then go to bed."

"Sounds good." A big turning point in their relationship. The sleepover.

She let him wash her hair because his big hands felt awesome massaging her scalp. But Gavin didn't stop there. He took a long time washing her breasts, making sure not to miss a spot with all that soap. And her belly, her legs, her ass.

"This is the best ass I've ever seen," he said, standing chest to chest against her as he cupped her butt in his hands. He kissed her, then lifted her against the wall.

"The water's getting cool," she managed in between kisses.

"Better get you warmed up. Wrap those ankles behind my back. Yeah, like that."

A few minutes later, panting and dirty all over again, she agreed. "Shower sex, definitely a yes."

"Definitely." He panted. "Now let's clean up for real and hit the sheets. I think I'm too exhausted to dream tonight."

"Me too." She yawned, turned off the water, and stepped out of the shower. "But we need to be at Josh's house tomorrow at nine."

"Huh? Who's Josh?"

"Some guy."

She had a hard time focusing as they dried off, then stumbled into bed. She fit in his arms like the perfect piece in a puzzle. Zoe sighed and put her head on his chest, listening to his heartbeat. She felt the kiss on top of her head and snuggled into him.

"Josh?" he whispered.

She slurred back, "Cleo's brother. You'll see."

Staring at the mounds of dog shit all over the guy's lawn, Gavin wanted to strangle Josh Brewer, cop or no cop. No wonder he hadn't locked his back fence. With the many minefields all over the place, the guy was in no danger of criminals underfoot. Because whatever made that yard mess had to be *huge*.

"This? This is what you tricked me into doing with you? Cleaning up the dog piles from a crappy lawn?"

"No. Our job is to take care of Mauler."

He blinked. "Who?"

She opened the back door with a key, and a black Great Dane lumbered out. It had pointed ears and a white diamond on its chest. The damn thing came to Zoe's sternum.

"Hey, Mauler."

It woofed in a deep bass and rose to its hind legs, planting its paws on her shoulders while it licked her.

She laughed and stroked the thing's huge head.

"Whenever you're done dancing, want to introduce me?"

At the sound of his voice, the dog left Zoe's shoulders and growled at him.

Whoa.

"Mauler, be nice. This is Gavin." She drew the dog toward him, holding it—being dragged by it—by the collar.

Gavin did nothing to alarm it, holding out a hand to let the dog sniff. After a few moments, the dog licked his palm. Then, to Gavin's dismay, it stuck its huge head in his crotch. Hard.

He moaned and clutched himself while Zoe laughed.

And she laughed a lot, not a soft hint of amusement, but a deep belly laugh.

When he could catch his breath, he scowled and said, "Glad you think this is funny."

"S-sorry." She wiped her eyes. "There's just something about a nut shot I find really funny."

"Nut shot?" He blinked, now able to focus past the pain between his legs.

Mauler had gone to add to the mess out back and returned with a happy grin.

"Appropriate, eh?" She watched the dog and shook her head. "I'm going to have to let Josh know his new guy isn't doing his job. He hires someone to clean up his yard every few days."

"There's a business for that?"

"Yep. Come on, Gavin. This is Seattle. There's an entrepreneur born here every minute."

"True."

"Now let's go feed Mauler and make sure his water bowl is full. Josh will be back later today. I volunteered for dog-walking duty and fun time with Mauler because Cleo was busy. You remember Cleo."

"Your best friend, the cutie with the mouth. Yeah."

"So glad you noticed."

He smiled at the bite of jealousy he liked to believe he heard. "Hey, she's cute. You're gorgeous. Now tell me again why Officer Josh isn't minding his own dog."

"He's working out of town at the moment. Helping a buddy in Idaho. Don't ask. I don't know the details. What I do know is Cleo and Matt, her other brother, have been caring for Mauler at Matt's place. But Matt had to go away this weekend, so Cleo asked if I could swing by if Matt dropped him off here. Because Josh will be back today, and she's busy with something else."

"My head hurts from that convoluted explanation, but okay. So let's go entertain Mauler. Great name for a dog, by the way."

"I like it."

"You would. What's your nickname? Bruiser York?"

"Only at work."

"And in bed," he added under his breath.

"What was that?"

"Nothing, Mistress. Nothing at all."

After she'd gathered the leash and a few dog treats, as well as some bags for any more of Mauler's piles, they moved back into her car, with Mauler sprawled across her entire backseat, which she'd covered with an old blanket.

"I see you've done this before." He sat in the passenger seat, hoping the dog wouldn't drool all over him.

"Yep." She smiled. "I don't have a pet right now, but I'd like to get one someday, when I have more time." She gave him a side-look. "Or when I get a boy toy to

take care of him. You know, make love to me, rub my
feet, cook my meals, take care of the dog. Maybe even
clean the house for me. The important things."

"Going down on you?"

"I said make love. Same thing."

"That's true." He winked, amused that she constantly
blushed when talking about sex. This from the woman
who'd worn a boobless bustier. "And we all know how
much I love making love to your fine, delicious, p—"

"*Gavin,* I get it." She cleared her throat.

"I was going to say person. Geez, Zoe. Get your mind
out of the gutter." Mauler barked. "Now let's get going.
You heard the dog."

They drove toward an off-leash dog park Zoe wanted
to take him to.

"Gavin?"

"Yeah?"

"How did you sleep last night?"

He turned to her and smiled. "Better than I have in a
long, long time."

"No nightmares?"

"Not a one." He paused. "Except when I saw your
hair this morning." She snorted. "I didn't want to say
anything, but a rat's nest comes to mind."

"I'm the nightmare?" She laughed, cheery, a spark
in her eyes. "Try your breath, buddy. It was like Satan
vomited in your mouth and then set it on fire. Burned my
eyebrows nearly off when you rolled over and huffed a
good morning."

"See, now that was clever. I can't understand how
you could think only Aubrey was the creative one in
your schemes. You? Straight man? No way."

She paused, and he wondered if he'd made a mistake mentioning her sister.

But Zoe's slow smile enthralled him. "She'd have liked you, Gavin."

"I know I'd have liked her. But not more than you."

She took his hand to her lips and kissed it.

Not to be outdone. Mauler leaned forward and slobbered a tongue in Gavin's ear.

"So romantic. Not. Ew," Gavin complained and wiped his ear, shoving Mauler's huge head back and scratching his ears. Secretly, he thanked the dog. Because if Mauler hadn't made that move, Gavin might have done something stupid. Like told Zoe how much he cared for her. How he thought he might…love her.

And wouldn't that be a disaster?

Zoe spent the next week with Gavin. They worked separately, of course. But she met him at the gym for workouts when he could squeeze her in between clients. For all that he'd said he hadn't intended to work at the gym as long as he had, he seemed a natural fit for training. The gym patrons loved him, and so did Mac.

For her part, she loved watching him move those sexy muscles. The man could seriously rock those gym outfits. Unfortunately, Mac now seemed to have a store of red gym shirts in all sizes, so Gavin had no choice but to wear them.

The prank wars had managed to come to an end. Landon was still incensed that he and Ava hadn't been invited to the pregnant dinner prank, but whatever. Gavin and Zoe reigned supreme. Ava told her Landon had actually been amused by the whole thing, especially about Linda losing to the "new girl."

Today, Sunday afternoon, Gavin planned on spending the day with Theo while Zoe spent some much-needed girl time with Cleo. Piper had extended her East Coast trip through July, so only Cleo and Zoe shared Sunday tea and cakes in her flourishing garden.

"So, tell all," Cleo ordered as she munched on a Twinkie.

"Really? I made scones." Zoe frowned. "You didn't have to bring your own snacks."

"Snack *cakes*. And sorry, but those scones taste like paste. Use sugar next time. Here. Have a Ho Ho."

"What did you call me?"

Cleo shook her head. "I think all that sex you're having has messed with your funny bone. You and the jokes lately."

"Good, aren't they?" Zoe bit into a scone. Cloe didn't know what she was talking about.

Cleo laughed. "They're so bad they're good. You look great, Zoe. And you're always smiling. I think Gavin is turning you into a real girl. I'm glad you have him, though I miss hanging out with you."

"I'm sorry."

"Don't be. I know what it's like. All that newness, the excitement, getting laid after an eternity of cobwebs taking root in your hoohah."

"Oh, that's an image."

Cleo laughed. "Ain't it though? That's a Scottism."

"So how is he?"

Cleo sighed. "Still in Germany. Still not coming home yet. It's weird how his orders keep getting delayed. But if the Army needs him there, then that's where he has to be." She shrugged. "So tell me, how are Sir Gavin and his fine ass today?"

"I knew it was a mistake to have you join the gym."

"Zoe, my God. The man's ass should have shrines and statues built to worship it. Two round, rock-hard globes of that magnitude… Just…amazing."

"Stop."

"So do you ever just want to climb him and put a flag between his cheeks, then do a big old Matterhorn victory dance? Like you've conquered Mount Donnigan, all by yourself?"

Zoe choked down a blueberry and had to hold herself, laughing so hard it hurt while Cleo continued to poke fun.

"Are you finished?" Zoe wheezed.

"My work here is done." Cleo wiped her hands and took another Twinkie from the pack. "I'm kidding, of course. I like Gavin a lot. I'm so glad you guys are together. He's good for you."

Zoe had gone back and forth about it, but Cleo's advice would help. She bit the bullet. "Can I ask you something?"

"Shoot."

"When did you know you loved Scott?"

Cleo gaped. "The l-word? *No way*."

"Answer the question."

"God, this is so great! Okay, okay. Um, Scott. I think it was after we'd been going out for a few months. But remember, we didn't see each other as much as you and Gavin do. Those first few months after I met him, he would come to visit his sister while looking for a place to rent. He still had weeks before his reassignment to Fort Lewis. I want to say it was our fifth or sixth date. I knew he was cute and I liked him, but until he told me he loved me, it hadn't clicked." She sighed. "Then it was magical. And that was two years ago tomorrow."

"So romantic." Zoe had met Scott a few times. He'd seemed nice enough, a good-looking, hardworking soldier. But something about him... She couldn't put her finger on it. Maybe because Cleo was so outspoken and vibrant, and Scott had been so quiet. A little boring, to tell the truth.

"Yeah. So you and Gavin. You're feeling it for him? That's a big step."

"I know." Zoe kicked back and put her feet up on the chair next to her. "At first it was his charm. He nagged me into going out with him."

"For which I still think you're nuts. One word out of his mouth, and I'd have been all, 'Hell yeah!'"

"Then it was the amazing sex. Because, damn, it's amazing."

They high-fived.

"But being with him is so much fun, Cleo. I like him as a person. He's down-to-earth, exciting, kind. He makes my heart race whenever I'm near him. And when I'm not, I want to be with him. I've never felt like that before. Typically I just want my space. But he sleeps over, and I'm totally fine with that."

"Wow. So you love him."

"I really do." *Oh my God. I do.*

"Now hold on. I can see the panic setting in. Zoe, think. You love this man. Does he love you?"

"I don't know. Maybe."

"Does it matter if you do and he doesn't?"

"Hell yes, it matters."

"Okay, yeah, that was dumb. I guess what you really need to ask yourself is, what are you going to do about it?"

The million-dollar question.

"I don't know." Zoe sighed. "I want to tell him."

"So do it."

"He's always giving me these intimate smiles, these looks. He strokes my hair and kisses my head when he thinks I'm sleeping. He makes me coffee first thing in the morning. He's not threatened by my job or success. And he's not trying to outdo me with a career."

"He can't be making a ton of money at the gym," Cleo pointed out.

"I know. I asked him about that. He's comfortable, and he gets a small amount as retirement."

"He's retired? I thought he was thirty-one."

"Thirty-two. And it's a medical retirement. We don't talk about it, but he got shot when he was in the Marine Corps. I think he saw a lot of bad stuff there."

Cleo's eyes widened. "Wow."

"Yeah. He has money to go to college if he wants, from the military. But it's not bugging him that he didn't go. And I couldn't care less. When we go out to do stuff, he's always happy to pay. But I insist we take turns."

"Of course you do." Cleo rolled her eyes.

"But that doesn't bother him. He's really mellow about a lot of stuff. It's like he balances me out."

"That's great. Still doesn't answer the question about what you plan to do with the big love bubble in the air."

"I want to tell him. Should I tell him? What if I do and he doesn't feel the same? That's a lot of pressure."

"Look. Just because you say it doesn't mean he has to say it back. You've always been bold, not afraid to take a risk—at work. Why not apply the same policy at home? That's logical, right?"

She nodded, thinking. "And it's something Aubrey would do." Lately, around Gavin, she felt more okay about her sister's loss.

Cleo tapped her fingers on the table. "Do you think Aubrey would like him?"

"Yes. I bet she'd have met him and made a play for those delicious glutes from day one," Zoe teased.

"You got that right. You're just lucky my heart is already taken."

"By hunky Mark Swanson, you mean?"

"Hey." Cleo stuck out a cream-covered tongue.

"Ew."

"That's what you get for ruining my sugar high. Yeah, if you put a muzzle over Swanson's mouth, then he's a god. But he talks too much and has too high an opinion of himself to ever be Mr. Right."

"That's true."

They sat in silence while the sun blazed overhead, butterflies danced in the garden, and the scent of lavender and honeysuckle mingled in the air.

"You're going to tell him, aren't you?"

"I have to. I'm all full inside, and I need to say it. Go big or go home, right?" WWAD—What Would Aubrey Do? She'd tell the man to his face. In big, bold letters. *I. Love. You.*

Zoe could do that. And she planned to. Later that night.

But when Gavin joined her that evening, they laughed through a really bad Netflix movie. Zombies and zoos and leprechauns were too much to fit on any size screen, big or small. Then Gavin showed her what the *chill* part of that idiom should be used for. A glorious interpretation of the number sixty-nine.

After which, Zoe fell asleep and didn't wake up until her alarm the next day.

―◆◆◆―

At the early-morning Monday meeting, Cleo asked, "Did you tell him?"

Zoe flushed. "We got distracted."

"Mm-hmm."

Monday night followed the same pattern. But this time it was Gavin getting out of the shower and strutting around in front of her that provided the distraction.

Tuesday night, he didn't sleep over.

Wednesday night, they worked out together, a run around Green Lake that turned into a race. She didn't like him winning and rubbing her nose in the loss. That was her right as ultimate victor. So she'd challenged him at home in games until she won. Then she made him feel the pain through another night of delayed gratification that had him begging her to finish him.

Thursday, after bringing him dinner at the gym and going home—to her home, now one she kind of thought of as theirs—she waited. She bit her nails. She weeded and re-weeded. But when he returned, tired and carrying a red rose for his thorny chick of a girlfriend, she chickened out.

"You okay?" he asked as they snuggled after another

marathon session of sex. God, if she hadn't been on the pill, she felt sure he'd have knocked her up already. The man had stamina.

"Great." She sighed. "Just tired."

"Oh, okay. You've seemed distracted lately."

"Only in the best way." She kissed his chest and hugged him.

She heard him sigh and felt him kiss her hair, then hug her back.

She woke later in the dark of early morning to him moving around, restless in his sleep. He moaned, and at first she thought she'd hurt him.

"Gavin?"

Groggy, she didn't realize he'd been caught in a nightmare until he started moaning, "No, no. Don't get in the truck, damn it. It's not safe."

She quietly crept out of bed and got him a cup of water. When she returned, she turned on a side light and saw him clearly distressed.

"Oh, Gavin. It's okay, baby. I'm here."

He didn't seem to hear her, frowning and straining. Then… "Zoe?"

Was he dreaming or awake? She stayed where she was, by the side of the room, just in case.

"Fuck, Zoe," he muttered. "Don't go."

She blinked, surprised to find her eyes burning. She sipped the water she'd fetched for him and watched him ease back to sleep. When she'd given him a good ten minutes, she moved tentatively back to his side.

He turned over, took her in his arms, and sniffed her neck.

"Gavin?" She stroked his hair.

He sighed, murmured, "Zoe," then fell back asleep.

"I love you." Finally. She had no trouble saying it. And he couldn't hear her.

She didn't have to work hard to imagine what Aubrey's response to that would have been—*Lightweight*.

Chapter 16

SATURDAY EVENING, GAVIN GLANCED AROUND ZOE'S FANCY work party, holding a glass of punch in his hands. The nonalcoholic kind, available because apparently he wasn't the only person who didn't want to booze it up. Then again, with the many doctors hanging around the place, it made sense some of them might have to be sober if on call.

"So, Gavin. Nice to see you again." Mark Swanson—his archenemy. Not really, but he felt the need to laugh.

"Igor. How's it hanging?"

Swanson blinked. "Igor?"

"The brains behind the Frankenstein outfit, or so I once witnessed during an incredibly bad musical about the guy, the doctor, and a bean."

"Ah. So I'm not the only one who was forced to watch *Frank Got Beans But Igor Got Brains*. A theatrical masterpiece, or a mistake? You decide."

Gavin blinked. "You saw that?"

"My sister forced me to go as her date many, many years ago. Sadly, hers stood her up when he realized she planned to watch a musical. Of course, the guy was sixteen and had better taste than amateur theater. I wanted to scrape my own eyes and ears out after the spectacle."

Gavin laughed. "It was awful. My mom made me go because my little brother played the part of the bean."

Swanson actually cracked a smile. "Does he still act?"

"Hell no. Thank God. Just graduated high school a few years ago. He's figuring out what to do next."

"A rough age." Swanson nodded, then glanced around. "I take it you're here with Zoe?"

"Yep. She's…mingling."

"She's good at that. Keeps the peace around here often enough." He grimaced when Cleo Brewer walked by. "Unlike others." Beyond the loathing in the guy's eyes, Gavin saw heated interest. *So, that's the way the wind blows, eh, Swanson?*

"But she's so tiny," he said, lifting his glass at Cleo. "How can she make trouble?"

Swanson raised a brow. "You've met her, and you have to ask?"

Zoe's friend had a mouth on her Gavin appreciated. "Good point."

"So what do you do at the gym, Gavin? I know you were a Marine."

"*Am* a Marine."

"Excuse me?"

"Haven't you heard, once a Marine, always a Marine?"

"No, but then, I've been stuck in business and medical texts for way too much of my life, it seems. I tend to miss a lot."

Gavin considered the guy. Medical texts? "Are you a doctor? I thought Zoe said you were a clinic manager."

"I am. I tried a year of medical school before realizing it wasn't my thing. So I went back for a master's in business. Now I'm invested in the medical group, doing my best to get rid of our laggy procedures. Our clinics are top-notch."

"So I hear." Zoe loved her job. "But you know, you don't look like you spend too much time in books. You look like you work out."

"It helps me balance. The job can get stressful."

"I'll bet. Being in the Corps, exercise was part of the job. But I've found it really helps me deal with everything better."

Swanson nodded. "Exactly. There are so many benefits to exercise and good nutrition. I'm not talking diet fads or fitting into pant sizes. I'm talking about the coexistence of physical and mental well-being."

"Huh. Makes sense."

As Swanson continued to preach, Gavin agreed with everything the guy had to say, adding his own two cents from what he'd learned in the Corps and seen at the gym. Shocker, but Swanson wasn't such a loser after all. And he didn't seem to be panting after Zoe, so Gavin didn't have to hurt him. Another bonus.

"I'm so sorry, Gavin," Zoe apologized as she breezed up to them. "Dr. Garrison would not leave me alone."

"Want me to shove his head through a wall?" Gavin asked lightly. Meaning it.

She blinked. Swanson narrowed his eyes.

"Ah, no. He was actually badgering me, in a good way, about some training concerns. But I told him to talk to Mark." She smiled at Swanson. "You're welcome."

"Yep. A real ballbuster." He grunted and turned to leave. "Oh, Gavin, if you ever feel like a game of racquetball, let me know. I'd love to continue our conversation. You have a real head for exercise science, you know. Some great ideas in an area I've been pursuing with one of our CEOs. I'd like to talk to you again about it."

"Thanks. Great. Yeah, I'm game for racquetball. Never played, but it can't be hard to learn." He held up his drink in salute as Swanson left, then turned to see Zoe staring at him. "What?"

"Did Mark just ask you out?"

"Shut up, Zoe."

She laughed, wearing some clingy thing she called an A-line skirt and a silk blouse he wanted to peel off her shoulders, then lick his way down to her creamy center. Better than a Twinkie any day, and that was saying something.

"Gavin. Stop looking at me like that."

"Like what?"

"Like you want to take me into the nearest closet and do me."

"Oh? And where would that nearest closet be?" he teased. The Hotel Monaco was a pretty fancy place. The party had gourmet appetizers, high-end booze, and classy service. No question the medical group wanted to hold on to their people, as Zoe had told him on the way over. Nothing but the best for the doctors and staff at SMP Medical.

With Zoe running all over the place hobnobbing with folks, he'd had little to do but look pretty standing next to her. Then she'd gone off to talk to someone else, one of her bosses.

So except for his time with Swanson, Gavin had been bored stiff.

But Zoe had asked him to come. She'd made it seem like no big deal if he didn't want to, but Gavin took it as a sign she wasn't embarrassed to be seen with him. Sure, he was good looking. But she wanted him around her brainy friends and coworkers. She introduced him like he was God's gift to fitness, respect in her voice, warmth in her gaze.

His stomach fluttered as he looked into her eyes. So fucking beautiful. And his.

The unworthy thoughts he continued to have came less of late. He thought he might finally be getting over the past. Even the lone nightmare he'd had last week hadn't been so bad. Because Zoe erased the past, promising a future.

He hoped.

God, he hoped.

She continued to stare at him. Then she nodded and plucked a glass of champagne and a napkin from a tray going by. "Follow me. I was here earlier and found out where they're keeping our coats. In a small closet in the back. But there's a restroom near it that's not too crowded."

"Oh, sure." Gavin followed her down the side hall toward the restrooms. Then she turned again. "Before that, let me show you something."

With any luck, her etchings, he thought with amusement.

She turned once more, and he wondered where the hell they were going. This seemed like a section of more conference rooms, from the map he'd seen earlier. "Um, Zoe?"

"Almost there." She headed for a door that looked slightly ajar. Then she opened it to reveal a large, dark room set with long tables and chairs. As he'd figured, a conference room.

She pulled him in with her, then shut the door behind them. Except for the faint light from the hallway under the door and the exit sign above it, he couldn't see too much. But Zoe had been cast in a faint red light, and adjusting to the darkness, he could make her out no problem.

"O-kay." Gavin glanced around. "So what did you want to show me?"

She sighed, then reached under her skirt and stepped out of her panties. "Do I need to spell it out for you?"

He stared, wide-eyed. "Um, no. Not at all." Suddenly rock hard and ready, he took her drink with his and set them down on a nearby table, then came back to her and unzipped his pants.

"No, let me. You deserve it."

"I do?" He moaned when she crouched in front of him and took his dick between her lips. In a darkened hotel conference room anyone could walk into? *Jesus*. "Oh, I do." He watched her bob over him, pulled back her hair to see her more clearly, then started fucking her mouth.

His personal fantasy come to life.

She closed her eyes, her lashes thick shadows on her cheeks as she blew him. And fuck, those ripe lips sure the hell hugged him in all the right ways. Ready to come, and from a few tugs of her mouth. She stroked him with her tongue, and he jerked.

Zoe gave a low moan.

"Not yet," he whispered, more to himself than to her. He stopped her with a hand to her shoulder, then pulled out. "Turn around and bend over."

She licked her lips and looked up at him. So damn sexy. Smiling, she rose and slowly pulled her tight skirt up over her hips, exposing that perfect ass.

He prodded her to step away from the wall and bend over, then widened her stance. With her skirt around her waist, she had more room to move.

And after shoving down his pants and underwear, so did he.

Gavin was breathing hard, trying to be quiet, and so turned on it hurt. "You ready for me, baby?" he whispered as he prodded her pussy from behind.

So hot. He pushed, slowly, and had no trouble sliding inside her. "Touch yourself. Get off when I fill you up," he ordered.

She reached down, pleasuring herself.

"Stroke that tight little clit," he growled. "Harder."

Gavin fucked her. Rapid strokes in and out as he pumped into his lover. Her breathing grew choppy, her tiny moans louder.

"Shh. Quiet, Mistress, or someone will hear us. You ready to come, baby? Because I'm just about there."

"Yes, yes," she hissed and rocked back, slamming into him. And then she must have come, because her body clamped down hard, and she shuddered.

Gavin had reached his end. "*Fuck*." He gripped her hips tight while he came, the climax stretching out while he gave her everything he had. He couldn't have said why he was so shaken, but when he withdrew from her, he felt unsteady.

She took the napkin he'd settled over the champagne glass and wiped herself, not looking at him. Zoe stepped back into her panties, straightening her skirt and clothes, then flipped her hair back.

She looked like a siren, her lips shiny, her eyes sparkling, smiling, bathed in the faint red light from above.

He just stared at her, bemused.

"Here. Let me tuck you in." She gently put his cock back into his underwear, swiped a finger through his slit, then licked it.

"*Zoe*." He kissed her while she set the rest of his clothes to rights. When he pulled back, he continued to stare down at her, unable to look away.

"Gavin?"

"Yes?" he answered, his voice as hushed as hers.

"I love you." Her eyes widened, as if surprising herself. "You don't have to say it back. I just wanted you to know."

Then, before he could even think of how to respond, she pushed open the door and left him alone with a dozen empty tables and chairs in the darkened room. Just a glass of champagne, a cup of punch, and a dirty napkin for company.

———— ⁓ ————

Gavin didn't say much to Zoe on the ride back to her house after the party. She didn't know if she'd freaked him out or what, but she'd had to tell him. She couldn't keep it in any longer. He'd been so patient, so great about coming with her to a work party. No complaints, no acting wounded or jealous surrounded by a bunch of pompous doctors and heads of departments. Just a sweetheart who supported her. Had she said the word, she knew he really would have put Garrison's head through the wall.

But now, in the privacy of her home, she didn't know if she'd done the wrong thing.

"Are you okay?" she asked him.

He didn't speak, just walked down the hallway, stripping out of his sport coat, shirt, and tie. Talk about looking like a million bucks. He was hot in shorts and T-shirts. But in a suit? She'd had to tell more than one person at the party to keep their grubby hands to themselves. Yeah, because that's how Zoe 2.0 rolled. No messing with her man. Telling him she loved him after boning him at the company party in a dark room. Classy all the way.

She covered her eyes. No more drinks for her at work. Oh God.

Yet she couldn't blame the alcohol on her need to be honest with Gavin. He meant so much to her. She was done playing it safe. The time had come to put her heart on the line. Go big or go home. WWAD? Yeah, her sister would be proud of her for sharing herself, for experiencing love and taking a risk.

She kicked off her heels, yet her steps grew smaller as she moved to accept the repercussions from taking that big risk.

When she reached the bedroom, she wasn't prepared to get jumped.

She shrieked as Gavin grabbed her in his arms and proceeded to seduce her. More like ravage her. He didn't say a word. He just kissed her, stripping her out of her clothes with a fierceness that shocked and delighted her. Then he had her on the bed, and he was pounding into her while he stared into her eyes. He never looked away, and his honest need aroused her unbearably.

She came just as he did. His carnal agony lit her up, and she squeezed him tight and dragged him down for another kiss. She nipped his lip, tasted blood, and kept kissing him, only coming up for air when he let her.

Time meant nothing as they rolled around, tasting, touching. He had her on her hands and knees, his fist in her hair dragging her head back, the bite of pain both scary and fulfilling at the same time. Then he took her harder, hammering while he said naughty, raunchy things about what he planned to do to her for their encore.

She came crying his name, barely able to stay upright. But he didn't come. Instead he pulled out and flipped her onto her back.

"We're not done," he growled.

And round three started.

She lost track of time after that.

But sometime in the morning, with the sun shining through her window, she woke to a gentle kiss on her lips, a hand stroking her hair. "Gavin?" She blinked her eyes open.

He smiled, his gaze soft. "Hey, baby. I have to get to the gym. I'm on today. I'll see you later, okay?"

"Hmm. Love you."

He didn't answer. And then he was gone, and Zoe went back to sleep.

———

Gavin didn't know how to feel, so he concentrated on work. He helped those at the gym, worked through some training clients, did his own reps and a short three-mile run—for speed, not endurance.

But the run only made it easier to think about Zoe and her scary-ass confession.

I love you.

Well, fuck. Hadn't he been feeling the same for awhile now? So in love with the witchy black-haired woman that he'd do anything to make her happy? She talked about Aubrey with tears in her eyes and a smile. She confronted pushy doctors and put them in their place. She'd totally taken on his family and conquered Linda, for God's sake. The queen of victory had actually conceded the win to Zoe.

So unselfish, so sweet, so cute in her bloodthirsty need to trounce him at something, then taunt him about losing.

How could he not love a woman like that?

But he was scared to tell her the truth of his feelings. To open himself and give her his whole heart—because it wasn't whole yet. He still hadn't talked to Nicole, still hadn't gotten the closure that might finally allow him to put his past to rights. How could he give Zoe any less than all of him? He needed to talk to Lee again. He might have gone to Ava, but he didn't want her talking about him to Landon. He knew she'd try not to, but she worried about him almost as much as his big brother did.

No, he didn't want to pressure Ava with his issues. He wanted to stop being a damn pussy and just meet Nicole for lunch. Something simple, where they could share stories about the guys, laugh, maybe cry a little because yeah, they all missed them. Then they'd all move on, Gavin would realize even fucked-up dudes needed love, and he'd get the balls to talk Zoe into a more committed relationship.

Hell, as it was, they spent all their time together. He practically lived at her place, and going out and doing fun stuff together wasn't cheap. He needed to figure out what to do with the rest of his life, career-wise. He had a few thoughts about that, but he'd been putting everything off, knowing he needed to be settled in his mind first.

"Yo, Gavin. You got a minute?" Mac asked, and Gavin realized he'd run a good mile past his three-mile cutoff.

"Sure." Gavin slowed the machine to a walk, then stopped it and stepped off.

Mac handed him his towel, and he dried off his sweat and guzzled his water bottle.

"Mac?"

Mac was staring at him. "Oh…sorry. You look good, Gavin. A little frazzled, as usual, but not like you used to be."

Gavin shook his head.

Mac frowned. "What?"

"Mac, I hate to tell you this, but I'm not interested. I have a girl, and I'm pretty sure Maggie loves you. If you left her for me, it would break her heart. Plus, I hear Elliot already called dibs."

"You are such an asshole." Mac scowled.

Gavin laughed. "That's what they say."

"Follow me, shithead." Mac hustled away from the main gym down the corridor toward his office.

Gavin followed, hoping he hadn't done anything to piss Mac off, yet not really caring, his mind too full of Zoe and how to make things right with her.

"Sit down."

"You don't outrank me, Top." Top—what Marines called master sergeants in the Marine Corps.

"Funny. Sit your ass down, *please*."

"Okay. But I'm kind of sweaty. But maybe you like that, some Gavin left in your office after I'm gone, so you won't miss me as much. Kinky, but okay."

Mac threw up his hands. "Fine, stand." He started laughing. "You are *such* a pain in my ass."

"I live to serve." He saluted, then started stretching so he wouldn't tighten up.

Mac rounded the desk and leaned against the wall, watching him. "Maggie thinks I should fire you."

Gavin froze. "What?" What had he done to annoy Mac's cute little wife? He couldn't think of a thing.

"I know, right? She's insane. But don't tell her I said that. She's pregnant, and her hormones are all over the place."

Gavin sat on the floor, his legs outstretched though he no long reached for his feet. "Did I do something wrong?"

"No, no. Shit. I'm not saying this right." Mac pulled a chair close and sat, and they both pretended it was because he wanted to, and not because the guy's knee ached. "Gavin, you're the best trainer in the place. You work harder than everyone else. Everyone loves you, and the only reason you don't have as many clients as Pete is because Pete has the schooling behind him that some of these folks want."

"The science behind the training. I get that." Which was why he wanted to talk to Mark Swanson again about the guy's thoughts on exercise science.

"You're smart. You could have that if you wanted. What I'm trying to say is, are you happy here? Maggie thinks it's too easy for you, and that if I fired you, you'd go back to school or get a better job that would truly suit you."

"But I love my job here." Surprisingly, he did. He'd finally found a place where he fit in.

"Good." Mac smiled. "But be honest. It's easy, isn't it?"

"Yeah. But sometimes easy is good. You know I was in a bad way when I started working here. I couldn't handle anything too taxing. *Exercising* my demons away, helping others do the same, it was just what I needed."

"You're not the only guy who came back with issues, you know. We all have them. Even my man Shane."

"Really?"

"Well, maybe not. He's a real Boy Scout. But he also isn't as good at taking orders as he needs to be sometimes. And come on, he was an officer. He and Landon didn't really work that hard in the Corps."

"True." They smiled, bonding as only hardworking enlisted men could.

"I really appreciate you taking me on, Mac. I know Landon put you up to it."

"Landon? Nah." Mac leaned back. "I was—"

"Please. Don't bullshit a bullshitter. I know it was Big Brother behind it. But you said yes. So thank you."

Mac flushed. "No big deal. It's not like you're a charity case, you know. In case it's escaped your notice, I pay you for the work you do."

"Well, since that pay is so minuscule, I did wonder."

"Ha-ha."

"Look, this place has given me the time and space to get my head together. I still want to work here, but I do have plans to do a little more in the future. So tell Maggie not to get rid of me yet."

"Christ. Don't breathe a word of what I told you to her. I'll just say we talked and you're good. If she knew

I'd told you what she'd said, she'd feel terrible, then cry forever. And man, I do not do tears well."

"Oh. Right." Maggie was a beautiful, sweet, and now apparently pregnant blond. He didn't think he'd be able to handle seeing her cry either. "We never talked. Everything is just great. I love my job." Mac nodded, so Gavin continued. "You're giving me a raise, and—"

"Whoa, Marine. Nice try."

Gavin stood slowly and shrugged. "It was worth trying." He laughed and pulled Mac to his feet. "Thanks, old man. I really do appreciate everything."

"Shut up. Old man? I'm only a few years older than you, asshole. Now get out of my office and go home. You stink."

"Thanks so much." Gavin headed to the door, then turned and paused. "And Mac? You know, if you let us go back to our own gym clothes, or at least get a better color and T-shirt manufacturer than this, I might be able to quiet those rumors about you and Elliot hooking up." He plucked his shirt. "The material sucks, and the color is awful."

Mac shot him the finger. "Ha-ha. But come on, man. They're Marine Corps colors. Scarlet and gold."

"This is fire-engine red with white lettering. Try again."

"Fine. You're not the only one to complain. We'll go with the more expensive shirts," Mac said with disgust. "And now I'm going to have to hear it from Maggie and Shane about how wrong I was. I hate the smug *I told you so*."

"You and me both, brother." Gavin whipped off his shirt. "But damn. I told you so a month ago."

"Get out."

"Leaving, boss, leaving."

Gavin left, a new spring in his step and a real sense of purpose. He needed to talk to Lee, and to keep it together with Zoe until he did. He might not be ready to tell her what was in his heart, but he could show her. As he had been by loving her until neither could move, night after night.

He glanced at the clock on his way back to her place…to home.

And smiled as he thought about his plans for tonight—that bottle of chocolate syrup, the whipped cream, and Zoe. Three of his favorite things.

Chapter 17

ZOE DIDN'T KNOW WHAT WAS GOING ON WITH GAVIN. He hadn't said anything about her two *I love you's* so she hadn't asked. And that was uncharacteristic of her. She knew that, but she also knew Gavin needed to be handled differently. He'd grown more skittish, sometimes lost in thought, and startled easily. But he didn't suffer nightmares, so she had a feeling his preoccupation had to do with something else. Her? His job? That weird get-together he'd had with Mark this morning?

Since Gavin was currently at his counseling session, she couldn't ask him about it. Mark had been close-mouthed about their time, only saying that Gavin was indeed a natural athlete. And if the bastard practiced much more, he might actually beat Mark—an impossible feat.

She grinned at the thought, then sobered. She couldn't keep ignoring the big, fat loving elephant in the room. She'd said *I love you*. He had not, and now he spent each night making love to her until she could barely breathe.

Granted, she had no complaints about being screwed silly six ways from Sunday, but at some point they would need to talk before his dick fell off.

Gavin texted her that he planned on staying at his home alone this evening, needing to think through some things Lee had told him.

No problem, she texted back, wishing he would share

more but understanding he needed his space to work things out. Dealing with Aubrey's loss got easier as time passed, but Zoe still missed her twin. Gavin, on the other hand, had seen some horrible things and was dealing with a lot more than just death. She never wanted to be someone who'd stand in the way of another getting well. The fact that Gavin sometimes seemed withdrawn or quiet about his therapy told her he felt some sense of shame about it. Oh, he joked and acted as if outing himself as the "family screwup" was no big deal. But she knew better.

She called Ava and asked about getting together tonight for some wine and received an invitation to join Ava and Landon at Ava's place. Zoe arrived two hours later after stopping by the store for a plate of cheese and crackers. Following the directions, she walked past the unlocked iron gate and entered the covered condo hallway, then walked down the stairs to Unit 2B. She'd barely knocked before Landon answered, grabbed the food from her hands, and pointed her to the shoe mat. "Shoes. Coat goes in there." He nodded to the closet, then walked away with the tray, already prying it open.

Ava stood in the living room with her hands on her hips, her hair pinned up in a loose bun, glasses on her face, looking very doctor-like, even in loose cotton pants and a sweatshirt. She huffed. "Great hospitality, Landon. Good Lord. No wonder no one ever invites us over."

He shrugged and shoved a large square of cheese in his mouth. "Meh. She's family. She doesn't care. Besides, I'm starved. You wouldn't let me eat any of our dinner, and she tempted me with cheese. I blame both of you," he said with his mouth full and disappeared into another room.

"Come in, Zoe. Sorry about that." Ava waved in his direction.

Zoe laughed. "No problem. You really do have to feed them, Ava. Or you chance them going rabid."

"Seriously." Ava laughed and removed her glasses. She set them on the table behind the couch and motioned Zoe in. "This is the place. Living room here. In there's the tiny galley kitchen." She pointed to the doorway where Landon had disappeared. As Zoe neared, she saw the main area had an L shape. The living room bent into an open dining area with a large pass-through, making the kitchen visible. But what struck Zoe was the lovely view of the park and Lake Union past the wall of windows behind Ava.

"Wow. That's so pretty."

"Yeah. The condo isn't that big, so we'll eventually need to move. But we have kind of a flipped unit. The living area and kitchen are here, and downstairs we have a bedroom, study/spare room, and two bathrooms. Oh, and if you need it, the upstairs bathroom is over there." She pointed to a small powder room behind Zoe.

"This place is beautiful."

"We like it." Landon came out of the kitchen holding a glass of wine for her. "Sorry. Low blood sugar. Gavin's like this too, so if he's acting like a jerk, feed him." He grinned at Ava. "Or give him lots of sex. That helps too."

"Landon." Ava sounded scandalized.

"Easy, Doc. I'm kidding." He leaned closer to Zoe, winked, and whispered, "I'm really not."

She chuckled. "Thanks, Landon. For the wine, not the advice."

"Whatever. I tried to help."

Ava yanked him out of her way. "Put on some music, would you? And Zoe, sit down."

"I just came for wine and company. You didn't have to go all out."

"I made a late dinner, and I've been wanting to have you over for a while. Two birds, one stone. Have you eaten?"

"Late night for me too." She sipped the wine, a crisp white, and sat at the dining table. Landon put the tray of goodies, now accompanied by olives and some more crackers, in the center of the table and joined her with a beer. "Gavin is staying at his place tonight, processing his therapy," she blurted. "I'm worried about him."

"We all are," Landon said quietly. "Lee's been good for him, though. Christ, you should have seen Gavin when he first got back. He was a hot mess."

"Landon." Ava joined them at the table. "He's not wrong about Lee, though. I told Gavin about him, in hopes Gavin would see him. He's been going weekly for a while, but you know that."

She nodded. "Gavin told me."

"Lee's been a real help. Not that Lee told me; it's just what I've seen from Gavin. He's more open, clear, and he seems a lot more in control."

"His nightmares aren't so bad either," Landon said. He stared at Zoe.

She didn't want to tell his secrets, but Landon and Ava loved him. She wanted their help to better understand.

"He's had one with me. Just one. And he's never been violent. He just seems sad."

Landon sighed. "Yeah. Poor little brother. He ever tell you what he saw over there?"

"No. And I didn't ask."

"Good," Ava said. "He's not ready to share that. He might never be ready. And that's okay. That doesn't mean he doesn't care enough to share, but that he shouldn't dredge up that kind of trauma."

"But he doesn't share anything about his feelings either. I mean, I know if he's happy and laughing. He's fun to be around, and he's always in a good mood. Unless he's quiet. We rarely argue."

"He's always been like that though," Landon mused. "Even before the Marine Corps, Gavin wasn't the type to fight a lot. He's sneaky and jokey, always laughing. When he gets really mad, he's super quiet."

"I don't think he's been mad at me. Confused, maybe. Quiet, like he's not sure what to do."

"Oh?" Ava leaned forward.

Zoe glanced at Landon. She really didn't want to confess what she'd said to Gavin in front of his brother. To Ava, a girlfriend, sure.

"Hell no. I'm not going anywhere if we're talking about Gavin. I've stayed out of his business for way longer than I planned, because the doc here"—he pointed to Ava—"told me to butt out. But I'm worried too, damn it. Zoe, what the hell is going on with him? He seems so much better, almost normal. But he's also more withdrawn, and I'm a little freaked. I've caught him at the gym a few times this week just staring at nothing."

Zoe tilted her head back, praying for strength. She

stared at Landon, then Ava. "You have to promise not to tell anyone. Not anyone. Gavin already knows, and that's who needs to know."

"Fine, fine." Landon said. Ava nodded.

"Well." Zoe swallowed a mouthful of wine. "Last weekend we went to a work party. He came with me, all dressed up. And wow, he was so handsome. So sweet to come there as my date."

"Oh, I'd love to see him in a suit."

"Ava," Landon growled.

"Sorry. Go on." Her eyes sparkled.

Zoe smiled. She wanted that, what Landon and Ava shared, with Gavin. "Well, he was just so great. And I've been feeling close to him for a while now. It just popped out. We had a moment alone, and then…I said it."

"Oh." Ava sighed.

"What? Said what?" Landon looked baffled.

"For someone so smart, you can be so dense." Ava rolled her eyes. "She told him she loves him, bonehead."

"Oh. *Oh*." He gave a wide smile. "Nice."

"I didn't give him time to say it back. It just kind of popped out. But after that, we haven't talked about it. I said it once more. Not to make him say it back, but because I feel it." She sighed. "I really love him. I don't want to stress him out or anything. But I think I did. Because he's been quieter since."

"So how did he respond?" Landon asked. "He just ignored you telling him that? Yeah, that can hurt." He glared at Ava.

"Please. I did not ignore you. I broke up with you, but you refused to accept it." Ava sniffed. "I apologized later."

"True." He grinned, then turned back to Zoe with a straight face. "Zoe, Gavin is really into you. Big time. I know my brother, and he's never, ever been so into a chick before. But he's—"

"Messed up." Zoe tapped her temple. "I know. He told me. I don't care. We're all messed up."

"Well, I was going to say 'traumatized by what he saw and did overseas,' but 'messed up' works." Landon nodded. "I wasn't privy to the missions he went on. But I heard about some of them. And I have to say, Little Brother was a badass. He did some serious shit over there. Specialized shit, where people died and small regimes disappeared before they could become bigger problems.

"Did you know he was healing from a punctured lung when his friends got blown up? Yeah, some dumb luck all four of them happened to be back in the same province, assigned to the same unit after being separated for a few years. Gavin's all stoked to see his best buds, and then he's on a mission where he gets hit. The guys razzed him about it, he told me. Then they left him, and he never saw them again."

Landon coughed, cleared his throat, and continued. Ava put a hand over his, and he squeezed it. "I don't know what Gavin goes through, but I know how hard it was for me to lose Marines I was responsible for. You feel this huge weight, like how come they died and not me? Like survivor's guilt. Then you think, *Shit. I didn't protect them*. And it's just as bad. More guilt."

"Landon's got issues, but his are nowhere near what Gavin suffered," Ava said softly. "*Suffers*, probably. Lee is helping him, but I don't know that Gavin's ever going to be what he was before he left."

"He shouldn't be," Zoe said. "Life changes all of us."

"Yeah." Landon gave a wan smile. "Exactly. Don't give up on Gavin, Zoe. He's gotten so much better. He's good with you."

"But you can't stay with him out of fear he'll get worse if you leave," Ava said bluntly. "Gavin's mind and moods are Gavin's to deal with, not yours, Zoe."

"I know that."

"Good. Sorry. It's my therapist coming out," she admitted with a wry smile. "I see too many spouses or partners of military men and women who take on too much. And that hurts everyone."

"Do you think I'm hurting him by being too emotional or something?" Had her loving him hurt him?

"*No*. Not at all. You're the one constant in Gavin's life that's turned him from being uneven to stable."

Landon nodded. "He might act like a goof, but he's pure to the bone, deep down. He'd do anything for the people he cares about."

She sniffed. "I know. That's part of why I love him so much. I want to help, but I know he has to help himself. I just don't want to be another responsibility. He should want to be with me."

"He does." Landon nodded and patted her shoulder. "Seriously. He's so gone over you. He smiles all the time. Well, when he's not being a moody bastard. Give him space, and he'll be good to go in no time."

"And if he isn't," Ava added, being the voice of reason, "it's not because of anything you did, but because Gavin can't be there in here." Ava tapped her head. "Now how about we talk about something else, because I am not having Zoe cry on me twice within two weeks."

"Huh?"

Zoe laughed and accepted the tissue Landon pulled from a nearby box for her. "How about we talk about a mutual hottie we both know and love?"

"Zoe, I don't know if I'm comfortable with you calling me that in front of my intended," Landon said.

"I meant Elliot Liberato. That hottie."

Ava straightened, her smile bright. "Oh, you met Elliot?" The oven timer dinged. "Landon, get that. So how did you meet my cousin?"

Zoe told them about him messing with Mac, and they all had a laugh. A shared meal and stories about Ava's funny cousins and Zoe's funnier twin added an intimacy to the evening. One Zoe had been missing.

She only hoped she'd get to share more times like these with Gavin.

Gavin had sat through Lee's therapy. He'd asked Lee a bazillion questions, speaking in terms of Zoe and Zoe's loss as if it were his own. Though Lee hadn't thought Gavin ready to face his friends' loved ones, it had obviously helped that Gavin had talked about them with Zoe.

Except he hadn't. And he also hadn't been so chatty about his past. Unlike Zoe, Gavin had buried his feelings like a scared jackass.

But he couldn't go to Zoe half a man. No longer could he ignore that broken part of himself. So he would confront his fears, as Zoe had. He'd arranged to meet the ladies on their turf.

Nicole had invited him to meet with her and Amanda, Luke's sister. Nancy, John's mother, hadn't been able to come, too busy looking after Jane, her granddaughter and John's daughter.

Gavin had dressed in jeans and a nice shirt, along with a sport coat. He wanted to look nice for his friends' families. And he promised himself to be normal with them, to give them the closure they—and he—needed.

Nicole answered the door right away. She looked thinner and more tired than she used to. But joy glowed in her big, brown eyes when she saw him. "Gavin!" She hugged the breath out of him, and he thought today might not be so bad after all.

He followed her inside and saw Amanda, looking so damn pretty, so much older, and so like Luke.

He blinked, forced himself to man up, and said, "Well, well. Look who's all grown up."

"Dummy." She wiped her eyes and blew her nose into the tissue she'd been holding. A big box of them sat on the coffee table. Good thinking. "I just saw you two years ago, and I was already this grown-up and gorgeous."

"Obviously." He smiled, loving her attitude. Still the same Amanda. "And what's this? A ring?"

She smiled, showing off her engagement ring and bringing him up to date on her life. She worked as an executive at a finance place—Amanda had always been a brain—and had found the love of her life. He mentioned the gym, what he'd been up to, but he couldn't bring himself to discuss Zoe. He needed to keep her separate, because he knew if he started talking about her, he'd fuck up everything he'd set out to accomplish today.

Nicole joined them and set down a platter of coffee and cups.

"Damn, Nic. I could have gotten those." He frowned.

She gave him a beatific smile. "I missed you, Gavin. So bossy all the time. And it used to drive Mick nuts when you called me Nic, because he always thought you were talking to him."

"Mick and Nic. Yeah, I know." He chuckled, feeling a stab go right through his heart. Mick and Nic, sides of the same coin, they used to say. He saw the sadness in her eyes, but she muddled through and gave him a watery smile. "Good call on all the tissues."

She laughed and blew her nose.

"You still sound like a goose when you do that."

"Still a charmer," Amanda teased, laughing and wiping away more tears.

"What about you, Nic? What have you been up to?" He hadn't seen her kid. Wasn't sure he could handle it, honestly.

"I've been super busy wrangling a toddler." She made a face. "I was three months along when…well, when Mick left us. I had him last August, you know. He'll be one in a two months." She smiled. "He's just like Mick. Eats a lot, throws tantrums, a real momma's boy." She wiped the tears on her cheeks. "Sorry. I'm not this weepy usually. It's just seeing you brings it all back."

"Yeah." He nodded, his voice gruff. He blinked a lot, trying not to cry.

"Oh please." Amanda shoved a tissue at his face. "It's manly to cry, dipshit."

He chuckled and wiped his eyes. "Jesus. Does your fiancée know what a hard-ass you are?"

"No, and don't you tell him either." She glanced at Nicole. "I—"

"So tell us about yourself, Gavin," Nic interrupted. "Anyone special in your life?"

"What about you?" He ignored her question. "Amanda's got a new man. How about you?"

She blushed. "No. It wouldn't be right."

"Bullshit."

Both women looked taken aback by his outburst.

"What?" Nic leaned back.

"Mick, Luke, and I all knew the risks over there. We'd smoke and joke, but we all knew the score. Whoever made it back had to tell you ladies to move on." He cleared his throat, knowing it shouldn't have been him giving the rah-rah speech. "I'm sorry I wasn't here sooner, and that I missed the birth." He felt like shit. "I-I was in a bad way, and I didn't want you guys to see that. It was ugly. I was a huge ass, more than I usually am." He tried to joke, but it fell flat.

"Oh, Gavin." Nicole touched his shoulder, and it burned through the jacket.

"Gavin, no," Amanda said.

He glanced around, finally seeing pictures of Nic and her baby, of Mick, of all the guys standing arm in arm around a keg. On a holiday, one where Amanda had shown up with a few giggly teenage girlfriends. Nic and her mom and dad with the baby, all smiling. But he could see the grief she carried, a weight around her neck he couldn't make go away.

"Yeah. So you two need to cut that sad shit out right now. Amanda at least has a brain. Shocking but true."

She smiled. "Gavin, not nice."

"But Nic, you're stupid if you hide away. You're beautiful, smart, and you made a great kid." He nodded to the mantel and all the pictures there. "Mick would expect you to go get laid at least."

She blushed. Amanda laughed through tears.

"Well, he would. Always said you were insatiable."

"That's not true."

"No, he said *nympho*, but we all knew what he meant."

Nic smiled, and her joy made him hurt all the worse, because she should have been having a conversation with her husband, not his sorry ass. "Funny."

"I mean it though. The part about you going out and finding someone to love. You're so special, you and Amanda and Jane." John's baby girl, now four or five, if he recalled. "You're the best of them," he said, his voice breaking. He stood and paced. *Gotta keep it together, man. Stop. Now they're crying harder*. "Sorry."

"Oh, Gavin. I miss him so much." Nic went to hug him, and he threatened to break into tiny pieces. Then Amanda hugged him too, all three of them locked in a crying, snotty embrace.

"If you wipe your nose on my shirt, I'll slug you," Amanda said, breaking the mood.

Thank God.

He chuckled and went to grab the tissues, passing them around.

"Okay, Gavin. I'll go out and get laid right away," Nic said and hiccupped, now smiling through her tears.

"Good. You do that."

"You volunteering?"

He must have looked as horrified as he felt, because both ladies started laughing hysterically.

"Oh my God, your face," Amanda said.

"Shut up." This time he did wipe his nose on a sleeve—his own.

"I was kidding, Gavin. Ew. That would be like sleeping with my brother." Nic made a face. "But maybe you should take some of our own advice. Find a nice girl." She narrowed her eyes. "Or have you?"

He felt his cheeks heat. "There's someone special. I like her a lot, but, well…" He shrugged. "She can do a lot better than me."

Amanda frowned. "Is this where we're supposed to chime in and list all your good qualities?"

"Hell no."

"Because no one as handsome, strong, kind, and funny as you should ever have a girlfriend," Nic teased.

"Yeah, those fine manners and that protective streak that any woman would kill to have are so yesterday," Amanda said.

"Stop." He wiped a hand over his mouth.

"And those gray eyes, that firm chin, that—"

A baby's cry saved him.

"Thank God."

Nic and Amanda snickered while Nic went to grab her baby.

"Seriously, Gavin. Let yourself find happiness." Amanda socked him in the arm. "Because if I can get over my brother—the last member of my family standing—being gone, then you can too. How's hunky Landon, by the way?"

He told her about his brother and Ava, about Hope and Theo. She laughed at Theo's orange mohawk.

He glanced around. "What is taking her so damn long?" He was itching to leave, because he felt drained.

As much as he loved seeing his friends' family looking happy and living life, he needed to decompress from the tightness in his chest.

"Here I am. Had to settle him down." She came out carrying a little blond boy. "This is little Mick. I call him Mikey."

"Oh man. He's so cute." *Mick, dude, your kid is incredible.*

The boy saw Gavin and stilled. Big, brown eyes looked him over, and Mikey reached out a hand.

Gavin gave him a finger to grab onto. "Strong grip."

"Like his daddy."

Gavin swallowed the lump in his throat. "So he'll be one in August?"

"Yep. August twenty-eighth."

Mikey reached both arms toward Gavin. The boy let out a garbled command Gavin didn't understand. But he knew what that reach meant.

"Go on." She held the boy over.

Gavin took him, felt the unfamiliar weight of a child, and stared at the boy in wonder.

"Gavin, meet Michael Gavin Lucas Duncan. I also managed to finagle a John onto his birth certificate, but it's a little wordy to fit in there." Nic smiled.

Shocked, he felt tiny hands on his cheeks, then his nose and hair. The boy wanted down, and Gavin followed the little guy's orders without thought.

Then Nic hit him with another emotional two-by-four. "Gavin, can you… Can you tell us if it's true how they died?"

"What?"

"The Marine Corps told us the men were in a routine

convoy when they ran over land mines. That it was all over in an instant. No one suffered. That's true, isn't it? It wasn't friendly fire or a cover-up, and they weren't in agony when they died?"

"Fuck, Nic." She was crying again. Amanda was wiping her cheeks too. "You know I wasn't with them. I was in the medical bay—more like a tent. I was there for two weeks before it happened. Took another four before I could go back to active duty. And even then it was limited." He took a deep breath, then let it out. "But I investigated the hell out of that incident. Talked to the few guys at the back of the convoy who survived. The roads should have been cleared. They still think we got faulty intel, that the insurgents talked to someone inside the camp and knew where we'd be heading eventually. If not Mick and the guys, then it would have happened to another convoy a day later." He rubbed his eyes. "Such fucking bad luck. But they went instantly. No suffering, no pain."

A flat-out lie, because they'd worked on John for hours but couldn't save him. Mick had been thrown from the wreck and broken his neck, his body on fire. Luke immolated. No chance of saving him.

And all while Dumbass Donnigan lay on a stupid hospital cot, hearing the terrible news as it came in, and knowing he'd never see his friends for that promised poker game or their next shared liberty together. It had been the worst night of his life, up there with the first time he'd had to kill.

"I'm glad," Nic said.

"Me too. Thanks, Gavin." Amanda nodded.

"I know this wasn't easy," Nic continued. "And

it might be too much to ask, but we'd like to see you every now and then. We love you, Gavin. We miss you. I know the guys are gone. We miss them too."

"Even Luke," Amanda teased. "Now who's going to walk me down the aisle?" She paused. "I was planning to invite you to the wedding, if that's okay."

Oh fuck.

Nic grabbed his arm before he could flee. "But if you can't, it's okay," she said, as much to him as Amanda, it seemed. "We love you, Gavin. Whether we ever see you again or not, you'll always be a part of us."

"Yeah." Amanda nodded. "We love you. And we're so glad you're okay. With you and us around, the gang is always here with us. You know?"

"I do." He was suffocating. "I, um, I need to go."

"Sure." Nic walked him to the door and tugged him into a hug before he left. "Be happy, Gavin. Have a good life. You deserve it."

He nodded and left, knowing he'd never heard anything more untrue.

Chapter 18

ZOE DIDN'T KNOW WHAT TO THINK. SHE'D GOTTEN A TEXT from Gavin saying he'd see her in a few days, that he had more to work out. Then nothing.

A call to Ava yielded a similar answer. Gavin hadn't been at the gym either. Everyone wanted to know where he was, but no one had an answer other than the old not-feeling-well excuse he'd given Mac.

Zoe worried about him, but she'd also grown angry. She had no idea what bothered him because he didn't talk to her. She could understand posttraumatic stress issues. The survivor's guilt Landon had mentioned. She appreciated that Gavin had sought treatment for his problems.

But no communication with someone you loved didn't make sense. Would this be the way of their relationship? Gavin had issues, so he'd disappear for days in a cone of silence, and Zoe would just need to deal?

So by Tuesday night, after *four days* of not one phone call, text, or message from Gavin, she'd gone from worried to nervous to angry. And still in love with the jerk.

A knock at her door surprised her. Had Gavin come to beg forgiveness after all?

Her heart thundered as she went to the door, glad she hadn't undressed for bed yet. If Gavin thought they could take up their sexual play without talking this time, he'd be in for a rude surprise.

But the Gavin standing outside her door didn't have sex on his mind. He had a hollow-eyed, gaunt look, and his expression made her want to cry. He cleared his throat. "Hi, Zoe. Can I come in?"

She stood back and let him enter, then automatically locked the door behind him. "Hi."

He stood with his hands in his pockets, so unsure, so…lost.

"Do you want something to drink?" she asked.

"Water would be good."

She grabbed some water and handed it to him. He took the glass, but then he put it on the counter and pulled her in for a hug.

The desperation in the gesture allowed her to swallow her anger. Instead she only wanted to alleviate his hurt. He held on tight, and to her horror, she felt her shoulder grow damp. From his tears?

She pulled back. "Gavin? Are you okay?"

Watery gray eyes blinked at her. "I've been better."

"Sit down." She took his hand in hers and sat with him. "Now what the hell is going on?"

He gave a short laugh, but there was no mirth in it. "God, where to start?"

He sat staring at her, studying her features with an almost hopeless, hungry look. As if she was all he ever wanted but could never have.

"Talk to me. Is this because I said 'I love you'?" She hadn't meant to ask that so soon. "I'm sorry. I didn't mean to put pressure on you."

"But you did. And I'm glad." He held her hand in his. "Zoe, I…" His eyes grew damp again. "Do you have any tissues?"

She hurried to grab a box and handed them to him.

"Thanks." He blew his nose. "Been doing this a lot lately. Crying. I fucking hate it."

"Oh, Gavin."

"Don't be nice to me," he warned.

"I won't." He was breaking her heart, looking so sad and trying to be so strong. She blinked back her own tears. "So talk. What the hell happened, and where have you been?" *And is this where you break up with me? God, please, no. Not when I've finally found you.*

"A week ago, in a dark conference room in that snazzy hotel at your office party, you told me you loved me."

"I do."

"But you don't know me. The real me." He tapped his heart, looking so sad. "Zoe, you brought me back to life. You make me smile. Make me happy." He sighed. "I wanted to be the guy that does the same for you."

"So be that guy."

"I thought if I could put the past behind me, could move on, I could give you what you need. But I'm such a fuckup. I don't think I can."

Panicked as well as concerned, she just listened.

"I talked to Lee a lot. He thought I wasn't ready to confront the past. That I should learn to cope with it and deal with stress instead. But you didn't. You went straight at your pain head on. You're sad when you talk about Aubrey, but you don't sweep away the hurt." He grew more animated. "You love her; you miss her. You own that pain."

"Yes."

"You still miss her right now, but it's an honest emotion. It's real."

Where was he going with this? And why did he worry her?

"When my friends died, when they got blown up because their convoy took the right trail instead of the left, it was awful. They didn't survive. They were good guys, friends I'd grown up with. Guys I'd spent years in the Corps with. Some I'd even fought back-to-back with through the shit." Tears streamed down his cheeks, but she didn't think he noticed them anymore. He was looking at her, but not seeing her.

"And I was in a med unit. Because I'd been shot on a mission. So they all died, but I survived. But why me? They weren't out doing anything wrong. They weren't crushing the people. Weren't demolishing governments or stealing natural resources. They tried to protect, to do good."

He hung his head in his hands.

She tried to touch his knee, but he pulled away and stood.

"Gavin, I'm so sorry."

"No, I'm sorry. I don't deserve you, Zoe. I knew that when we started, but I thought... I'd hoped maybe I did. So I tried to deal with the past. I went to therapy. I saw Nicole and Amanda, the families left behind when Mick, Luke, and John died."

Oh boy. "What happened?" she asked gently.

"They were happy to see me." He looked puzzled. "Just laughing and crying and pleased that I was there. But I never should have been there. I did bad things, things a good man won't do. I killed people, Zoe," he whispered. "I was the best fucking sniper and special teams guy they had. I did my job. I struck first before the enemy could." His tears came in earnest. "But Mick and the guys, they protected. They helped. They saved lives. And they died. So why did I come home? Why do I get to fall in love with the pretty girl? Why do I get a chance at a future when they're in the ground?"

She wanted to comfort him, but he needed to get this out, a festering wound that would never heal until he did. Or so she hoped. She wanted like hell to get Ava over here, so that Zoe wouldn't do or say the wrong thing.

Then Gavin broke down, just lost all strength and sagged to his knees, his head in his hands. He sobbed. Huge tears that left a gaping hole in her heart. "I don't know. God, I don't know."

She hurried to him and took him in her arms, wishing him all the healing and love she could muster while she rocked him. "It's okay, Gavin. I love you. You're so worth it, baby. So worth it."

He cried for the longest time, and she held him, easing him down so that his face sat on her lap and she stroked his hair. When he ceased, shivering, so still, she eased out from under him after replacing her leg with a pillow.

"Just wait here. I'm going to get a blanket, okay?"

He didn't say anything, which concerned her even more.

She hurried to get a blanket and raced back, not wanting him to leave. Then, with an eye on him, she grabbed her phone and sent a text to Ava, asking her to come immediately, and to bring Landon as well.

Returning to Gavin, she put the blanket over him, then lay down with him and stroked his hair again. He'd closed his eyes, and she thought him asleep.

"I'm sorry."

She started and moved her hands to his shoulders, petting him, offering comfort through touch, even through the blanket. "It's okay."

"I didn't talk to you. I couldn't." He let out a watery breath, then opened his eyes. So tormented, so full of pain. "When Nic and Amanda asked if I had anyone, I couldn't say. I couldn't talk about you. Because when I did, I knew I was wrong. That I shouldn't have you." His eyes filled again. "But fuck it, I want you. I want to be happy. And I know I shouldn't. I'm so weak. I should let you go. Should just let it all go."

"Gavin—"

"But I can't. The guys would kill me if I offed myself. Biggest pussy move there is."

Thank God.

"But I don't know how to be happy. Every time I think I can be, I remember what I am."

"And what's that?"

He didn't answer at first. "Some of them didn't get a fair fight. I cheated. I took them out. And then I survived. Why did I survive?" He closed his eyes. "Jane is only a kid. Nic's baby isn't even one yet. Amanda has no one to w-walk her down the aisle."

She felt so awful for him. No way to help him through this. She had nothing but the truth.

"You listen to me, Gavin Donnigan. I don't know about all that stuff you did. I don't want to know. I don't need to know. I know you.

"The man who makes me laugh. Made me smile when all I wanted to do was curl into a ball and die. You're not the only who feels guilty. I used to think it should have been me who died. Aubrey was funnier, livelier, prettier. She was an artist. I work training people. How creative is that?" She gave a pained laugh and felt his fingers entwine with hers. "But that self-pity bullshit had to go. You and me, we're survivors, that's for sure. And we're strong. And we get sad. And then we get up and go on the next day. We can help people. You do it every day.

"So many people have been worried about you. Your family. Me. The people at the gym. Even Swanson asked about you yesterday. And that's not a burden, buddy. That's a gift. You make people smile and laugh. Nic and Amanda know you're special. Your friends knew it too."

"No."

"*Yes*." She gave him a fierce kiss and watched his eyes open wide before he shut them, shut *her* out. "If they had survived, you'd be up in heaven or down in hell," she teased, getting a faint twitch out of his lips, "and you'd be okay with them living on. Why? Because they were good people, and you're some big jerk? You're just a man with a guilty conscience. Just because your friends didn't do what you did during wartime doesn't mean they never did anything bad in their lives. Stuff they feel guilty for. No one is perfect. Everyone has regrets." She paused. "You know what mine is?"

He opened his eyes. "Me?"

"Yes." She watched him shut his eyes, as if he'd been waiting to hear her reject him. "Not telling you I loved you sooner... That's my regret. It was killing me. I had that love balled up inside me for a while. And then I told you in the tackiest way ever. After sex in a hotel conference room, for God's sake. That will haunt me forever."

He didn't say anything, but he pulled her down into his arms. And he held her there, her head tucked against his chest as they lay on the cold, hard floor.

He had to be uncomfortable. She was. But she didn't move until his breathing evened out. Then she heard a car pull up in front of her house.

She left Gavin lying on the floor, covered in a blanket, and hurried to let Ava and Landon in. She put a finger to her lips and waved them inside.

They took a few steps in, where they could see Gavin sleeping on the floor, tear tracks evident on his cheeks.

"Aw, Bro. Damn." Landon looked so sad.

"He'll be okay." Ava stroked his arm. "He's got us, and Zoe."

"Yeah. Come here." Zoe drew them with her into the kitchen and whispered what had happened.

"He wasn't ready," Ava murmured.

"Shit." Landon kept looking back in to check on his brother.

"Why don't you go sit with him?" Ava said kindly.

He left them.

Zoe started crying. "I'm sorry. But Ava, it was so awful. He's grieving so hard. I felt like my heart was breaking while he cried. And it's just…I love him so much. I felt helpless."

Ava enfolded her in a hug she needed, until Zoe stopped her useless tears. "Sorry."

"That's it. We're going to Costco in a few days, and I'm buying you a few dozen boxes of tissues."

Zoe wiped her eyes. "Now you know what to get me for my birthday."

Ava chuckled, then sobered. "He needed you. He

wanted you enough not to let his guilt get in the way, and that's saying something. Gavin fools everyone into thinking he's fine because he laughs a lot, but that laughter hides a well of pain. I'm not his therapist, but I think Lee would agree he needed this. Badly."

"Really?" Zoe felt a measure of hope.

"This, I think, will be his turning point. Where he can either learn to live with the guilt and forgive himself, or not. And nothing you or I or anyone else does can get him through this."

"That doesn't mean I can't be here, waiting for him to get better."

"You'd do that?"

Zoe nodded. "Well, not 'til I'm eighty. I do have some hope for a life. But I have time, and I'm not going anywhere at present." She paused. "And I know what it's like to hurt so deep inside you think you'll never get past it. But when you do, life is so much sweeter."

Ava hugged her again. "Now *that's* the truth I wish everyone knew."

Gavin felt like shit. He looked worse, and he hated that he'd broken down in front of Zoe. Hadn't he hoped to have the strength to break it off with her? Now he didn't have to. She'd probably never want to see his sorry ass again. *Fuck.* He hadn't just cried, he'd fallen, wept, and snotted all over the place. And man, he was an ugly crier.

Hell.

He sat in Lee's office, a week and two days after his meltdown. At his regularly appointed time. After he'd lost it Tuesday night, he'd slept for hours. Landon had eventually woken him the next day, only to pack his sorry ass home and shove him in bed. Then apparently he and the rest of the family had taken turns watching him while he slept. But not Zoe. She stayed away.

And that stabbed like a knife. Like a fucking KA-BAR through his spleen. He'd say *heart*, but he wasn't sure he had one anymore.

It was like his whole body ached. He had no energy, no desire to do anything but mope. He'd even slept through Independence Day, right through the fireworks last night. No worries about him losing it with those loud booms. Oo-fucking-rah.

But Landon had forced him to get up. Nagged and poked and prodded until Gavin had taken a weak swing at him. "God. I think our cousins hit harder than that," Landon had mocked. "And I'm talking about Cam, the weakest link."

"Dick."

The rudeness had made Landon smile, so Gavin had given him a litany of better, more thorough insults.

"Gavin, good to see you," Lee said.

Gavin sighed.

"Landon, I'd like you to stay."

"Sure."

So fat-ass sat right next to Gavin on the couch, thigh to thigh.

"Move over," Gavin said.

"Make me."

Gavin looked at Lee, then looked at Landon, as if to say, "You see what I put up with? Why I'm more nuts than usual?"

Lee didn't hide a grin for once. "I have brothers too, Gavin. I get it."

"Hey." But Landon moved over.

"I know what happened. Or at least, I heard what happened from others. Why don't you tell me?"

Gavin didn't want to talk in front of Landon. Honestly, he was surprised Lee had suggested it. Then he realized he had nothing to lose. Zoe was gone. He had to live through this mess. Somehow.

So he told it, all of it, and broke down again when he talked about Mick's kid. About Amanda's wedding. About losing Zoe, the reality of that pain making it hard to breathe.

"Now, Gavin. Look at me."

He glanced at Lee.

"How do you feel?"

"Feel? Like a train ran over me. It hurts."

"Good."

Psychotic bastard.

"I told you that you weren't ready for this. That we needed to work on coping skills before."

"Closure. Yeah. Blah, blah, blah. I get it." Which all would have sounded much more condescending if his throat hadn't been so scratchy and his nose so stuffed up from crying like a damn pussy.

"Shut up and listen." Landon smacked him in the back of the head.

But when Gavin turned to swear at his brother, he saw Landon's eyes full of tears too.

"The doc knows what he's talking about. So shut it."

Gavin hadn't seen Landon cry in forever. So he shut up and turned back to Lee.

"Your friends. Mick, Luke, John. They're gone. Forever. And their wives and sisters and children are moving on. Growing. Learning to live and love again. You told Nicole to find someone special. But you aren't allowed to?"

Gavin shrugged.

Landon smacked him again. "Answer him."

"Is this some alternative form of treatment?" Gavin asked, snappish. "Quit fucking hitting me."

"Answer the fucking question."

"Fine. Look, those women are good people at heart. I'm…not."

"Bull." Landon said before Lee could talk. "Whoever was in your crosshairs was not a good guy. So don't sell me that line. You and your stupid, warped sense of fair play. Look, when the enemy is ripe for the plucking, you fire. Period. And you save countless lives from being blown up or tortured the next day when the enemy's plans would have succeeded. You did your job. You killed. You survived. Fucking move on, or put the gun to your head and pull the trigger."

"Landon!" Lee stood up.

Now he's concerned?

"Make a fucking decision. We're Marines. We don't waffle. We don't second-guess. You do or you die. How can you not know that? If it came down to sniping a guy intent on gutting me tomorrow, would you do it?"

"Yes." Gavin didn't have to think about that.

"Then what the hell is your problem?"

"What if they weren't all guilty?"

"What if, what if. We don't play *what if*. We go with our orders and our guts, and we deal. Because *what if* is making you like this." Landon looked him over. "And you hate it, don't you?"

"Yeah."

"I hate it. Lee hates it."

"Well," Lee said. "I don't—"

"Zoe hates it too. She's waiting for you to get your head on straight and go grovel at her feet or some shit."

"She is?" She didn't hate him?

"Dumbass. I told you that like three times already, but you had to go sleep off another emotional bender." He grabbed Gavin by the shoulders and shook him. "That's your redo button. Use it. Get yourself together. Talk to Lee." Landon stood. "No more pity cards for you. Yeah, you were in the shit. Biggest shit there was, I bet. But it's over, Gavin. Decide to heal and move on. But make that decision and stick to it. Okay?"

Staring up at his big brother, hearing and understanding it was okay that he'd come through started to penetrate.

"We love you, Gavin," Landon said gruffly, his eyes still shining. A tear slipped free, and he angrily wiped it away. "Stop with all this bullshit, and get your ass back to the gym before Mac fires you. And for God's sake, get back with Zoe before she goes out with that loser who keeps sniffing around her asking what's wrong."

He blinked. "Swanson?"

"I don't know his name. But Ava said he was sexy. Not cool." Landon grabbed him by the collar and hauled him to his feet, then crushed him in a bear hug. Two seconds later, he left Gavin alone with Lee.

Lee shook his head. "Your brother. Quite a powerhouse, hmm? And Ava's marrying that?"

"Yeah." Gavin chuckled. "She is. She loves the guy. Go figure." And if she could handle Landon maybe, just maybe, Zoe could handle him. "So I guess I should talk some more?"

"That might be good. Tell me how you feel."

"I feel…" He thought about everything he'd been through, a wringer of an emotional mess. His past, his present, his possible future.

"You feel?"

Gavin looked at Lee and smiled. "Better, Lee. I feel better."

───※───

It had been two weeks since Zoe had seen Gavin. She missed him like crazy, but according to Ava, he was healing. Apparently, he'd really needed to let this pain go. It had been traumatizing but therapeutic, in a way his therapist—and Ava—hadn't figured.

Then too, apparently Landon had gotten through to his brother with some head slapping and blunt words, more wacky therapy Ava was convinced would only work with someone as hardheaded as a Donnigan.

Zoe sighed and looked up at the periwinkle-blue sky, thankful to Hope for the invitation to finish with her friend's gardens before the older lady returned. Hope thought Zoe had done such a great job that she'd invited Zoe to finish it. And needing her own kind of therapy to deal with missing Gavin so much, fending off Swanson's attempts to give his new people extra training over everyone else, and dealing with her nosy aunt's need to know if everything Cleo had told her was true— *last time I share with Cleo*—Zoe needed the break.

She hummed as she put a new lily in the container Hope had indicated. Apparently Hope was supposed to do it, but she'd killed off the last one after not watering it enough and not transplanting it in time.

Zoe cringed at the thought.

"Now what would you do if you were taken unaware, on your knees, and your attacker was a huge, buff guy standing just behind you?"

She blinked. Gavin?

"Yep. He's just waiting for you to turn so he can—*shit*." He dodged the trowel aimed for his groin—not that she would have hurt him for real—and disarmed her, then took her down to the ground, as gently as possible.

"Ah, is that how they normally interact, dear?" Peggy Bower asked.

The seventy-three-year-old owner of the house and her nephew stared at the spectacle outside by the flower bed.

"Um, not exactly," Hope said, wondering what the hell her brother thought he was doing. Had he lost his mind completely? *Romance, Gavin. Be romantic.*

Peering through the blinds from the side window of the house, the three of them had thought to watch two parted lovers unite. Hugs and kisses, some tears, all set against the backdrop of the neighborhood's most exquisite gardens.

Hope sighed. "It'll get better."

"I hope so," Mark said, shaking his head. "I'm a little disappointed in Zoe, I have to say. I expected much more than this. And really. Do any of us buy that she really could have taken Gavin out with that trowel? I've seen him on the racquetball court. He's a beast."

His aunt shook her head. "No. But the girl has moves."

"Shh." Hope held a finger to her lips. "Let's watch."

Zoe looked like she wanted to flip him to his back, but he held the upper hand. "Gavin?"

"Hey, Pink Yoga Pants." He smiled down at her choice of attire, approving. "How are you?"

"Isn't that my line?"

He held her wrists down, hoping she had no real plan to escape. God, she looked good. Gorgeous, sexy, a little bit thin, but if she'd let him, he planned to fatten her up as soon as he could.

He sighed, so in love with her. And *trying* to be worthy. "I'm so sorry, Zoe. It was not one of my better days."

"It explained a lot though." She looked so serious, so sad. "Aw, Smoky. I know how difficult all that was to say. I just wish you could have told me about some of it. Like, the feeling-guilty part. I know what that's like."

He sighed and let go of one wrist to run a finger down her cheek. Her eyes teared up, and he felt an answering burning behind his own. "Damn, Zoe. I'm sorry, baby. I missed you so much." He leaned back to stand and brought her to her feet. Then he hugged and kissed her, holding her tight. "After that night, I thought you'd hate me. I was all weak and broken. Such a damn loser about everything. I—*Ow*. Did you just pinch me?" He stared at her in amazement.

"I hear the purple nurple is a favorite of your sister's. And I can see why. Shut up. Just stop talking and listen."

"Okay."

"You are *not* a loser. Not a weak, pathetic fool."

"I don't think I said *fool*."

She held up her pinching fingers. "Not another word."

He stopped talking.

"I love you, you big moron. So much it hurts me inside. Life is so much better when you're with me. I even buy peanuts now, just in case you want a sundae. I have extra pink yoga pants, because the ones you used to tie me up lost their elasticity, and I'm saving them for our happy times at home. *Our* home. I don't know how you did it, but you wormed your way in here." She put his hand over her heart that beat like a frenzied drum.

He trembled, feeling emotional but doing his best to remain stoic, reserved. He hadn't lost her. *Thank you, God.*

"I want to say I can help you through everything that happened," she continued. "But I know I can't. Only you can forgive yourself. Only you can decide if you want to live with me. To love me."

She paused.

He didn't know if he should speak, so he waited.

<hr/>

What the hell was he waiting for? That was her big moment, the big speech, where he was supposed to sweep in with the grand "I love you."

"Well?" she snapped.

"Oh, I can talk now?"

She waved her hands at him. "Yes."

"I love you."

"Okay. And?"

"That's not enough?"

"Argh!" She clutched her hands in her hair, recalled she had soiled gloves on and threw them to the ground, then had to work to get the dirt out of her hair.

"Wait, stop." He was *laughing*. "Baby, stop. Zoe, I fucking love the shit out of you, okay? I'm a mental case with issues that I'm working through, but the biggest kicker to the whole mess was the thought of having to give you up. Because even if I was nothing, I had you. For a time. Then I got turned around and mixed up, and I thought, *No, I can't have her*. But I wanted you, so damn bad."

She had to kiss him. He had the same thought, because he leaned in at the same time she stood on tiptoe.

Once their lips met, it was like warmth returned to her soul. She hugged him, trying not to cry again. God, she'd cried so much the past few weeks. "I missed you."

"Oh, baby. I missed you too. I'm so sorry for—"

"No more apologies. Not today. Knowing you, you'll have plenty more to make in the days to come."

"In the days, weeks, months, and maybe if I'm lucky, years to come?"

She felt such joy she wanted to burst. "I'm game. But you need to talk to me when you need space. Not just take off for days, okay?"

"No more of that. Zoe, I'm making plans for the future." He swallowed. "For *our* future, if you'll have me."

She blinked. "Are you proposing?"

"Please. Without a ring? And still being a mental patient?"

"Would you stop calling yourself that?"

He laughed. "I'm pre-proposing. Life with you is

what I want. But I still have a ways to go to get better." He brushed more dirt from her hair.

She hoped she looked better than she thought she did. *Pre-proposing? Yes!* "So, um, don't you want my answer?"

"Not if it's a no. If it's a no, just wait until I can ask again, with flowers and a ring and maybe a degree in exercise science. I'm going back to school. I had a talk with Mark, and we have some really cool ideas for therapy through exercise. Like, mental therapy, not physical therapy. Stuff especially for veterans."

"You've been talking to Mark?" She blinked.

"Well, after I jacked him up to make sure he left you alone, I realized I'd been fed some bad intel. So then I apologized, explained I wasn't right in the head, and he got it. We talked. I played more racquetball and then realized his aunt owns this place and asked him for a favor. But somehow Hope got involved, and—"

"Surprise!" Hope, Mark, and an older woman walked out onto the porch. "So are you back in love now?" Hope asked.

"Well?" Mark checked his watch. "Hurry it up. I have things to do. Sorry, Aunt Peggy, I have to run. But I'll call you later."

"Yes, dear. Thanks for bringing me home." Aunt Peggy held up her thumb, then turned it down. "Which one?"

"Up," Zoe yelled and laughed when Gavin lifted her and whirled her around. "Oh, man, I'm getting dizzy."

"Love will do that." Gavin smiled.

"So will little to eat and going in circles."

"Oh." He set her down.

"Hey, Mark, are you single?" they heard Hope ask.

They didn't hear his answer as she followed him back into the house.

But Gavin shook his head. "No way."

"I agree. No." Yet, Mark wasn't a bad candidate for a break in Hope's supposed streak in dating losers. What could it hurt?

Then Zoe didn't care, because Gavin was kissing her and making plans for their happy reunion. And her pink yoga pants.

Chapter 19

IT WAS A BEAUTIFUL WEDDING. THE BRIDE HAD WALKED down the aisle with a handsome stud, and Zoe had beamed when he'd winked her way before handing Amanda off to her groom-to-be.

Hope sighed. She'd known Amanda for years, and now another of her friends had found true love and the man of her dreams, while Hope had a date who'd left early due to a problem at the office with a patient complaint.

But hey, at least she'd had a good-looking professional on her arm. Her other friends had been jealous, not realizing Mark had done her a favor for taking such good care of his aunt's place. Thank goodness for Zoe's gardening skills. Peggy was so thrilled she'd asked Hope to house-sit the next time she went away.

No fool, Hope had immediately agreed.

Too bad she didn't have the hot man to go with the cool house. She liked Mark, and he was sexy and rich, but he did nothing for her. She sighed.

Men. They all sucked.

Except for her family.

She joined Gavin, now looking happier than he had in a while, as he stood with Zoe and another woman, Nicole. She held an adorable little towhead in her arms. "Mikey, say hi to your Uncle Gavin and Aunt Zoe."

Gavin looked a little pale until Zoe wrapped her arm around his waist and smiled. "Gavin would just love to change his diapers, Nic. When can we babysit?" Then she and Nicole laughed at Gavin and told him to stop being an idiot. "I'm kidding," Zoe said. "Baby steps, okay?"

Nicole beamed. "I'll bother you two later. Mikey and I have to sucker Aunt Amanda and her new husband into sitting for us when they get back from Paris."

"Good luck," Gavin called out, then turned to Zoe, his heart in his eyes. "I love you so much, Pink Yoga Pants."

"I love you too, Smoky."

They kissed.

Hope wiped happy tears from her face. Another Donnigan brought down by the love of an amazing woman. Now that just left her and Theo to get out from under Linda's fat thumb.

She stayed at the party and pretended she was having fun, then left when no one would notice her leaving early. Honestly, that one groomsman had better learn to keep his hands to himself.

She didn't want to head back to her lonely apartment in Queen Anne, so she drove instead to Gas Works and parked, then walked to an unoccupied spot where she could look over Lake Union. The wind blew, but the warmth of the evening sun kept her comfortable enough. She didn't much care about the state of her outfit, the pink cocktail dress pretty but too trendy to keep.

Hope sighed. She was twenty-nine years old. Old enough to have a life, a relationship, a great job. So why was she still hopelessly single, living in just an okay place, and dissatisfied with life? She wasn't her cousin's charity case. She worked hard for Cameron's investment firm. Had learned a lot and even started to invest her own money wisely. And her cousin—her boss—treated her like a valued employee. She'd earned her place there.

But she had no special man in her life, just an endless string of disasters behind her. She only wanted to be loved and taken seriously. Geez, her family respected Theo more than they did her, and Theo was twenty and still not sure what he wanted to do with his life.

"So. This is where you spend your time slumming now."

Startled, she shot to her feet. "Greg?" She glanced around. Most of those who'd been milling close by were departing. She wouldn't be noticed unless someone stood directly below the hill she was on.

He smirked. "Not so tough now without your brothers, are you, bitch?" He took a step closer. He had at least a hundred pounds on her and an attitude she'd dumped. "How about telling me I'm sorry and meaning it? Or better yet, showing me how sorry you are?" He leered at her breasts and smirked.

She didn't wait for him to attack first. Hope punched him right in the nose, grabbed his arm and twisted, then kicked him in the side of the knee.

He went down with a startled yelp and clutched his face. *Wow! That self-defense class actually worked.*

A shadow suddenly covered her, and she saw the giant behind Greg, staring at her in shock.

Oh my God, it's him. Del's brother. That hot hunk of man who had *mistake* written all over him. The gorgeous tattoo artist and possibly the worst man she should lust after, considering her track record. Also the reason she kept her distance from her McCauley cousins as best she could, Mike and Del especially.

"Ah, need some help?" J.T. Webster asked in that rich baritone that sent shivers down her spine. Between her legs. Oy.

Dark, sexy, and built. And those eyes. A dark, melty brown that seemed to invite a girl to take off her clothes before she knew what she was doing.

Hope coughed. "Nah, I'm good. Thanks." She stepped over Greg, then turned to ask, "Greg, why are you here?"

He responded in a nasal whine, "To tell you to get your brothers to lay off."

She frowned. "Huh?"

"They put a beatdown on him months ago." J.T. frowned. "They're still bugging you, douche bag?"

"Put a tire iron to my car last night," Greg said through a bloody nose. "Wrote me a threatening note too."

"Not my brothers. They're too busy to deal with you, dickhead." Hope turned on her heel and walked back down the hill, too fast, toward her car.

Just as she stumbled, J.T. grabbed her.

She clutched his thick forearm and stared at his hand, seeing his darker skin against hers. Noticing how graceful and long his fingers were. How sensual… Heat sizzled along every nerve in her body.

She refused to meet his gaze, though she felt it burning through her like a laser. He guided her down the hill, then slowly let go, his fingers trailing her arm to her wrist, then the back of her hand, a whisper of touch.

He walked her back to her car in silence.

"Th-thanks."

He nodded. "I was passing by and saw some guy going up the hill, but the woman at the top—you—didn't seem to know he was there. He watched you before he walked up. I didn't get a good vibe."

"Oh. Yeah, he's an old ex." She frowned. "Not sure what he's talking about with my brothers. They wouldn't be bothering with him. Heck, *I* haven't heard from the guy in months."

"Odd." He nodded, looking her over. "You look pretty."

"Thanks." They just stared at each other. "I was at a wedding."

He glanced at her fingers. "Obviously not yours."

"Right. Pink dress. Not white." She pointed to herself.

He smiled. "I like pink."

Oh God. He was flirting with her. *Danger! Danger!* Everything feminine in her preened and counted down a timeline to when she could legitimately audition to be his personal mattress. First date? Third?

Just another potential bad decision on her list of bad decisions.

Nope. Not this time. Not this girl. "Thanks again." She smiled, waved, and rushed into her car so fast he blinked and she was gone. She checked her rearview as she drove away and saw him staring after her.

Man, her mother would burst a blood vessel if Hope brought him home. J.T. Webster—a man with a questionable background, rumors of jail time, a *tattoo artist*, and a giant who looked like he ate mean for breakfast. Now to stop thinking how amazing it would be to flaunt him under Linda's nose and instead focus on better life choices.

She pulled into her apartment complex and parked, then checked her phone, only to see *more* haranguing from Queen Linda, the Donnigan matriarch who had never made a mistake in her whole damn life.

Thoughts played through Hope's brain, the flickering of plans made and refined. Like what kind of tattoo she planned to get the next time Linda jumped her case.

She smiled. "Bring it, Linda. And I bring *him*."

Here's a taste of Marie Harte's
new Halloween romance!

All I Want for Halloween

"YO, SUCKFEST. WHAT ABOUT THAT ONE?"

Harrison "Gear" Blackstone silently counted to ten before answering his younger brother. He noted his sister standing by a dress dummy, trying to pretend she wasn't listening in on the conversation. Just an ordinary day at Fair of Dreams—costume shop to the stars, or so Iris liked to brag after having dressed the local weatherman once for a party.

"I am not going as a gladiator," he enunciated to his brother. "I don't want everyone staring at my bare arm and asking about the Sahara tattoo I'm missing." *No, I'll leave all the ass-kissing to Brian, that lying, cheating, fuckhead of a backstabbing—*

"I still don't understand why Sahara wanted you to get a fake tattoo of her on your bicep," his sister said. "Your other arm is full of them, but your bare arm looked stupid with her face on it. You know I'm right."

"Of course I know."

"The minute you showed it on camera, you were sunk. I mean, now you have to get a real one to show it was real all the time, or you're just a poser." Iris blinked. "Er, well, you're not a poser. I mean, you don't... Because she, um... You..." She coughed. "Brian—Ah..." She trailed off as he stared at her.

A moment of awkward silence filled the dressing room. Then Thor said, "So no to Spartac-*ass*?" He guffawed, holding up the costume with one short-as-fuck skirt. "Gear, you of all people could pull this off. The ass part, I mean."

"I'm sorry, *Thorvald*. Are you seriously trying to make fun of *me*?"

His brother glowered. "It's Thor, knuckle-dragger."

"You wish." Gear laughed, cheered when Thor hung the outfit back on the rack, then moved to another one, muttering under his breath. So easy to get one over on his brother. Thor might not be as mighty in presence as a Norse god, but the guy had a brain like a computer. If anyone could figure a way for Gear to escape the mess that had become of his life, Thor could. "Oh, come on. I'm kidding. It's not like you haven't heard that since birth."

"True," Iris had to add. "He's just upset because the new girl laughed when she heard his name." To Thor, she said, "You should be over that by now."

"I am." Thor gave them a smug look. "Please. I might not be Chris Hemsworth, but I'm rich, handsome, successful, smart, driven—"

"Verbose," Iris interrupted. "Arrogant."

Gear cut in, "And crazy if you think I'm wearing

anything you've been holding up." He sighed. "Do I have to go to this party?"

"Yeah. You do," Iris said, no-nonsense. "It's in your contract that you go, but not that you have to be seen all night. You show up wearing that"—she pointed to Batman's archvillain, the Joker costume—"show your face, growl, and act like the complete jerk you are on *Motorcyle Madnezz*."

"I'm not a jerk."

"Uh-huh, keep telling yourself that," Thor said drily.

"After some time on camera, duck away, change into something with a mask, stay for the rest of your mandated time, then check out with the producer before you leave. And bingo, you followed the terms of your contract."

The last terms. Thank God the contract had been up for renewal. Delaying the agreement had pushed back filming, but it had allowed him to take a hard look at what his life had become. The dream of running one of the best custom shops on the West Coast had come true, but at a cost.

Just thinking about the shit Sahara and Brian had put him through, letting him take the blame while they gloried in looking like sunshine and fucking roses, made him want to hurt someone. Two someones. If he hadn't been raised not to hit women, he'd have decked Sahara. That he hadn't been hurt by her so much as pissed told him they'd been over for a while. But the betrayal he felt at Brian's deception, that still stung. The fucker.

"Stop it. You're scaring away my good vibes," Thor complained.

"Good vibes?"

Iris cleared her throat. "What our brother is trying to

say is that he's been envisioning a future for you filled with good things. A happy life, a fine woman to love, three children, one of whom you will name Thor Jr., and a return to the fold."

Thor nodded, smiling. "Like you read my mind."

Iris snorted. "More like I sat through Mom's latest lectures on positive thinking and the way of the hippie."

Gear chuckled. "Glad I missed that one."

Iris gave him a mean smile. "Oh, you'll be getting it when they see you for brunch on Sunday. It'll happen. I'm *envisioning* it for you." She snickered. "Ah yes, I see you coming back, adding to the show. Making your wicked bikes a part of the act. Gear the Magnificent rides again…"

"Not no, but *hell no*." Gear had run fast and far from the family business years ago. His gift with all things mechanical had transformed into a love for the motorcycle—only the finest mode of transportation known to man. His mistake had been in sharing that art with his family, letting them use his funky motorized bikes in the jousting part of their medieval show.

Since then, his father had been on his ass to come back home and leave his glamorous TV life alone. His mother kept trying to zen him into believing life would be good to him if only he believed.

"Click your heels together and wish upon a star," he muttered, remembering her more nutty advice. He loved Orchid Blackstone, but by God, the woman had dropped some crazy drugs in her day. Probably why she tolerated his father though. Otis was one scary motherfucker, a badass biker to the bone with the clichéd heart of gold. It would have been cheesy if it weren't so obvious anytime his dad glanced at his mom, his big heart in his eyes.

For years Gear had itched to leave all their positive energy BS behind. Then when he did, he landed in a black hole steadily sucking away his identity, creativity, and happiness. Hell, maybe Orchid and Otis were onto something after all.

"I know that look." Thor shook his head. "No, you are not joining back up with the Blackstone circus."

"Steampunk fair," Iris corrected, sounding peeved. Gear knew she had a pet peeve about anyone talking down on the family business.

Thor ignored her. "Gear, you will avoid the temptation to join up with Satan's jesters. You and Otis nearly came to blows the last time you tried to help out."

"True," Gear had to admit.

"You will get out of this mess. We'll find a way, Bro, don't worry. And you'll be even better for it. The parental unit will only drive you insane." Thor shot a sly glance at their sister. "Look at what they've done to Iris."

"I would flip you off, but that's negative." She threw a tiny pillow at his head instead. "Now embrace the love I just sent you, and piss off."

Thor laughed. "You haven't had a good insult for me in like, five years. Try again, or—" An alarm on his phone interrupted him, and he turned it off. "Damn. Gotta get to class. Talk to you guys later." Thor darted away with a light punch to Iris's arm and a high five for Gear. As usual, Professor Blackstone would be late to lecture.

Gear grunted. At least some things hadn't changed. His brother still tried to boss everyone around with his super brain while being unable to understand how time worked. His sister continued to design amazing costumes for the show while picking on their younger brother, and their parents remained loving, crazy, and humming with positivity while they recovered and prepared for next season's Renaissance Daze.

"So this party," Gear said with a sigh. He sat on a stool and watched Iris trace chalk over the fabric on the dummy. "I really don't want to go."

"I know, sweetie." She paused. "They keep replaying that punch on TV. It's like it happened yesterday." It had happened two months ago. "Man, you knocked Brian into tomorrow. Nice. He's such an asshole. Didn't I tell you he was no good? But did you listen to me?"

He groaned. "Please. Not again."

"Biggest mistake you ever made was letting that bitch convince you to let her partner up with you guys. You know the only reason they didn't go it alone as soon as she signed on is because you're the talent."

"And they're the charm," he growled, having heard that since they'd started Madnezz three years ago. "I know."

"Nope. They're not charming. She has giant fake boobs and bottle-blond hair, and he has a straight white smile under that fake tan. That's all they have going for them."

He grunted. "Thanks."

"So you're going to go to the party, and you're going to ignore the rumors about you cheating on her first, that Brian was just defending her honor, and that you've been trying to break up the business to steal clients for a solo show. Instead, you're going to hold your head—"

"*What?*"

"You really need to watch *Entertainment Tonight*

more often." She sighed, filled him in on what that con-niving ex-fiancée of his had been up to, and heard him out as he swore, punched *through* the wall, then punched it again.

After he'd knocked a second hole through the dry-wall and bloodied his knuckles, he sat back on the stool, breathing hard.

"Sorry to have been the one to have to tell you, but it could have been worse."

"How?"

"Well, you could have married her, then found out she and Brian would get custody of your lovechild as well as access to half of everything you own. Now you don't have to split the kid too. Just start over without them."

"Start over? With what? There's nothing left." God, he wanted to destroy something before he broke down at the hopelessness of it all. His entire life spent working toward a goal, only to have it crumble because he'd put his faith in the wrong people.

Fuck.

Iris put a hand on his shoulder. "You listen to me, Harry." Only she could get away with calling him that. "You've always been upfront about who you are and what you want. The people who are your friends know this. So you see who's still around after your house of cards tumbles. And then you pick up, start over, and kick those fuckwads in the ass with the best new chop shop on the West Coast."

He felt himself smiling. "It's not a chop shop, Iris. Those are illegal."

"Whatever. Get it done. And if you still hate me calling you Harry, wait until I start calling you Harrison.

Or, you know, your *other* name. That which should never be said."

He shuddered. "Fine. I swear. I'll man up and deal. But I won't like it."

"Don't. Get mad, get even, but don't get played for a fool again."

He nodded. "Yeah. That." And that's why Gear would go to the damn party. Because the studio would throw Brian and Sahara at him, using his loss to drum up ratings for the new show without him, making him a scapegoat for the crap he hadn't done so they could salvage viewers. He'd go tonight, but on his own terms. Sahara he'd ignore. Brian... With any luck, he would refrain from blackening Brian's face all over again.

Gear sighed. "What should I wear to the party?"

"I thought you'd never ask." Iris cheered, came over to hug him, then shoved away Thor's awful choices and found him two costumes. A villain for the press, the other to hide in.

He smiled at the second, warming to the idea of the party more and more.

COMING OCTOBER 2017

*Here's a sneak peek at book four in
the Body Shop Bad Boys series*

*COLLISION
COURSE*

"TWO DOZEN RED ROSES AND 'I'M SORRY I SCREWED YOUR
sister'?" Josephine "Joey" Reeves stared over the counter at the thirty-something guy who badly needed a haircut, thinking she must have misheard him.

"Yeah, that doesn't sound so good." He sighed,
combed back his trendy bangs with his fingers, and
frowned. "I was going to go with 'Sorry I fucked your
sister,' but that's a little crude. Probably just 'I slept with
your sister,' right? That's better."

She blinked, wondering at his level of stupidity. "Um,
well, how about ending at just 'I'm sorry'?"

He considered that and nodded. "Hey, yeah. That'll
work. Do I need to sign the card? Maybe you could
write that for me. My handwriting sucks."

*So does your ability to be in a committed relation-
ship.* Joey shrugged. "It's your call. But if it was me, I'd
prefer a note from the person who's sorry, not from the
woman selling him flowers."

Her customer brightened and chose a note card from

the stack on the counter. "Good call. Hey, add another dozen while you're at it. She loves roses."

Joey tallied up the order while he signed it, then took the handwritten card. The guy really did have crappy handwriting. After he paid and left, she tucked the note into the folder of orders due to go out by two, in another two hours. For a Monday, the day had gone as expected, and then some. Not chockful of customers, but not empty either. Late spring in Seattle had most people out and about working on their gardens, not inside shopping for hothouse blooms.

Still, enough anniversaries, birthdays, and relationship disasters had brought a consistent swell of customers into S&J Floral to make Stef, her boss, more than happy.

Joey hummed as she organized the orders, thrilled that she'd gotten the hoped-for promotion to manager that morning. She'd worked her butt off for it, and that diligence had paid off. She wanted to sing and dance, proclaim her triumph to the masses.

Except it was just her, Tonya in the back putting together floral arrangements, and a half-dozen shoppers perusing the store. It had been Joey's idea to add some upscale gifts to their merchandise selection. Teddy bears, pretty glass ornaments, and knickknacks went hand in hand with flowers. S&J had seen a boost in revenue since last December, when they'd implemented the big change.

Thank God it had worked. Joey appreciated Stef taking a risk by believing in her. And now…a promotion to manager and a $50K salary! With this money, she and Brandon could finally move out of her parents' place and start fresh, away from the history of mistakes her family never let her forget. She couldn't wait to tell her best friend Becky about it.

"Well, hello there."

She glanced up from the counter and froze.

"You work here?" A large grin creased a face she'd tried hard to forget.

The man who'd been haunting her sleep, who'd dogged her through a wedding and sizzled her already frazzled nerves, looked even better in the hard light of day.

"H-hello." She coughed, trying to hide the fact that she stuttered. When she could breathe without hyperventilating, she said, "Sorry. What can I do for you today?"

The look he shot her had her ovaries doing somersaults and her brain shutting clean off.

The first time she'd seen him had been on a visit to her first-ever wedding client, and she'd been *floored*. The guys who worked at Webster's Garage all looked larger than life, covered in tattoos, muscles, and that indefinable sense of danger they wore like a second skin. But it had been this guy, the tall, Latin hunk with dark brown eyes and lips made for kissing, who had snared her.

He had a way of raising one brow in question or command that turned her entire body into his personal cheering section.

"…for some flowers. I dunno. Something that looks like I put thought into it?"

Focus, Joey. Be professional. This isn't personal. Don't get all gooey on the man. "Ah, budget?"

He sighed. "For Stella, it has to be decent. Girl is like a human calculator when it comes to anything with value. If I skimp, she'll know," he said, still grinning. He took the binder she slid to him and leafed through the floral selections. "I'm Lou Cortez, by the way."

"I remember." He'd only introduced himself once, months ago in the garage while she'd been going over flower choices with his boss. But Joey had never forgotten those broad shoulders, chiseled chin, or bright white smile. Talk about too handsome for her own good.

She'd kept her distance, or at least tried to. She'd been invited to the wedding, having become friends with the bride. Of course, all the woman's employees had been invited as well. Joey had done her best to steer clear of the man women seemed to drool over. Talk about trouble she didn't need.

She realized he'd stopped looking through the binder and was staring straight at her. More like through her. Wow. How did he do that? Bring so much concentration and intensity, she felt as if his gaze reached out and wrapped around her, holding her still?

And why, when confronted with all that masculinity, did she want to stammer and obey any darn thing he said? She had to force herself to be strong, to speak. But she just stared, mute, at so much male prettiness.

His smile deepened. "And *your* name would be…?" God, a dimple appeared on his left cheek.

A dimple. Kill me now. Breathe, dummy. You can handle this. It's business. "Oh, right. I'm Joey."

"You don't look like a Joey," he murmured.

Her heart raced, and she forced herself to maintain eye contact. "Short for Josephine. So the flowers. Did you find anything you like?"

A loaded question, because his slow grin widened as

he looked her over. Then he turned back to the binder and shook his head. "Nah. I need something original. Do you design bouquets?"

"Yes." More comfortable on a professional level, she nodded. "We have some amazing florists and—"

"No. *You*. Do you put flowers together?"

"Yes."

"Good. I want you to do it." He shrugged. "Del, my boss at Webster's, you remember her?"

She nodded. How could she forget the woman with the cool gray eyes, tattoo sleeves, and funky ash-blond hair braided in twists? The same woman she'd made friends with not long after meeting. Heck, she'd attended Del's wedding.

"She said you were amazing. My sister needs something amazing right now."

The flowers were for his sister. *Oh man. He's sexy as sin, has a body to die for, and now he's buying flowers for* his sister?

She softened toward him. "Do you know if she has a favorite flower or color? A scent maybe? Did you want sophisticated or simple? How old is she?"

"Ah, something cool. I don't know. She's gonna be twenty-three." He rattled off a few ideas, and she made quick notes.

"I can have this for you by…" She paused to check the computer. "Tomorrow. Would that work?"

"Hell. I really need them today. Her birthday isn't until Friday, but she got some shitty news, so I wanted to give them to her when I see her later. I'm willing to pay extra, no problem."

Adding *charming* and *thoughtful* to the Lou List, Joey

did her best not to moon over the man and kept a straight face. "Well, if you can wait until the end of the day, I'll try to fit them in. We close at seven. Is that okay?"

He broke out into a relieved smile. "*Gracias*, Joey. You're doing me a huge favor."

Ignoring his smile, she called on her inner manager. "Well, you're doing something nice for your sister. And I know all about crappy days."

"Yeah?" He leaned closer, and she caught a whiff of motor oil and crisp cologne, an odd blend of manly and sexy that nearly knocked her on her ass. "Who tried to ruin your day, sweetheart? I can fix that."

She blew out a shaky breath and gave a nervous laugh. "Ah, I just meant I've had those kinds of days before. Not now. It's just a regular Monday for me." A great Monday, considering her promotion.

He didn't blink, and she felt positively hunted.

"Well, if anyone gives you any trouble, you let me know and I can talk to them for you. Nobody should mess with a woman as pretty and nice as you." He stroked her cheek with a rough finger before she could unglue her feet from the floor and move away.

Then he glanced at the clock behind her, straightened, and said something in Spanish.

"Sorry, Joey." Her name on his lips sounded like a caress. "Gotta go. I'll be back at seven to pick them up, okay? Thanks. I owe you."

"You don't owe me anything," she said. "But I'll probably have to charge you extra for the short notice. It's a rush order," she blurted, not wanting him to think she was giving him special favors.

"I'll pay, no problem." He slid a card toward her.

"My number in case something comes up with the flowers. Or a customer bothers you." He nodded to it. "You're a sweetheart. I'll see you soon."

He left, and she could breathe again. Still processing the overwhelming presence that had been Lou Cortez—mechanic, paint expert, and all around heartthrob—Joey tried to calm her racing heart.

One of their regulars plunked a few items on the counter, her blue eyes twinkling, her white hair artfully arranged around her face. "Don't know how you let that one get away. If I was a few years younger, I'd have been all over him." She wiggled her brows. "Then again, he looked like he might be open to an octogenarian with loads of experience. Think he'd mind if you gave me his number?"

They both laughed, even as Joey tucked the card into her pocket and rang up Mrs. Packard's items. The thing burned in her pocket, a link to a man she knew better than to step a foot near. She'd throw it away after he picked up his flowers. Joey had made mistakes with a charmer a long time ago, and she had no intention of ever going down that road again. Nope, not ever.

COMING JANUARY 2018

Acknowledgments

Deepest thanks to those who helped me with the research for this book. Any mistakes are mine alone. To Dr. Elizabeth Leeburg, for your help with some of the psychological factors. To Julie Drey, for patiently explaining to me what EMR and the medical speak was about. And to all the folks at Sourcebooks for helping this book come together, I truly appreciate your expertise.

About the Author

Caffeine addict, boy referee, and romance aficionado, *New York Times* and *USA Today* bestselling author Marie Harte is a confessed bibliophile and devotee of action movies. Whether hiking in Central Oregon, biking around town, or hanging at the local tea shop, she's constantly plotting to give everyone a happily ever after. Visit marieharte.com and fall in love.